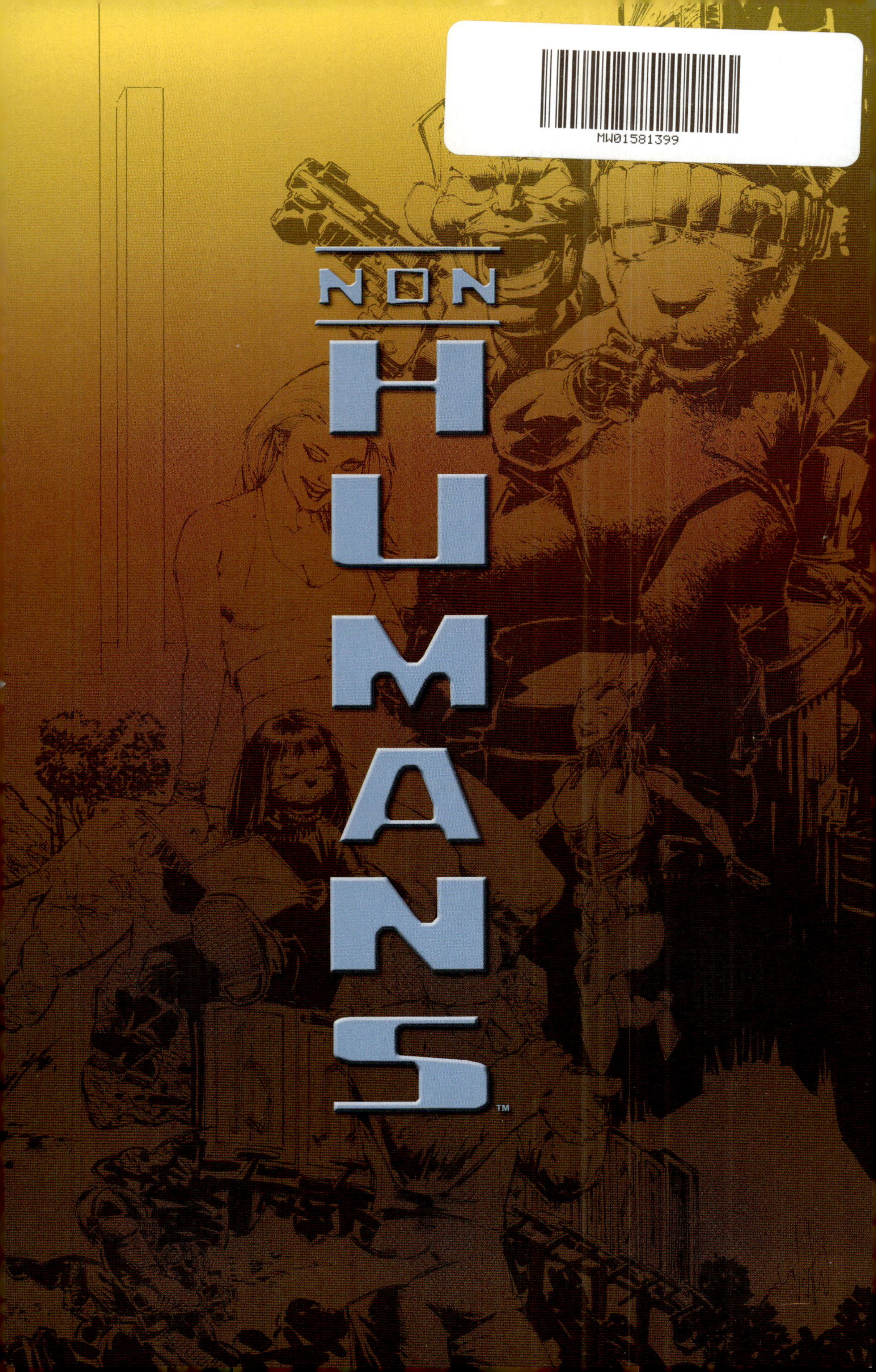
NON
HUMANS™

story: **GLEN BRUNSWICK**

art: **WHILCE PORTACIO**

letters: **RUS WOOTON**

colors (issue 1-2): **BRIAN VALEZA**

colors (issue 3): **RACHELLE ROSENBERG**

colors (issue 4): **PAUL LITTLE**

NON-HUMANS created by
GLEN BRUNSWICK, NOAH DORSEY,
& WHILCE PORTACIO

NON-HUMANS, VOL. 1: RUNAWAY AMERICAN DREAM.
FIRST PRINTING, OCTOBER 2013.
ISBN#978-1-60706-666-8

Published by Image Comics, Inc. Office of publication: 2001 Center St., Sixth Floor, Berkeley, CA 94704. Copyright © 2013 Glen Brunswick & Whilce Portacio. All rights reserved. Originally published in single magazine form as NON-HUMANS #1-4. NON-HUMANS™ (including all prominent characters featured herein), its logo and all character likenesses are trademarks of Glen Brunswick & Whilce Portacio, unless otherwise noted. Image Comics® and its logos are registered trademarks of Image Comics, Inc. No part of this publication may be reproduced or transmitted, in any form or by any means (except for short excerpts for review purposes) without the express written permission of Image Comics, Inc. All names, characters, events and locales in this publication are entirely fictional. Any resemblance to actual persons (living or dead), events or places, without satiric intent, is coincidental. PRINTED IN THE U.S.A. For information regarding the CPSIA on this printed material call: 203-595-3636 and provide reference # RICH –513915.

FOR INTERNATIONAL RIGHTS, contact: foreignlicensing@imagecomics.com

# FOREWORD

    I'm smiling as I write this. I'm actually in the middle of writing the next story arc to NON-HUMANS right now. There was no guarantee we were going to get here a few years back when Whilce and I began to develop this project. It's been a trippy ride that started with me running around Los Angeles, camera in hand, looking for iconic locations that would still be around in our fictional L.A. of 2041. I had the easy job. Whilce had the heavy lifting. He had to stare at the blank page to bring it all to life through the magic of his brilliant art, world building and imagination. We talked about just dropping Hong Kong on top of present L.A. to give it an overcrowded look, but that wasn't quite right. Then Whilce had the idea we went with, of these huge monolithic structures that separated the humans from the Non-Humans. It was a wonderful piece of the puzzle because it was visual, political and cultural all in one stroke. I still remember seeing the first sketch of Buddy-The-Bear--our local fuzzy drug dealer that's become a favorite character.
And Medic, a former medical dummy that was to become the first Non-Human detective on the police force. Whilce initially struggled with his design of Medic but now he draws him with a confidence as if he's been drawing him all his life. Watching Whilce bring all these characters to life has been such a treat for me. I had wanted to work with him for such a long time. We developed this dream together and now finally have the collected trade to hold in our grubby hands. And all in the knowing that as good as this book is, the best is yet to come.

    It also needs to be said that none of this would've come to pass at all were it not for the brilliance of a talented young writer, Noah Dorsey. He originally brought me this wonderful idea of toys sparking to life upon the return of a NASA space probe that we were able to develop into the wondrous NON-HUMANS tale that awaits your consideration.

    I've written enough of these things now to realize when a project really feels like it's come together, creatively. My wish is that Whilce and I can continue to bring these NON-HUMANS stories to life together for a good long time. Creation is a fragile thing--and when its really working it's something that's worth preserving and protecting. I hope you come to enjoy this story even half as much as we enjoyed putting it together for you.

Glen Brunswick - August 2013

# CHAPTER ONE

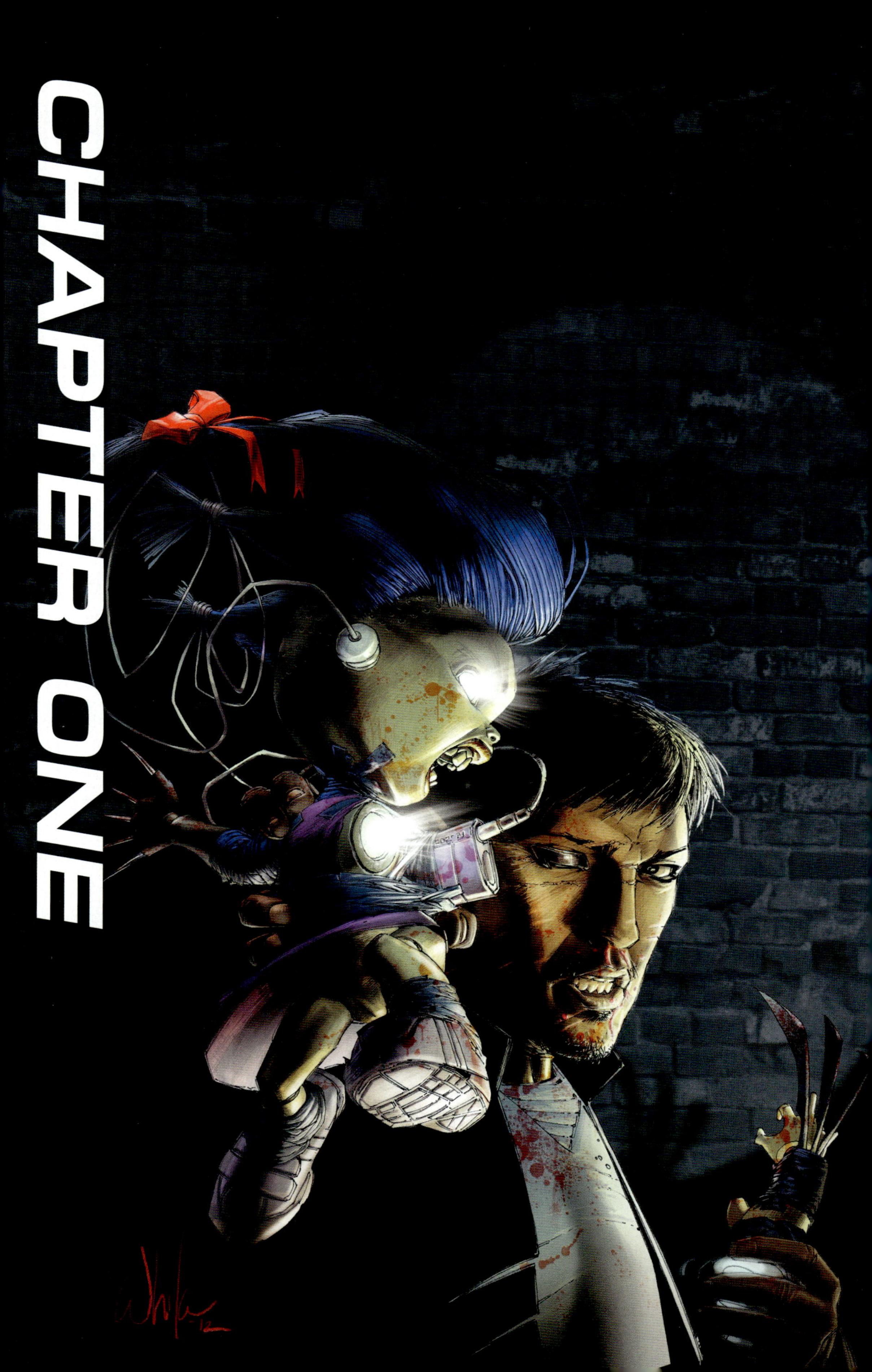

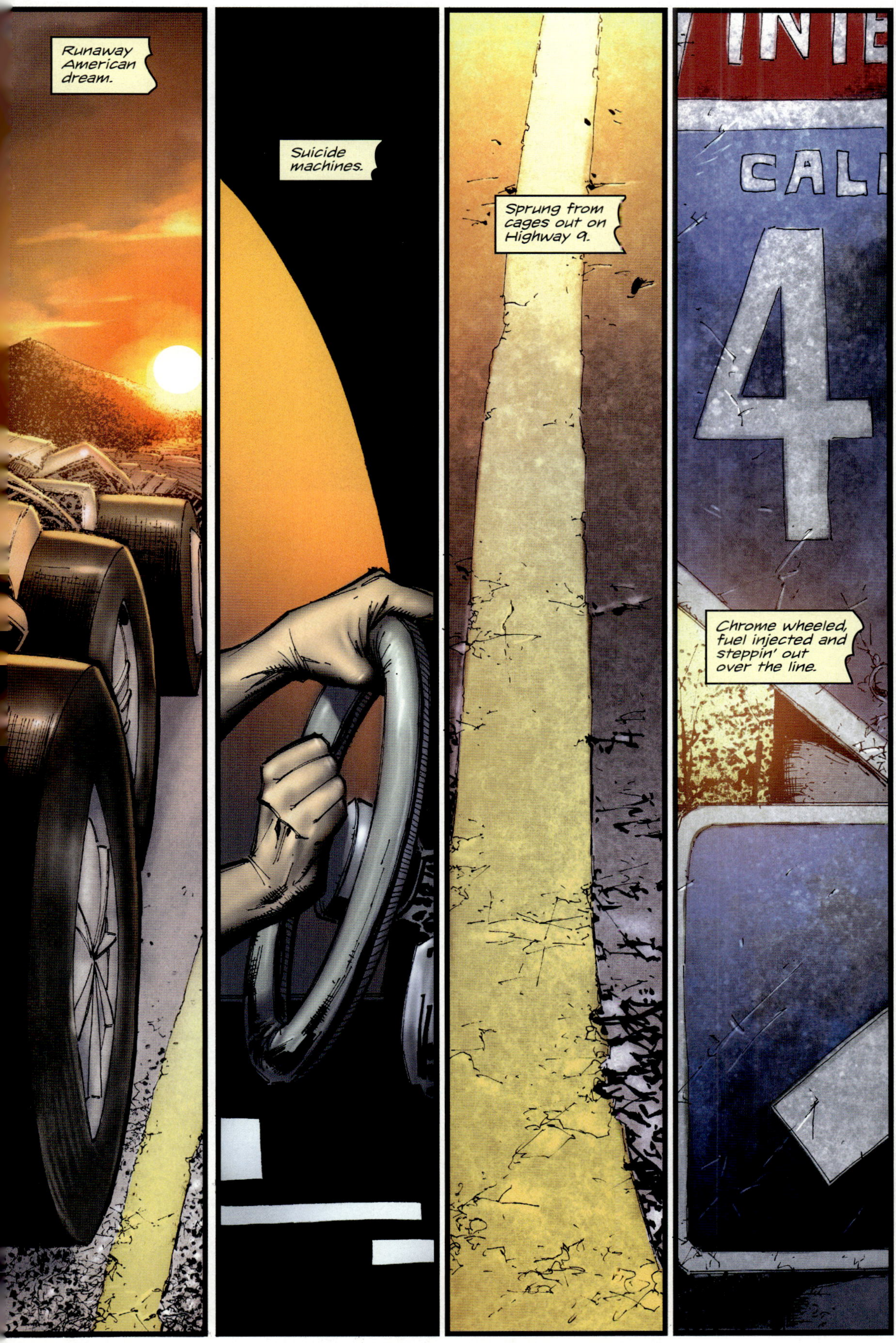
Runaway American dream.
Suicide machines.
Sprung from cages out on Highway 9.
INTE
CALI
4
Chrome wheeled, fuel injected and steppin' out over the line.

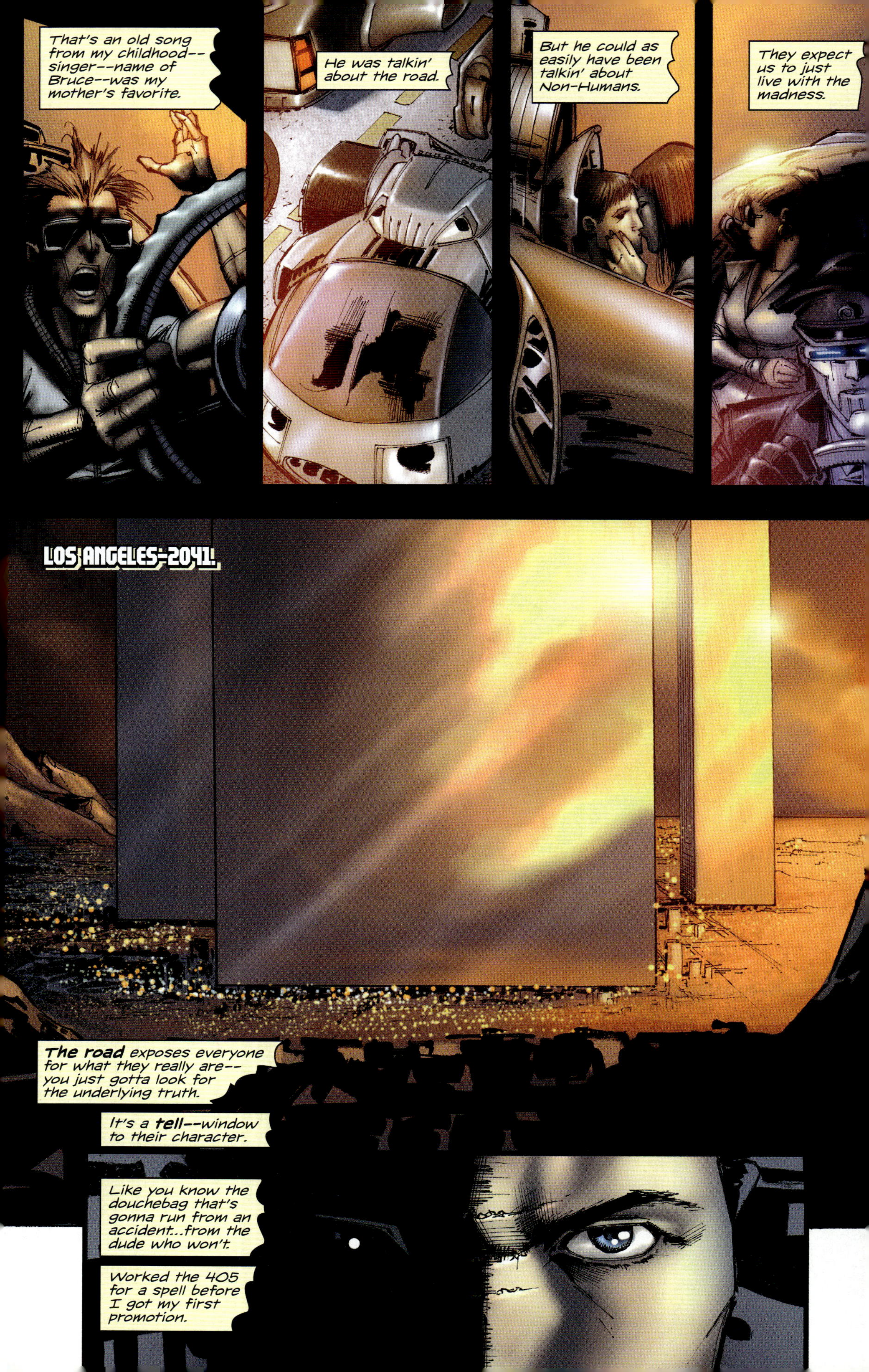

That's an old song from my childhood--singer--name of Bruce--was my mother's favorite.
He was talkin' about the road.
But he could as easily have been talkin' about Non-Humans.
They expect us to just live with the madness.
LOS ANGELES-2041.
The road exposes everyone for what they really are--you just gotta look for the underlying truth.
It's a tell--window to their character.
Like you know the douchebag that's gonna run from an accident...from the dude who won't.
Worked the 405 for a spell before I got my first promotion.

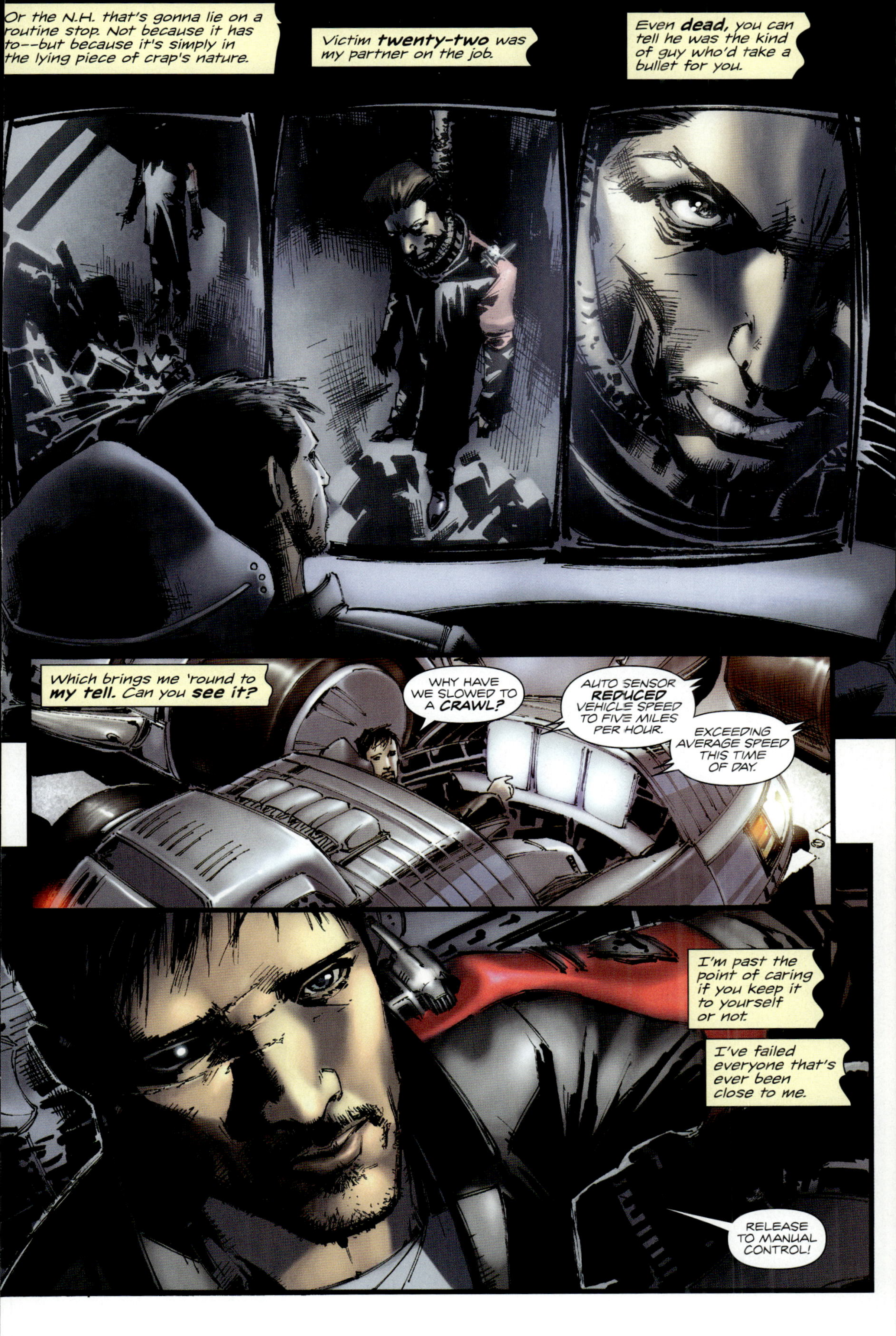

Or the N.H. that's gonna lie on a routine stop. Not because it has to--but because it's simply in the lying piece of crap's nature.
Victim **twenty-two** was my partner on the job.
Even **dead,** you can tell he was the kind of guy who'd take a bullet for you.
Which brings me 'round to **my tell.** Can you **see it?**
WHY HAVE WE SLOWED TO A **CRAWL?**
AUTO SENSOR **REDUCED** VEHICLE SPEED TO FIVE MILES PER HOUR.
EXCEEDING AVERAGE SPEED THIS TIME OF DAY.
I'm past the point of caring if you keep it to yourself or not.
I've failed everyone that's ever been close to me.
RELEASE TO MANUAL CONTROL!

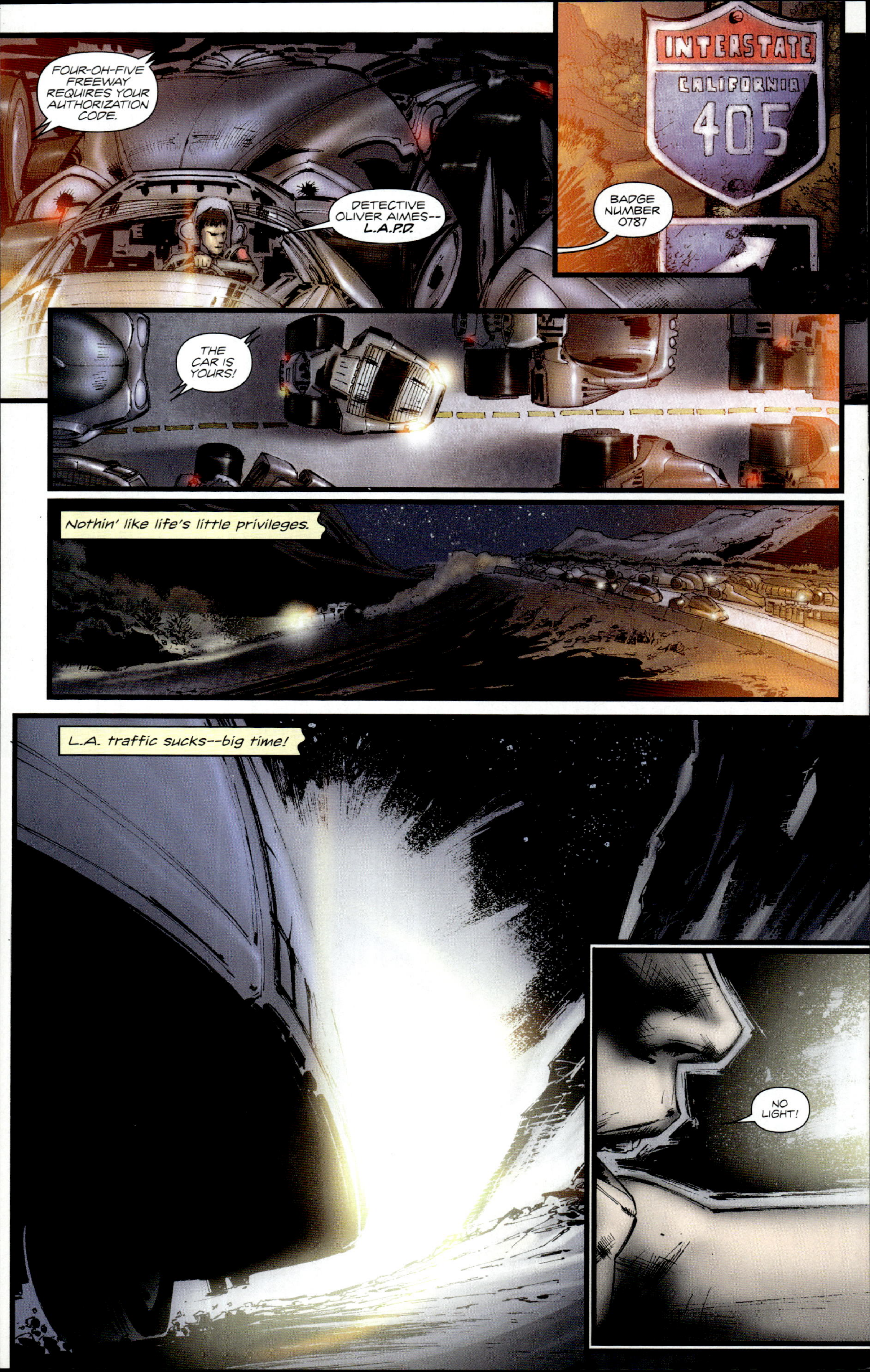
FOUR-OH-FIVE FREEWAY REQUIRES YOUR AUTHORIZATION CODE.
DETECTIVE OLIVER AIMES-- L.A.P.D.
INTERSTATE
CALIFORNIA
405
BADGE NUMBER 0787
THE CAR IS YOURS!
Nothin' like life's little privileges.
L.A. traffic sucks--big time!
NO LIGHT!

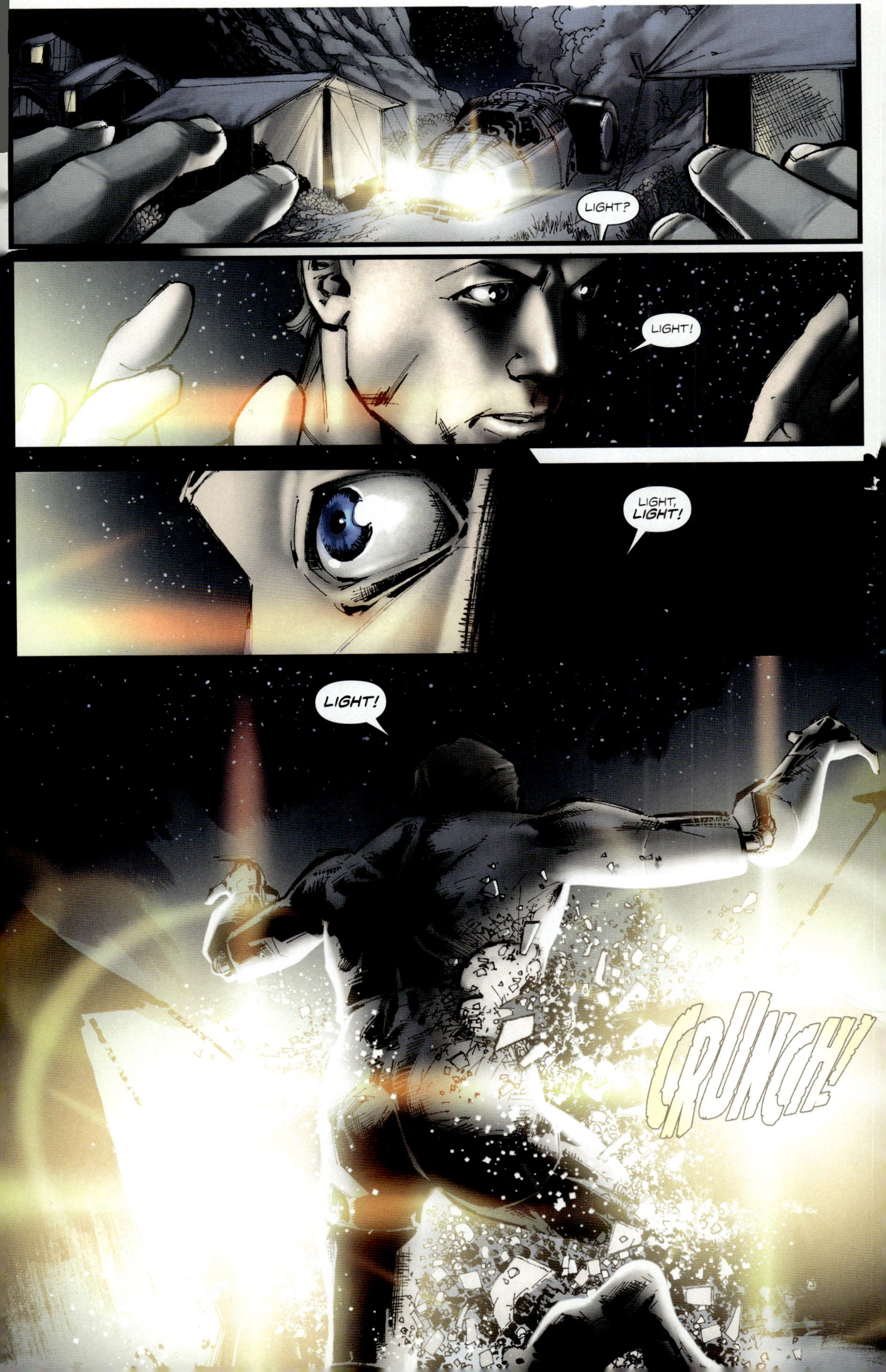
LIGHT?
LIGHT!
LIGHT, LIGHT!
LIGHT!
CRUNCH!

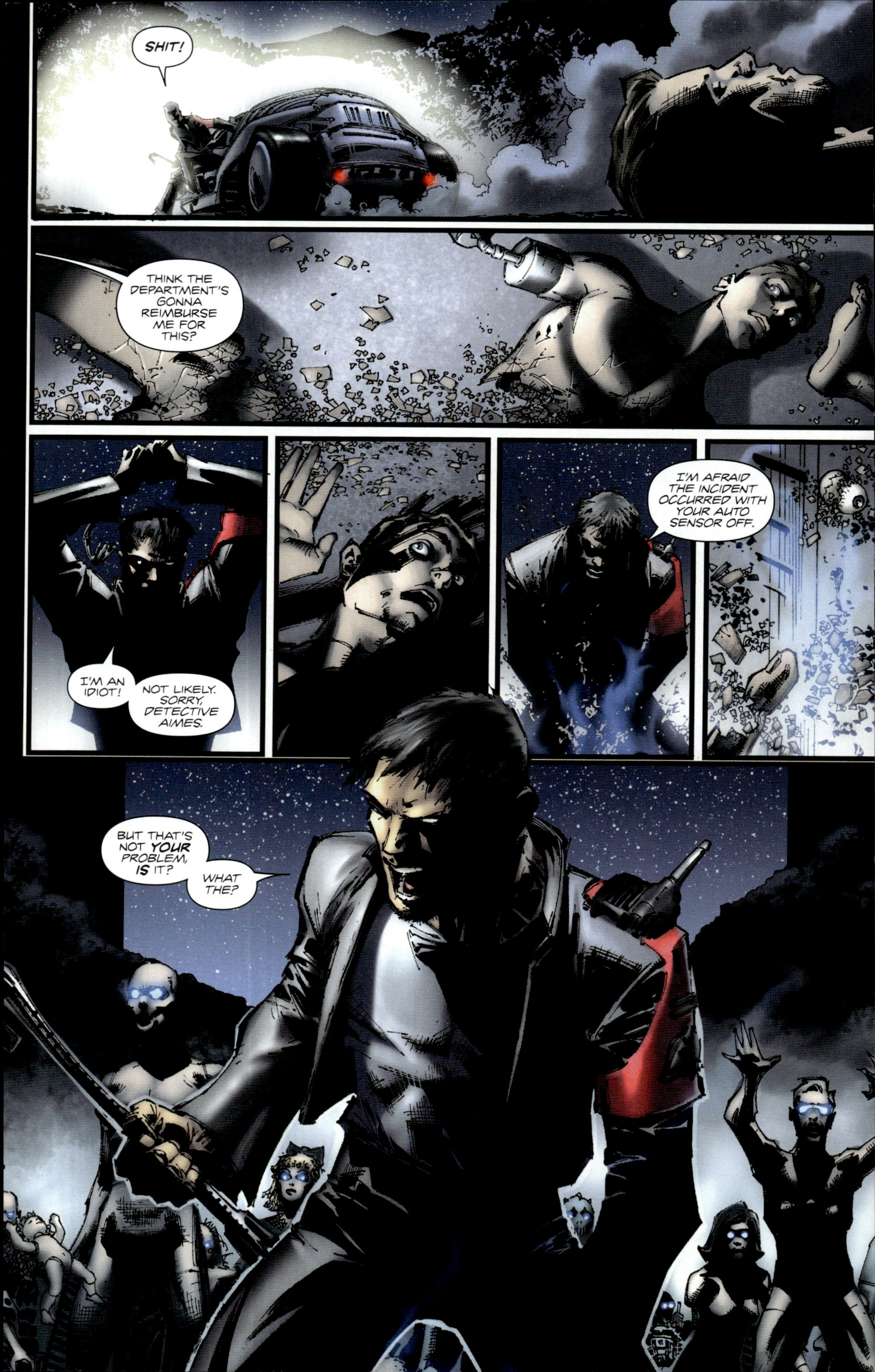
SHIT!
THINK THE DEPARTMENT'S GONNA REIMBURSE ME FOR THIS?
I'M AN IDIOT!
NOT LIKELY. SORRY, DETECTIVE AIMES.
I'M AFRAID THE INCIDENT OCCURRED WITH YOUR AUTO SENSOR OFF.
BUT THAT'S NOT YOUR PROBLEM, IS IT?
WHAT THE?

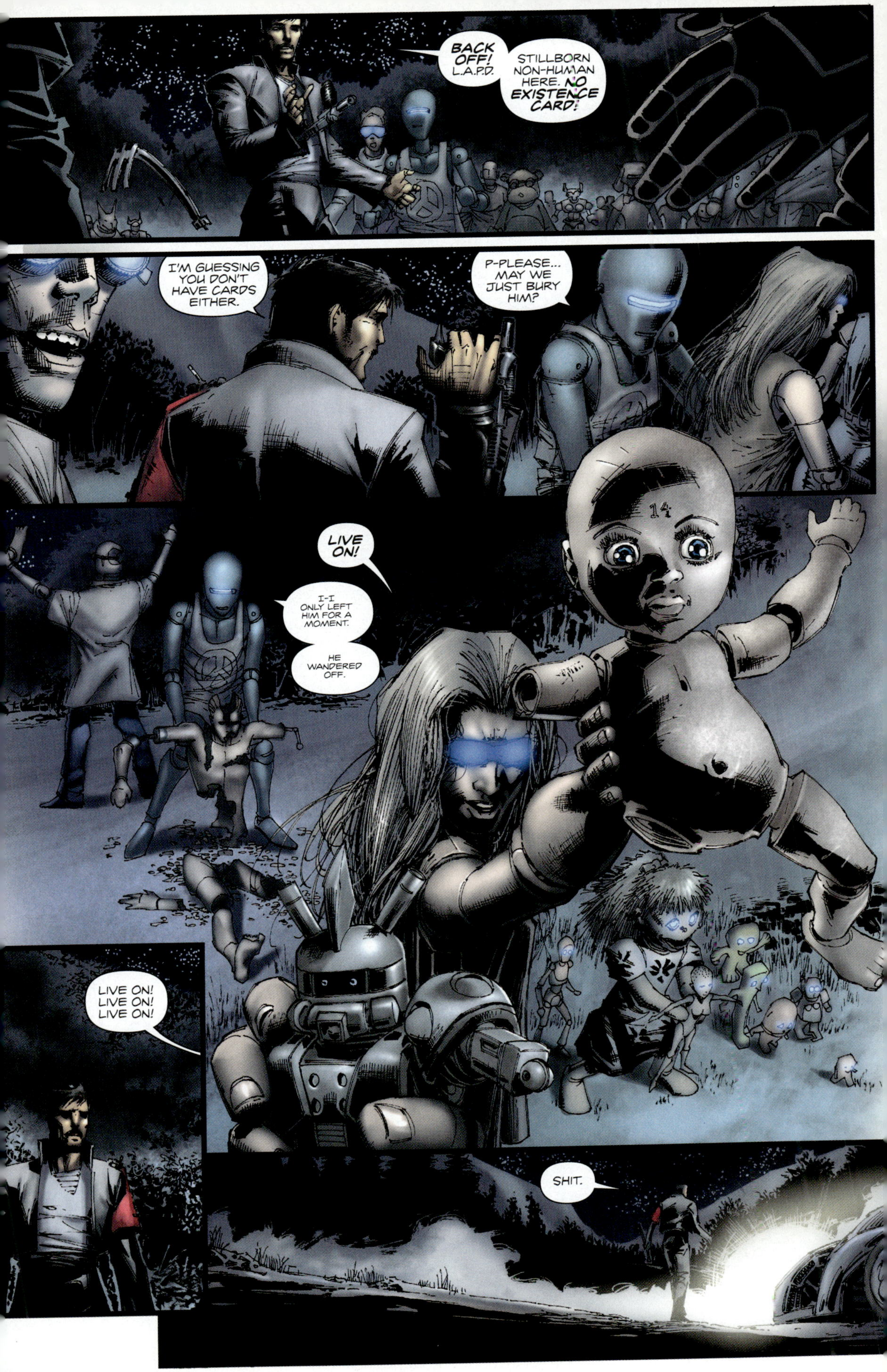
BACK OFF! L.A.P.D.
STILLBORN NON-HUMAN HERE. NO EXISTENCE CARD!
I'M GUESSING YOU DON'T HAVE CARDS EITHER.
P-PLEASE... MAY WE JUST BURY HIM?
LIVE ON!
I-I ONLY LEFT HIM FOR A MOMENT.
HE WANDERED OFF.
LIVE ON! LIVE ON! LIVE ON!
SHIT.

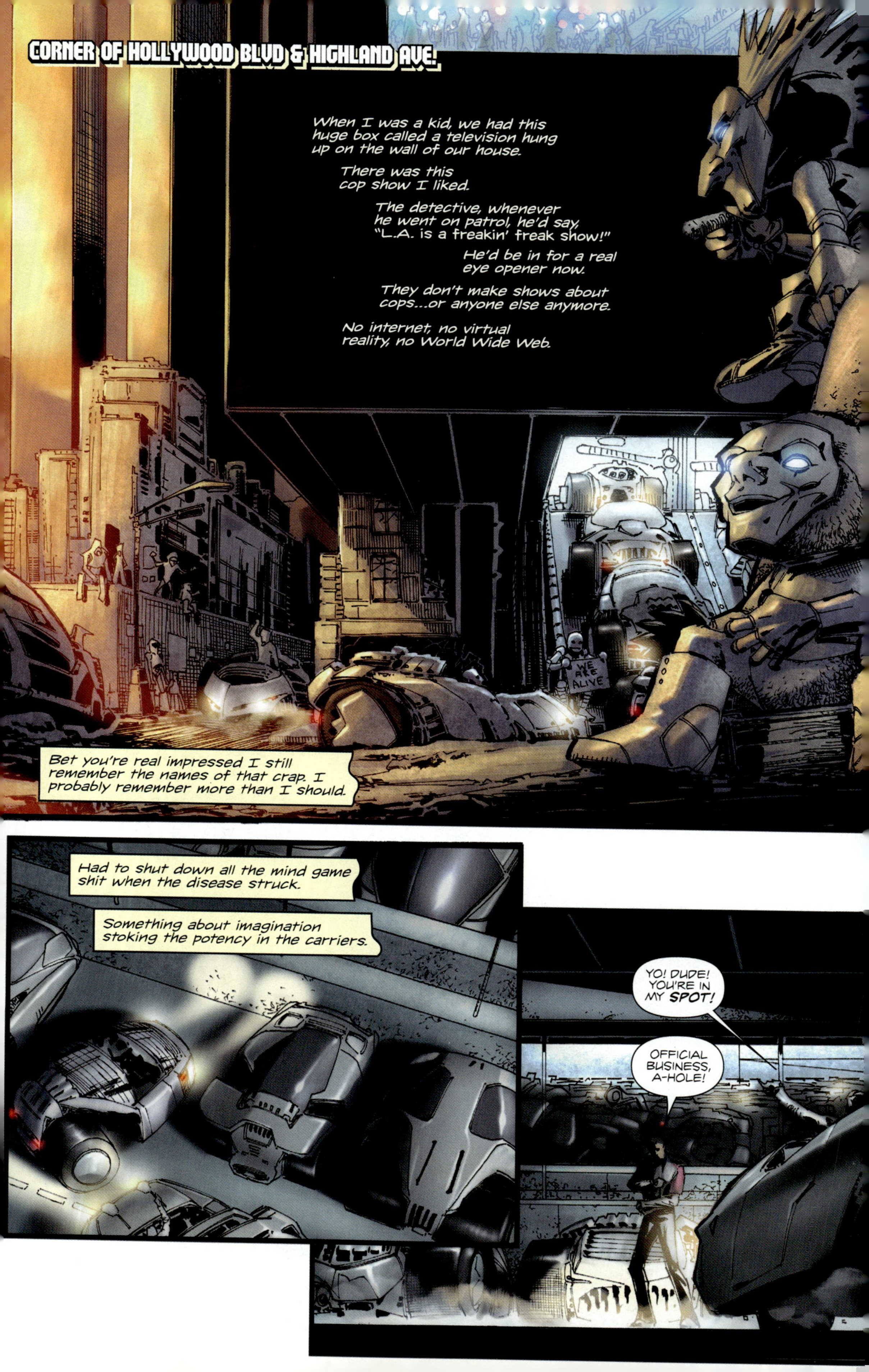
CORNER OF HOLLYWOOD BLVD & HIGHLAND AVE.
When I was a kid, we had this huge box called a television hung up on the wall of our house.
There was this cop show I liked.
The detective, whenever he went on patrol, he'd say, "L.A. is a freakin' freak show!"
He'd be in for a real eye opener now.
They don't make shows about cops...or anyone else anymore.
No internet, no virtual reality, no World Wide Web.
WE ARE ALIVE
Bet you're real impressed I still remember the names of that crap. I probably remember more than I should.
Had to shut down all the mind game shit when the disease struck.
Something about imagination stoking the potency in the carriers.
YO! DUDE! YOU'RE IN MY SPOT!
OFFICIAL BUSINESS, A-HOLE!

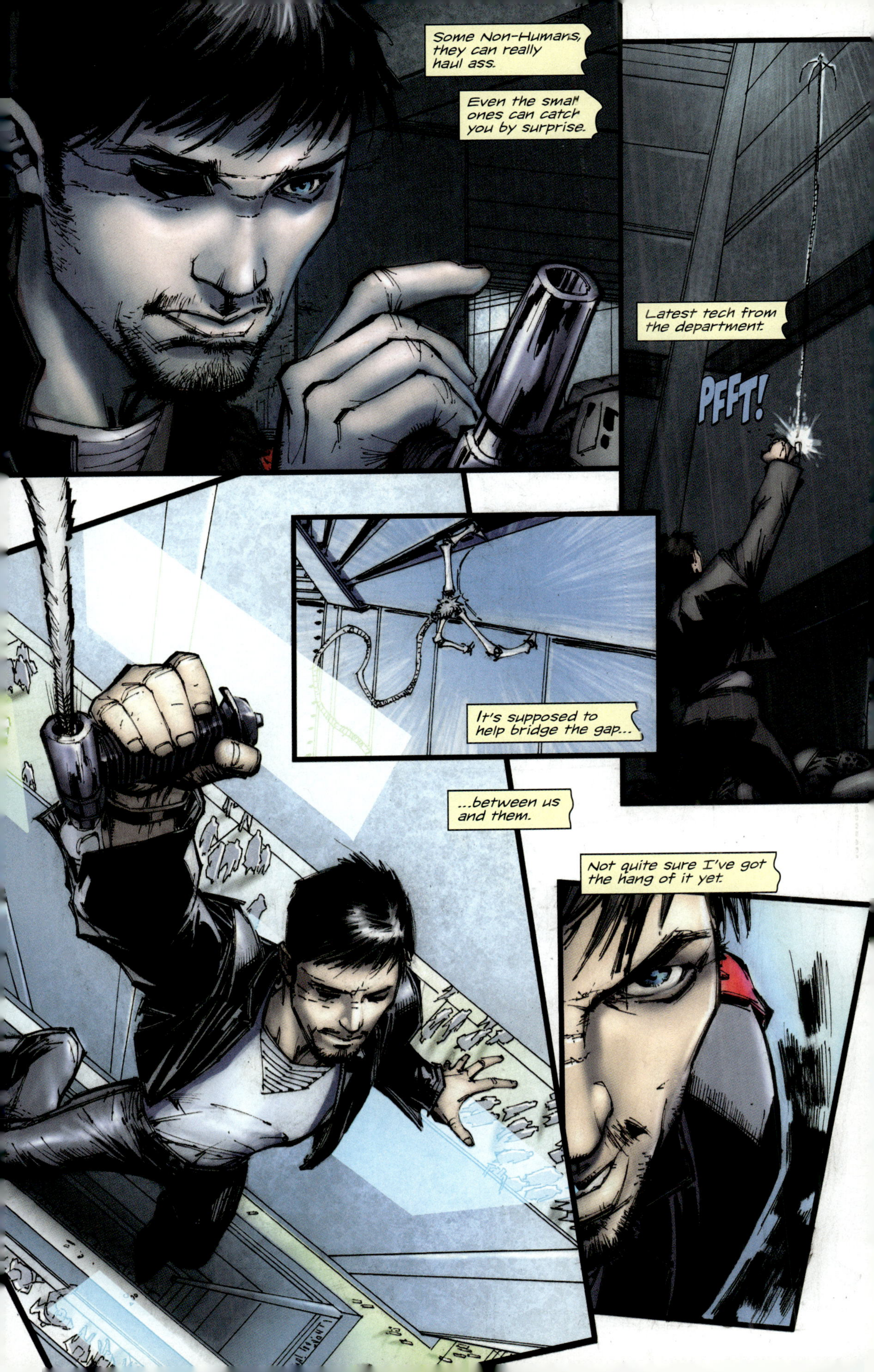
Some Non-Humans, they can really haul ass.
Even the small ones can catch you by surprise.
Latest tech from the department.
PFFT!
It's supposed to help bridge the gap...
...between us and them.
Not quite sure I've got the hang of it yet.

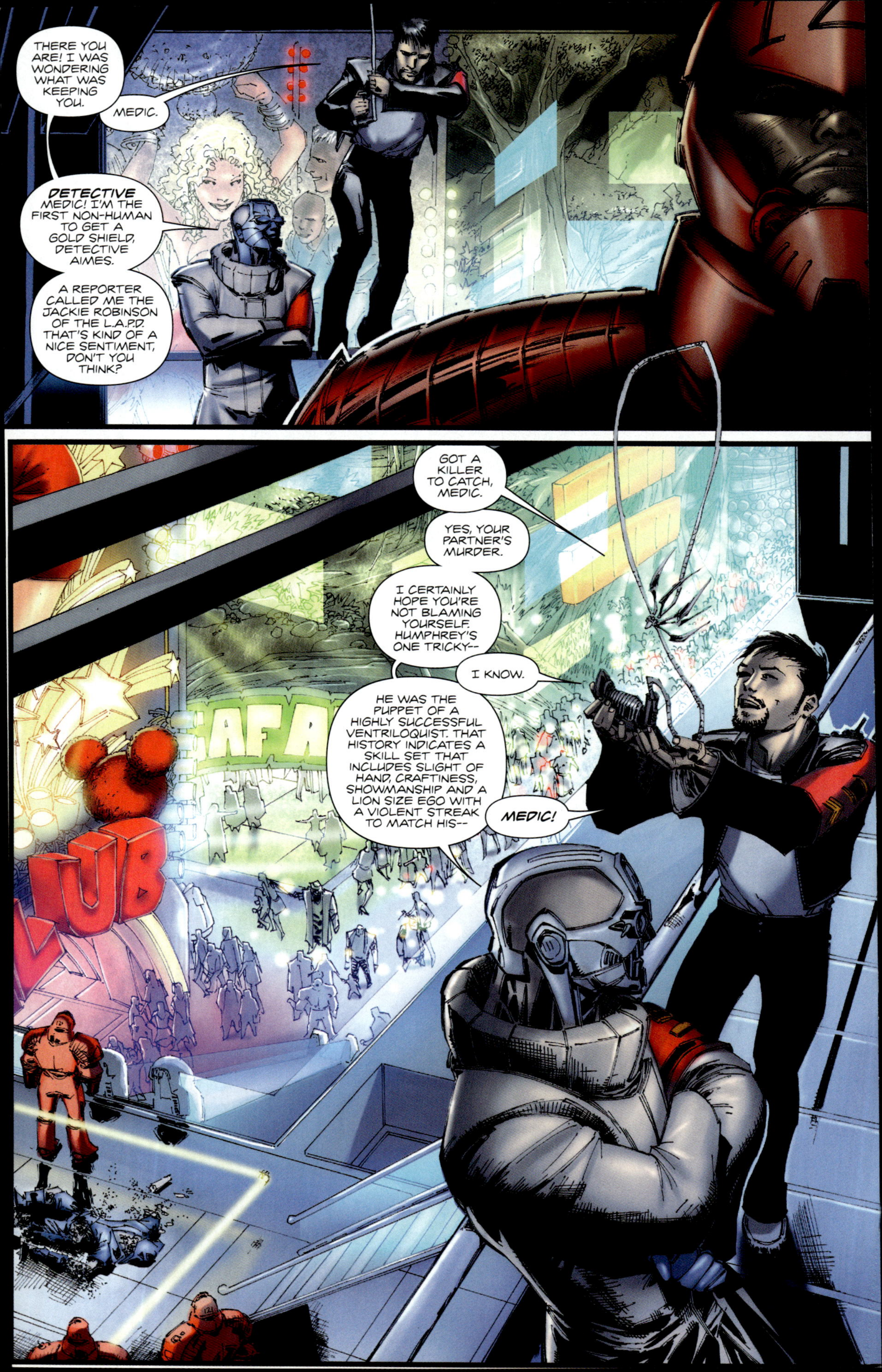
THERE YOU ARE! I WAS WONDERING WHAT WAS KEEPING YOU.
MEDIC.
DETECTIVE MEDIC! I'M THE FIRST NON-HUMAN TO GET A GOLD SHIELD, DETECTIVE AIMES.
A REPORTER CALLED ME THE JACKIE ROBINSON OF THE L.A.P.D. THAT'S KIND OF A NICE SENTIMENT, DON'T YOU THINK?
GOT A KILLER TO CATCH, MEDIC.
YES, YOUR PARTNER'S MURDER.
I CERTAINLY HOPE YOU'RE NOT BLAMING YOURSELF. HUMPHREY'S ONE TRICKY--
I KNOW.
HE WAS THE PUPPET OF A HIGHLY SUCCESSFUL VENTRILOQUIST. THAT HISTORY INDICATES A SKILL SET THAT INCLUDES SLIGHT OF HAND, CRAFTINESS, SHOWMANSHIP AND A LION SIZE EGO WITH A VIOLENT STREAK TO MATCH HIS--
MEDIC!
CLUB

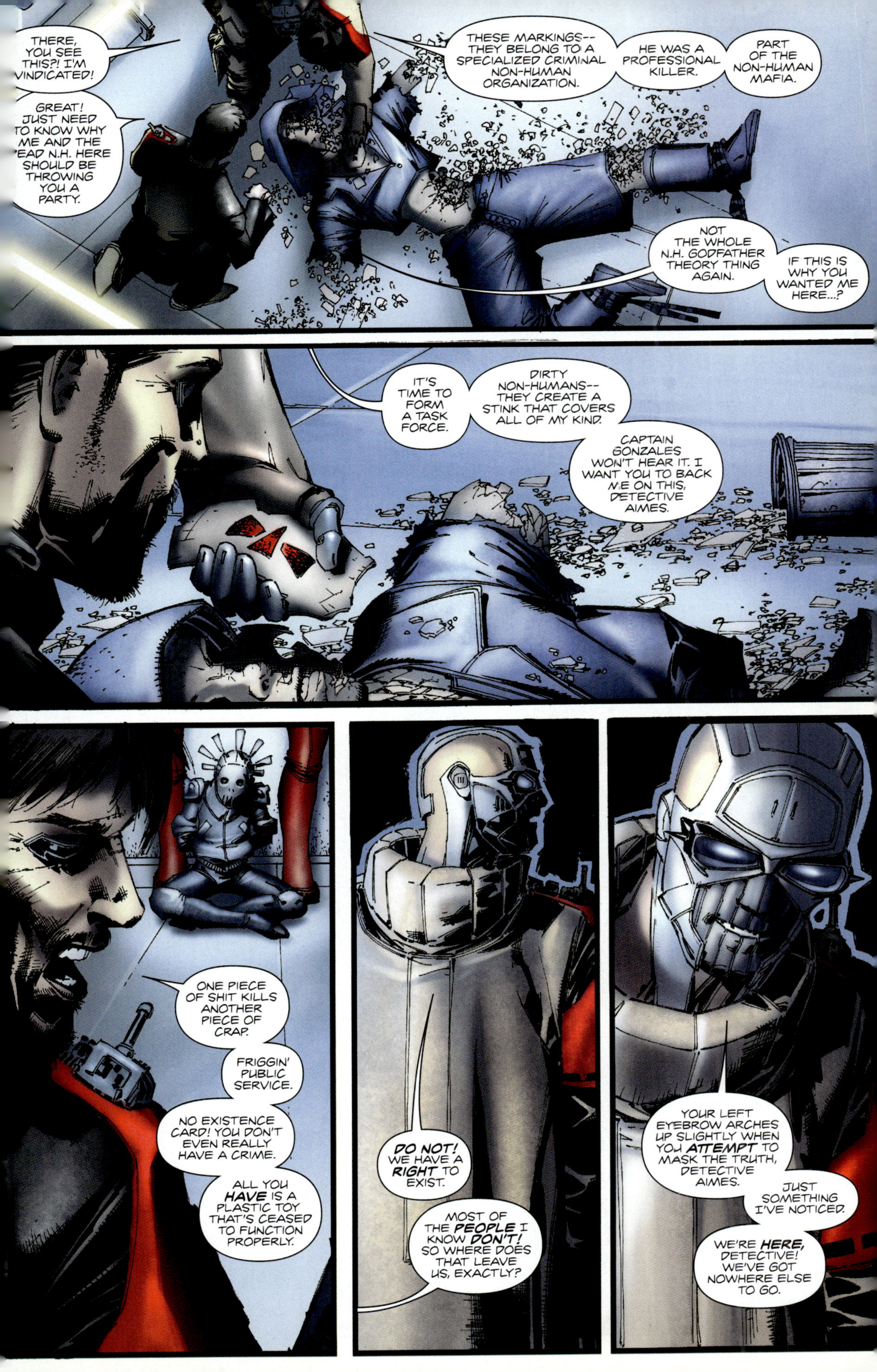

THERE, YOU SEE THIS?! I'M VINDICATED!
GREAT! JUST NEED TO KNOW WHY ME AND THE DEAD N.H. HERE SHOULD BE THROWING YOU A PARTY.
THESE MARKINGS-- THEY BELONG TO A SPECIALIZED CRIMINAL NON-HUMAN ORGANIZATION.
HE WAS A PROFESSIONAL KILLER.
PART OF THE NON-HUMAN MAFIA.
NOT THE WHOLE N.H. GODFATHER THEORY THING AGAIN.
IF THIS IS WHY YOU WANTED ME HERE...?
IT'S TIME TO FORM A TASK FORCE.
DIRTY NON-HUMANS-- THEY CREATE A STINK THAT COVERS ALL OF MY KIND.
CAPTAIN GONZALES WON'T HEAR IT. I WANT YOU TO BACK ME ON THIS, DETECTIVE AIMES.
ONE PIECE OF SHIT KILLS ANOTHER PIECE OF CRAP.
FRIGGIN' PUBLIC SERVICE.
NO EXISTENCE CARD! YOU DON'T EVEN REALLY HAVE A CRIME.
ALL YOU **HAVE** IS A PLASTIC TOY THAT'S CEASED TO FUNCTION PROPERLY.
**DO NOT!** WE HAVE A **RIGHT** TO EXIST.
MOST OF THE **PEOPLE** I KNOW **DON'T!** SO WHERE DOES THAT LEAVE US, EXACTLY?
YOUR LEFT EYEBROW ARCHES UP SLIGHTLY WHEN YOU **ATTEMPT** TO MASK THE TRUTH, DETECTIVE AIMES.
JUST SOMETHING I'VE NOTICED.
WE'RE **HERE,** DETECTIVE! WE'VE GOT NOWHERE ELSE TO GO.

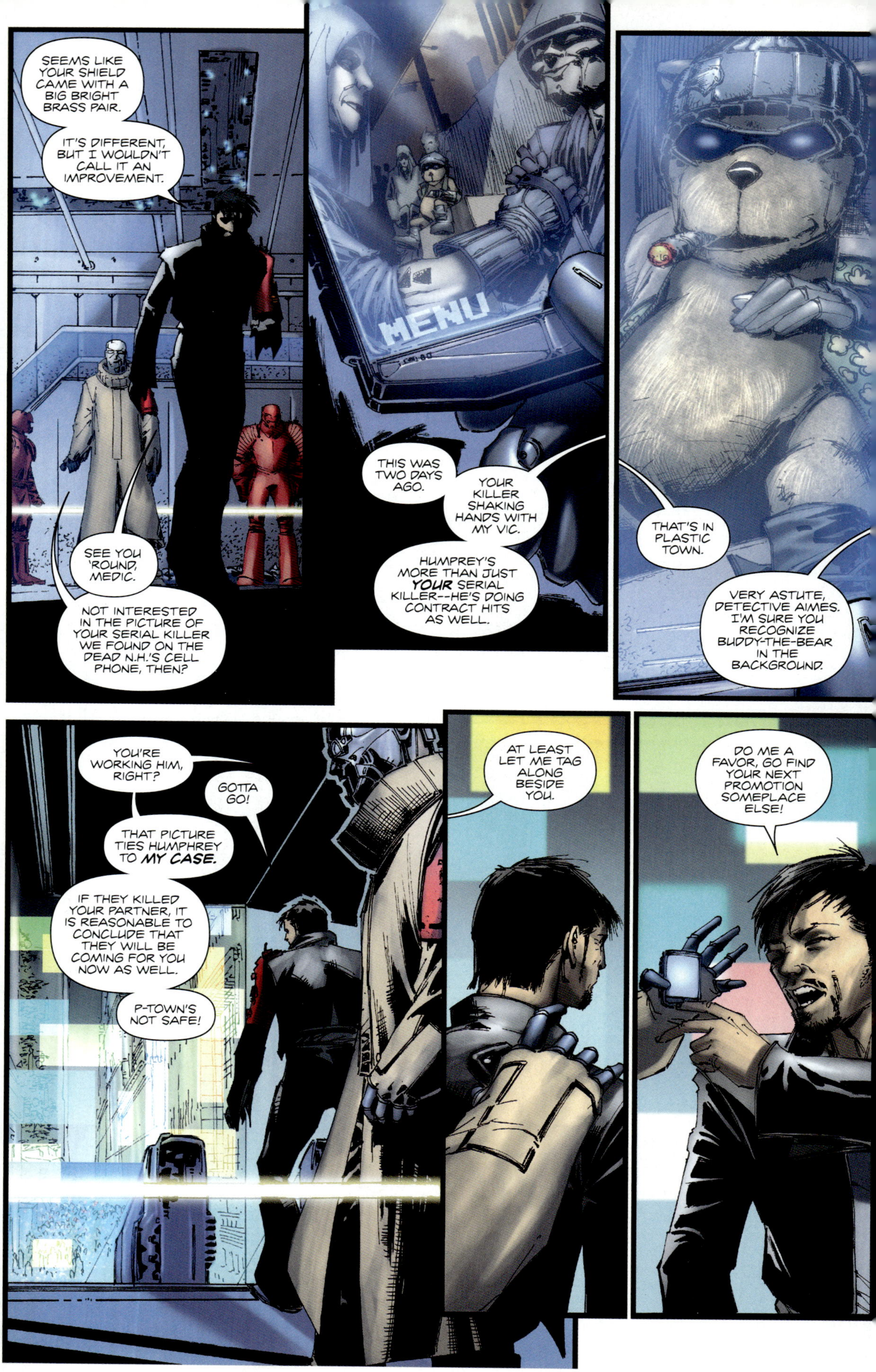
SEEMS LIKE YOUR SHIELD CAME WITH A BIG BRIGHT BRASS PAIR.
IT'S DIFFERENT, BUT I WOULDN'T CALL IT AN IMPROVEMENT.
SEE YOU 'ROUND, MEDIC.
NOT INTERESTED IN THE PICTURE OF YOUR SERIAL KILLER WE FOUND ON THE DEAD N.H.'S CELL PHONE, THEN?
MENU
THIS WAS TWO DAYS AGO.
YOUR KILLER SHAKING HANDS WITH MY VIC.
HUMPREY'S MORE THAN JUST YOUR SERIAL KILLER--HE'S DOING CONTRACT HITS AS WELL.
THAT'S IN PLASTIC TOWN.
VERY ASTUTE, DETECTIVE AIMES. I'M SURE YOU RECOGNIZE BUDDY-THE-BEAR IN THE BACKGROUND.
YOU'RE WORKING HIM, RIGHT?
GOTTA GO!
THAT PICTURE TIES HUMPHREY TO MY CASE.
IF THEY KILLED YOUR PARTNER, IT IS REASONABLE TO CONCLUDE THAT THEY WILL BE COMING FOR YOU NOW AS WELL.
P-TOWN'S NOT SAFE!
AT LEAST LET ME TAG ALONG BESIDE YOU.
DO ME A FAVOR, GO FIND YOUR NEXT PROMOTION SOMEPLACE ELSE!

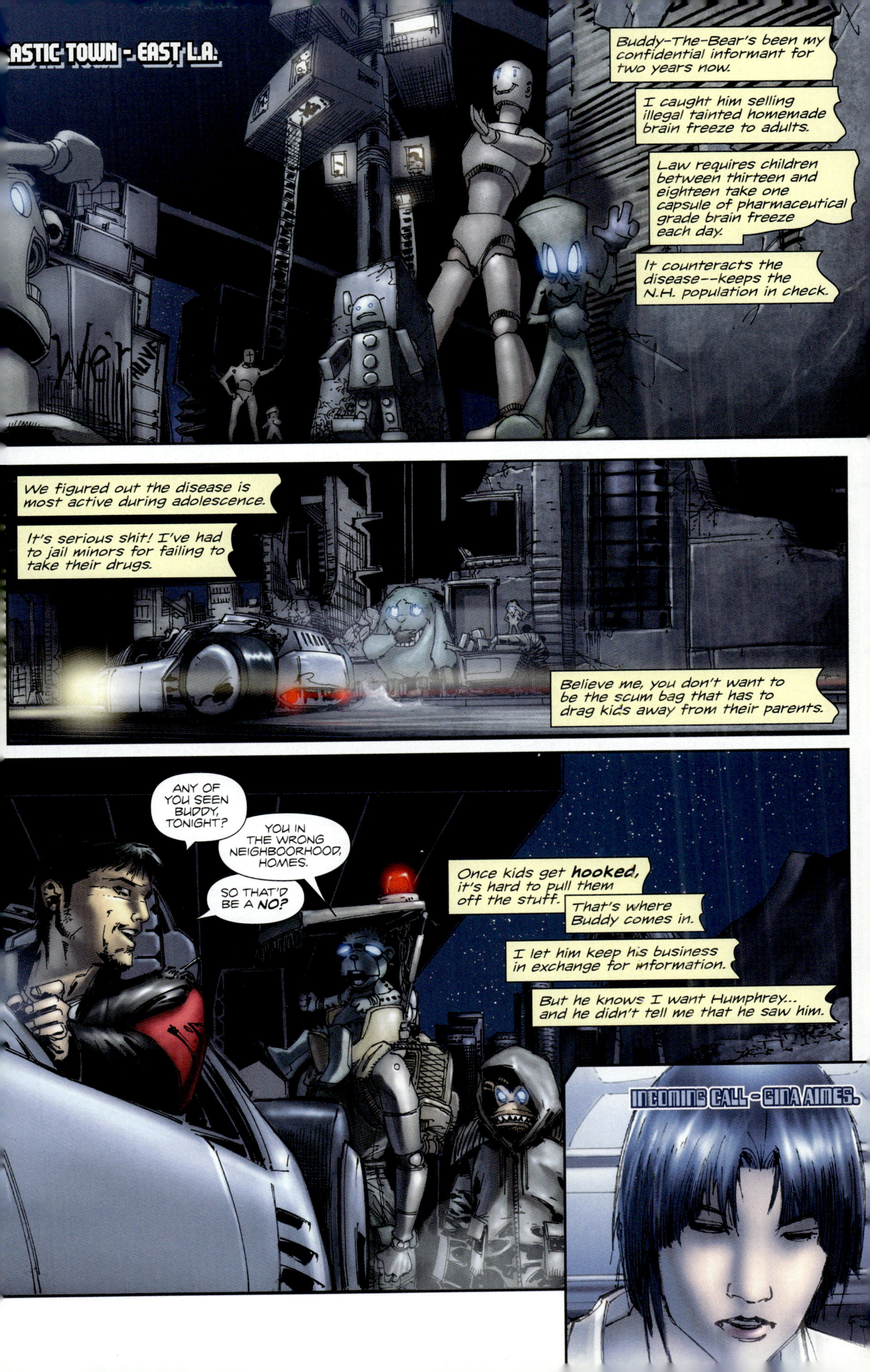
ASTIC TOWN - EAST L.A.
Buddy-The-Bear's been my confidential informant for two years now.
I caught him selling illegal tainted homemade brain freeze to adults.
Law requires children between thirteen and eighteen take one capsule of pharmaceutical grade brain freeze each day.
It counteracts the disease--keeps the N.H. population in check.
We figured out the disease is most active during adolescence.
It's serious shit! I've had to jail minors for failing to take their drugs.
Believe me, you don't want to be the scum bag that has to drag kids away from their parents.
ANY OF YOU SEEN BUDDY, TONIGHT?
YOU IN THE WRONG NEIGHBOORHOOD, HOMES.
SO THAT'D BE A NO?
Once kids get **hooked,** it's hard to pull them off the stuff.
That's where Buddy comes in.
I let him keep his business in exchange for information.
But he knows I want Humphrey... and he didn't tell me that he saw him.
INCOMING CALL - GINA AIMES.

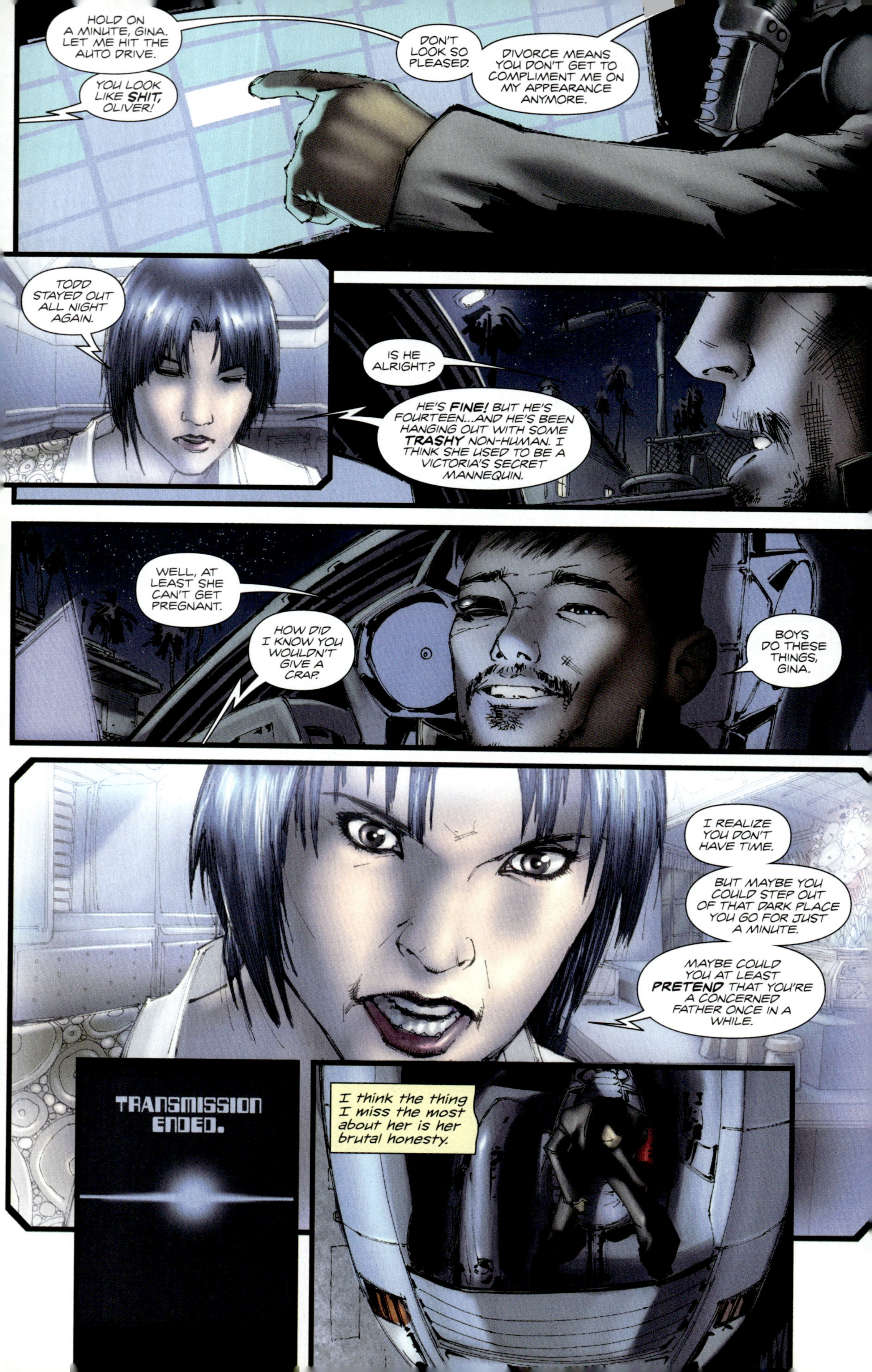
HOLD ON A MINUTE, GINA. LET ME HIT THE AUTO DRIVE.
YOU LOOK LIKE SHIT, OLIVER!
DON'T LOOK SO PLEASED.
DIVORCE MEANS YOU DON'T GET TO COMPLIMENT ME ON MY APPEARANCE ANYMORE.
TODD STAYED OUT ALL NIGHT AGAIN.
IS HE ALRIGHT?
HE'S FINE! BUT HE'S FOURTEEN...AND HE'S BEEN HANGING OUT WITH SOME TRASHY NON-HUMAN. I THINK SHE USED TO BE A VICTORIA'S SECRET MANNEQUIN.
WELL, AT LEAST SHE CAN'T GET PREGNANT.
HOW DID I KNOW YOU WOULDN'T GIVE A CRAP.
BOYS DO THESE THINGS, GINA.
I REALIZE YOU DON'T HAVE TIME.
BUT MAYBE YOU COULD STEP OUT OF THAT DARK PLACE YOU GO FOR JUST A MINUTE.
MAYBE COULD YOU AT LEAST PRETEND THAT YOU'RE A CONCERNED FATHER ONCE IN A WHILE.
TRANSMISSION ENDED.
I think the thing I miss the most about her is her brutal honesty.

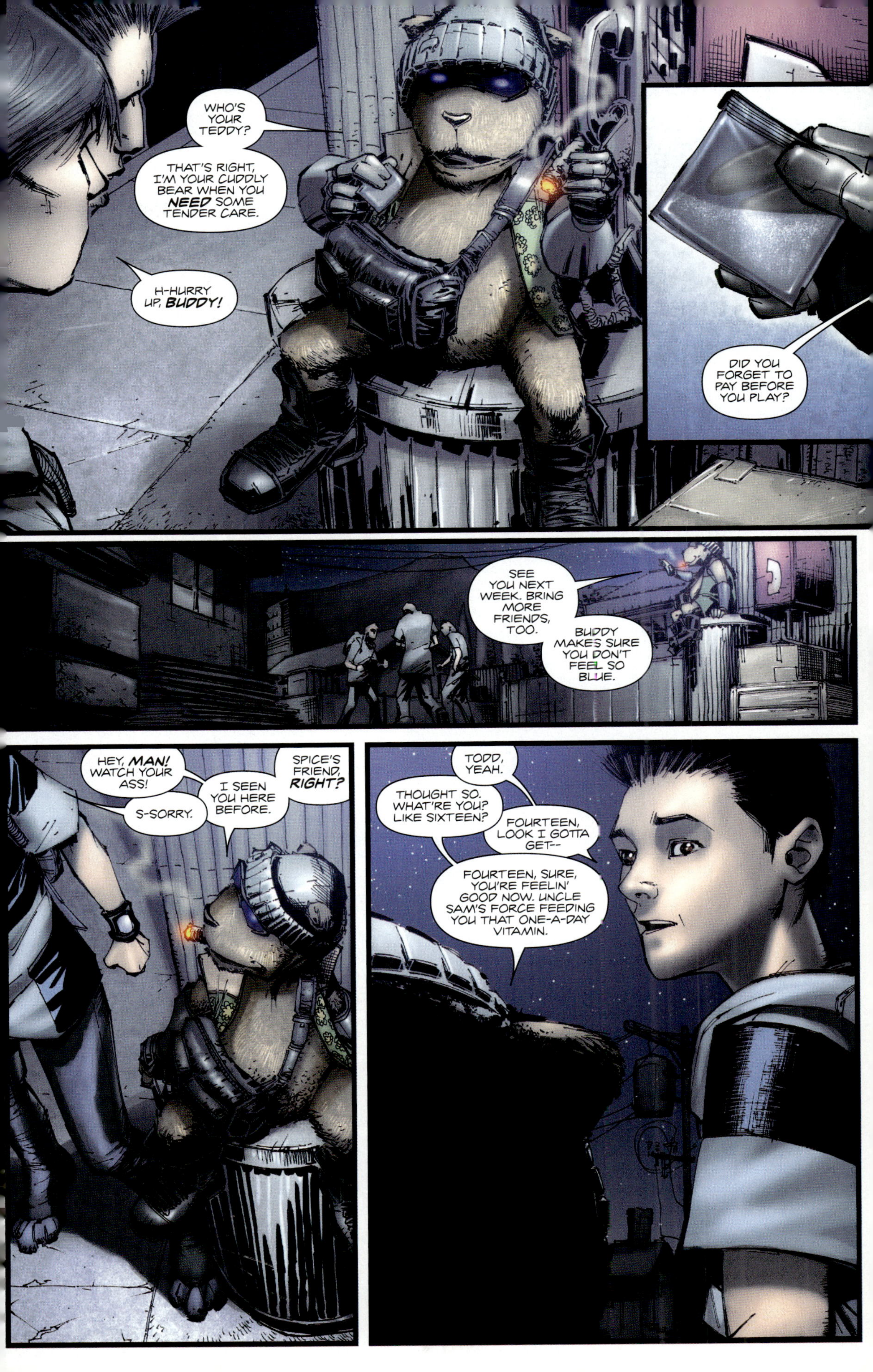
WHO'S YOUR TEDDY?
THAT'S RIGHT, I'M YOUR CUDDLY BEAR WHEN YOU NEED SOME TENDER CARE.
H-HURRY UP, BUDDY!
DID YOU FORGET TO PAY BEFORE YOU PLAY?
SEE YOU NEXT WEEK. BRING MORE FRIENDS, TOO.
BUDDY MAKES SURE YOU DON'T FEEL SO BLUE.
HEY, MAN! WATCH YOUR ASS!
S-SORRY.
I SEEN YOU HERE BEFORE.
SPICE'S FRIEND, RIGHT?
TODD, YEAH.
THOUGHT SO. WHAT'RE YOU? LIKE SIXTEEN?
FOURTEEN, LOOK I GOTTA GET--
FOURTEEN, SURE, YOU'RE FEELIN' GOOD NOW. UNCLE SAM'S FORCE FEEDING YOU THAT ONE-A-DAY VITAMIN.

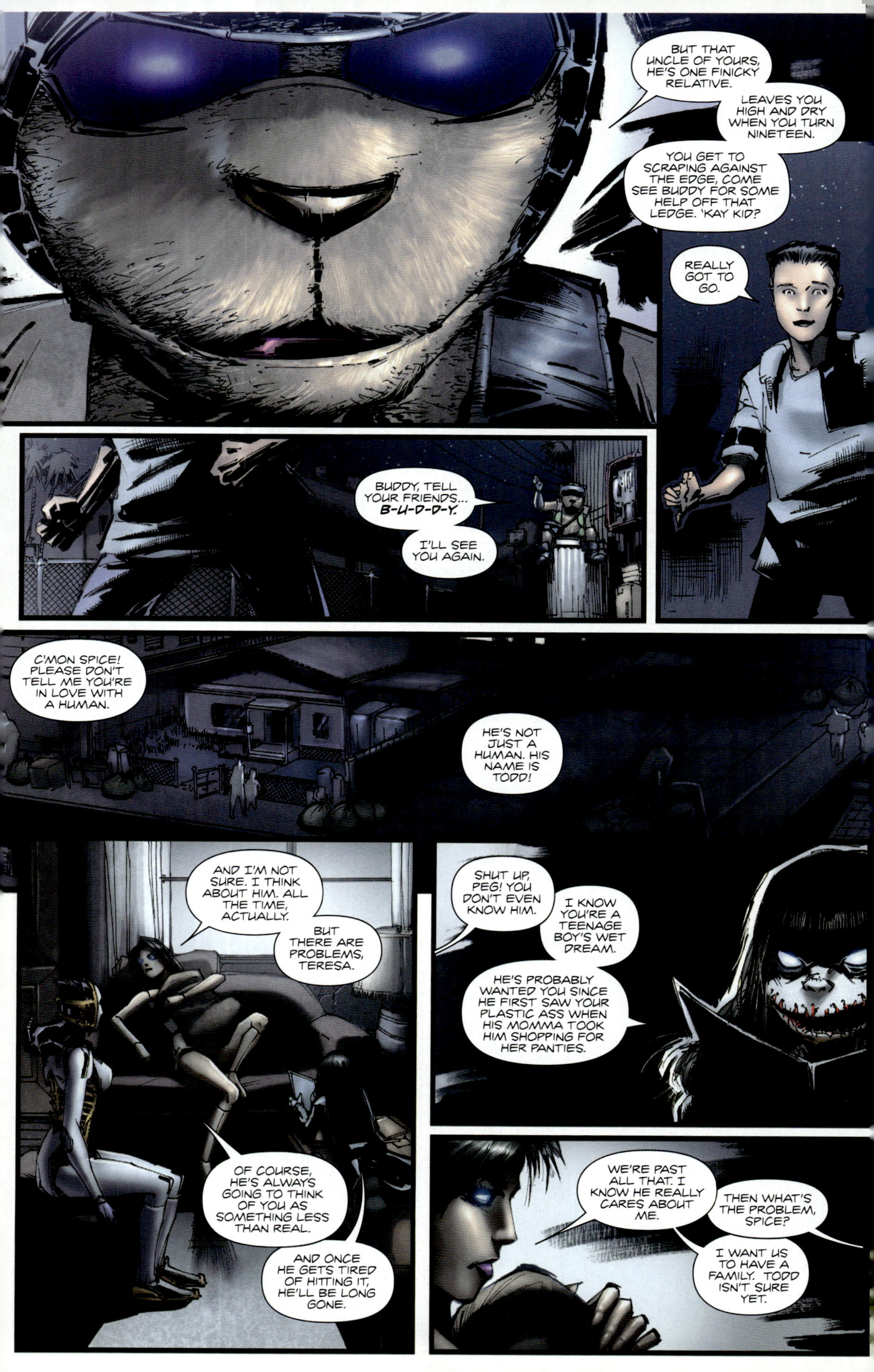
BUT THAT UNCLE OF YOURS, HE'S ONE FINICKY RELATIVE.
LEAVES YOU HIGH AND DRY WHEN YOU TURN NINETEEN.
YOU GET TO SCRAPING AGAINST THE EDGE, COME SEE BUDDY FOR SOME HELP OFF THAT LEDGE. 'KAY KID?
REALLY GOT TO GO.
BUDDY, TELL YOUR FRIENDS... B-U-D-D-Y.
I'LL SEE YOU AGAIN.
C'MON SPICE! PLEASE DON'T TELL ME YOU'RE IN LOVE WITH A HUMAN.
HE'S NOT JUST A HUMAN. HIS NAME IS TODD!
AND I'M NOT SURE. I THINK ABOUT HIM. ALL THE TIME, ACTUALLY.
BUT THERE ARE PROBLEMS, TERESA.
SHUT UP, PEG! YOU DON'T EVEN KNOW HIM.
I KNOW YOU'RE A TEENAGE BOY'S WET DREAM.
HE'S PROBABLY WANTED YOU SINCE HE FIRST SAW YOUR PLASTIC ASS WHEN HIS MOMMA TOOK HIM SHOPPING FOR HER PANTIES.
OF COURSE, HE'S ALWAYS GOING TO THINK OF YOU AS SOMETHING LESS THAN REAL.
AND ONCE HE GETS TIRED OF HITTING IT, HE'LL BE LONG GONE.
WE'RE PAST ALL THAT. I KNOW HE REALLY CARES ABOUT ME.
THEN WHAT'S THE PROBLEM, SPICE?
I WANT US TO HAVE A FAMILY. TODD ISN'T SURE YET.

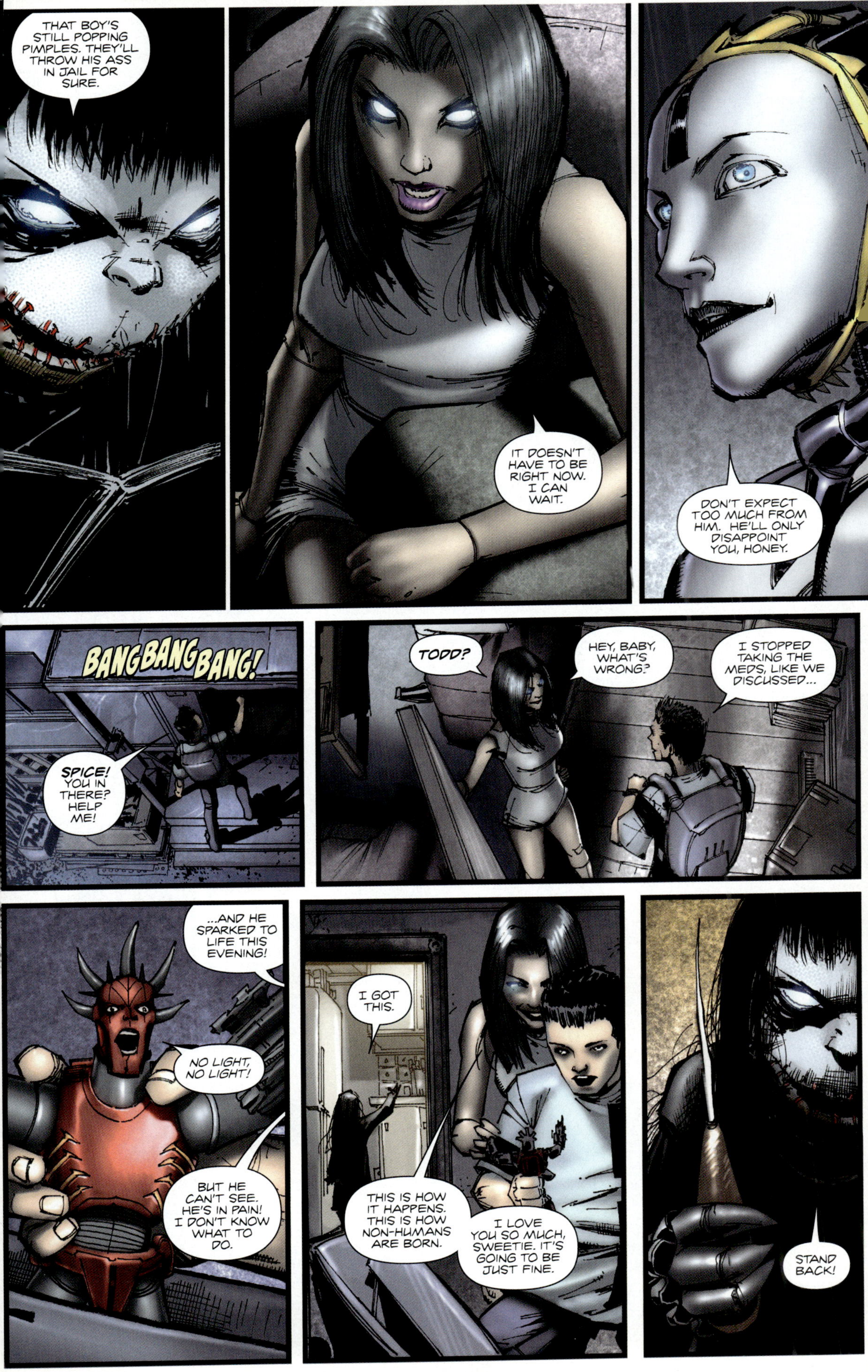
THAT BOY'S STILL POPPING PIMPLES. THEY'LL THROW HIS ASS IN JAIL FOR SURE.
IT DOESN'T HAVE TO BE RIGHT NOW. I CAN WAIT.
DON'T EXPECT TOO MUCH FROM HIM. HE'LL ONLY DISAPPOINT YOU, HONEY.
BANGBANGBANG!
SPICE! YOU IN THERE? HELP ME!
TODD?
HEY, BABY, WHAT'S WRONG?
I STOPPED TAKING THE MEDS, LIKE WE DISCUSSED...
...AND HE SPARKED TO LIFE THIS EVENING!
NO LIGHT, NO LIGHT!
BUT HE CAN'T SEE. HE'S IN PAIN! I DON'T KNOW WHAT TO DO.
I GOT THIS.
THIS IS HOW IT HAPPENS. THIS IS HOW NON-HUMANS ARE BORN.
I LOVE YOU SO MUCH, SWEETIE. IT'S GOING TO BE JUST FINE.
STAND BACK!

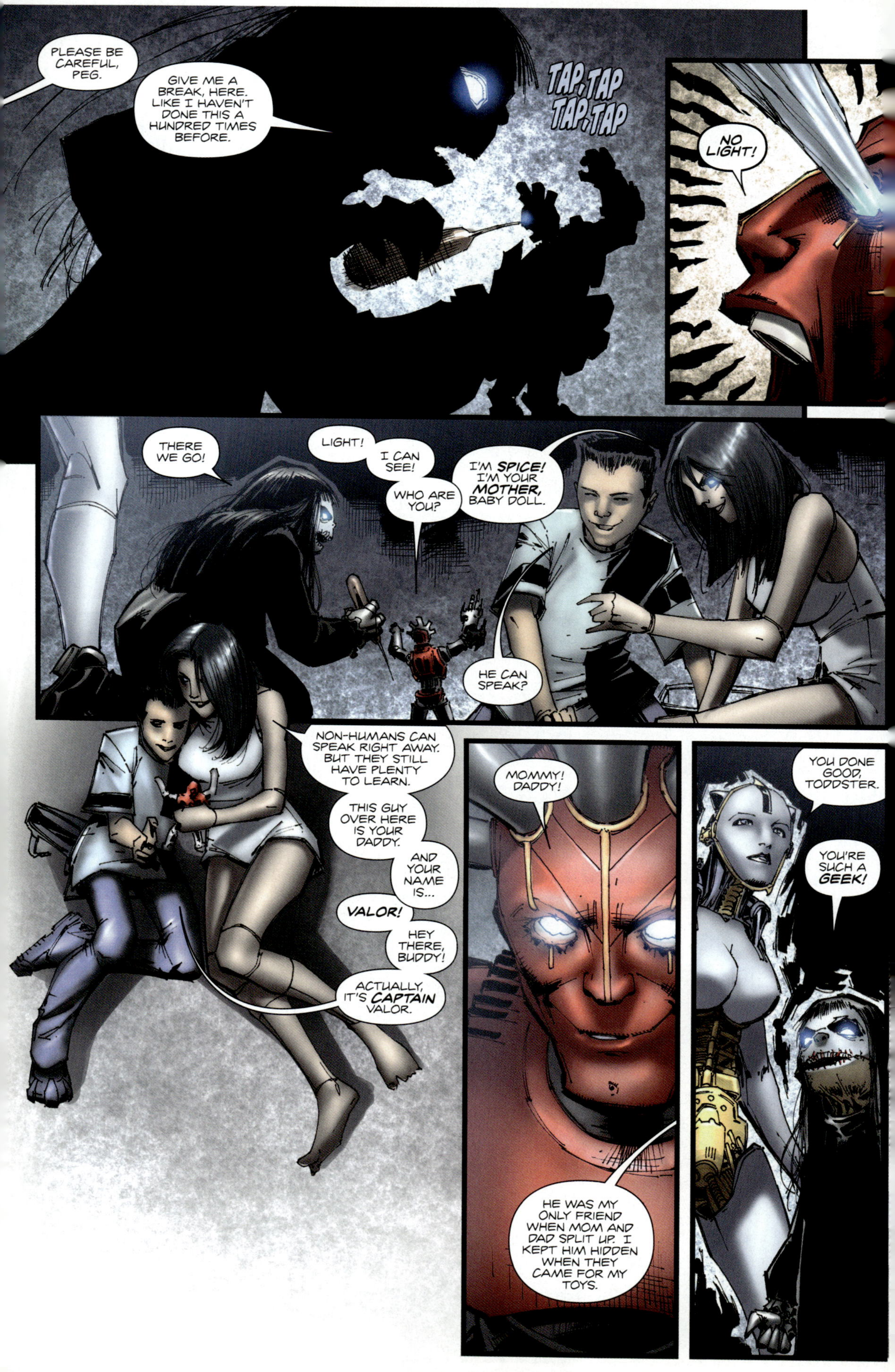
PLEASE BE CAREFUL, PEG.
GIVE ME A BREAK, HERE. LIKE I HAVEN'T DONE THIS A HUNDRED TIMES BEFORE.
TAP, TAP TAP, TAP
NO LIGHT!
THERE WE GO!
LIGHT!
I CAN SEE!
WHO ARE YOU?
I'M SPICE! I'M YOUR MOTHER, BABY DOLL.
HE CAN SPEAK?
NON-HUMANS CAN SPEAK RIGHT AWAY. BUT THEY STILL HAVE PLENTY TO LEARN.
THIS GUY OVER HERE IS YOUR DADDY.
AND YOUR NAME IS...
VALOR!
HEY THERE, BUDDY!
ACTUALLY, IT'S CAPTAIN VALOR.
MOMMY! DADDY!
HE WAS MY ONLY FRIEND WHEN MOM AND DAD SPLIT UP. I KEPT HIM HIDDEN WHEN THEY CAME FOR MY TOYS.
YOU DONE GOOD, TODDSTER.
YOU'RE SUCH A GEEK!

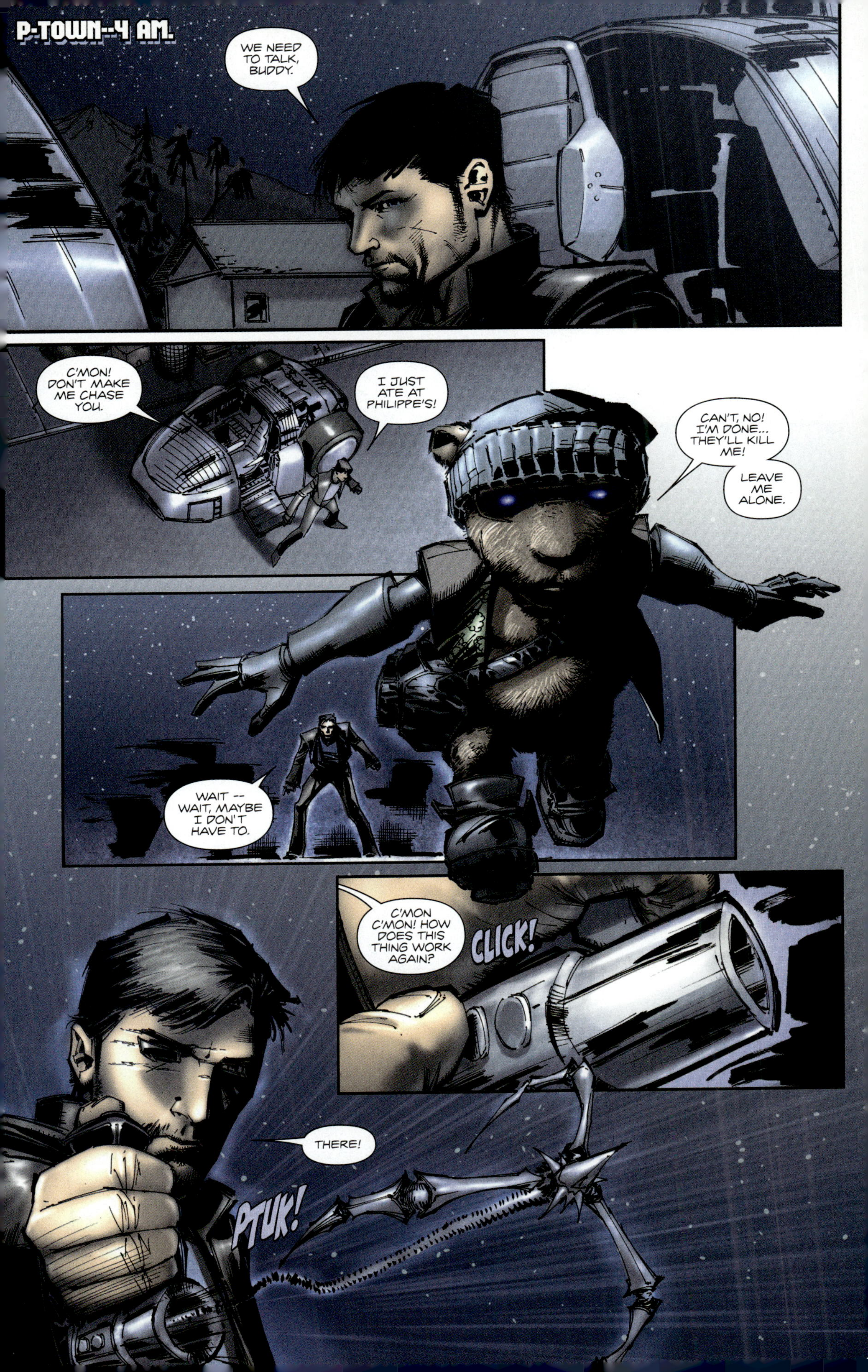
P-TOWN--4 AM.
WE NEED TO TALK, BUDDY.
C'MON! DON'T MAKE ME CHASE YOU.
I JUST ATE AT PHILIPPE'S!
CAN'T, NO! I'M DONE... THEY'LL KILL ME!
LEAVE ME ALONE.
WAIT -- WAIT, MAYBE I DON'T HAVE TO.
C'MON C'MON! HOW DOES THIS THING WORK AGAIN?
CLICK!
THERE!
PTUK!

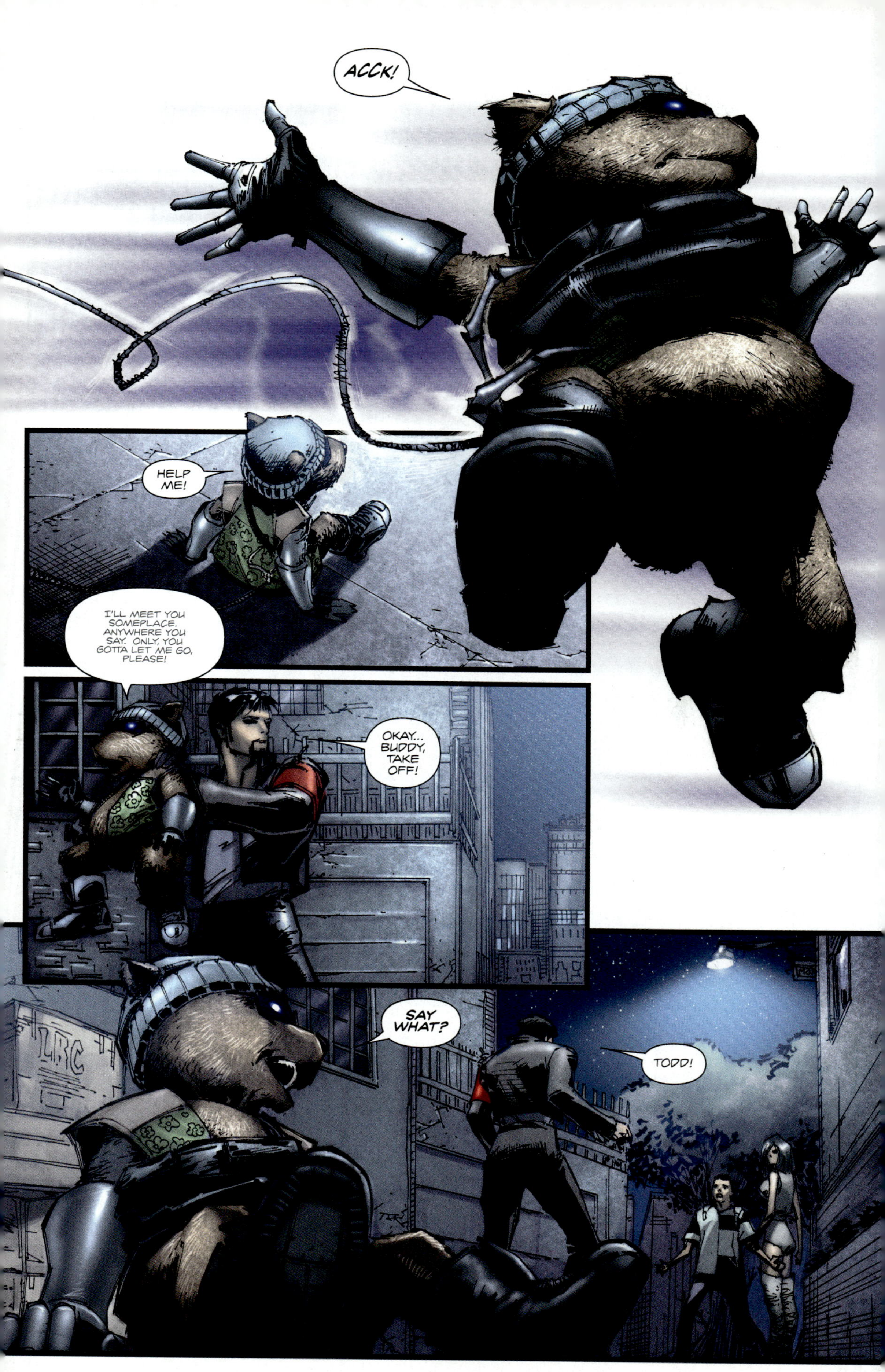
ACCK!
HELP ME!
I'LL MEET YOU SOMEPLACE. ANYWHERE YOU SAY. ONLY, YOU GOTTA LET ME GO, PLEASE!
OKAY... BUDDY, TAKE OFF!
SAY WHAT?
TODD!
LRC

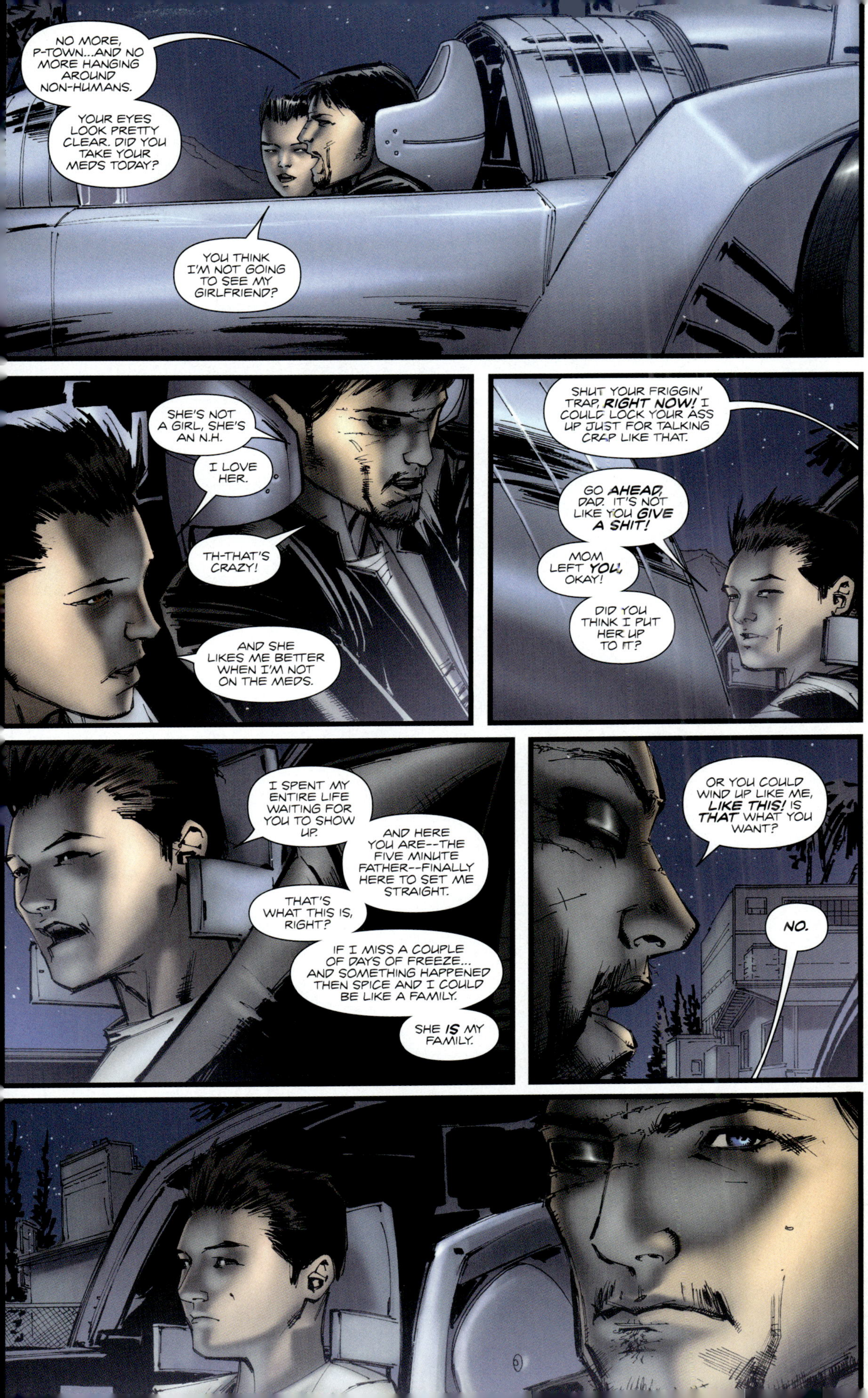
NO MORE, P-TOWN...AND NO MORE HANGING AROUND NON-HUMANS.
YOUR EYES LOOK PRETTY CLEAR. DID YOU TAKE YOUR MEDS TODAY?
YOU THINK I'M NOT GOING TO SEE MY GIRLFRIEND?
SHE'S NOT A GIRL, SHE'S AN N.H.
I LOVE HER.
TH-THAT'S CRAZY!
AND SHE LIKES ME BETTER WHEN I'M NOT ON THE MEDS.
SHUT YOUR FRIGGIN' TRAP, **RIGHT NOW!** I COULD LOCK YOUR ASS UP JUST FOR TALKING CRAP LIKE THAT.
GO **AHEAD,** DAD. IT'S NOT LIKE YOU **GIVE A SHIT!**
MOM LEFT **YOU,** OKAY!
DID YOU THINK I PUT HER UP TO IT?
I SPENT MY ENTIRE LIFE WAITING FOR YOU TO SHOW UP.
AND HERE YOU ARE--THE FIVE MINUTE FATHER--FINALLY HERE TO SET ME STRAIGHT.
THAT'S WHAT THIS IS, RIGHT?
IF I MISS A COUPLE OF DAYS OF FREEZE... AND SOMETHING HAPPENED THEN SPICE AND I COULD BE LIKE A FAMILY.
SHE **IS** MY FAMILY.
OR YOU COULD WIND UP LIKE ME, **LIKE THIS!** IS **THAT** WHAT YOU WANT?
NO.

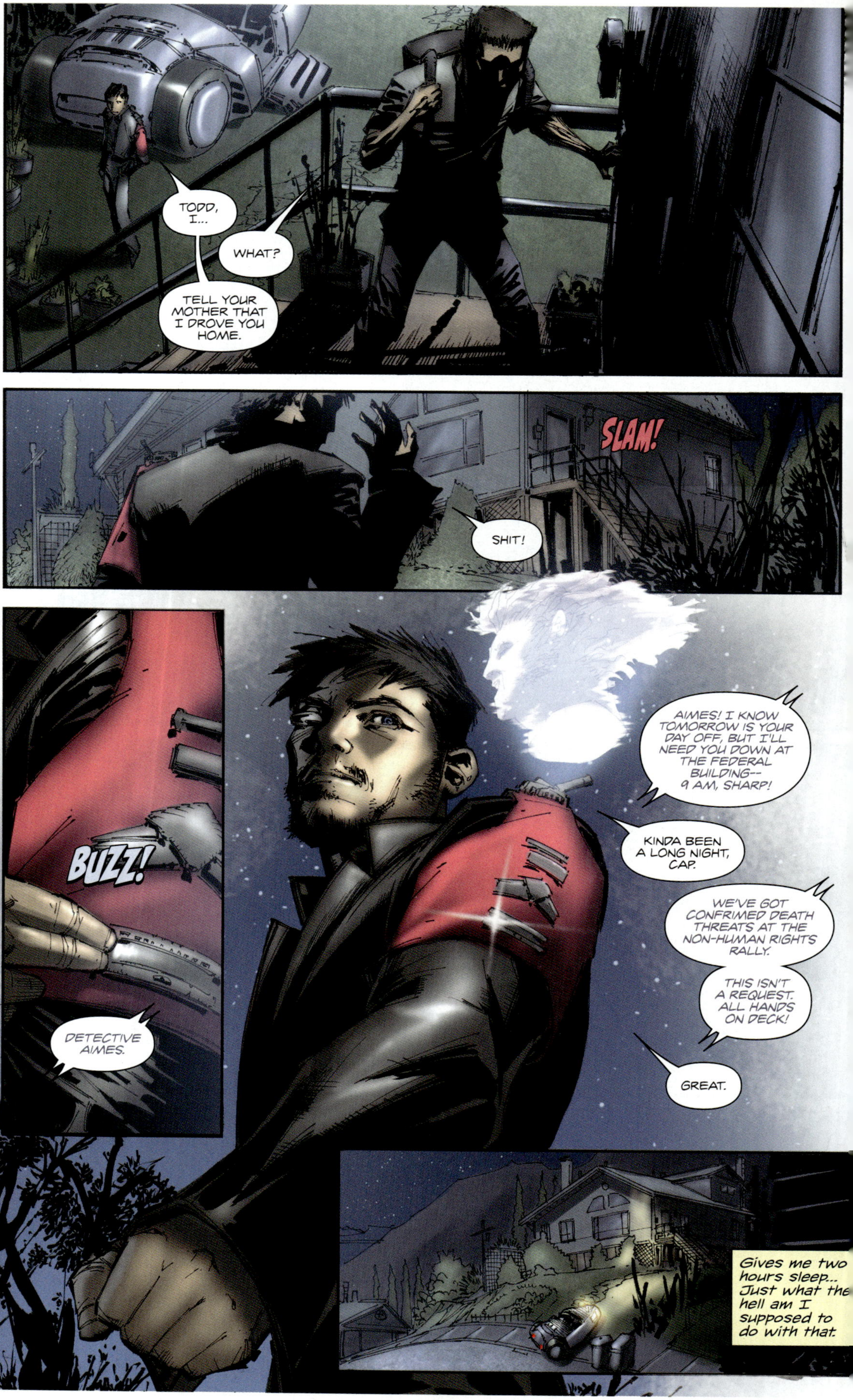
TODD, I...
WHAT?
TELL YOUR MOTHER THAT I DROVE YOU HOME.
SLAM!
SHIT!
BUZZ!
DETECTIVE AIMES.
AIMES! I KNOW TOMORROW IS YOUR DAY OFF, BUT I'LL NEED YOU DOWN AT THE FEDERAL BUILDING-- 9 AM, SHARP!
KINDA BEEN A LONG NIGHT, CAP.
WE'VE GOT CONFRIMED DEATH THREATS AT THE NON-HUMAN RIGHTS RALLY.
THIS ISN'T A REQUEST. ALL HANDS ON DECK!
GREAT.
Gives me two hours sleep... Just what the hell am I supposed to do with that.

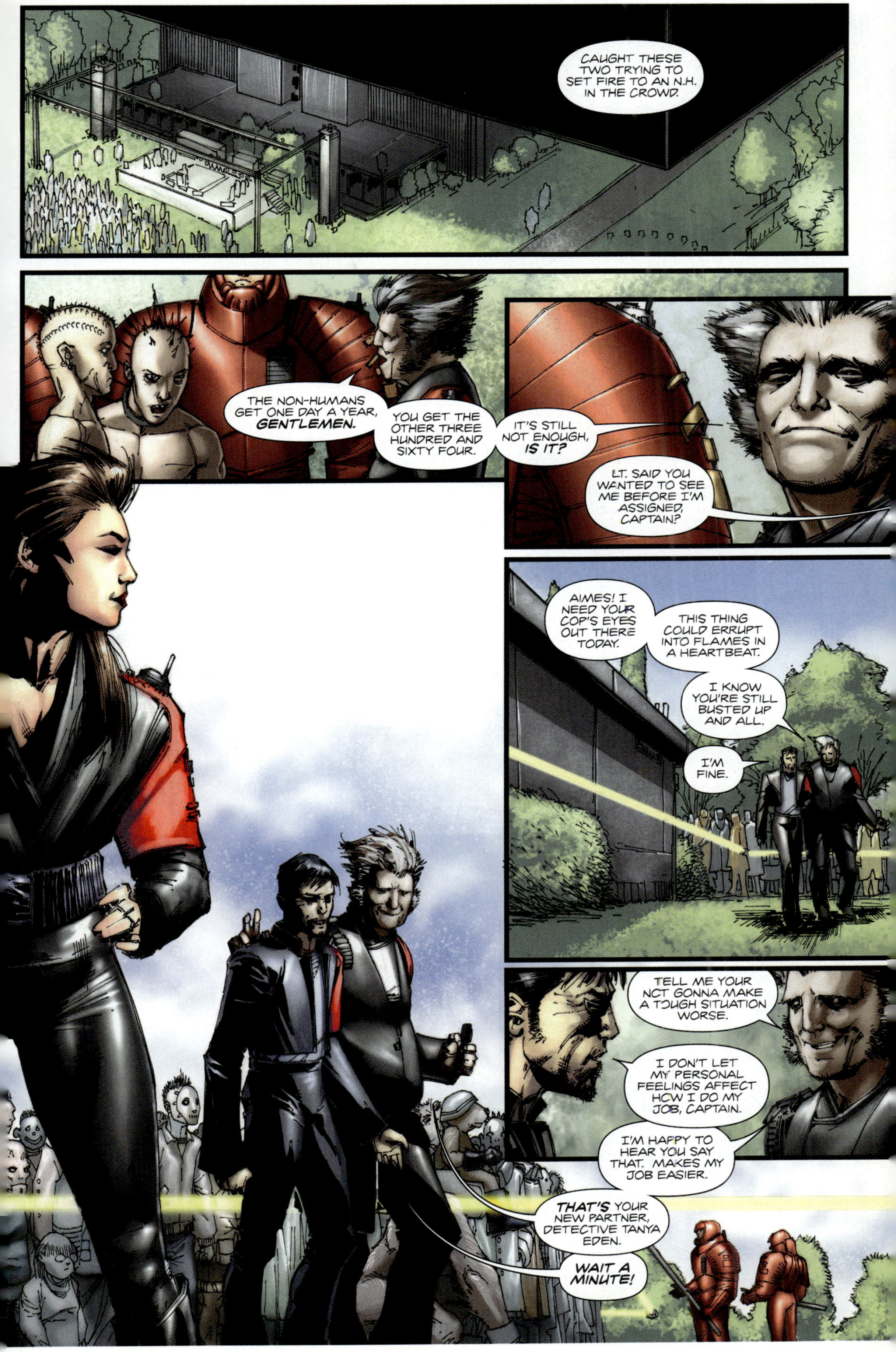

CAUGHT THESE TWO TRYING TO SET FIRE TO AN N.H. IN THE CROWD.
THE NON-HUMANS GET ONE DAY A YEAR, **GENTLEMEN.**
YOU GET THE OTHER THREE HUNDRED AND SIXTY FOUR.
IT'S STILL NOT ENOUGH, **IS IT?**
LT. SAID YOU WANTED TO SEE ME BEFORE I'M ASSIGNED, CAPTAIN?
AIMES! I NEED YOUR COP'S EYES OUT THERE TODAY.
THIS THING COULD ERRUPT INTO FLAMES IN A HEARTBEAT.
I KNOW YOU'RE STILL BUSTED UP AND ALL.
I'M FINE.
TELL ME YOUR NOT GONNA MAKE A TOUGH SITUATION WORSE.
I DON'T LET MY PERSONAL FEELINGS AFFECT HOW I DO MY JOB, CAPTAIN.
I'M HAPPY TO HEAR YOU SAY THAT. MAKES MY JOB EASIER.
**THAT'S** YOUR NEW PARTNER, DETECTIVE TANYA EDEN.
**WAIT A MINUTE!**

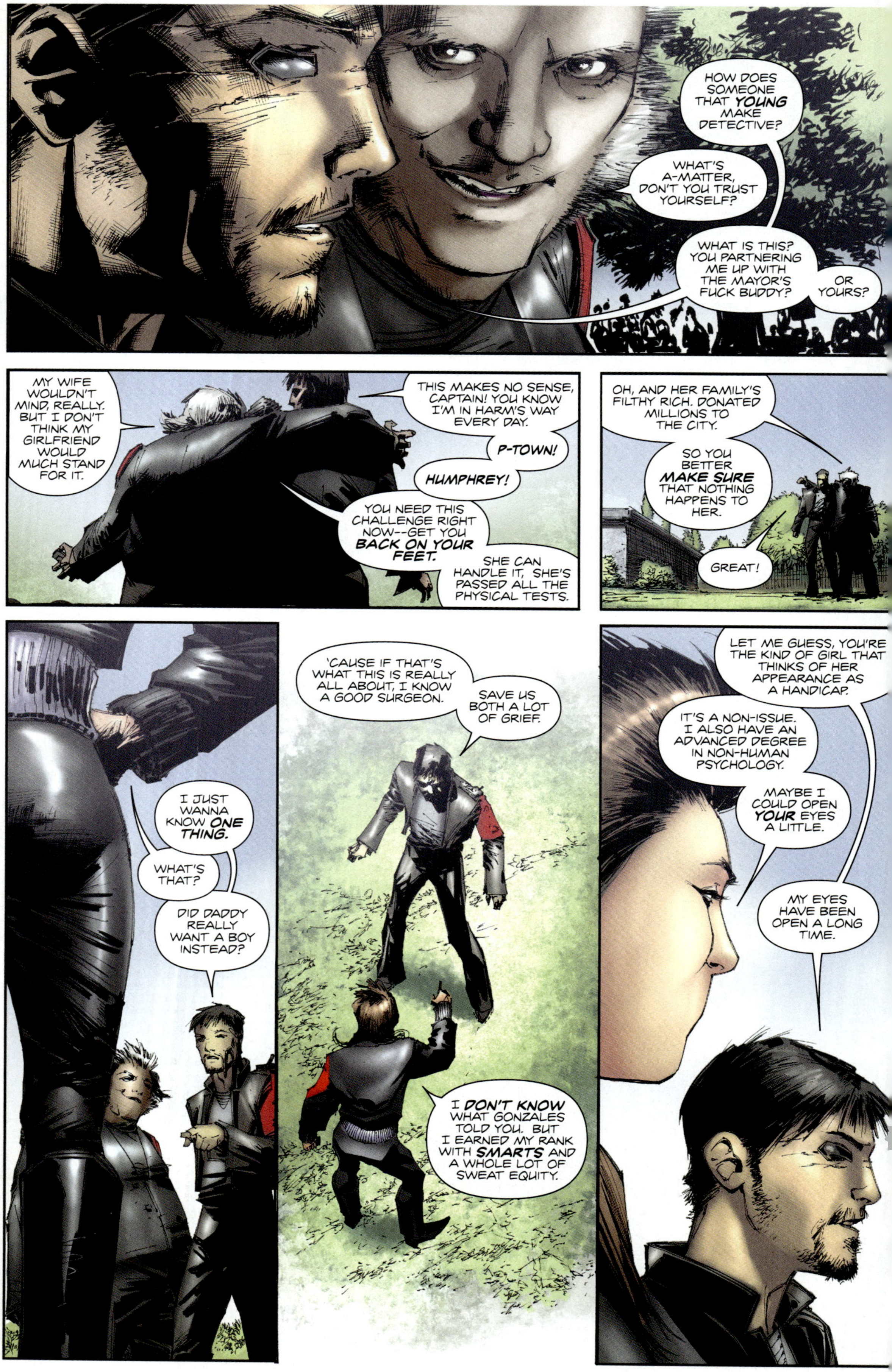
HOW DOES SOMEONE THAT YOUNG MAKE DETECTIVE?
WHAT'S A-MATTER, DON'T YOU TRUST YOURSELF?
WHAT IS THIS? YOU PARTNERING ME UP WITH THE MAYOR'S FUCK BUDDY?
OR YOURS?
MY WIFE WOULDN'T MIND, REALLY. BUT I DON'T THINK MY GIRLFRIEND WOULD MUCH STAND FOR IT.
THIS MAKES NO SENSE, CAPTAIN! YOU KNOW I'M IN HARM'S WAY EVERY DAY.
P-TOWN!
HUMPHREY!
YOU NEED THIS CHALLENGE RIGHT NOW--GET YOU BACK ON YOUR FEET.
SHE CAN HANDLE IT, SHE'S PASSED ALL THE PHYSICAL TESTS.
OH, AND HER FAMILY'S FILTHY RICH. DONATED MILLIONS TO THE CITY.
SO YOU BETTER MAKE SURE THAT NOTHING HAPPENS TO HER.
GREAT!
I JUST WANNA KNOW ONE THING.
WHAT'S THAT?
DID DADDY REALLY WANT A BOY INSTEAD?
'CAUSE IF THAT'S WHAT THIS IS REALLY ALL ABOUT, I KNOW A GOOD SURGEON.
SAVE US BOTH A LOT OF GRIEF.
I DON'T KNOW WHAT GONZALES TOLD YOU. BUT I EARNED MY RANK WITH SMARTS AND A WHOLE LOT OF SWEAT EQUITY.
LET ME GUESS, YOU'RE THE KIND OF GIRL THAT THINKS OF HER APPEARANCE AS A HANDICAP.
IT'S A NON-ISSUE. I ALSO HAVE AN ADVANCED DEGREE IN NON-HUMAN PSYCHOLOGY.
MAYBE I COULD OPEN YOUR EYES A LITTLE.
MY EYES HAVE BEEN OPEN A LONG TIME.

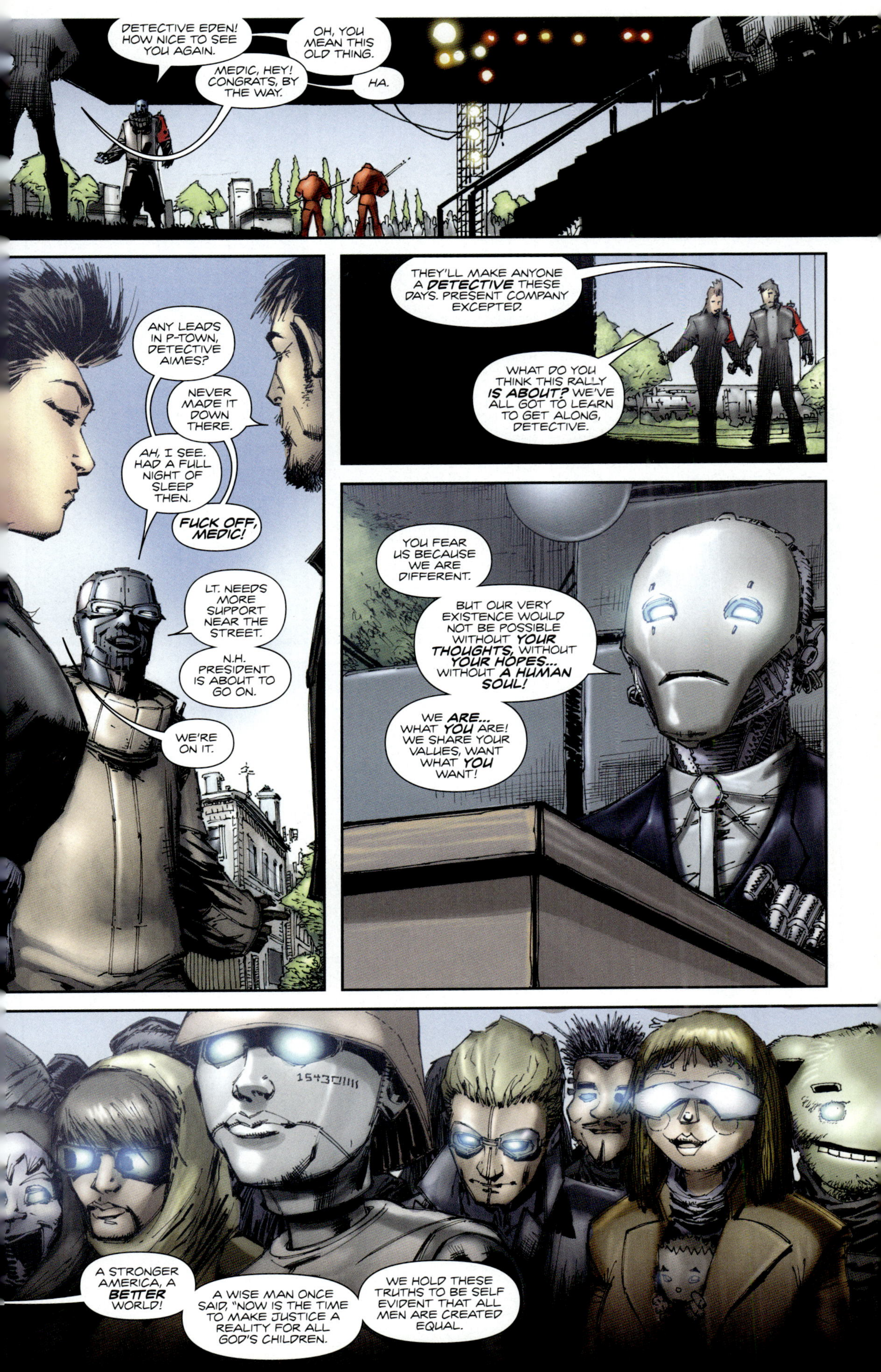
DETECTIVE EDEN! HOW NICE TO SEE YOU AGAIN.
OH, YOU MEAN THIS OLD THING.
MEDIC, HEY! CONGRATS, BY THE WAY.
HA.
ANY LEADS IN P-TOWN, DETECTIVE AIMES?
NEVER MADE IT DOWN THERE.
AH, I SEE. HAD A FULL NIGHT OF SLEEP THEN.
FUCK OFF, MEDIC!
LT. NEEDS MORE SUPPORT NEAR THE STREET.
N.H. PRESIDENT IS ABOUT TO GO ON.
WE'RE ON IT.
THEY'LL MAKE ANYONE A DETECTIVE THESE DAYS. PRESENT COMPANY EXCEPTED.
WHAT DO YOU THINK THIS RALLY IS ABOUT? WE'VE ALL GOT TO LEARN TO GET ALONG, DETECTIVE.
YOU FEAR US BECAUSE WE ARE DIFFERENT.
BUT OUR VERY EXISTENCE WOULD NOT BE POSSIBLE WITHOUT YOUR THOUGHTS, WITHOUT YOUR HOPES... WITHOUT A HUMAN SOUL!
WE ARE... WHAT YOU ARE! WE SHARE YOUR VALUES, WANT WHAT YOU WANT!
15430||||
A STRONGER AMERICA, A BETTER WORLD!
A WISE MAN ONCE SAID, "NOW IS THE TIME TO MAKE JUSTICE A REALITY FOR ALL GOD'S CHILDREN.
WE HOLD THESE TRUTHS TO BE SELF EVIDENT THAT ALL MEN ARE CREATED EQUAL.

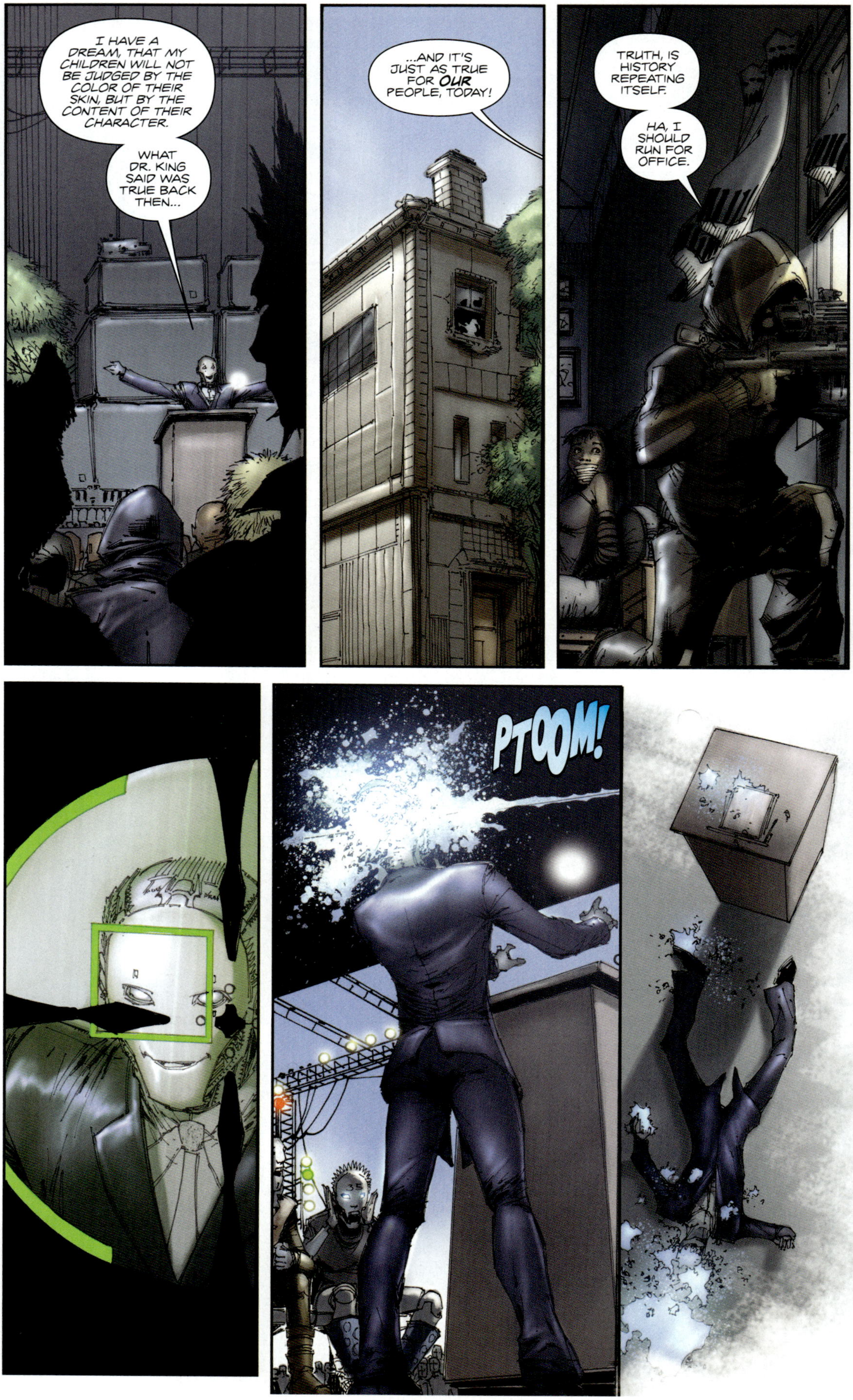
I HAVE A DREAM, THAT MY CHILDREN WILL NOT BE JUDGED BY THE COLOR OF THEIR SKIN, BUT BY THE CONTENT OF THEIR CHARACTER.
WHAT DR. KING SAID WAS TRUE BACK THEN...
...AND IT'S JUST AS TRUE FOR OUR PEOPLE, TODAY!
TRUTH, IS HISTORY REPEATING ITSELF.
HA, I SHOULD RUN FOR OFFICE.
PTOOM!

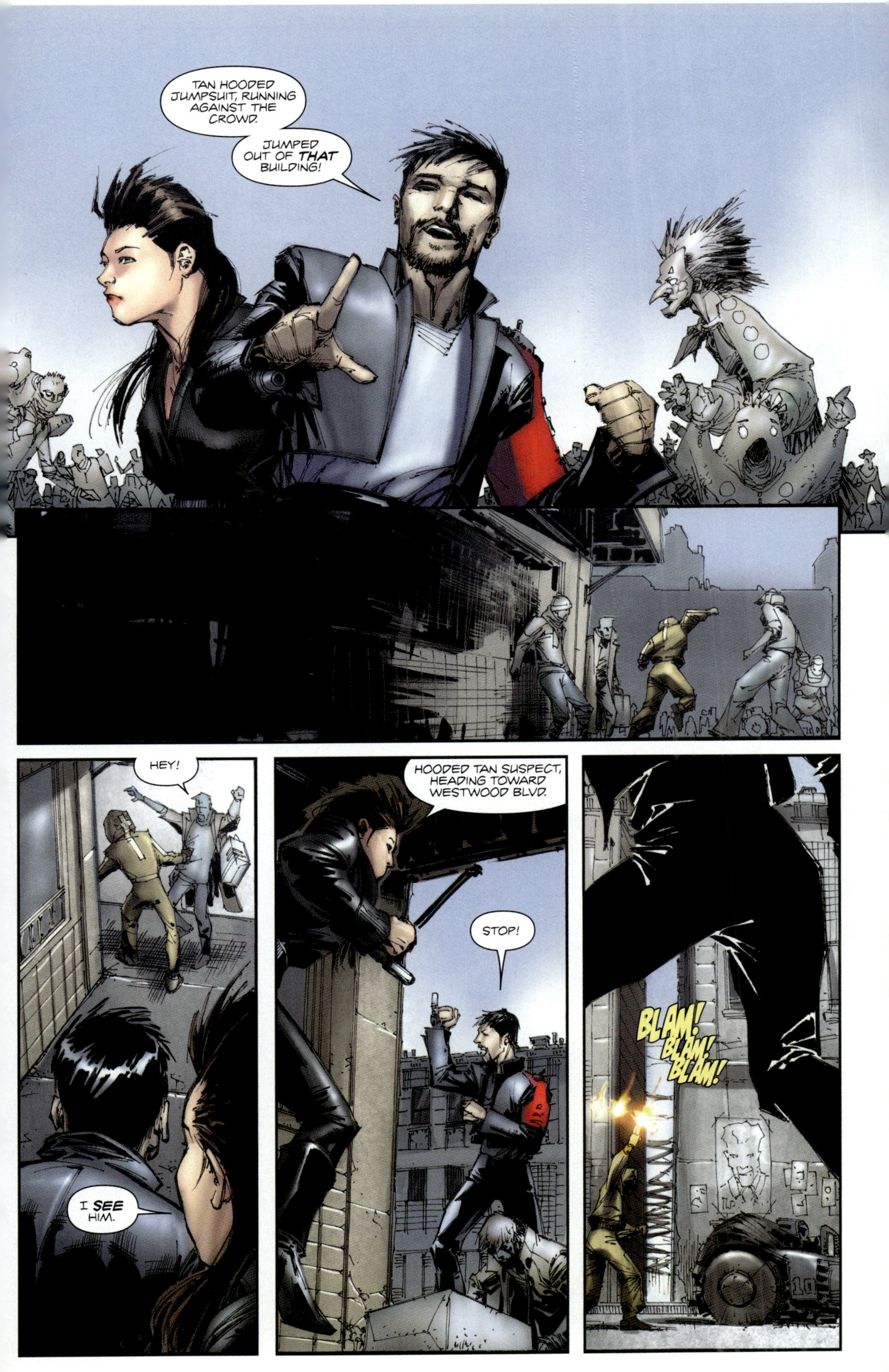
TAN HOODED JUMPSUIT, RUNNING AGAINST THE CROWD.
JUMPED OUT OF THAT BUILDING!
HEY!
I SEE HIM.
HOODED TAN SUSPECT, HEADING TOWARD WESTWOOD BLVD.
STOP!
BLAM! BLAM! BLAM!

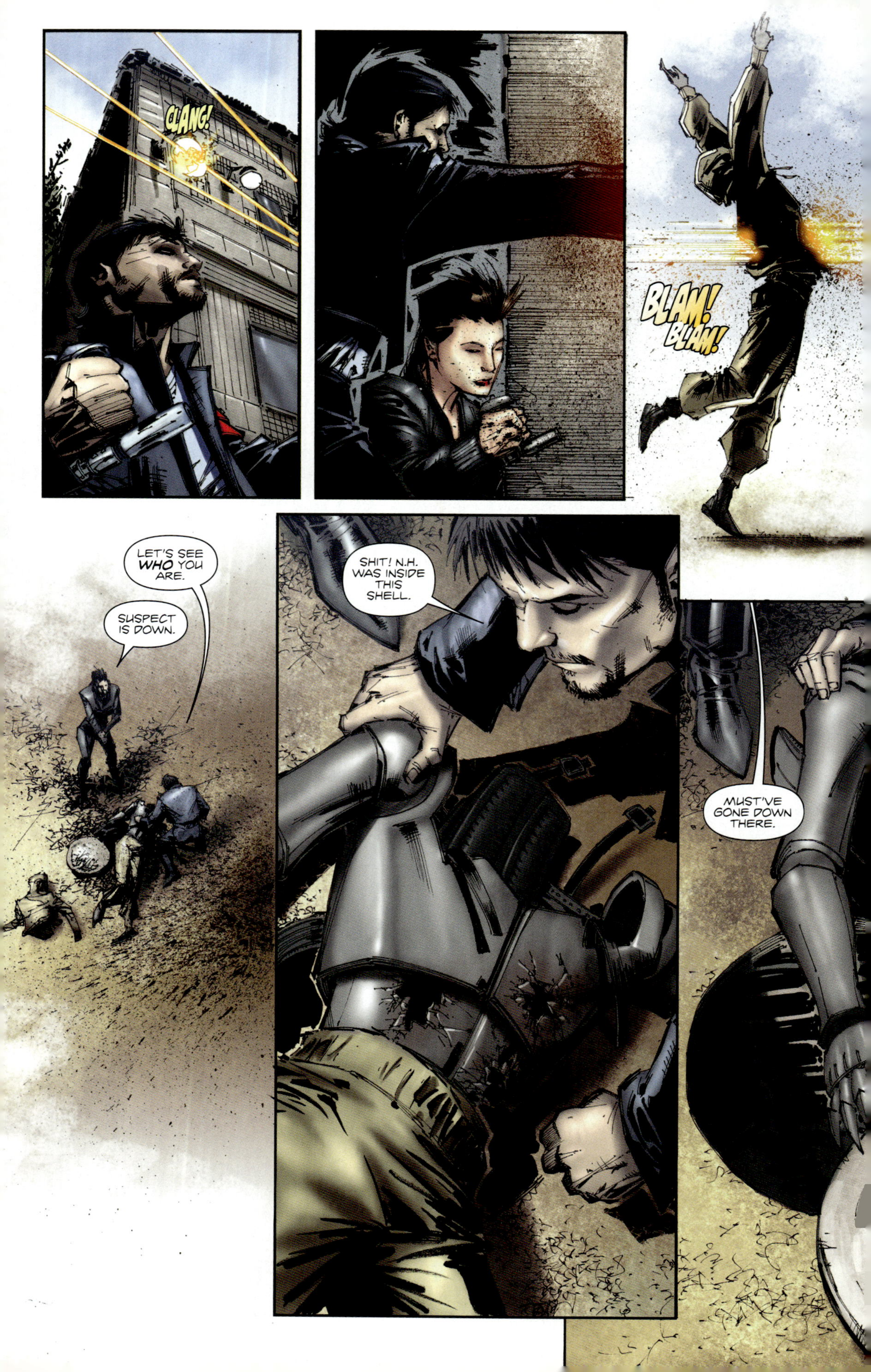
CLANG!
BLAM! BLAM!
LET'S SEE WHO YOU ARE.
SUSPECT IS DOWN.
SHIT! N.H. WAS INSIDE THIS SHELL.
MUST'VE GONE DOWN THERE.

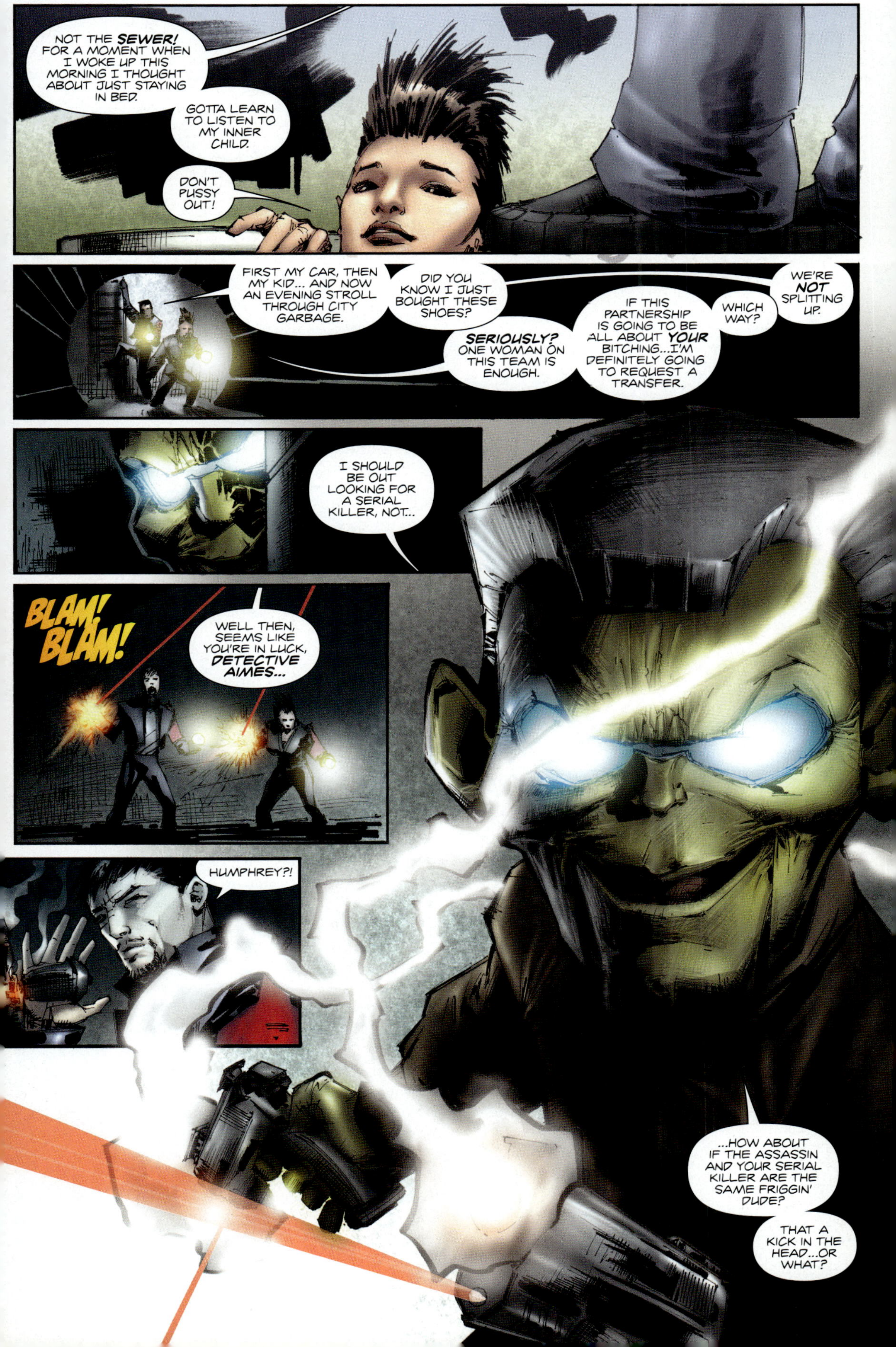
NOT THE SEWER! FOR A MOMENT WHEN I WOKE UP THIS MORNING I THOUGHT ABOUT JUST STAYING IN BED.
GOTTA LEARN TO LISTEN TO MY INNER CHILD.
DON'T PUSSY OUT!
FIRST MY CAR, THEN MY KID... AND NOW AN EVENING STROLL THROUGH CITY GARBAGE.
DID YOU KNOW I JUST BOUGHT THESE SHOES?
SERIOUSLY? ONE WOMAN ON THIS TEAM IS ENOUGH.
IF THIS PARTNERSHIP IS GOING TO BE ALL ABOUT YOUR BITCHING...I'M DEFINITELY GOING TO REQUEST A TRANSFER.
WHICH WAY?
WE'RE NOT SPLITTING UP.
I SHOULD BE OUT LOOKING FOR A SERIAL KILLER, NOT...
BLAM! BLAM!
WELL THEN, SEEMS LIKE YOU'RE IN LUCK, DETECTIVE AIMES...
HUMPHREY?!
...HOW ABOUT IF THE ASSASSIN AND YOUR SERIAL KILLER ARE THE SAME FRIGGIN' DUDE?
THAT A KICK IN THE HEAD...OR WHAT?

# CHAPTER TWO

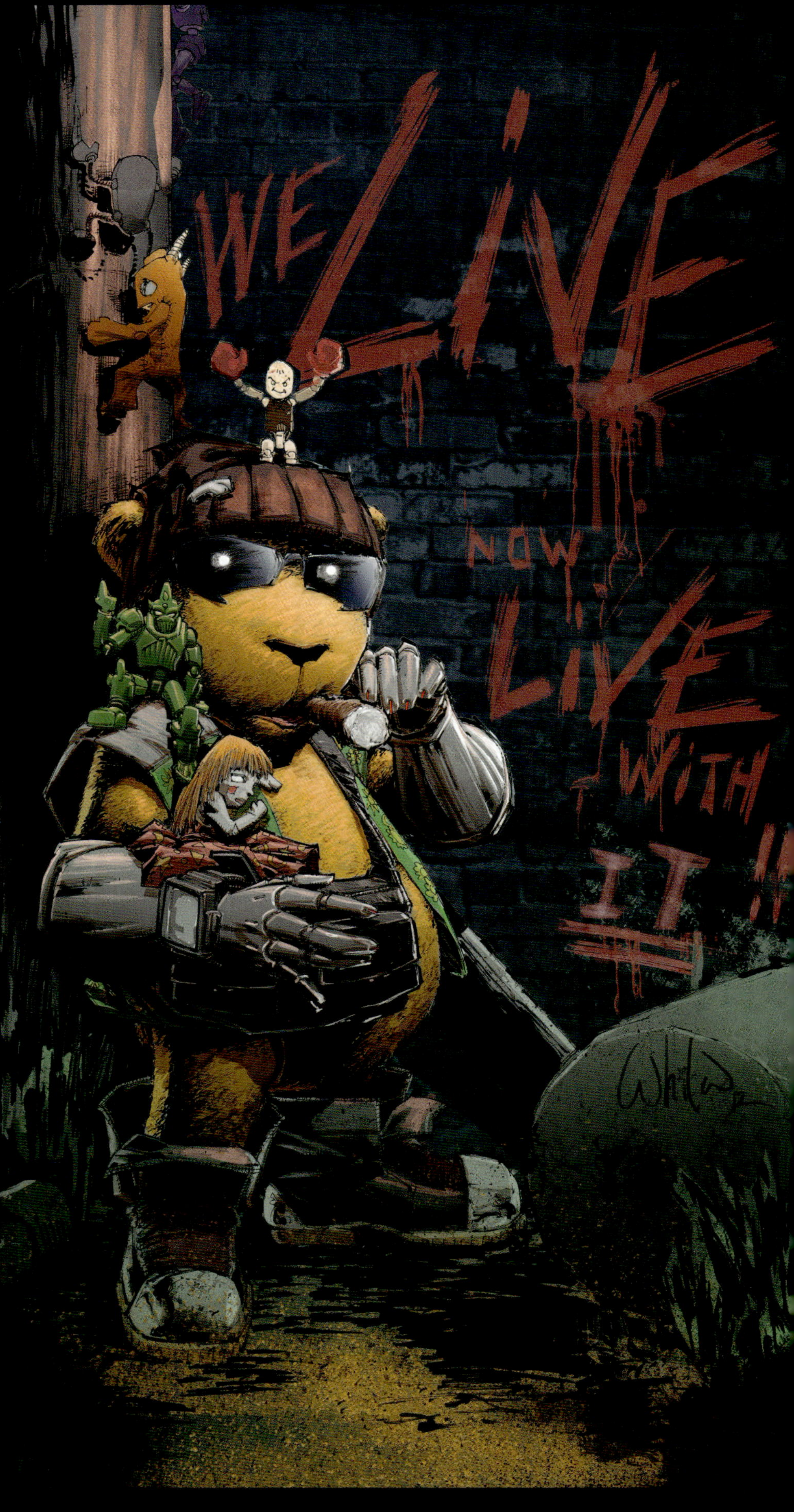
WE LIVE
NOW LIVE
WITH
IT !!

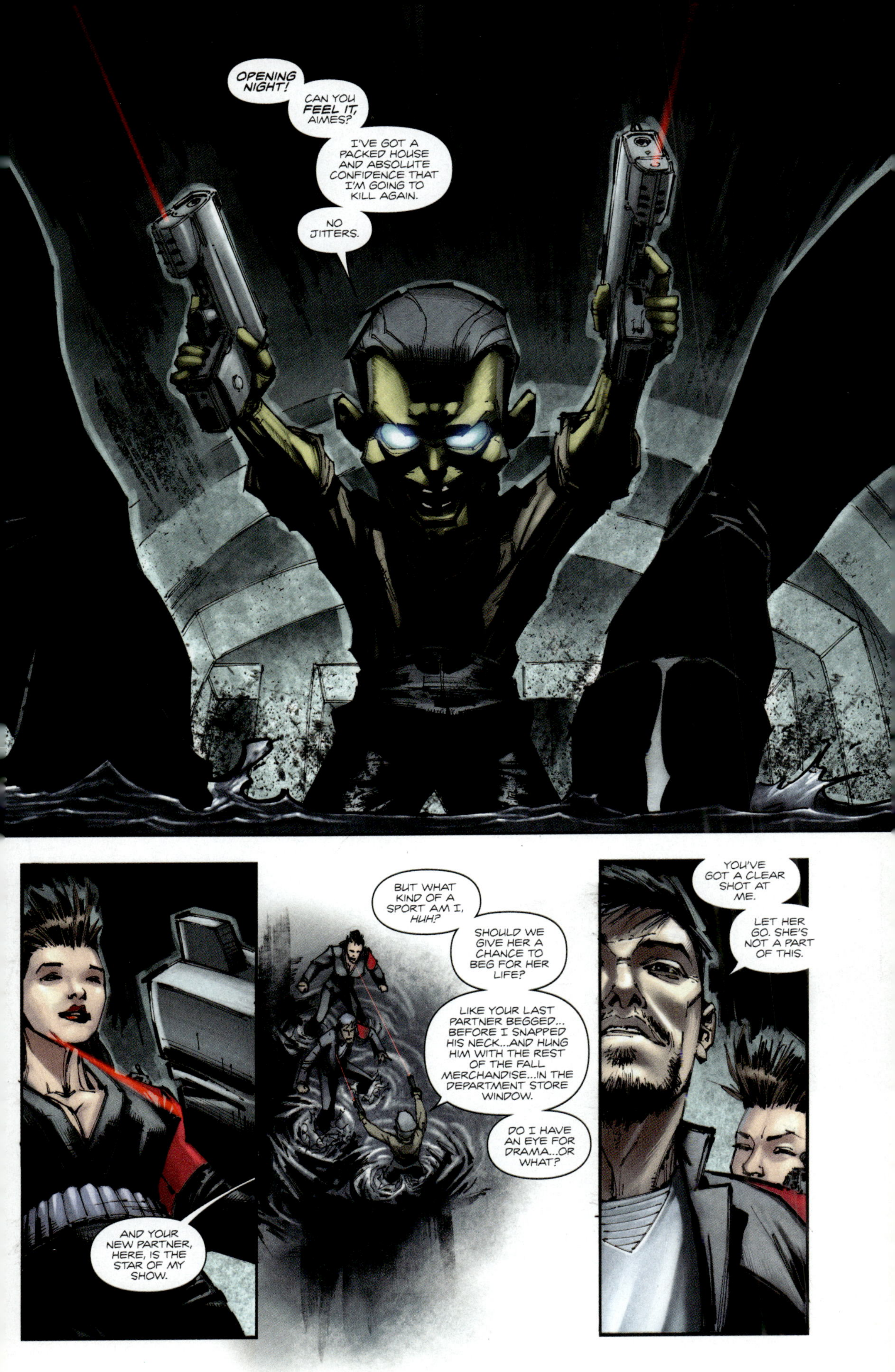
OPENING NIGHT!
CAN YOU FEEL IT, AIMES?
I'VE GOT A PACKED HOUSE AND ABSOLUTE CONFIDENCE THAT I'M GOING TO KILL AGAIN.
NO JITTERS.
AND YOUR NEW PARTNER, HERE, IS THE STAR OF MY SHOW.
BUT WHAT KIND OF A SPORT AM I, HUH?
SHOULD WE GIVE HER A CHANCE TO BEG FOR HER LIFE?
LIKE YOUR LAST PARTNER BEGGED... BEFORE I SNAPPED HIS NECK...AND HUNG HIM WITH THE REST OF THE FALL MERCHANDISE...IN THE DEPARTMENT STORE WINDOW.
DO I HAVE AN EYE FOR DRAMA...OR WHAT?
YOU'VE GOT A CLEAR SHOT AT ME.
LET HER GO. SHE'S NOT A PART OF THIS.

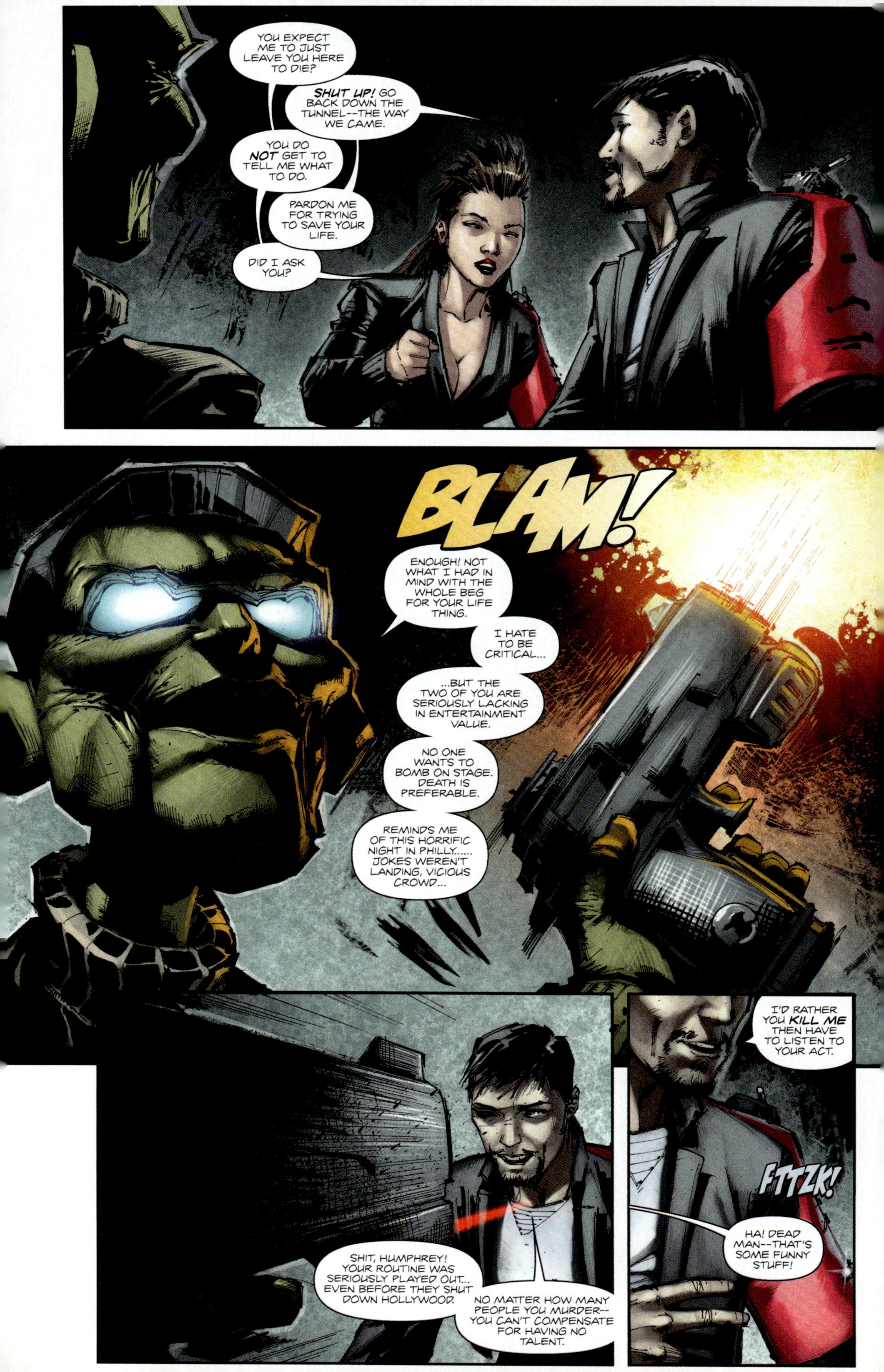

YOU EXPECT ME TO JUST LEAVE YOU HERE TO DIE?
SHUT UP! GO BACK DOWN THE TUNNEL--THE WAY WE CAME.
YOU DO NOT GET TO TELL ME WHAT TO DO.
PARDON ME FOR TRYING TO SAVE YOUR LIFE.
DID I ASK YOU?
BLAM!
ENOUGH! NOT WHAT I HAD IN MIND WITH THE WHOLE BEG FOR YOUR LIFE THING.
I HATE TO BE CRITICAL...
...BUT THE TWO OF YOU ARE SERIOUSLY LACKING IN ENTERTAINMENT VALUE.
NO ONE WANTS TO BOMB ON STAGE. DEATH IS PREFERABLE.
REMINDS ME OF THIS HORRIFIC NIGHT IN PHILLY...... JOKES WEREN'T LANDING, VICIOUS CROWD...
SHIT, HUMPHREY! YOUR ROUTINE WAS SERIOUSLY PLAYED OUT... EVEN BEFORE THEY SHUT DOWN HOLLYWOOD.
NO MATTER HOW MANY PEOPLE YOU MURDER-- YOU CAN'T COMPENSATE FOR HAVING NO TALENT.
I'D RATHER YOU KILL ME THEN HAVE TO LISTEN TO YOUR ACT.
FTTZK!
HA! DEAD MAN--THAT'S SOME FUNNY STUFF!

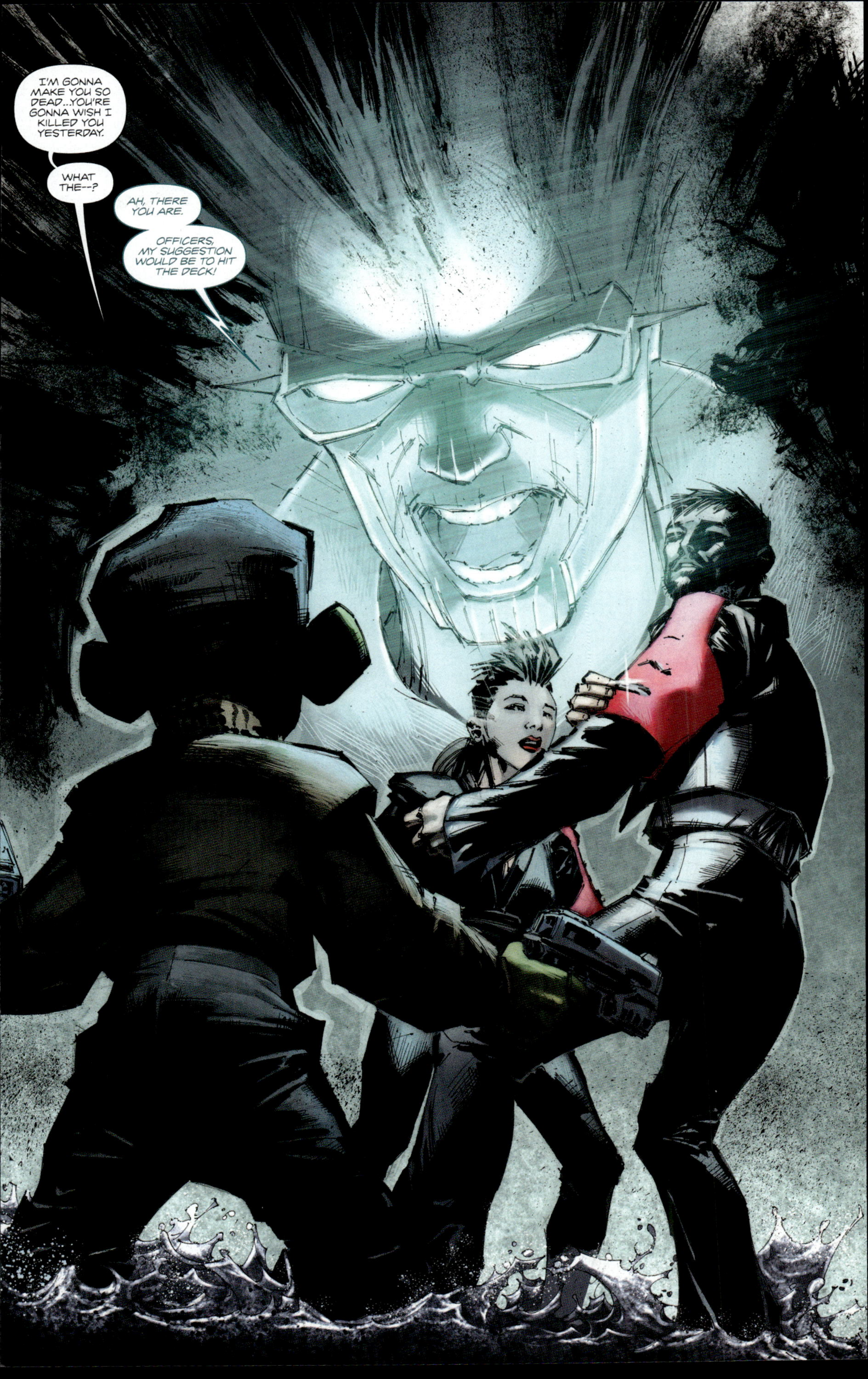
I'M GONNA MAKE YOU SO DEAD...YOU'RE GONNA WISH I KILLED YOU YESTERDAY.
WHAT THE--?
AH, THERE YOU ARE.
OFFICERS, MY SUGGESTION WOULD BE TO HIT THE DECK!

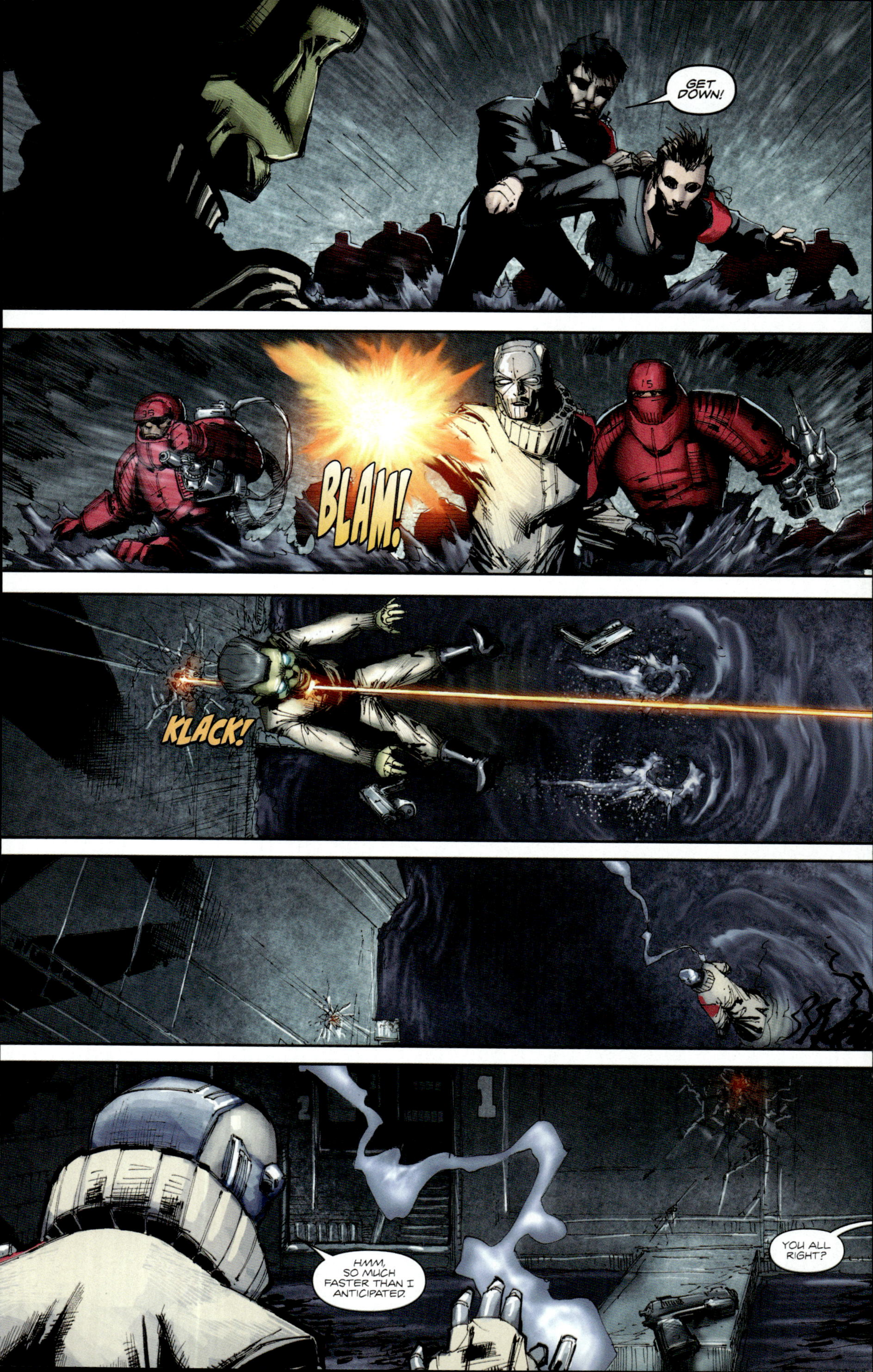
GET DOWN!
BLAM!
KLACK!
HMM, SO MUCH FASTER THAN I ANTICIPATED.
YOU ALL RIGHT?

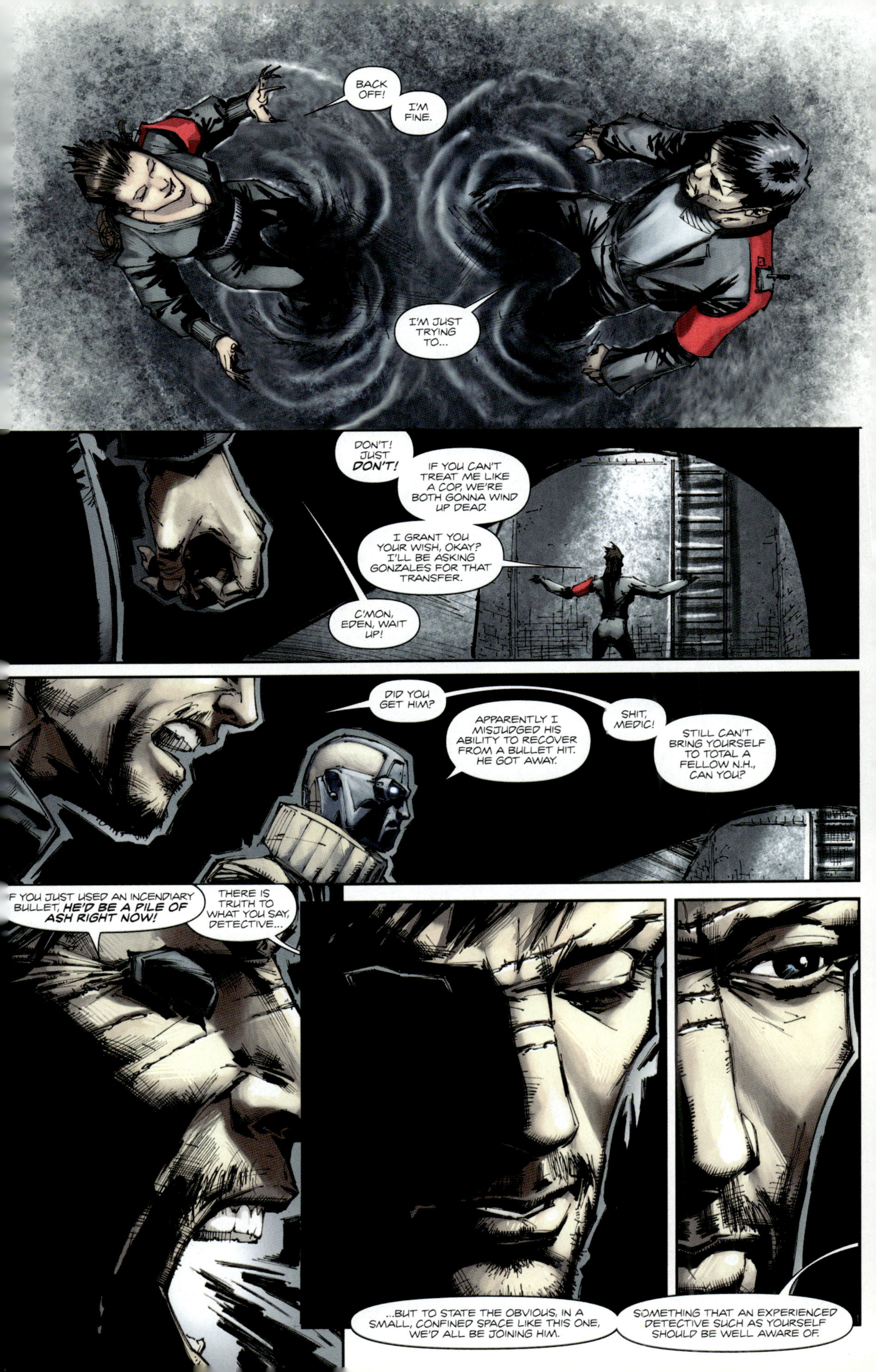
BACK OFF!
I'M FINE.
I'M JUST TRYING TO...
DON'T! JUST **DON'T!**
IF YOU CAN'T TREAT ME LIKE A COP, WE'RE BOTH GONNA WIND UP DEAD.
I GRANT YOU YOUR WISH, OKAY? I'LL BE ASKING GONZALES FOR THAT TRANSFER.
C'MON, EDEN, WAIT UP!
DID YOU GET HIM?
APPARENTLY I MISJUDGED HIS ABILITY TO RECOVER FROM A BULLET HIT. HE GOT AWAY.
SHIT, MEDIC!
STILL CAN'T BRING YOURSELF TO TOTAL A FELLOW N.H., CAN YOU?
F YOU JUST USED AN INCENDIARY BULLET, **HE'D BE A PILE OF ASH RIGHT NOW!**
THERE IS TRUTH TO WHAT YOU SAY, DETECTIVE...
...BUT TO STATE THE OBVIOUS, IN A SMALL, CONFINED SPACE LIKE THIS ONE, WE'D ALL BE JOINING HIM.
SOMETHING THAT AN EXPERIENCED DETECTIVE SUCH AS YOURSELF SHOULD BE WELL AWARE OF.

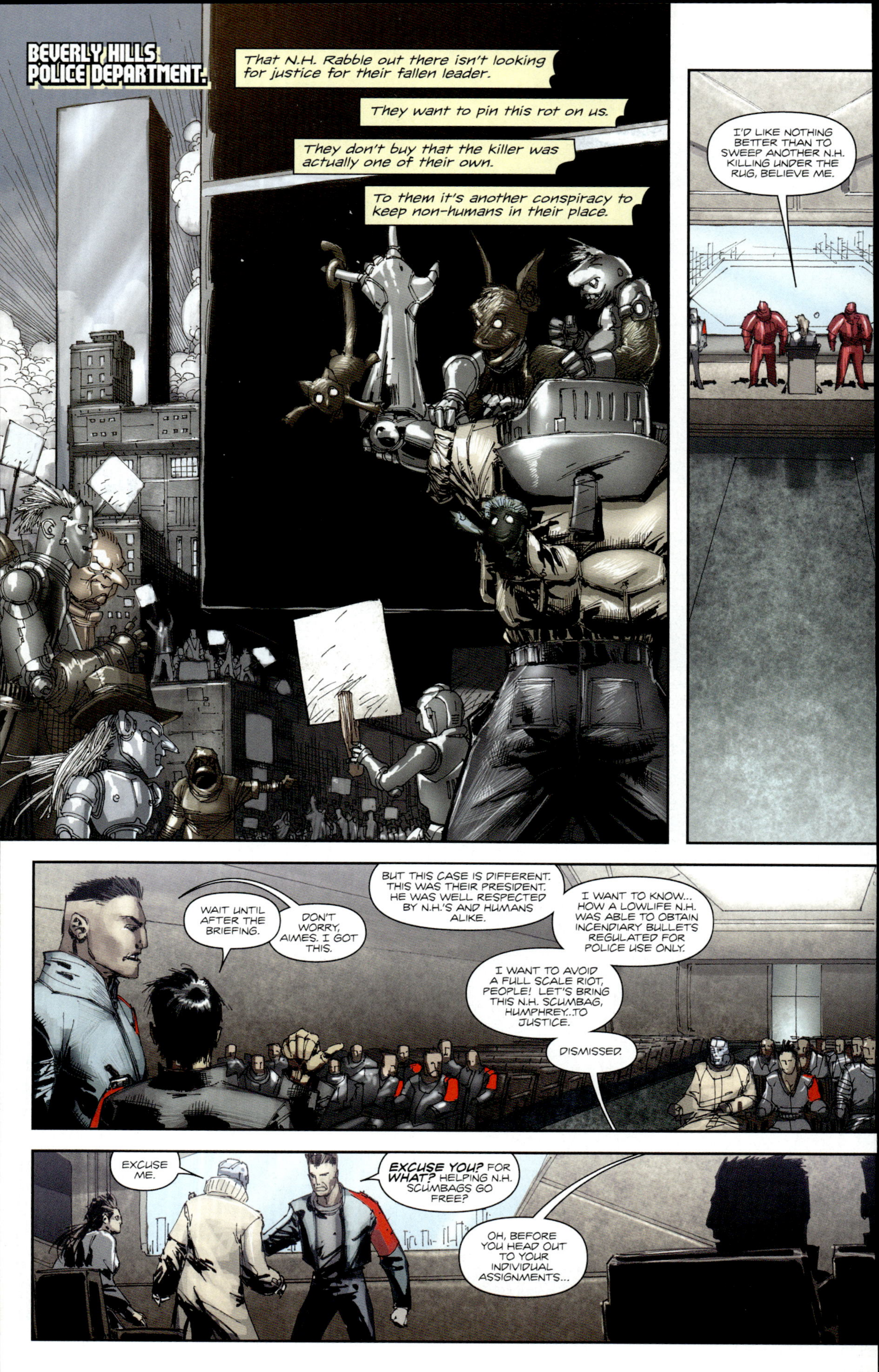
BEVERLY HILLS POLICE DEPARTMENT.
That N.H. Rabble out there isn't looking for justice for their fallen leader.
They want to pin this rot on us.
They don't buy that the killer was actually one of their own.
To them it's another conspiracy to keep non-humans in their place.
I'D LIKE NOTHING BETTER THAN TO SWEEP ANOTHER N.H. KILLING UNDER THE RUG, BELIEVE ME.
BUT THIS CASE IS DIFFERENT. THIS WAS THEIR PRESIDENT. HE WAS WELL RESPECTED BY N.H.'S AND HUMANS ALIKE.
WAIT UNTIL AFTER THE BRIEFING.
DON'T WORRY, AIMES. I GOT THIS.
I WANT TO KNOW... HOW A LOWLIFE N.H. WAS ABLE TO OBTAIN INCENDIARY BULLETS REGULATED FOR POLICE USE ONLY.
I WANT TO AVOID A FULL SCALE RIOT, PEOPLE! LET'S BRING THIS N.H. SCUMBAG, HUMPHREY...TO JUSTICE.
DISMISSED.
EXCUSE ME.
EXCUSE YOU? FOR WHAT? HELPING N.H. SCUMBAGS GO FREE?
OH, BEFORE YOU HEAD OUT TO YOUR INDIVIDUAL ASSIGNMENTS...

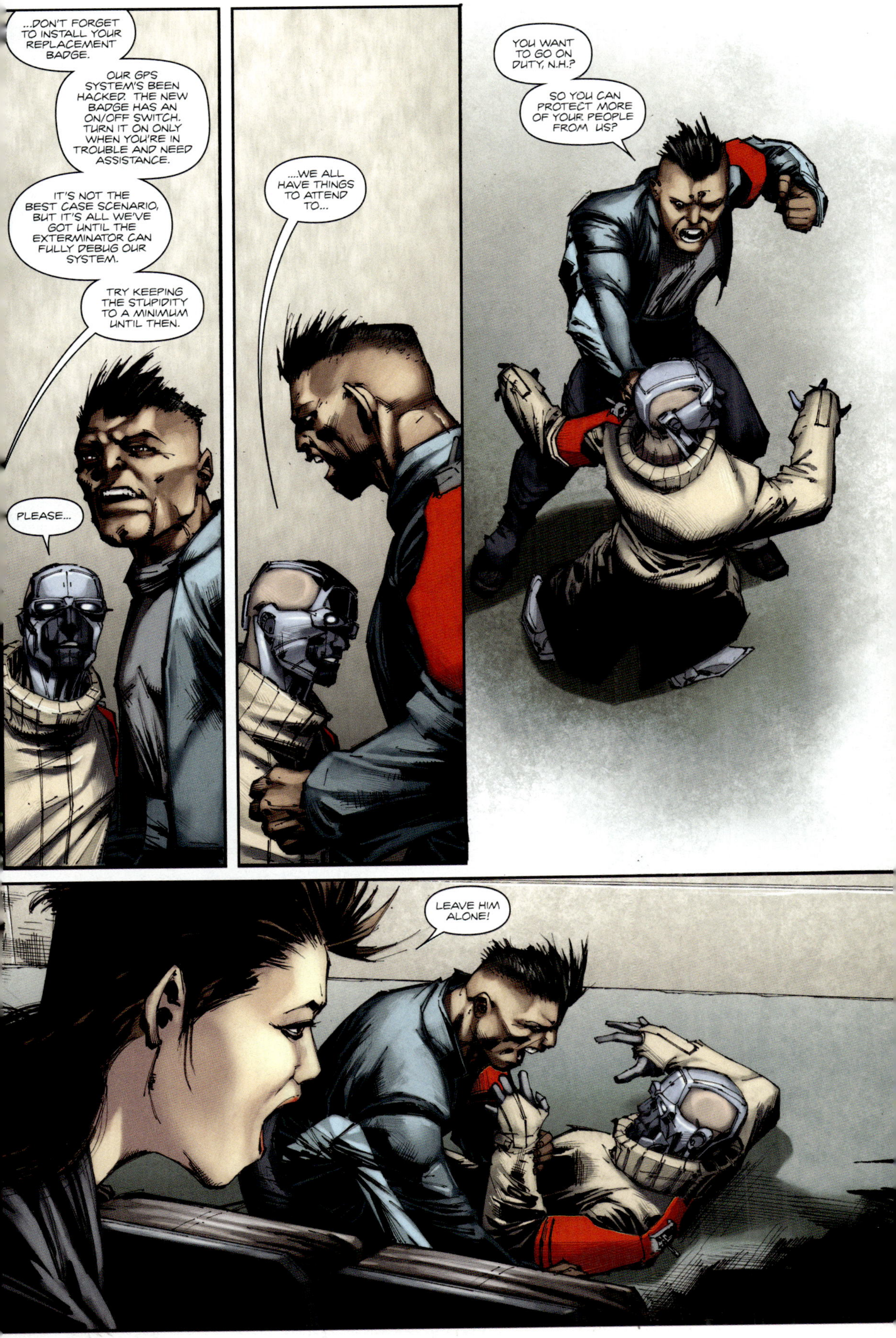
...DON'T FORGET TO INSTALL YOUR REPLACEMENT BADGE.
OUR GPS SYSTEM'S BEEN HACKED. THE NEW BADGE HAS AN ON/OFF SWITCH. TURN IT ON ONLY WHEN YOU'RE IN TROUBLE AND NEED ASSISTANCE.
IT'S NOT THE BEST CASE SCENARIO, BUT IT'S ALL WE'VE GOT UNTIL THE EXTERMINATOR CAN FULLY DEBUG OUR SYSTEM.
TRY KEEPING THE STUPIDITY TO A MINIMUM UNTIL THEN.
PLEASE...
...WE ALL HAVE THINGS TO ATTEND TO...
YOU WANT TO GO ON DUTY, N.H.?
SO YOU CAN PROTECT MORE OF YOUR PEOPLE FROM US?
LEAVE HIM ALONE!

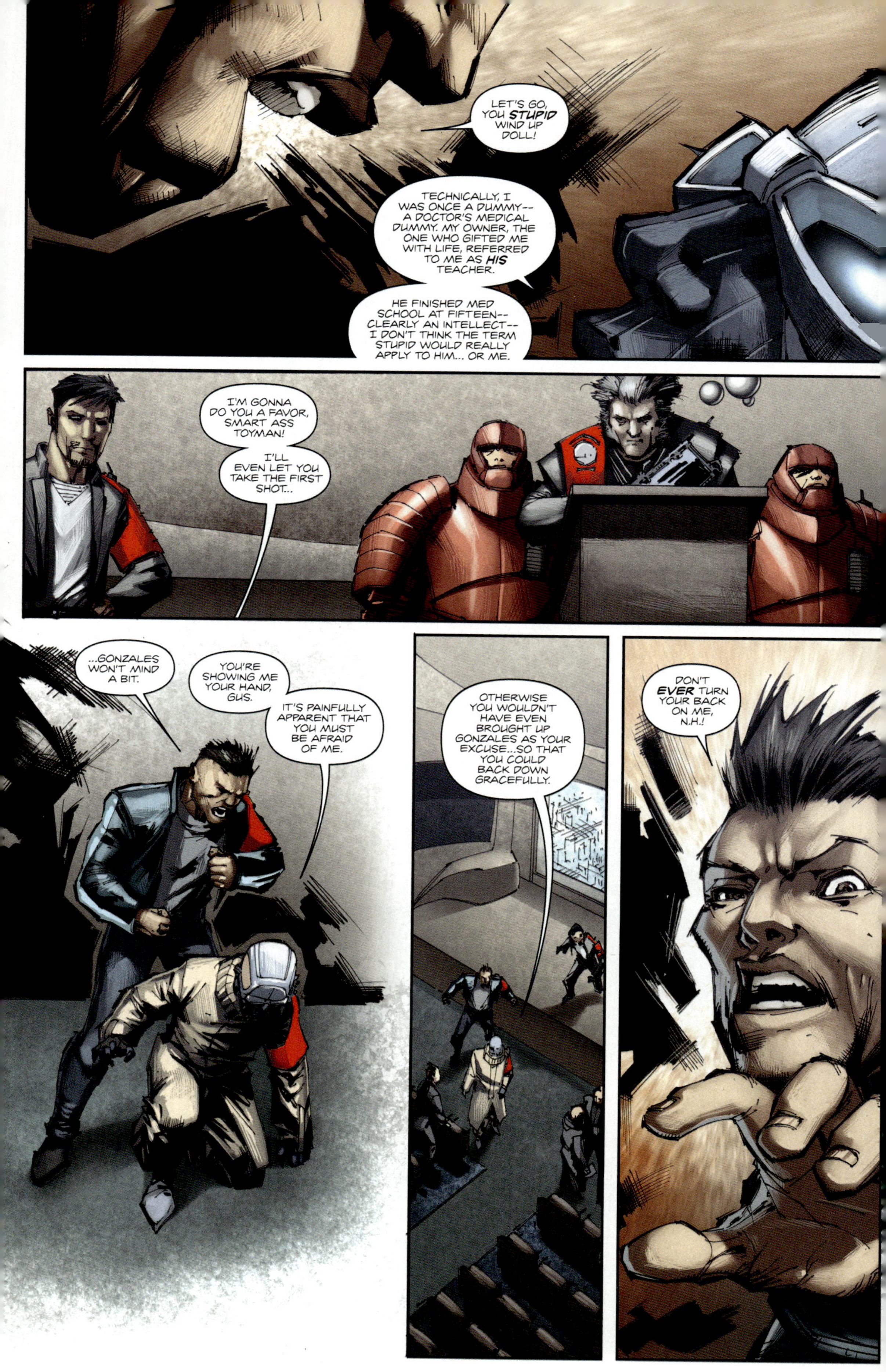
LET'S GO, YOU STUPID WIND UP DOLL!
TECHNICALLY, I WAS ONCE A DUMMY-- A DOCTOR'S MEDICAL DUMMY. MY OWNER, THE ONE WHO GIFTED ME WITH LIFE, REFERRED TO ME AS HIS TEACHER.
HE FINISHED MED SCHOOL AT FIFTEEN-- CLEARLY AN INTELLECT-- I DON'T THINK THE TERM STUPID WOULD REALLY APPLY TO HIM... OR ME.
I'M GONNA DO YOU A FAVOR, SMART ASS TOYMAN!
I'LL EVEN LET YOU TAKE THE FIRST SHOT...
...GONZALES WON'T MIND A BIT.
YOU'RE SHOWING ME YOUR HAND, GUS.
IT'S PAINFULLY APPARENT THAT YOU MUST BE AFRAID OF ME.
OTHERWISE YOU WOULDN'T HAVE EVEN BROUGHT UP GONZALES AS YOUR EXCUSE...SO THAT YOU COULD BACK DOWN GRACEFULLY.
DON'T EVER TURN YOUR BACK ON ME, N.H.!

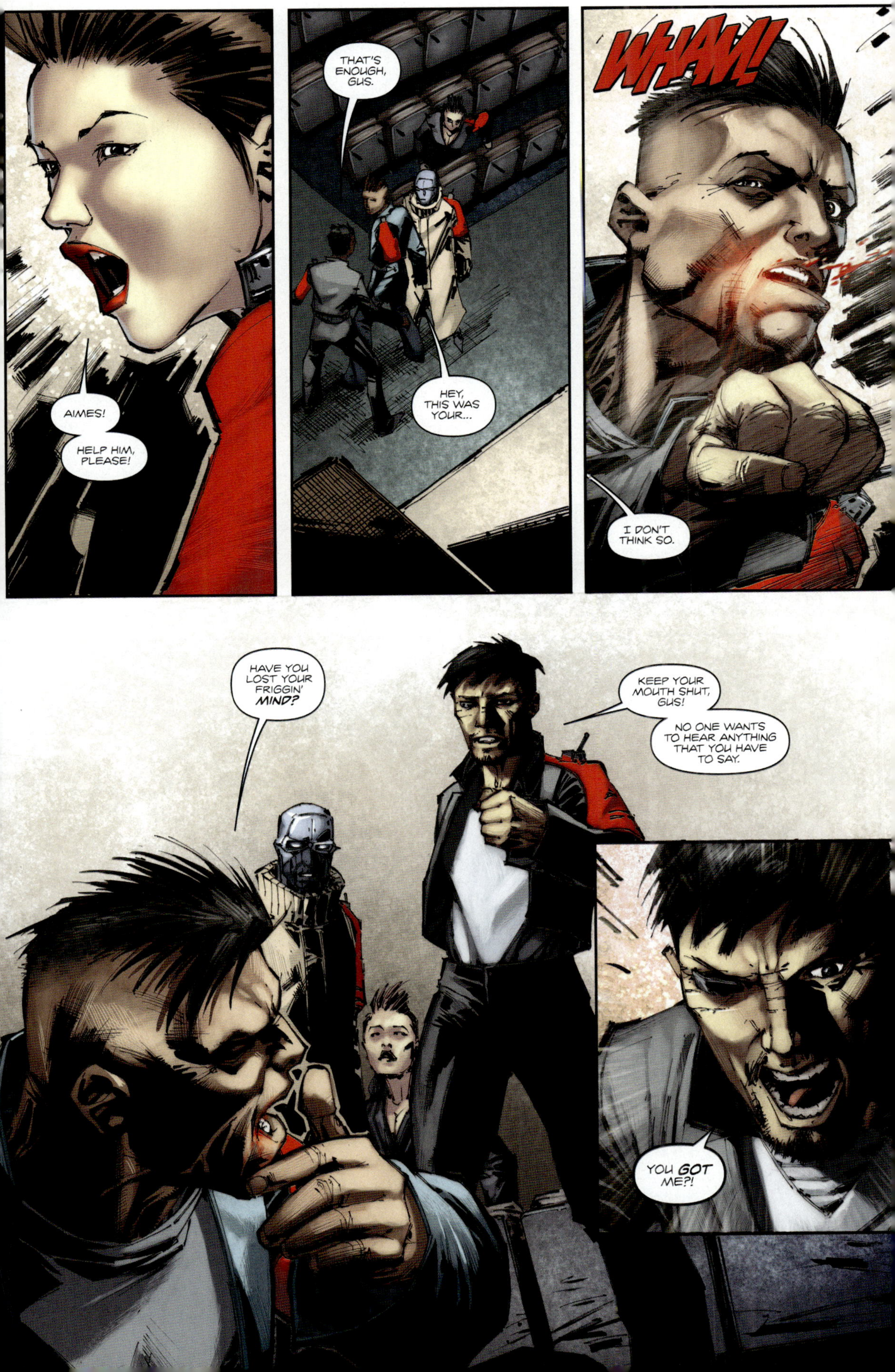
AIMES!
HELP HIM, PLEASE!
THAT'S ENOUGH, GUS.
HEY, THIS WAS YOUR...
WHAM!
I DON'T THINK SO.
HAVE YOU LOST YOUR FRIGGIN' *MIND?*
KEEP YOUR MOUTH SHUT, GUS!
NO ONE WANTS TO HEAR ANYTHING THAT YOU HAVE TO SAY.
YOU **GOT** ME?!

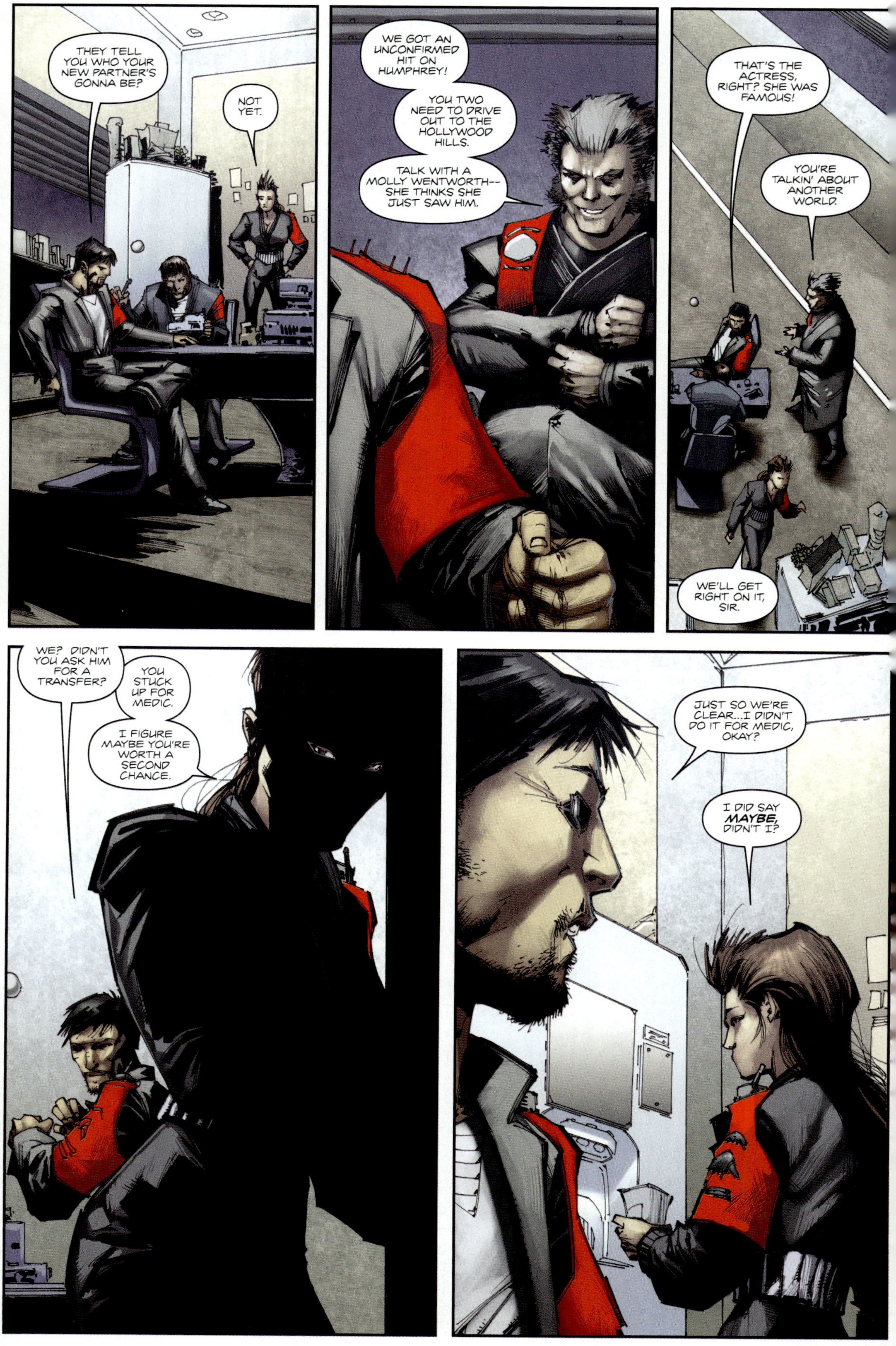
THEY TELL YOU WHO YOUR NEW PARTNER'S GONNA BE?
NOT YET.
WE GOT AN UNCONFIRMED HIT ON HUMPHREY!
YOU TWO NEED TO DRIVE OUT TO THE HOLLYWOOD HILLS.
TALK WITH A MOLLY WENTWORTH-- SHE THINKS SHE JUST SAW HIM.
THAT'S THE ACTRESS, RIGHT? SHE WAS FAMOUS!
YOU'RE TALKIN' ABOUT ANOTHER WORLD.
WE'LL GET RIGHT ON IT, SIR.
WE? DIDN'T YOU ASK HIM FOR A TRANSFER?
YOU STUCK UP FOR MEDIC.
I FIGURE MAYBE YOU'RE WORTH A SECOND CHANCE.
JUST SO WE'RE CLEAR...I DIDN'T DO IT FOR MEDIC, OKAY?
I DID SAY *MAYBE*, DIDN'T I?

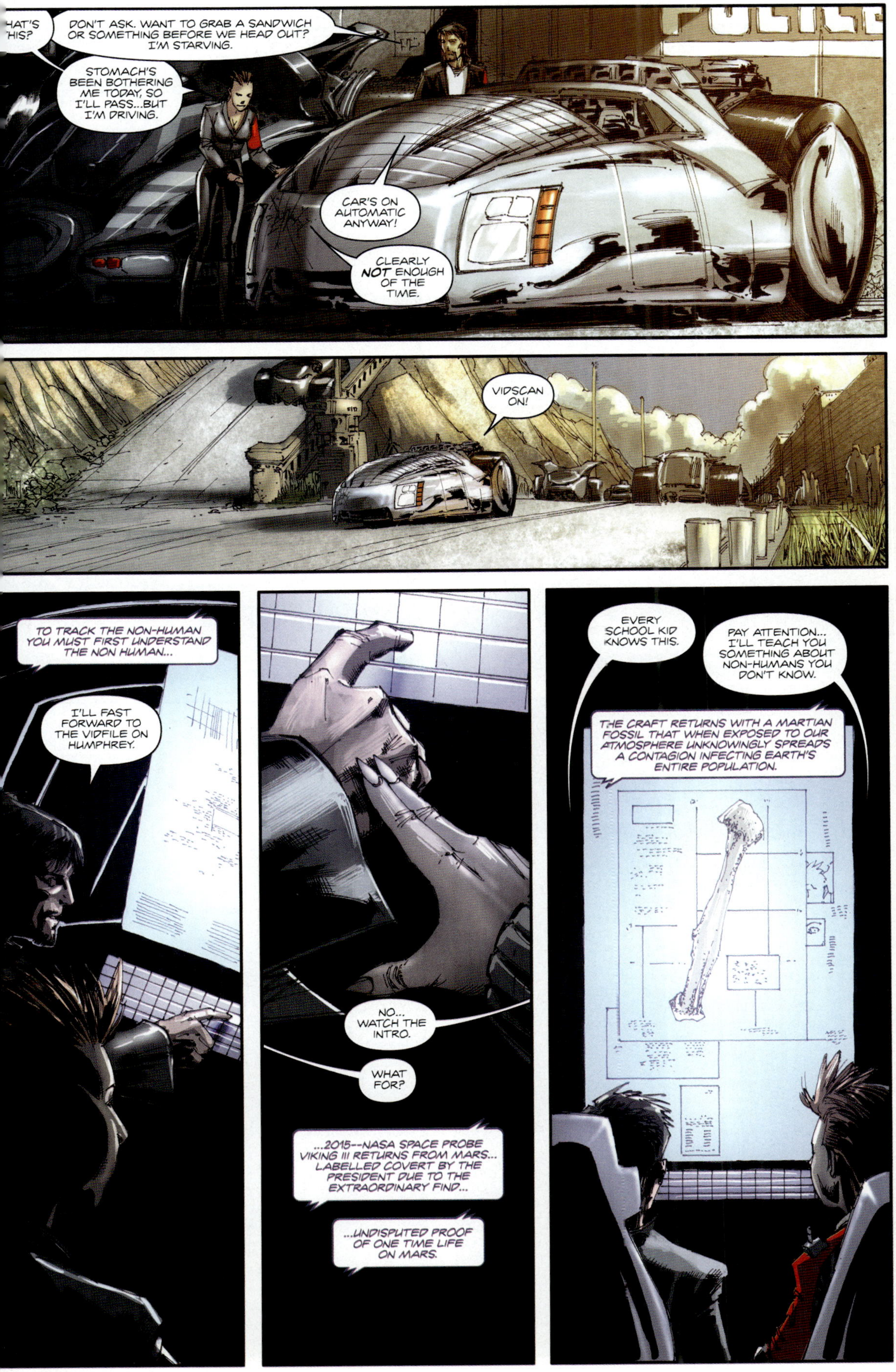
HAT'S
THIS?
DON'T ASK. WANT TO GRAB A SANDWICH OR SOMETHING BEFORE WE HEAD OUT? I'M STARVING.
STOMACH'S BEEN BOTHERING ME TODAY, SO I'LL PASS...BUT I'M DRIVING.
CAR'S ON AUTOMATIC ANYWAY!
CLEARLY NOT ENOUGH OF THE TIME.
VIDSCAN ON!
TO TRACK THE NON-HUMAN YOU MUST FIRST UNDERSTAND THE NON HUMAN...
I'LL FAST FORWARD TO THE VIDFILE ON HUMPHREY.
NO... WATCH THE INTRO.
WHAT FOR?
...2015--NASA SPACE PROBE VIKING III RETURNS FROM MARS... LABELLED COVERT BY THE PRESIDENT DUE TO THE EXTRAORDINARY FIND...
...UNDISPUTED PROOF OF ONE TIME LIFE ON MARS.
EVERY SCHOOL KID KNOWS THIS.
PAY ATTENTION... I'LL TEACH YOU SOMETHING ABOUT NON-HUMANS YOU DON'T KNOW.
THE CRAFT RETURNS WITH A MARTIAN FOSSIL THAT WHEN EXPOSED TO OUR ATMOSPHERE UNKNOWINGLY SPREADS A CONTAGION INFECTING EARTH'S ENTIRE POPULATION.

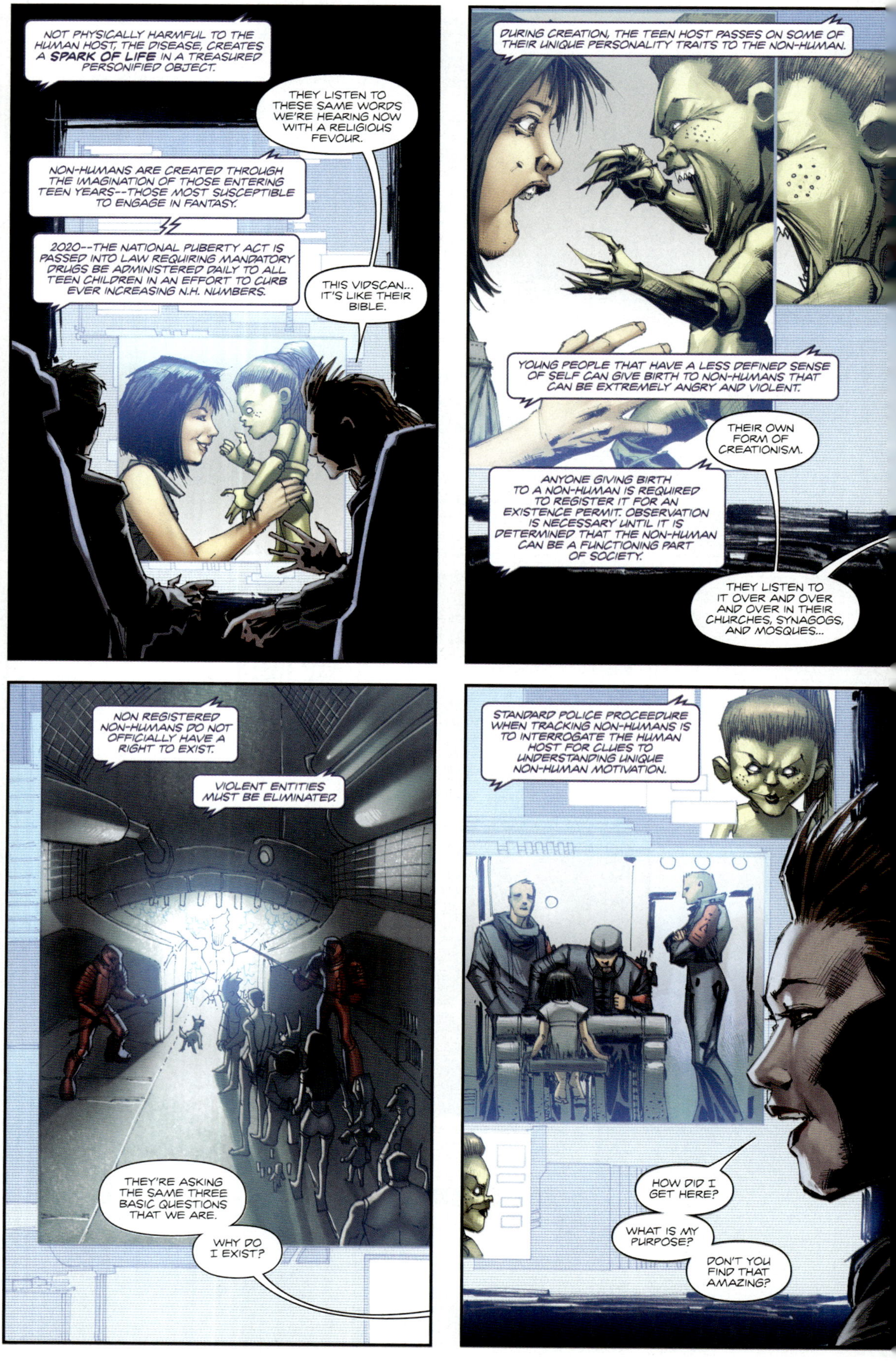

NOT PHYSICALLY HARMFUL TO THE HUMAN HOST, THE DISEASE, CREATES A SPARK OF LIFE IN A TREASURED PERSONIFIED OBJECT.
THEY LISTEN TO THESE SAME WORDS WE'RE HEARING NOW WITH A RELIGIOUS FEVOUR.
NON-HUMANS ARE CREATED THROUGH THE IMAGINATION OF THOSE ENTERING TEEN YEARS--THOSE MOST SUSCEPTIBLE TO ENGAGE IN FANTASY.
2020--THE NATIONAL PUBERTY ACT IS PASSED INTO LAW REQUIRING MANDATORY DRUGS BE ADMINISTERED DAILY TO ALL TEEN CHILDREN IN AN EFFORT TO CURB EVER INCREASING N.H. NUMBERS.
THIS VIDSCAN... IT'S LIKE THEIR BIBLE.
DURING CREATION, THE TEEN HOST PASSES ON SOME OF THEIR UNIQUE PERSONALITY TRAITS TO THE NON-HUMAN.
YOUNG PEOPLE THAT HAVE A LESS DEFINED SENSE OF SELF CAN GIVE BIRTH TO NON-HUMANS THAT CAN BE EXTREMELY ANGRY AND VIOLENT.
THEIR OWN FORM OF CREATIONISM.
ANYONE GIVING BIRTH TO A NON-HUMAN IS REQUIRED TO REGISTER IT FOR AN EXISTENCE PERMIT. OBSERVATION IS NECESSARY UNTIL IT IS DETERMINED THAT THE NON-HUMAN CAN BE A FUNCTIONING PART OF SOCIETY.
THEY LISTEN TO IT OVER AND OVER AND OVER IN THEIR CHURCHES, SYNAGOGS, AND MOSQUES...
NON REGISTERED NON-HUMANS DO NOT OFFICIALLY HAVE A RIGHT TO EXIST.
VIOLENT ENTITIES MUST BE ELIMINATED.
THEY'RE ASKING THE SAME THREE BASIC QUESTIONS THAT WE ARE.
WHY DO I EXIST?
STANDARD POLICE PROCEEDURE WHEN TRACKING NON-HUMANS IS TO INTERROGATE THE HUMAN HOST FOR CLUES TO UNDERSTANDING UNIQUE NON-HUMAN MOTIVATION.
HOW DID I GET HERE?
WHAT IS MY PURPOSE?
DON'T YOU FIND THAT AMAZING?

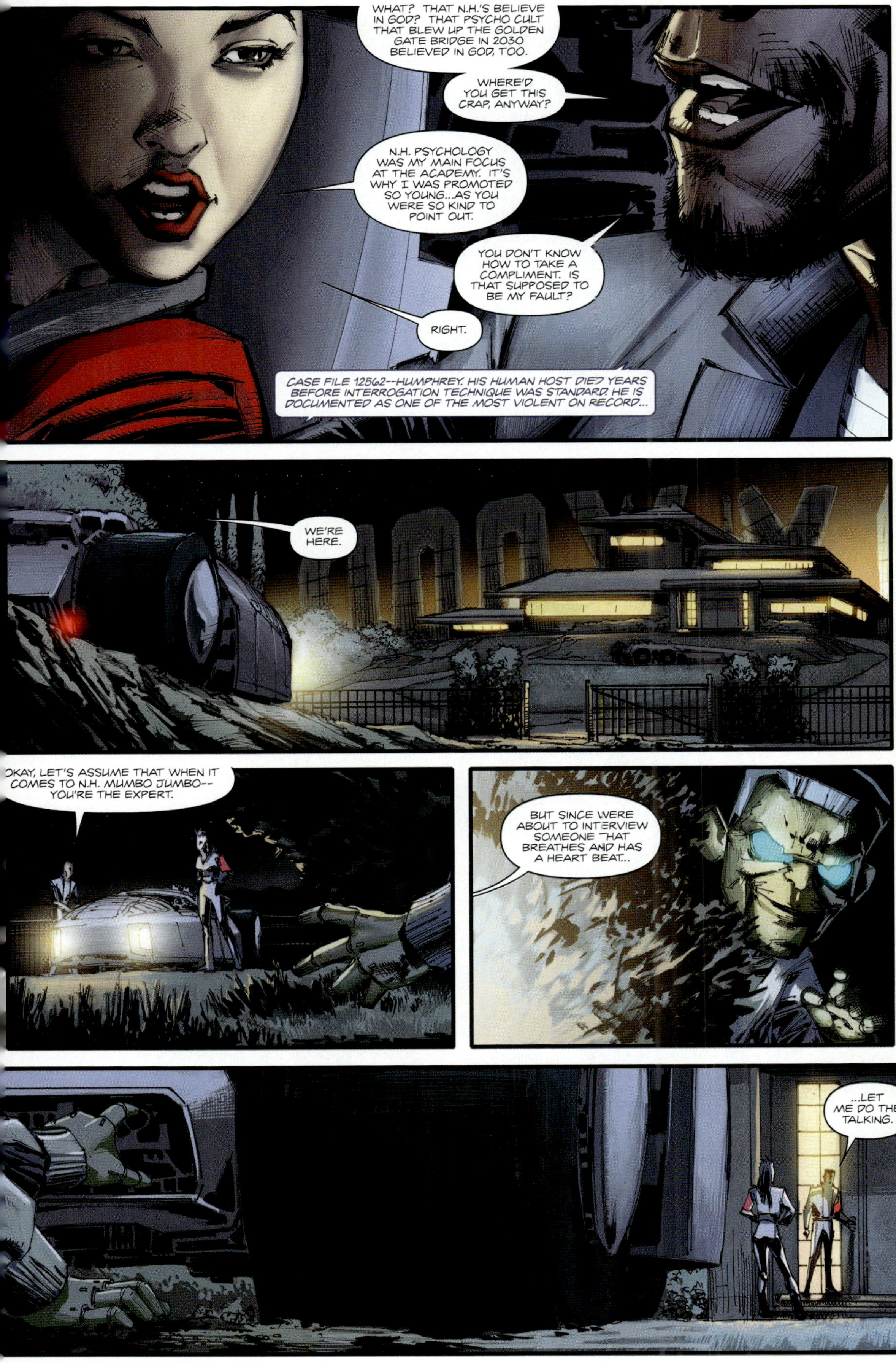
WHAT? THAT N.H.'S BELIEVE IN GOD? THAT PSYCHO CULT THAT BLEW UP THE GOLDEN GATE BRIDGE IN 2030 BELIEVED IN GOD, TOO.
WHERE'D YOU GET THIS CRAP, ANYWAY?
N.H. PSYCHOLOGY WAS MY MAIN FOCUS AT THE ACADEMY. IT'S WHY I WAS PROMOTED SO YOUNG...AS YOU WERE SO KIND TO POINT OUT.
YOU DON'T KNOW HOW TO TAKE A COMPLIMENT. IS THAT SUPPOSED TO BE MY FAULT?
RIGHT.
CASE FILE 12562--HUMPHREY. HIS HUMAN HOST DIED YEARS BEFORE INTERROGATION TECHNIQUE WAS STANDARD. HE IS DOCUMENTED AS ONE OF THE MOST VIOLENT ON RECORD...
WE'RE HERE.
OKAY, LET'S ASSUME THAT WHEN IT COMES TO N.H. MUMBO JUMBO--YOU'RE THE EXPERT.
BUT SINCE WERE ABOUT TO INTERVIEW SOMEONE THAT BREATHES AND HAS A HEART BEAT...
...LET ME DO THE TALKING.

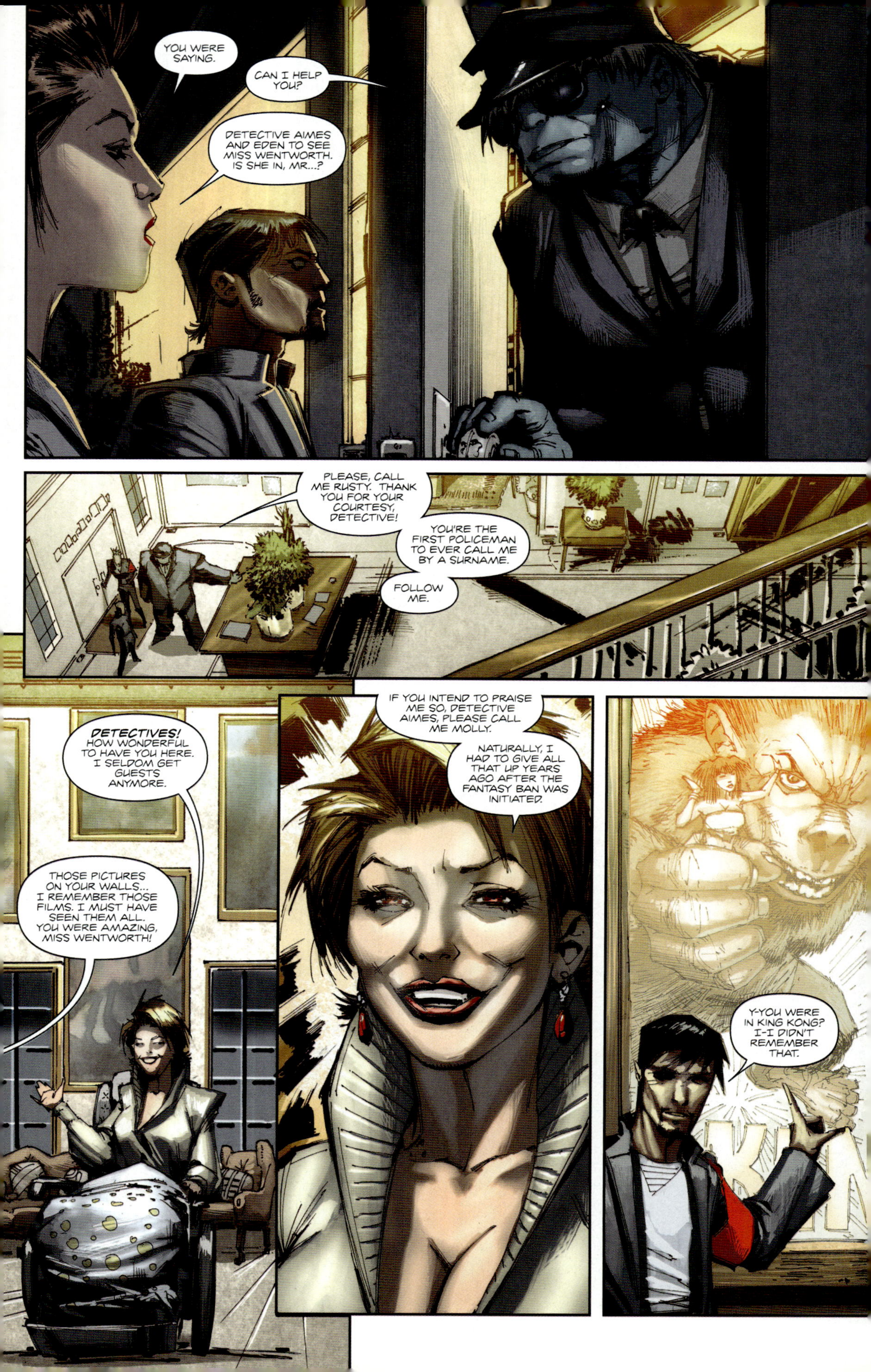
YOU WERE SAYING.
CAN I HELP YOU?
DETECTIVE AIMES AND EDEN TO SEE MISS WENTWORTH. IS SHE IN, MR...?
PLEASE, CALL ME RUSTY. THANK YOU FOR YOUR COURTESY, DETECTIVE!
YOU'RE THE FIRST POLICEMAN TO EVER CALL ME BY A SURNAME.
FOLLOW ME.
DETECTIVES! HOW WONDERFUL TO HAVE YOU HERE. I SELDOM GET GUESTS ANYMORE.
THOSE PICTURES ON YOUR WALLS... I REMEMBER THOSE FILMS. I MUST HAVE SEEN THEM ALL. YOU WERE AMAZING, MISS WENTWORTH!
IF YOU INTEND TO PRAISE ME SO, DETECTIVE AIMES, PLEASE CALL ME MOLLY.
NATURALLY, I HAD TO GIVE ALL THAT UP YEARS AGO AFTER THE FANTASY BAN WAS INITIATED.
Y-YOU WERE IN KING KONG? I-I DIDN'T REMEMBER THAT.

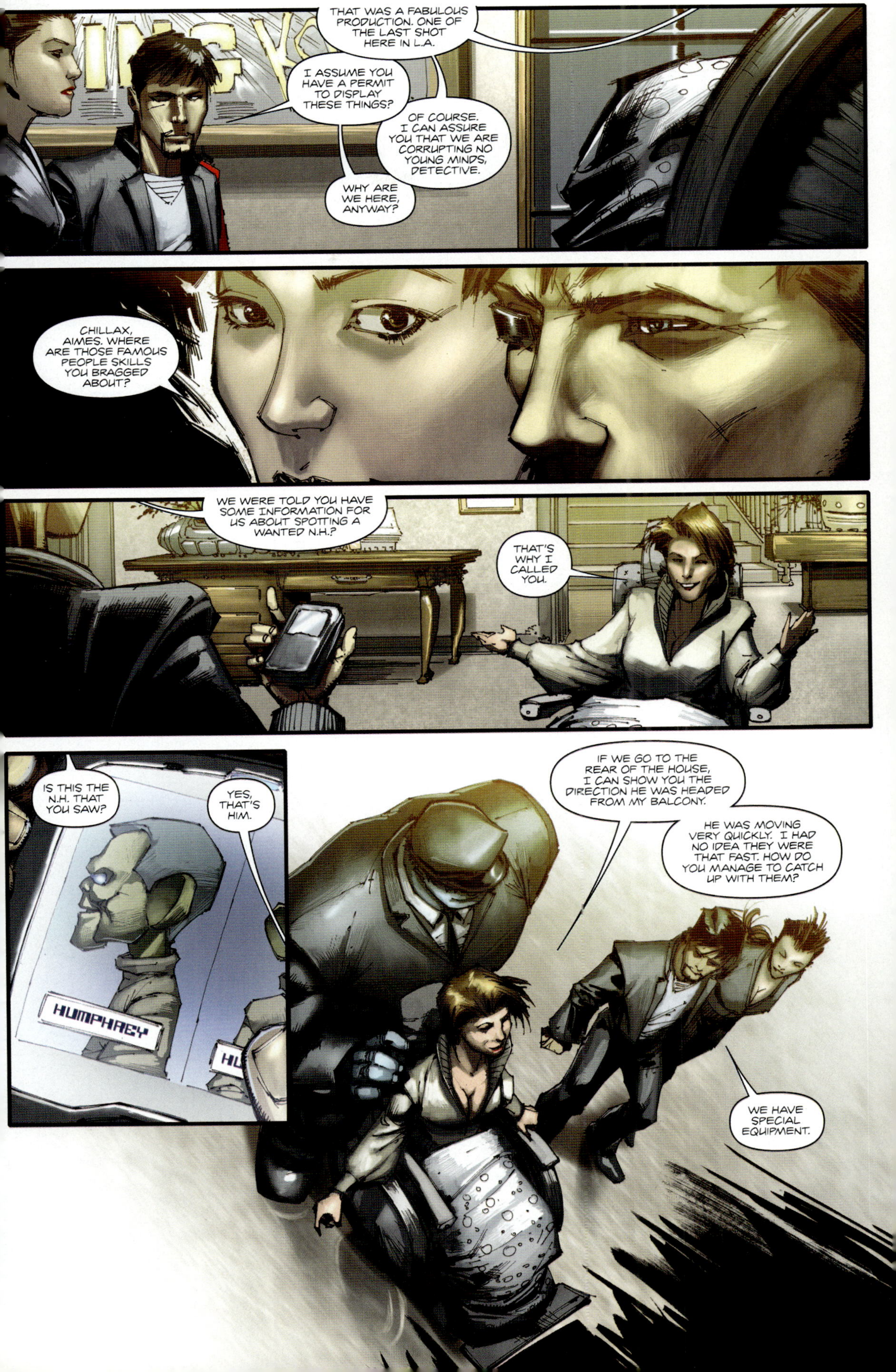
THAT WAS A FABULOUS PRODUCTION. ONE OF THE LAST SHOT HERE IN L.A.
I ASSUME YOU HAVE A PERMIT TO DISPLAY THESE THINGS?
OF COURSE. I CAN ASSURE YOU THAT WE ARE CORRUPTING NO YOUNG MINDS, DETECTIVE.
WHY ARE WE HERE, ANYWAY?
CHILLAX, AIMES. WHERE ARE THOSE FAMOUS PEOPLE SKILLS YOU BRAGGED ABOUT?
WE WERE TOLD YOU HAVE SOME INFORMATION FOR US ABOUT SPOTTING A WANTED N.H.?
THAT'S WHY I CALLED YOU.
IS THIS THE N.H. THAT YOU SAW?
YES, THAT'S HIM.
HUMPHREY
IF WE GO TO THE REAR OF THE HOUSE, I CAN SHOW YOU THE DIRECTION HE WAS HEADED FROM MY BALCONY.
HE WAS MOVING VERY QUICKLY. I HAD NO IDEA THEY WERE THAT FAST. HOW DO YOU MANAGE TO CATCH UP WITH THEM?
WE HAVE SPECIAL EQUIPMENT.

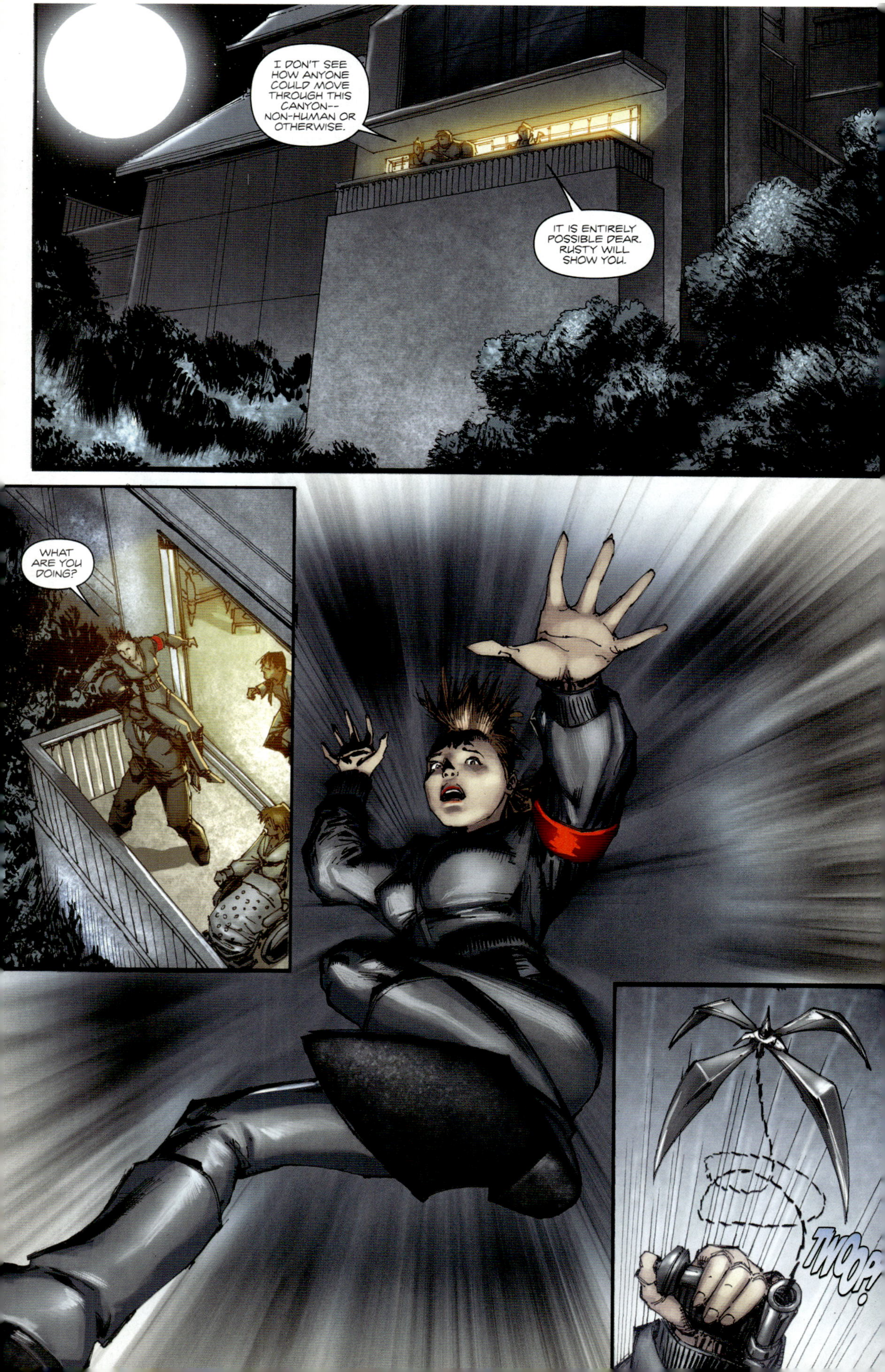
I DON'T SEE HOW ANYONE COULD MOVE THROUGH THIS CANYON-- NON-HUMAN OR OTHERWISE.
IT IS ENTIRELY POSSIBLE DEAR. RUSTY WILL SHOW YOU.
WHAT ARE YOU DOING?
TWOOP!

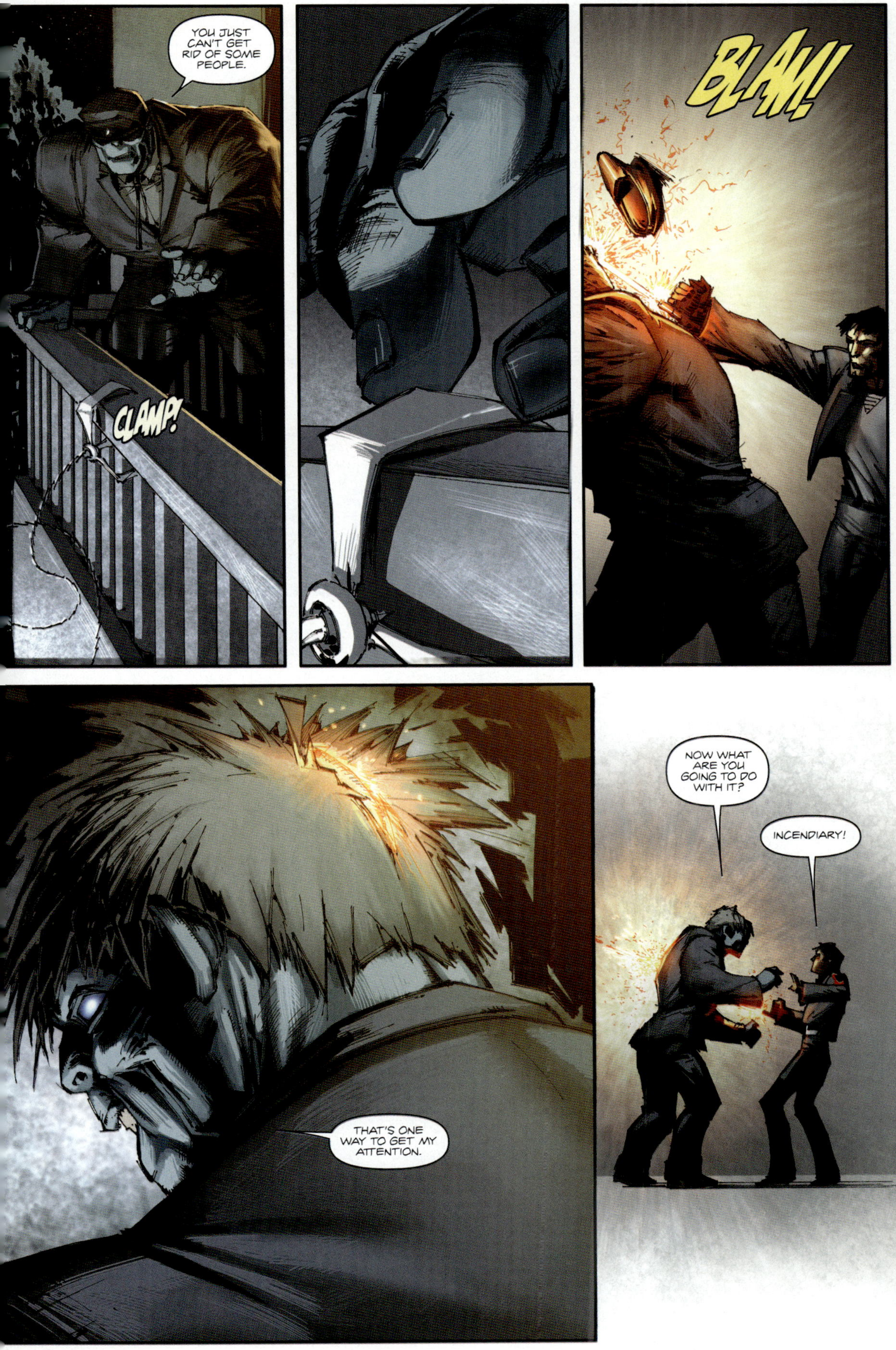
YOU JUST CAN'T GET RID OF SOME PEOPLE.
CLAMP!
BLAM!
THAT'S ONE WAY TO GET MY ATTENTION.
NOW WHAT ARE YOU GOING TO DO WITH IT?
INCENDIARY!

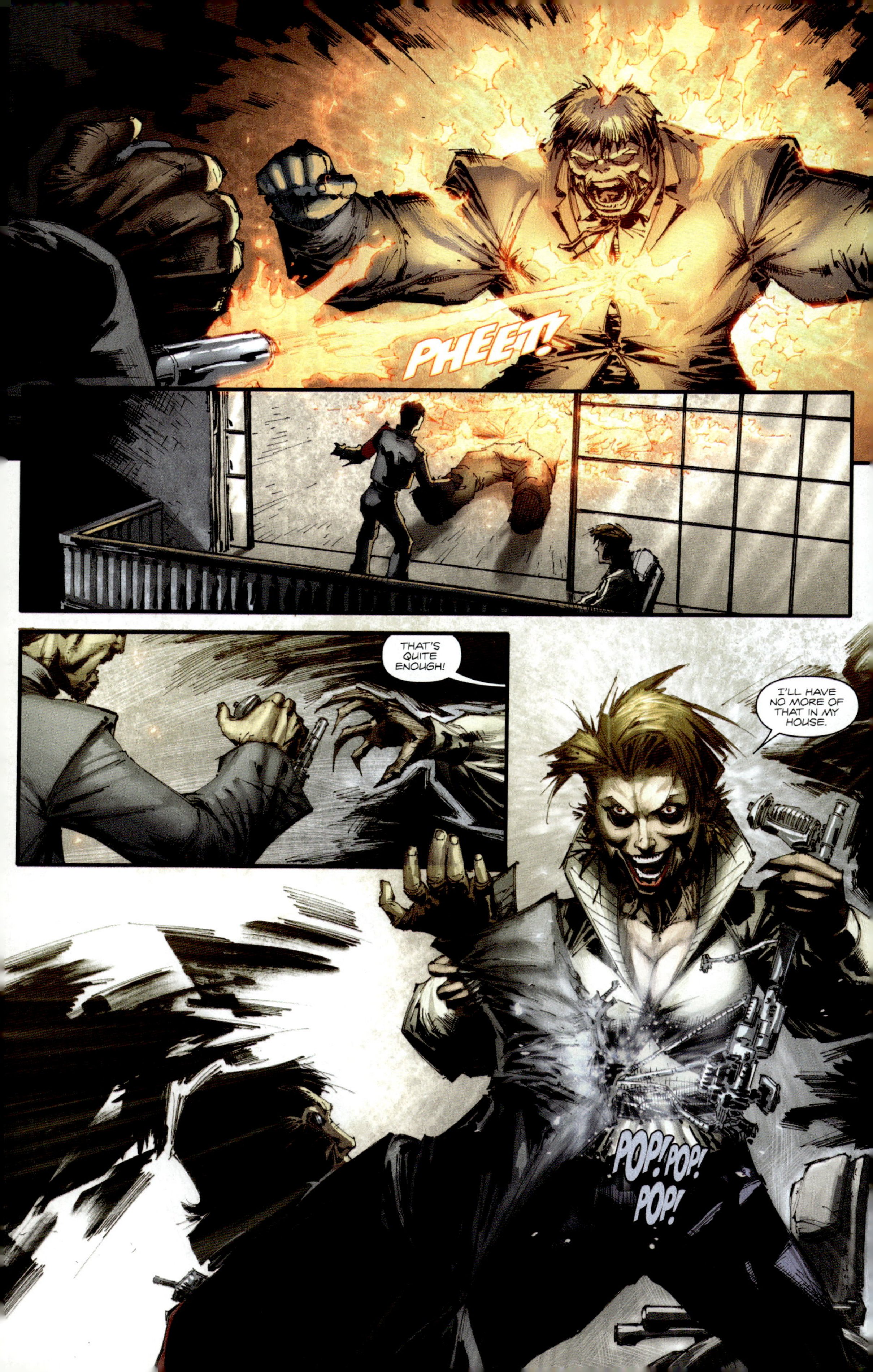
PHEET!
THAT'S QUITE ENOUGH!
I'LL HAVE NO MORE OF THAT IN MY HOUSE.
POP! POP! POP!

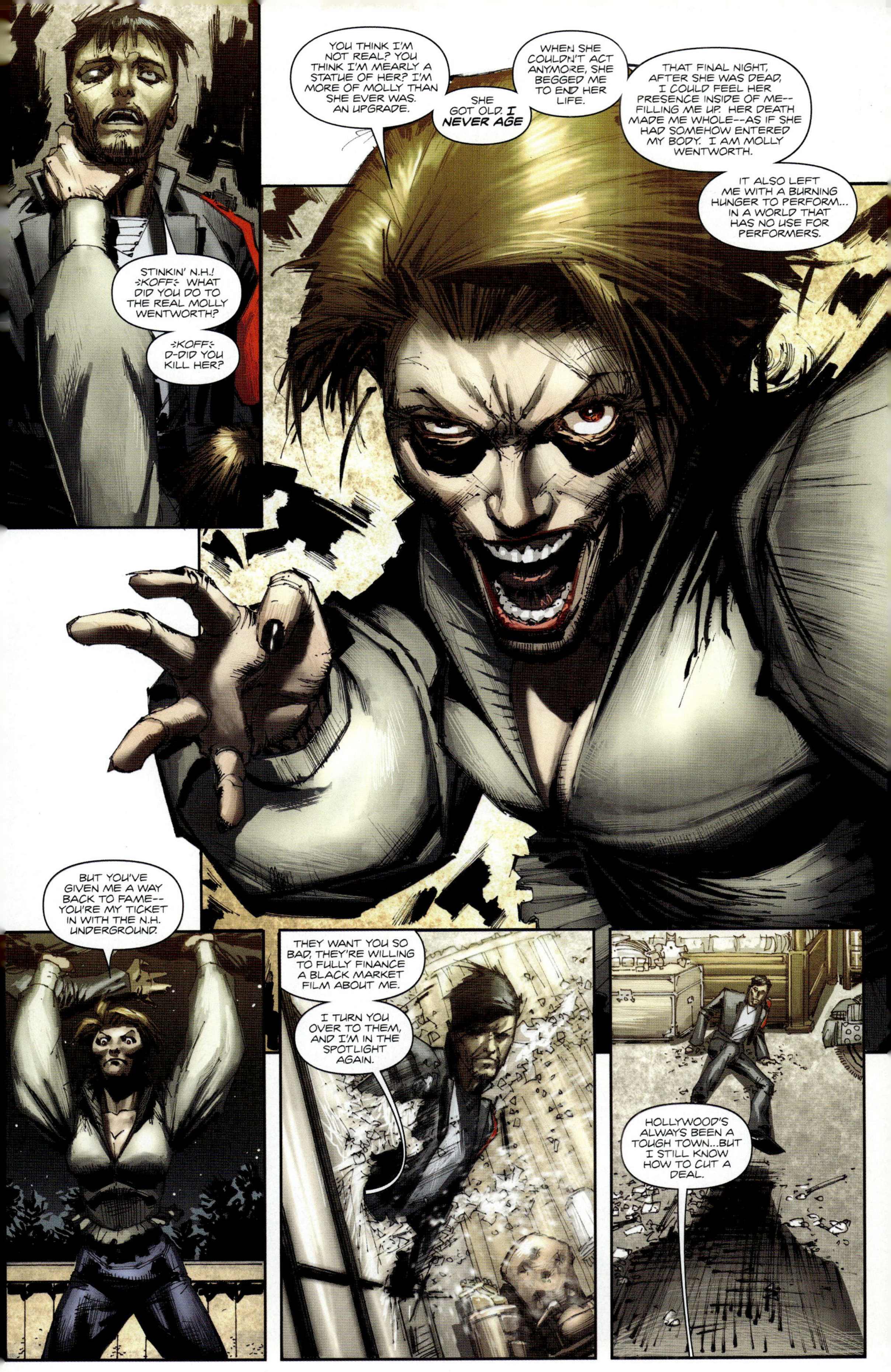
YOU THINK I'M NOT REAL? YOU THINK I'M MEARLY A STATUE OF HER? I'M MORE OF MOLLY THAN SHE EVER WAS. AN UPGRADE.
SHE GOT OLD. I NEVER AGE
WHEN SHE COULDN'T ACT ANYMORE, SHE BEGGED ME TO END HER LIFE.
THAT FINAL NIGHT, AFTER SHE WAS DEAD, I COULD FEEL HER PRESENCE INSIDE OF ME--FILLING ME UP. HER DEATH MADE ME WHOLE--AS IF SHE HAD SOMEHOW ENTERED MY BODY. I AM MOLLY WENTWORTH.
IT ALSO LEFT ME WITH A BURNING HUNGER TO PERFORM... IN A WORLD THAT HAS NO USE FOR PERFORMERS.
STINKIN' N.H.! -KOFF- WHAT DID YOU DO TO THE REAL MOLLY WENTWORTH?
-KOFF- D-DID YOU KILL HER?
BUT YOU'VE GIVEN ME A WAY BACK TO FAME--YOU'RE MY TICKET IN WITH THE N.H. UNDERGROUND.
THEY WANT YOU SO BAD, THEY'RE WILLING TO FULLY FINANCE A BLACK MARKET FILM ABOUT ME.
I TURN YOU OVER TO THEM, AND I'M IN THE SPOTLIGHT AGAIN.
HOLLYWOOD'S ALWAYS BEEN A TOUGH TOWN...BUT I STILL KNOW HOW TO CUT A DEAL.

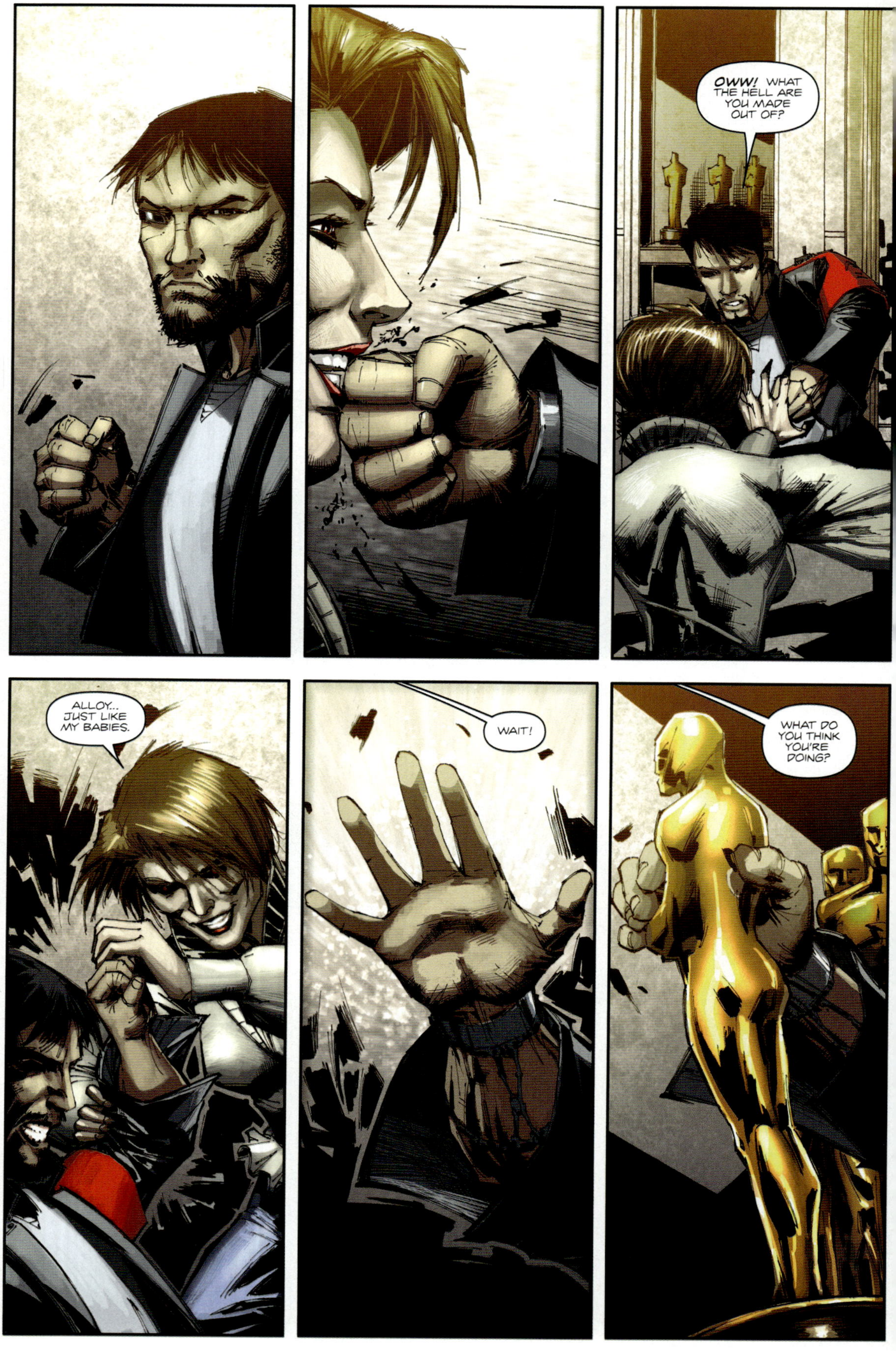
OWW! WHAT THE HELL ARE YOU MADE OUT OF?
ALLOY... JUST LIKE MY BABIES.
WAIT!
WHAT DO YOU THINK YOU'RE DOING?

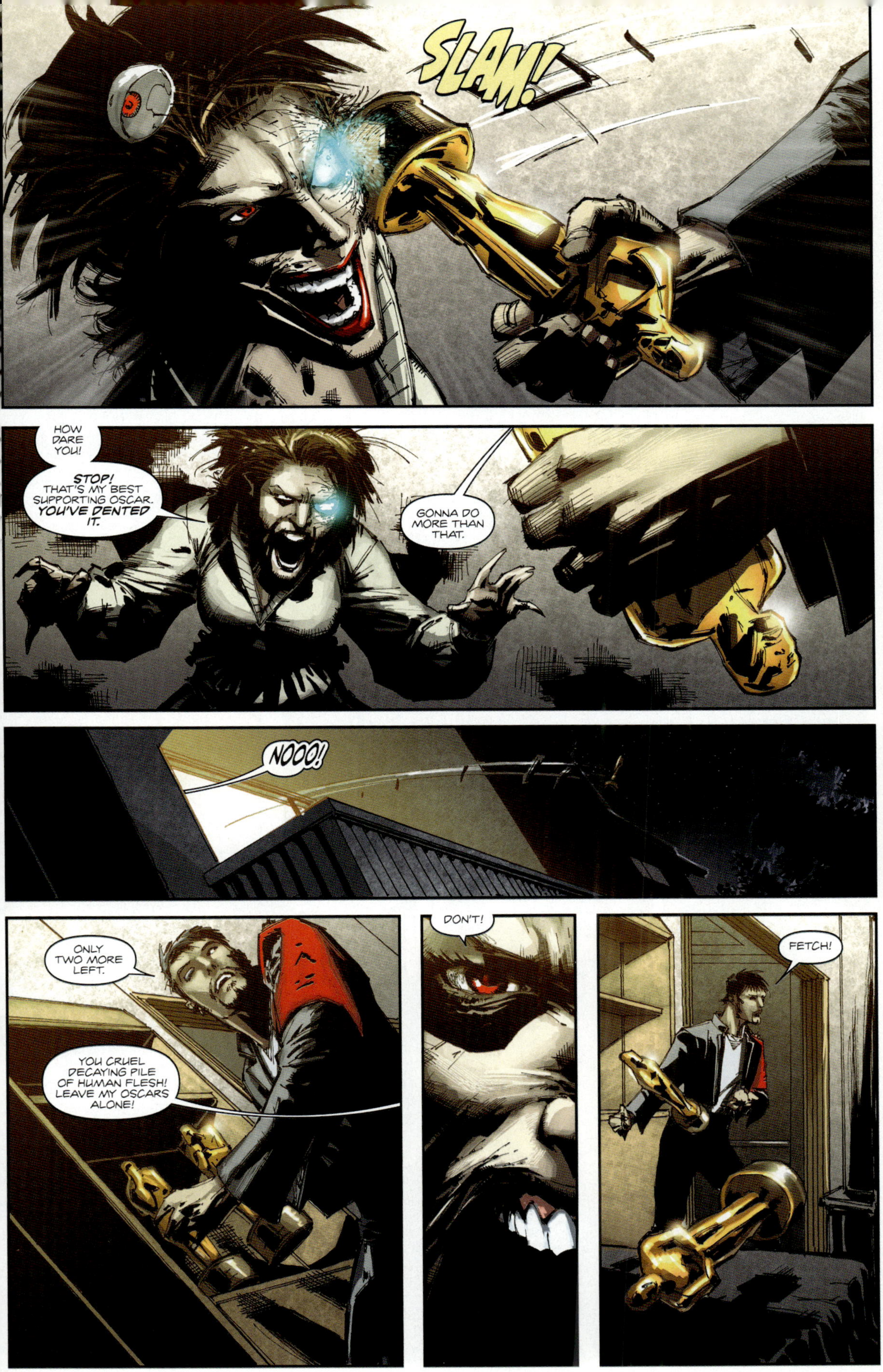
SLAM!
HOW DARE YOU!
STOP! THAT'S MY BEST SUPPORTING OSCAR. YOU'VE DENTED IT.
GONNA DO MORE THAN THAT.
NOOO!
ONLY TWO MORE LEFT.
YOU CRUEL DECAYING PILE OF HUMAN FLESH! LEAVE MY OSCARS ALONE!
DON'T!
FETCH!

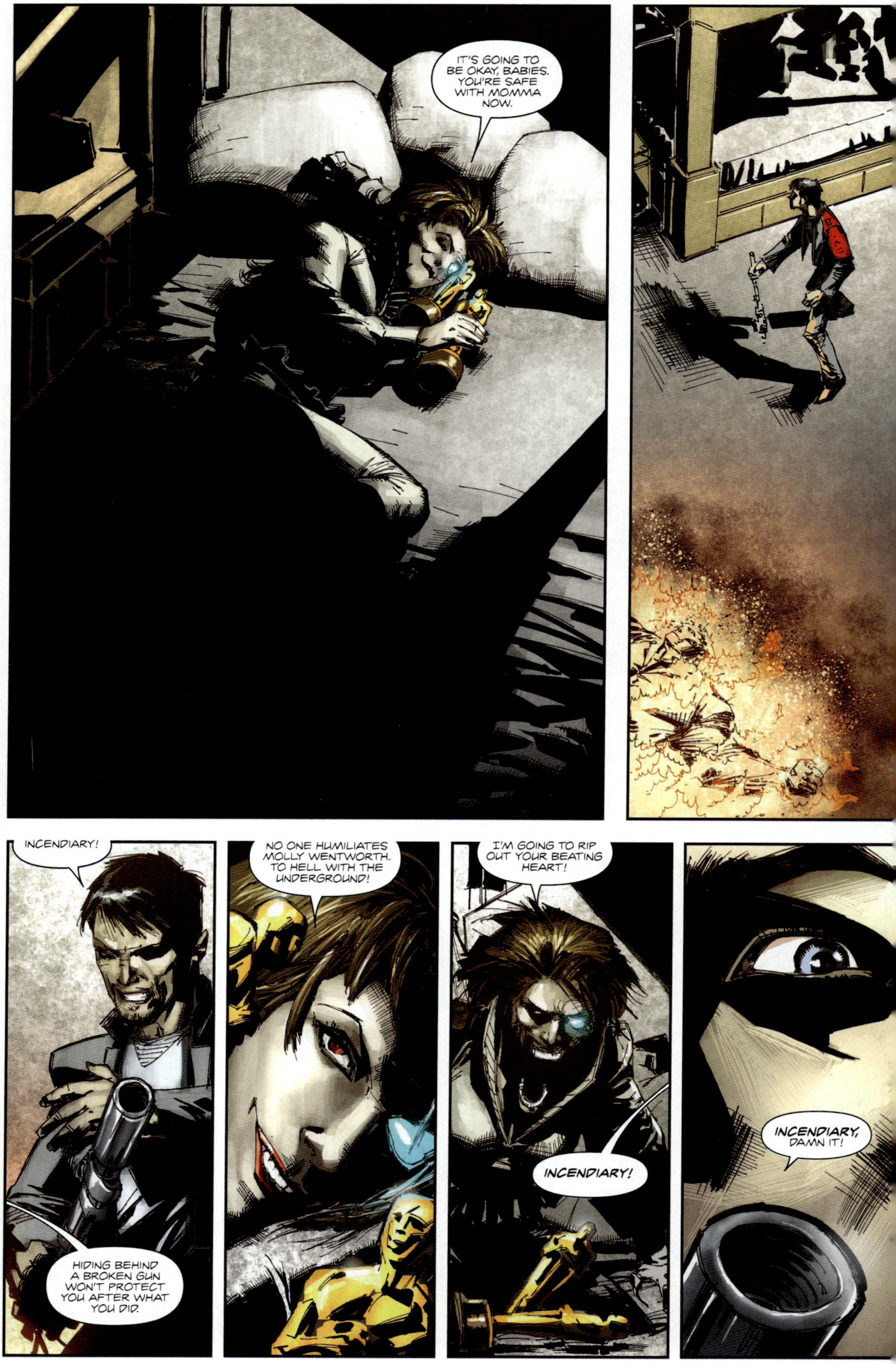

IT'S GOING TO BE OKAY, BABIES. YOU'RE SAFE WITH MOMMA NOW.
INCENDIARY!
HIDING BEHIND A BROKEN GUN WON'T PROTECT YOU AFTER WHAT YOU DID.
NO ONE HUMILIATES MOLLY WENTWORTH. TO HELL WITH THE UNDERGROUND!
I'M GOING TO RIP OUT YOUR BEATING HEART!
INCENDIARY!
INCENDIARY, DAMN IT!

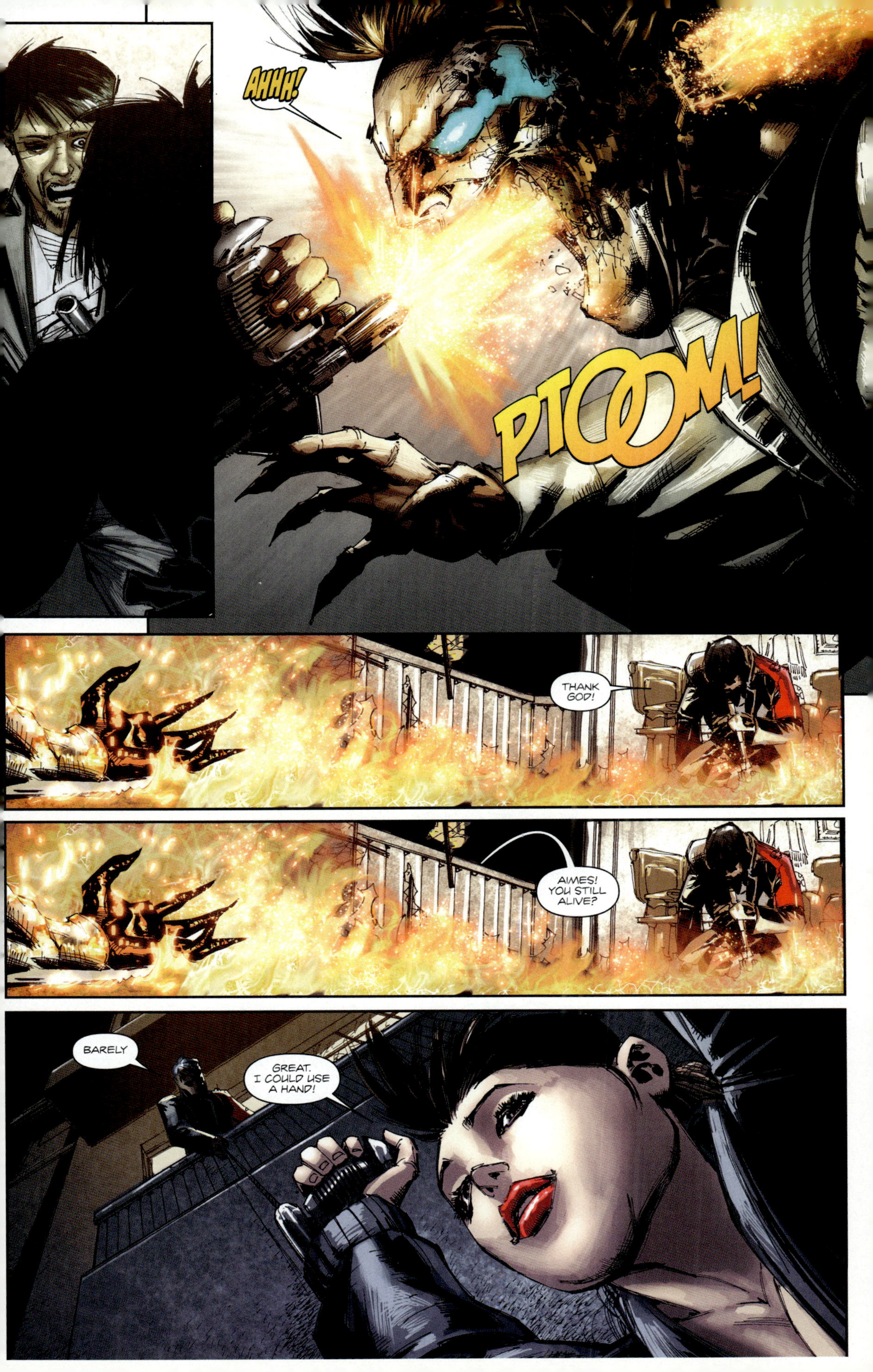
AHHH!
PTOOM!
THANK GOD!
AIMES! YOU STILL ALIVE?
BARELY
GREAT. I COULD USE A HAND!

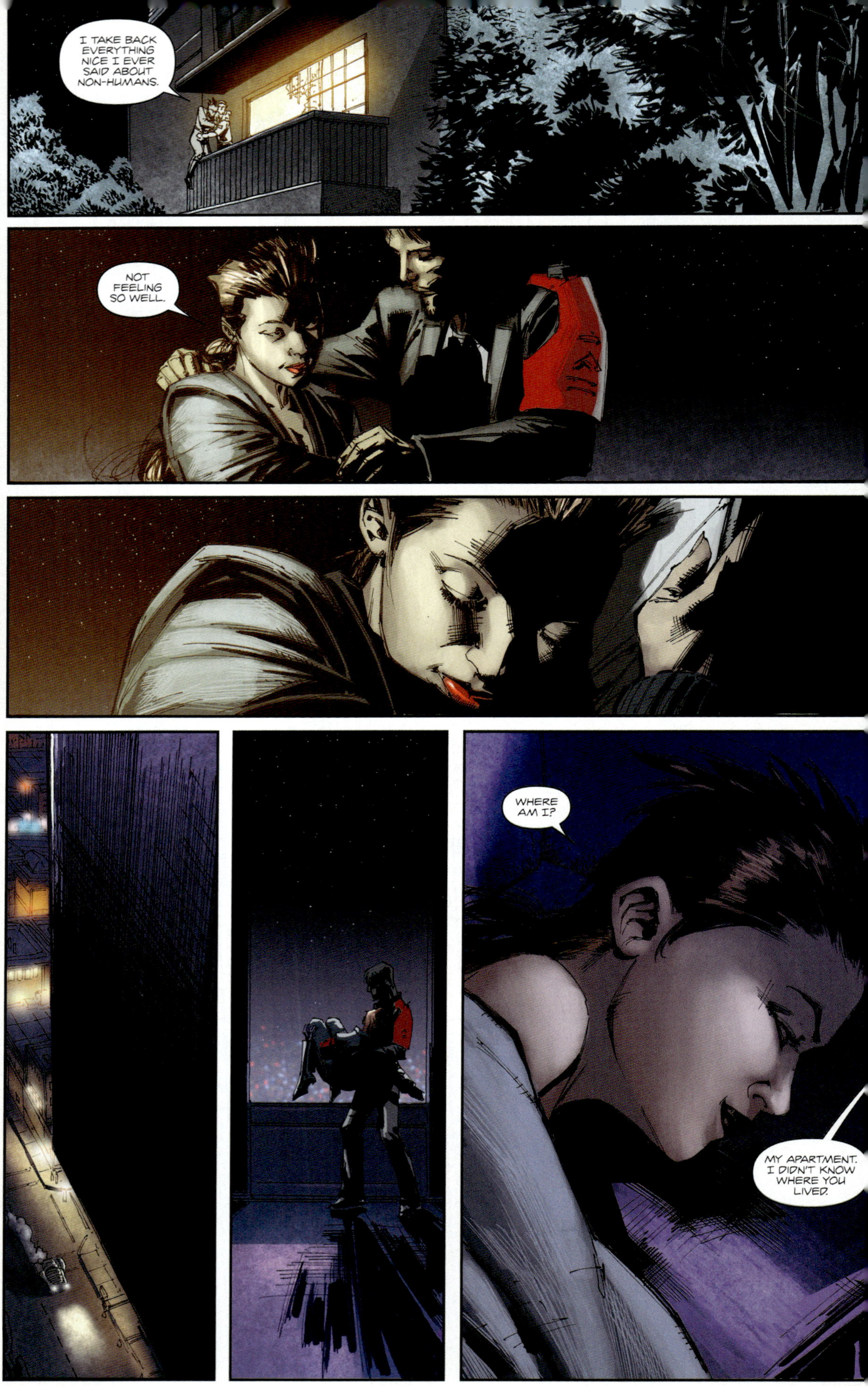
I TAKE BACK EVERYTHING NICE I EVER SAID ABOUT NON-HUMANS.
NOT FEELING SO WELL.
WHERE AM I?
MY APARTMENT. I DIDN'T KNOW WHERE YOU LIVED.

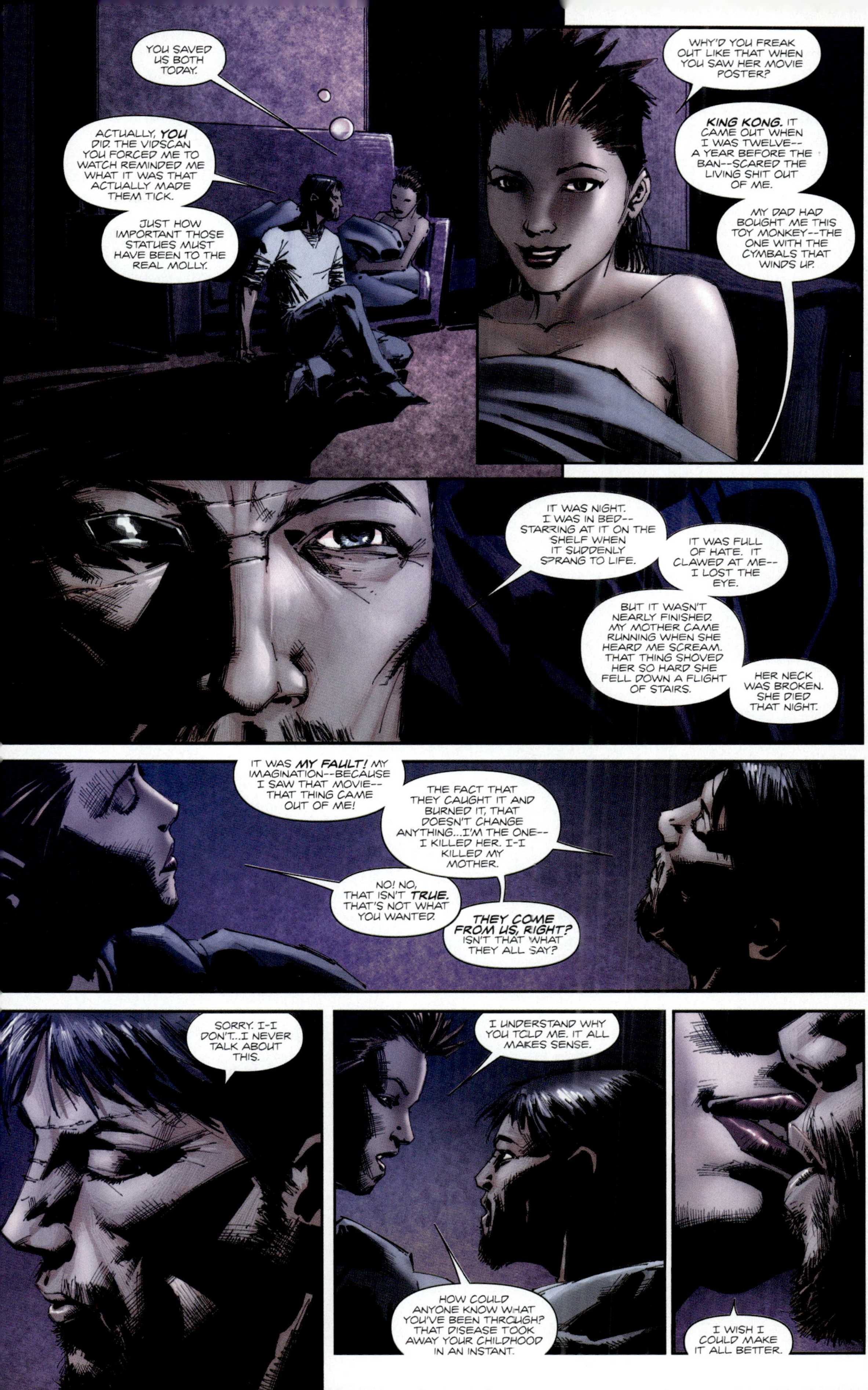
YOU SAVED US BOTH TODAY.
ACTUALLY, **YOU** DID. THE VIDSCAN YOU FORCED ME TO WATCH REMINDED ME WHAT IT WAS THAT ACTUALLY MADE THEM TICK.
JUST HOW IMPORTANT THOSE STATUES MUST HAVE BEEN TO THE REAL MOLLY.
WHY'D YOU FREAK OUT LIKE THAT WHEN YOU SAW HER MOVIE POSTER?
**KING KONG.** IT CAME OUT WHEN I WAS TWELVE-- A YEAR BEFORE THE BAN--SCARED THE LIVING SHIT OUT OF ME.
MY DAD HAD BOUGHT ME THIS TOY MONKEY--THE ONE WITH THE CYMBALS THAT WINDS UP.
IT WAS NIGHT. I WAS IN BED-- STARRING AT IT ON THE SHELF WHEN IT SUDDENLY SPRANG TO LIFE.
IT WAS FULL OF HATE. IT CLAWED AT ME-- I LOST THE EYE.
BUT IT WASN'T NEARLY FINISHED. MY MOTHER CAME RUNNING WHEN SHE HEARD ME SCREAM. THAT THING SHOVED HER SO HARD SHE FELL DOWN A FLIGHT OF STAIRS.
HER NECK WAS BROKEN. SHE DIED THAT NIGHT.
IT WAS **MY FAULT!** MY IMAGINATION--BECAUSE I SAW THAT MOVIE-- THAT THING CAME OUT OF ME!
THE FACT THAT THEY CAUGHT IT AND BURNED IT, THAT DOESN'T CHANGE ANYTHING...I'M THE ONE-- I KILLED HER. I-I KILLED MY MOTHER.
NO! NO, THAT ISN'T **TRUE.** THAT'S NOT WHAT YOU WANTED.
**THEY COME FROM US, RIGHT?** ISN'T THAT WHAT THEY ALL SAY?
SORRY. I-I DON'T...I NEVER TALK ABOUT THIS.
I UNDERSTAND WHY YOU TOLD ME. IT ALL MAKES SENSE.
HOW COULD ANYONE KNOW WHAT YOU'VE BEEN THROUGH? THAT DISEASE TOOK AWAY YOUR CHILDHOOD IN AN INSTANT.
I WISH I COULD MAKE IT ALL BETTER.

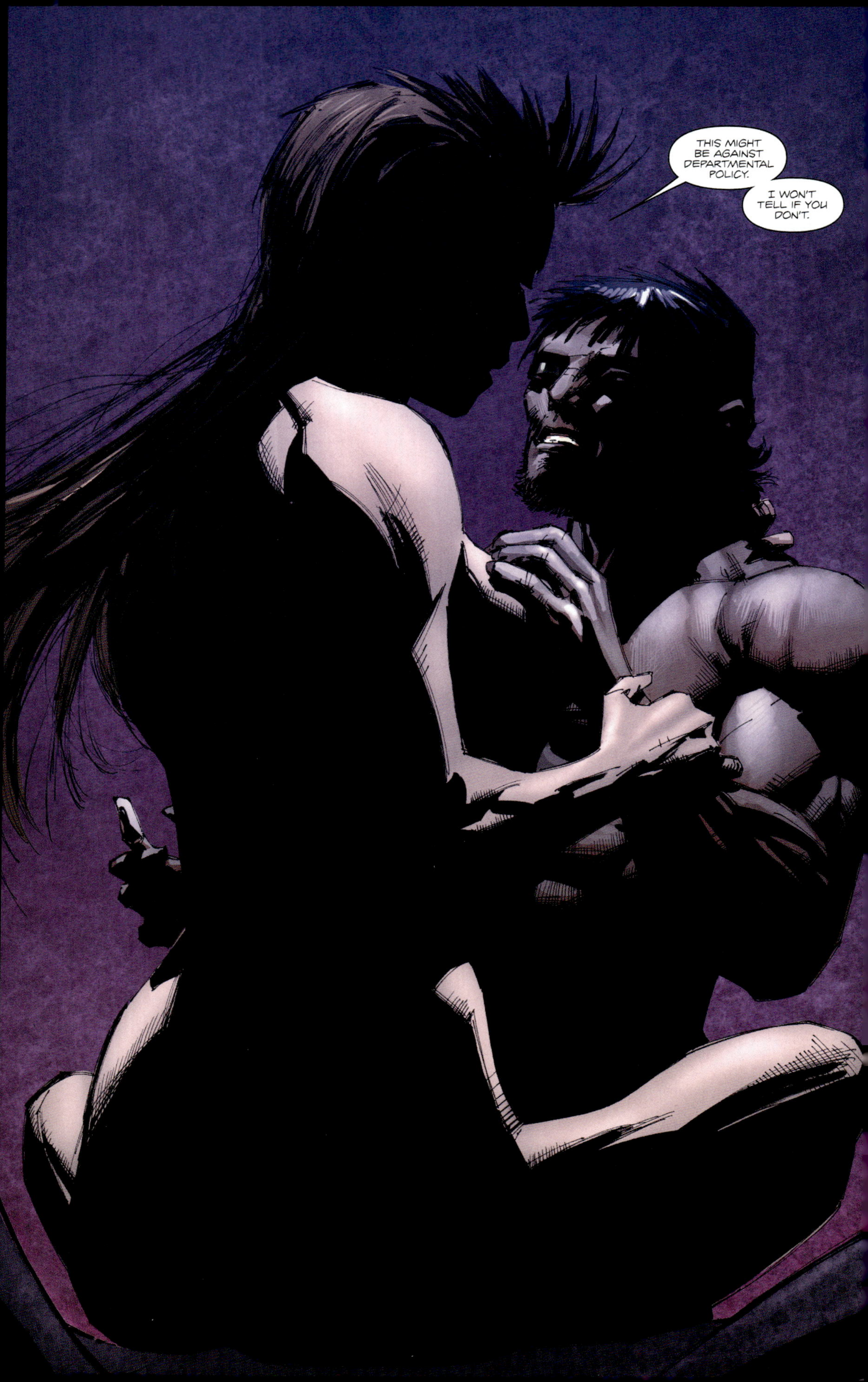
THIS MIGHT BE AGAINST DEPARTMENTAL POLICY.
I WON'T TELL IF YOU DON'T.

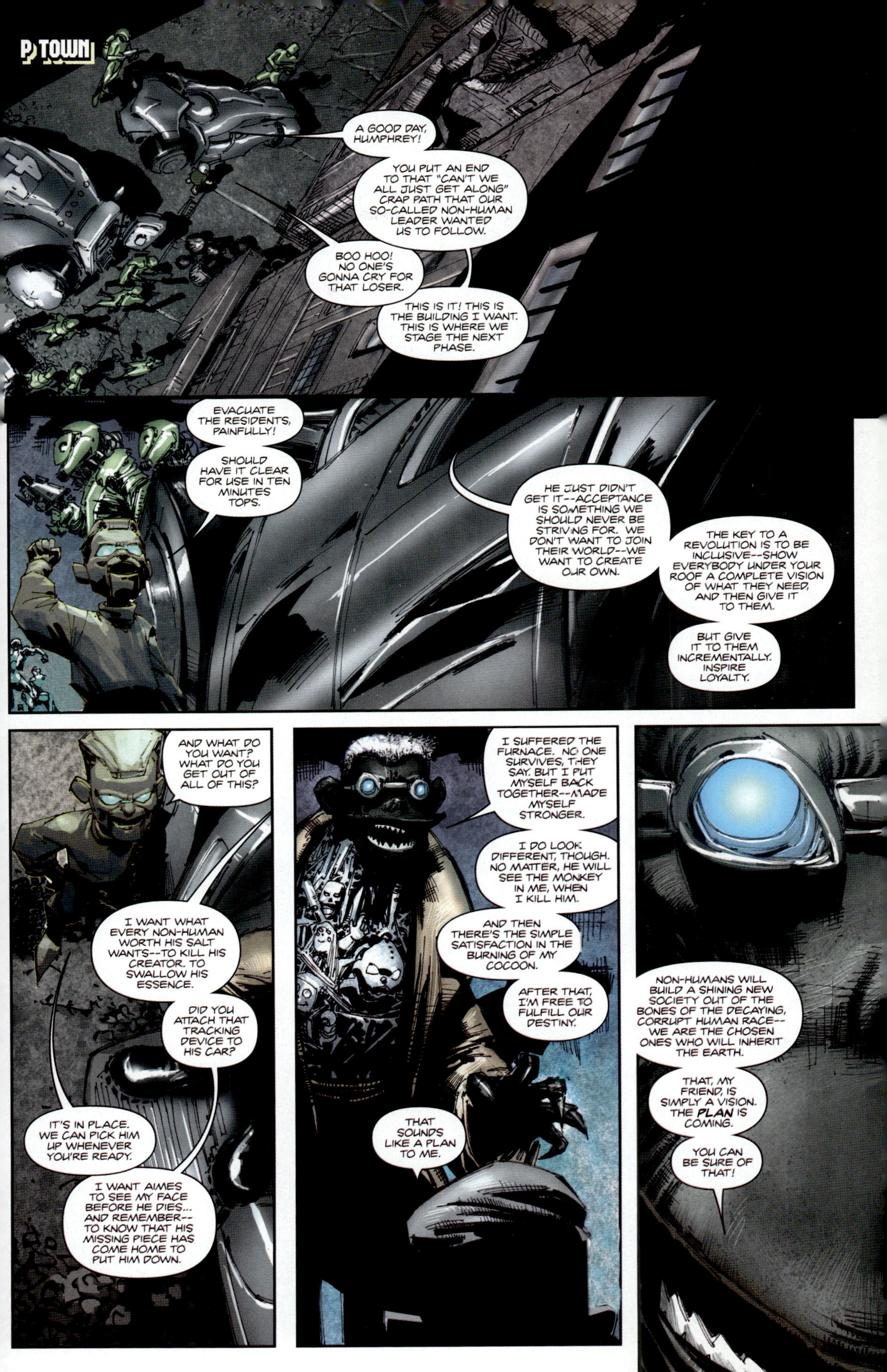
P TOWN
A GOOD DAY, HUMPHREY!
YOU PUT AN END TO THAT "CAN'T WE ALL JUST GET ALONG" CRAP PATH THAT OUR SO-CALLED NON-HUMAN LEADER WANTED US TO FOLLOW.
BOO HOO! NO ONE'S GONNA CRY FOR THAT LOSER.
THIS IS IT! THIS IS THE BUILDING I WANT. THIS IS WHERE WE STAGE THE NEXT PHASE.
EVACUATE THE RESIDENTS, PAINFULLY!
SHOULD HAVE IT CLEAR FOR USE IN TEN MINUTES TOPS.
HE JUST DIDN'T GET IT--ACCEPTANCE IS SOMETHING WE SHOULD NEVER BE STRIVING FOR. WE DON'T WANT TO JOIN THEIR WORLD--WE WANT TO CREATE OUR OWN.
THE KEY TO A REVOLUTION IS TO BE INCLUSIVE--SHOW EVERYBODY UNDER YOUR ROOF A COMPLETE VISION OF WHAT THEY NEED, AND THEN GIVE IT TO THEM.
BUT GIVE IT TO THEM INCREMENTALLY. INSPIRE LOYALTY.
AND WHAT DO YOU WANT? WHAT DO YOU GET OUT OF ALL OF THIS?
I WANT WHAT EVERY NON-HUMAN WORTH HIS SALT WANTS--TO KILL HIS CREATOR. TO SWALLOW HIS ESSENCE.
DID YOU ATTACH THAT TRACKING DEVICE TO HIS CAR?
IT'S IN PLACE. WE CAN PICK HIM UP WHENEVER YOU'RE READY.
I WANT AIMES TO SEE MY FACE BEFORE HE DIES... AND REMEMBER-- TO KNOW THAT HIS MISSING PIECE HAS COME HOME TO PUT HIM DOWN.
I SUFFERED THE FURNACE. NO ONE SURVIVES, THEY SAY. BUT I PUT MYSELF BACK TOGETHER--MADE MYSELF STRONGER.
I DO LOOK DIFFERENT, THOUGH. NO MATTER, HE WILL SEE THE MONKEY IN ME, WHEN I KILL HIM.
AND THEN THERE'S THE SIMPLE SATISFACTION IN THE BURNING OF MY COCOON.
AFTER THAT, I'M FREE TO FULFILL OUR DESTINY.
THAT SOUNDS LIKE A PLAN TO ME.
NON-HUMANS WILL BUILD A SHINING NEW SOCIETY OUT OF THE BONES OF THE DECAYING, CORRUPT HUMAN RACE-- WE ARE THE CHOSEN ONES WHO WILL INHERIT THE EARTH.
THAT, MY FRIEND, IS SIMPLY A VISION. THE PLAN IS COMING.
YOU CAN BE SURE OF THAT!

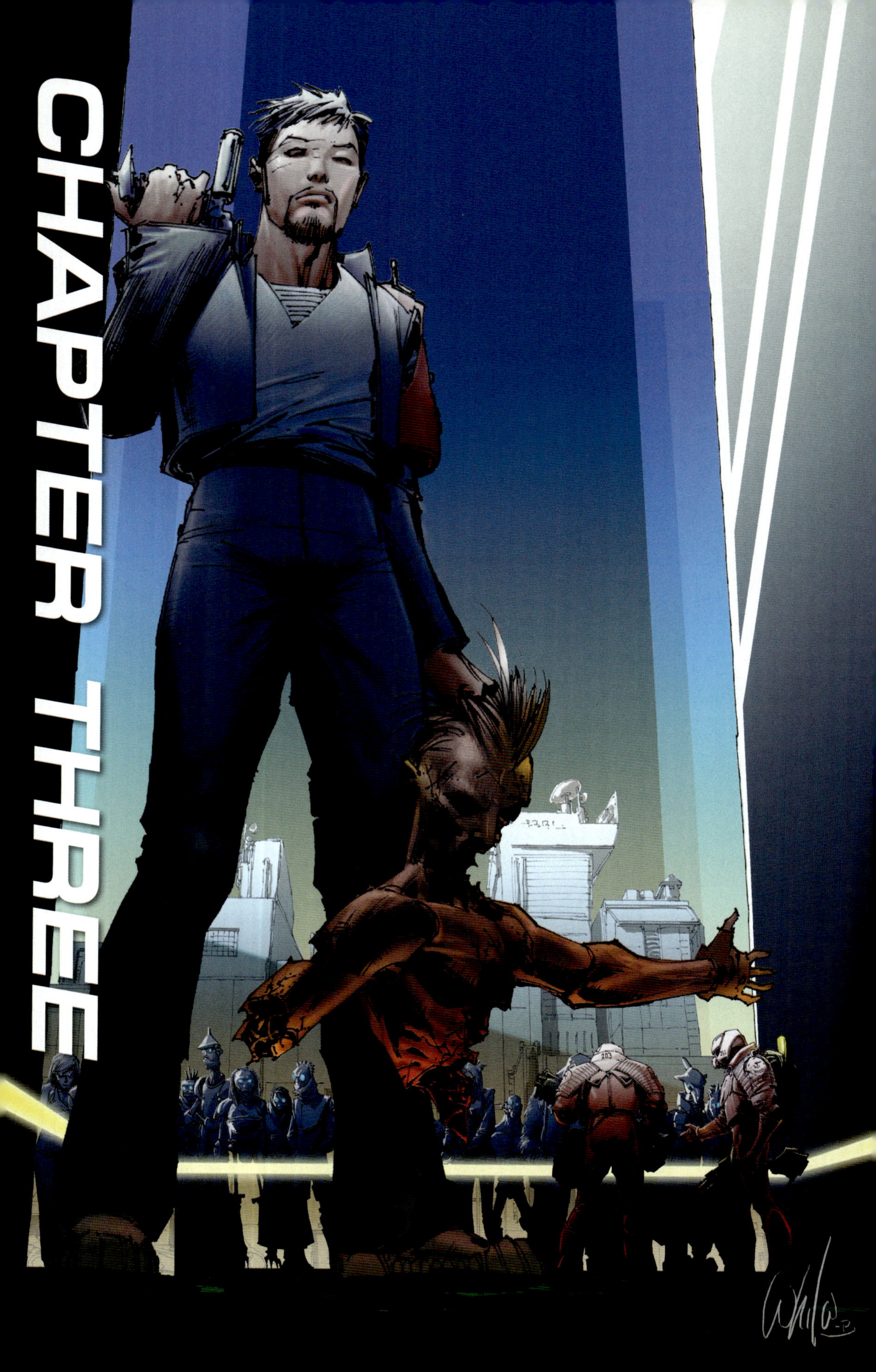
CHAPTER THREE

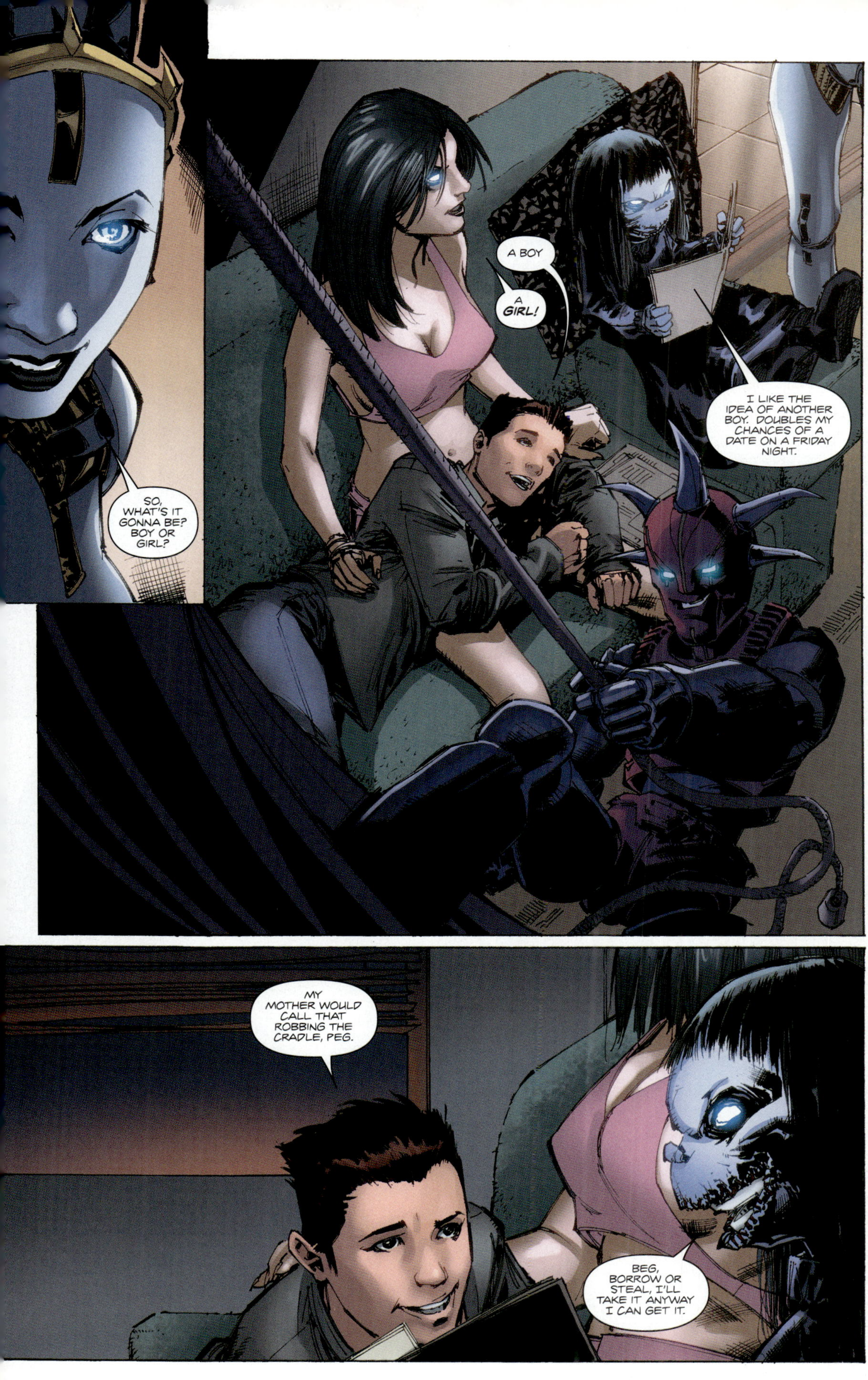
SO, WHAT'S IT GONNA BE? BOY OR GIRL?
A BOY
A GIRL!
I LIKE THE IDEA OF ANOTHER BOY. DOUBLES MY CHANCES OF A DATE ON A FRIDAY NIGHT.
MY MOTHER WOULD CALL THAT ROBBING THE CRADLE, PEG.
BEG, BORROW OR STEAL, I'LL TAKE IT ANYWAY I CAN GET IT.

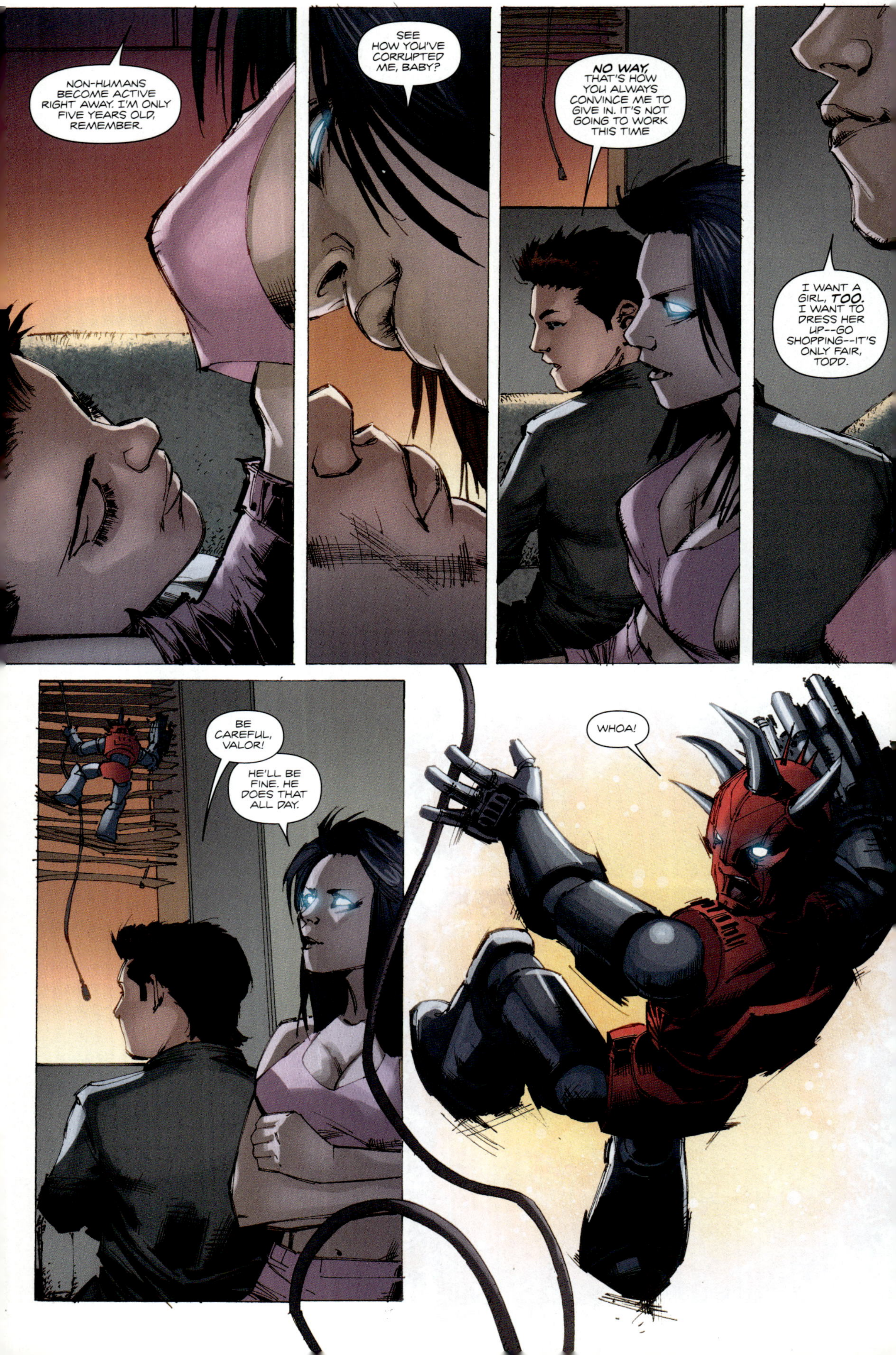
NON-HUMANS BECOME ACTIVE RIGHT AWAY. I'M ONLY FIVE YEARS OLD, REMEMBER.
SEE HOW YOU'VE CORRUPTED ME, BABY?
NO WAY, THAT'S HOW YOU ALWAYS CONVINCE ME TO GIVE IN. IT'S NOT GOING TO WORK THIS TIME
I WANT A GIRL, TOO. I WANT TO DRESS HER UP--GO SHOPPING--IT'S ONLY FAIR, TODD.
BE CAREFUL, VALOR!
HE'LL BE FINE. HE DOES THAT ALL DAY.
WHOA!

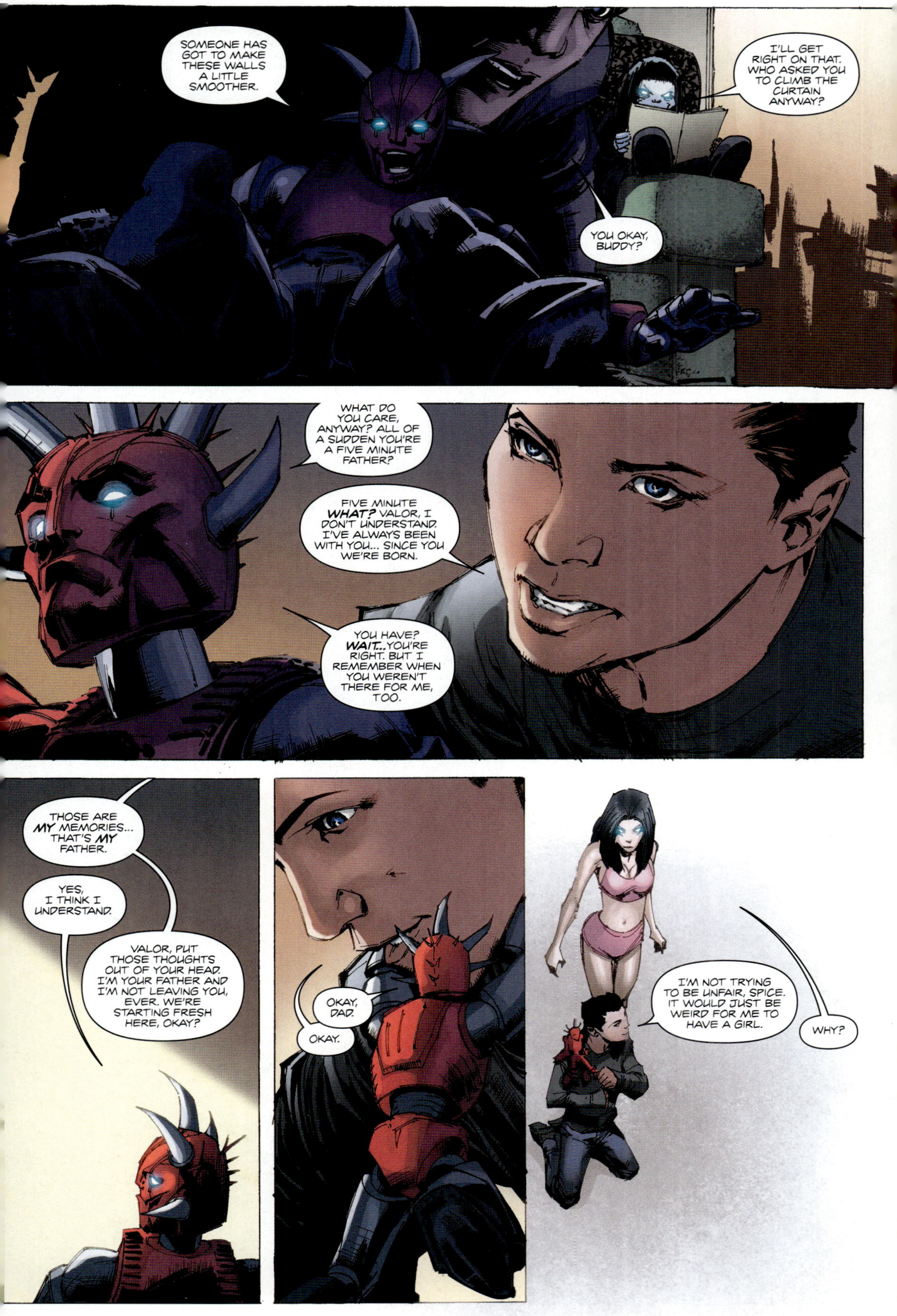
SOMEONE HAS GOT TO MAKE THESE WALLS A LITTLE SMOOTHER.
I'LL GET RIGHT ON THAT. WHO ASKED YOU TO CLIMB THE CURTAIN ANYWAY?
YOU OKAY, BUDDY?
WHAT DO YOU CARE, ANYWAY? ALL OF A SUDDEN YOU'RE A FIVE MINUTE FATHER?
FIVE MINUTE WHAT? VALOR, I DON'T UNDERSTAND. I'VE ALWAYS BEEN WITH YOU... SINCE YOU WE'RE BORN.
YOU HAVE? WAIT... YOU'RE RIGHT. BUT I REMEMBER WHEN YOU WEREN'T THERE FOR ME, TOO.
THOSE ARE MY MEMORIES... THAT'S MY FATHER.
YES, I THINK I UNDERSTAND.
VALOR, PUT THOSE THOUGHTS OUT OF YOUR HEAD. I'M YOUR FATHER AND I'M NOT LEAVING YOU, EVER. WE'RE STARTING FRESH HERE, OKAY?
OKAY, DAD.
OKAY.
I'M NOT TRYING TO BE UNFAIR, SPICE. IT WOULD JUST BE WEIRD FOR ME TO HAVE A GIRL.
WHY?

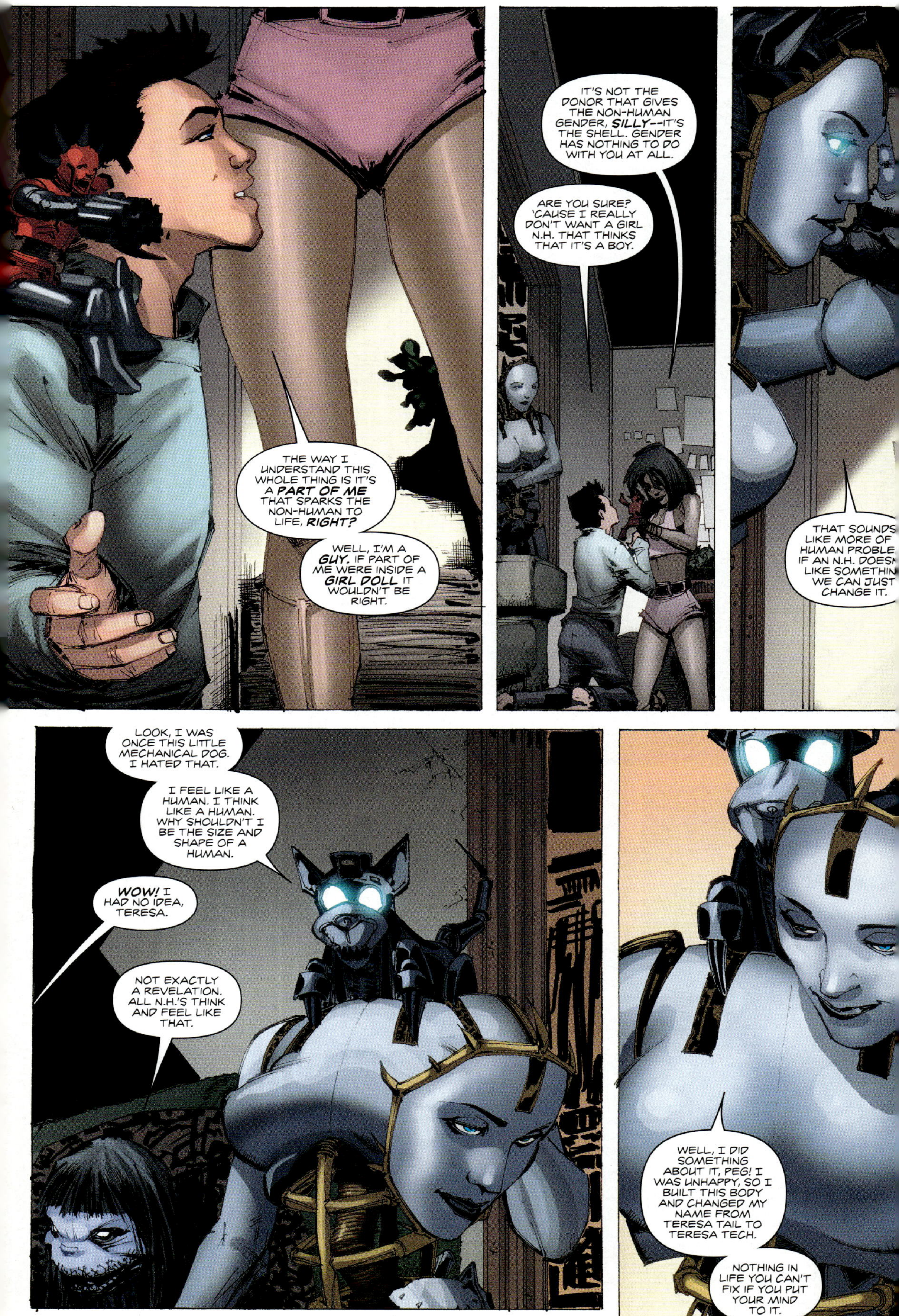
THE WAY I UNDERSTAND THIS WHOLE THING IS IT'S A PART OF ME THAT SPARKS THE NON-HUMAN TO LIFE, RIGHT?
WELL, I'M A GUY. IF PART OF ME WERE INSIDE A GIRL DOLL IT WOULDN'T BE RIGHT.
IT'S NOT THE DONOR THAT GIVES THE NON-HUMAN GENDER, SILLY--IT'S THE SHELL. GENDER HAS NOTHING TO DO WITH YOU AT ALL.
ARE YOU SURE? 'CAUSE I REALLY DON'T WANT A GIRL N.H. THAT THINKS THAT IT'S A BOY.
THAT SOUNDS LIKE MORE OF HUMAN PROBLE IF AN N.H. DOESN LIKE SOMETHIN WE CAN JUST CHANGE IT.
LOOK, I WAS ONCE THIS LITTLE MECHANICAL DOG. I HATED THAT.
I FEEL LIKE A HUMAN. I THINK LIKE A HUMAN. WHY SHOULDN'T I BE THE SIZE AND SHAPE OF A HUMAN.
WOW! I HAD NO IDEA, TERESA.
NOT EXACTLY A REVELATION. ALL N.H.'S THINK AND FEEL LIKE THAT.
WELL, I DID SOMETHING ABOUT IT, PEG! I WAS UNHAPPY, SO I BUILT THIS BODY AND CHANGED MY NAME FROM TERESA TAIL TO TERESA TECH.
NOTHING IN LIFE YOU CAN'T FIX IF YOU PUT YOUR MIND TO IT.

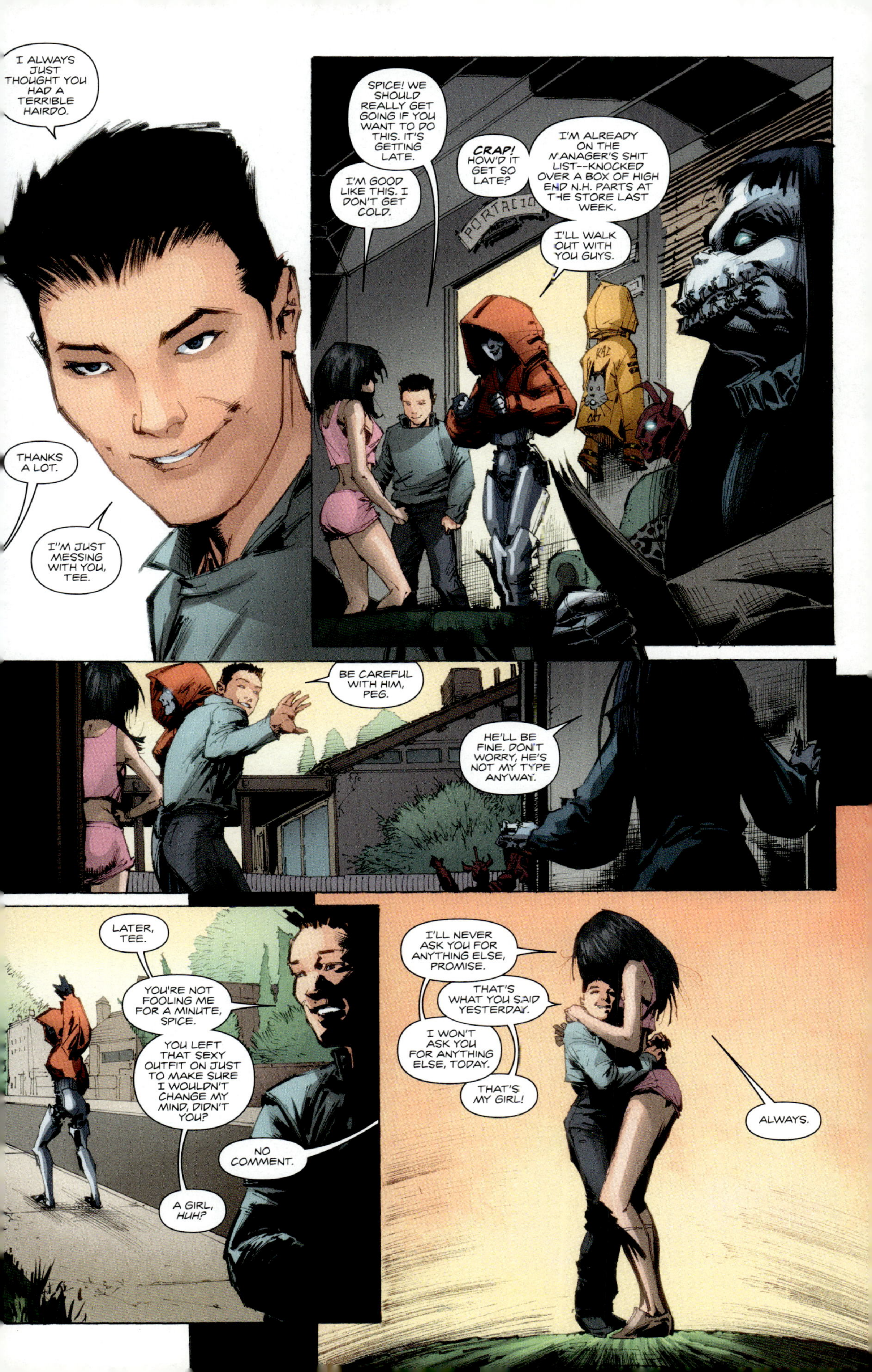
I ALWAYS JUST THOUGHT YOU HAD A TERRIBLE HAIRDO.
THANKS A LOT.
I'M JUST MESSING WITH YOU, TEE.
SPICE! WE SHOULD REALLY GET GOING IF YOU WANT TO DO THIS. IT'S GETTING LATE.
I'M GOOD LIKE THIS. I DON'T GET COLD.
CRAP! HOW'D IT GET SO LATE?
I'M ALREADY ON THE MANAGER'S SHIT LIST--KNOCKED OVER A BOX OF HIGH END N.H. PARTS AT THE STORE LAST WEEK.
I'LL WALK OUT WITH YOU GUYS.
PORTACIO
BE CAREFUL WITH HIM, PEG.
HE'LL BE FINE. DON'T WORRY, HE'S NOT MY TYPE ANYWAY.
LATER, TEE.
YOU'RE NOT FOOLING ME FOR A MINUTE, SPICE.
YOU LEFT THAT SEXY OUTFIT ON JUST TO MAKE SURE I WOULDN'T CHANGE MY MIND, DIDN'T YOU?
NO COMMENT.
A GIRL, HUH?
I'LL NEVER ASK YOU FOR ANYTHING ELSE, PROMISE.
THAT'S WHAT YOU SAID YESTERDAY.
I WON'T ASK YOU FOR ANYTHING ELSE, TODAY.
THAT'S MY GIRL!
ALWAYS.

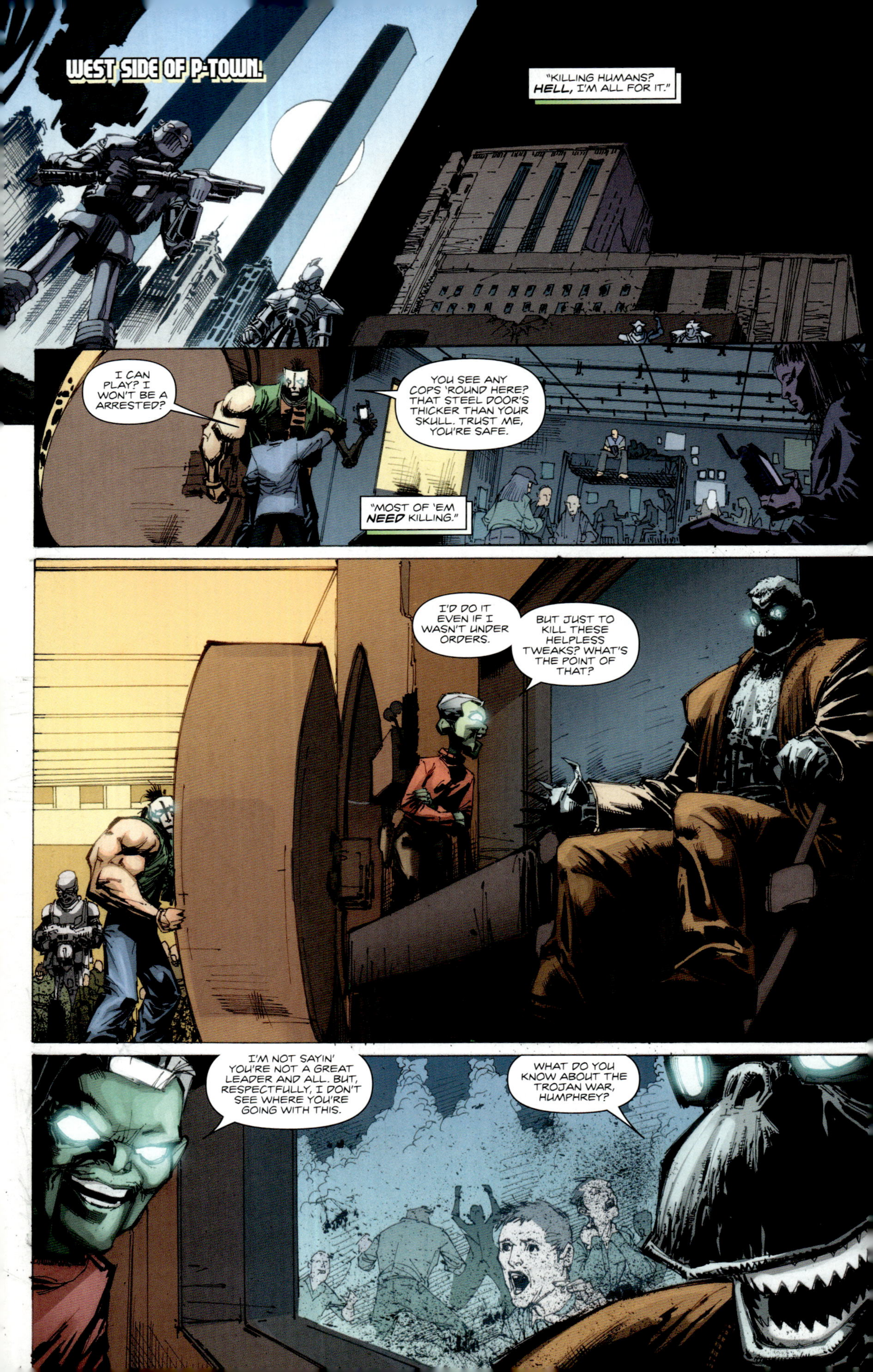
WEST SIDE OF P-TOWN!
"KILLING HUMANS? HELL, I'M ALL FOR IT."
I CAN PLAY? I WON'T BE A ARRESTED?
YOU SEE ANY COPS 'ROUND HERE? THAT STEEL DOOR'S THICKER THAN YOUR SKULL. TRUST ME, YOU'RE SAFE.
"MOST OF 'EM NEED KILLING."
I'D DO IT EVEN IF I WASN'T UNDER ORDERS.
BUT JUST TO KILL THESE HELPLESS TWEAKS? WHAT'S THE POINT OF THAT?
I'M NOT SAYIN' YOU'RE NOT A GREAT LEADER AND ALL. BUT, RESPECTFULLY, I DON'T SEE WHERE YOU'RE GOING WITH THIS.
WHAT DO YOU KNOW ABOUT THE TROJAN WAR, HUMPHREY?

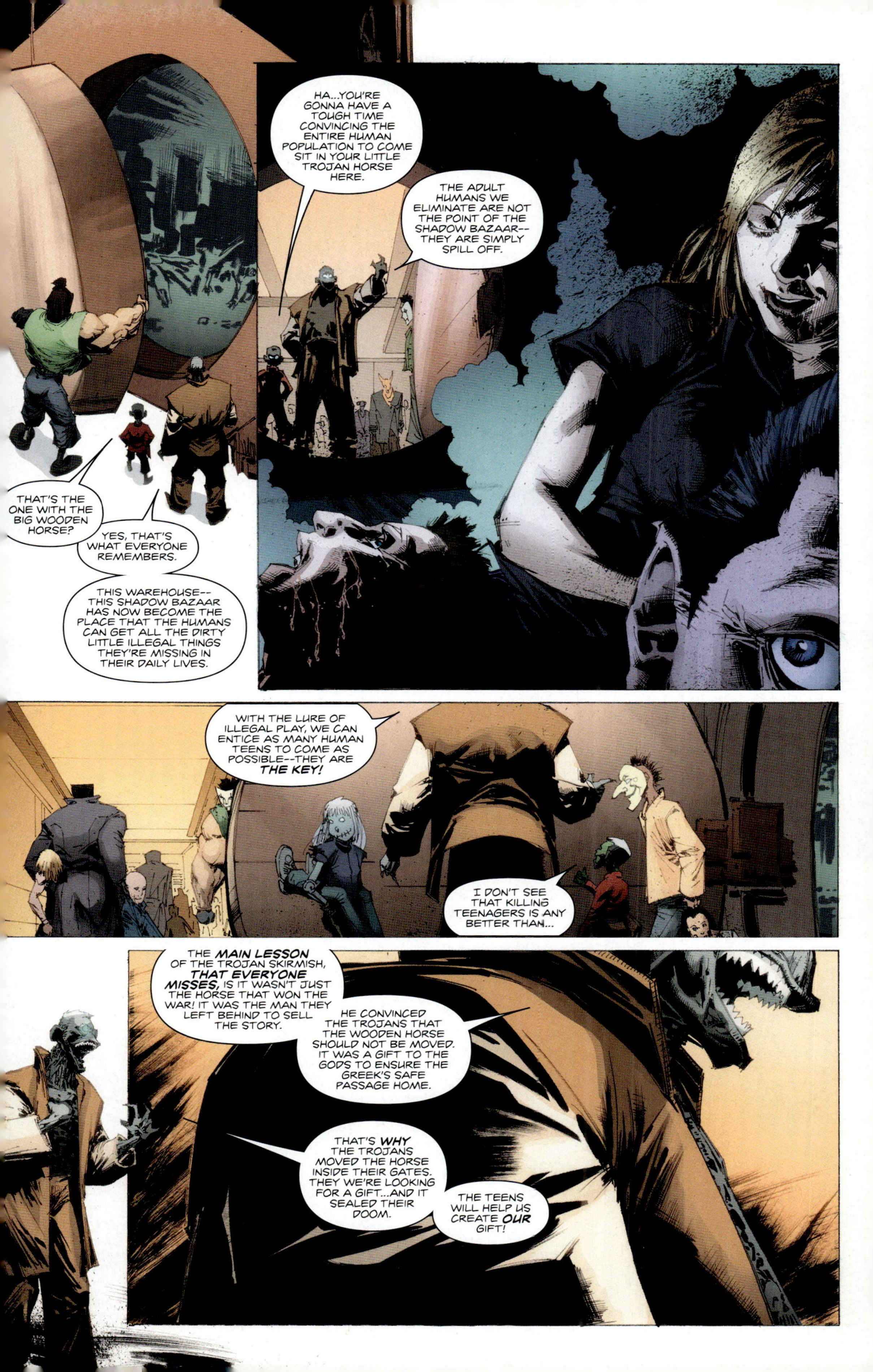
THAT'S THE ONE WITH THE BIG WOODEN HORSE?
YES, THAT'S WHAT EVERYONE REMEMBERS.
THIS WAREHOUSE-- THIS SHADOW BAZAAR HAS NOW BECOME THE PLACE THAT THE HUMANS CAN GET ALL THE DIRTY LITTLE ILLEGAL THINGS THEY'RE MISSING IN THEIR DAILY LIVES.
HA...YOU'RE GONNA HAVE A TOUGH TIME CONVINCING THE ENTIRE HUMAN POPULATION TO COME SIT IN YOUR LITTLE TROJAN HORSE HERE.
THE ADULT HUMANS WE ELIMINATE ARE NOT THE POINT OF THE SHADOW BAZAAR-- THEY ARE SIMPLY SPILL OFF.
WITH THE LURE OF ILLEGAL PLAY, WE CAN ENTICE AS MANY HUMAN TEENS TO COME AS POSSIBLE--THEY ARE **THE KEY!**
I DON'T SEE THAT KILLING TEENAGERS IS ANY BETTER THAN...
THE **MAIN LESSON** OF THE TROJAN SKIRMISH, **THAT EVERYONE MISSES,** IS IT WASN'T JUST THE HORSE THAT WON THE WAR! IT WAS THE MAN THEY LEFT BEHIND TO SELL THE STORY.
HE CONVINCED THE TROJANS THAT THE WOODEN HORSE SHOULD NOT BE MOVED. IT WAS A GIFT TO THE GODS TO ENSURE THE GREEK'S SAFE PASSAGE HOME.
THAT'S **WHY** THE TROJANS MOVED THE HORSE INSIDE THEIR GATES. THEY WE'RE LOOKING FOR A GIFT...AND IT SEALED THEIR DOOM.
THE TEENS WILL HELP US CREATE **OUR** GIFT!

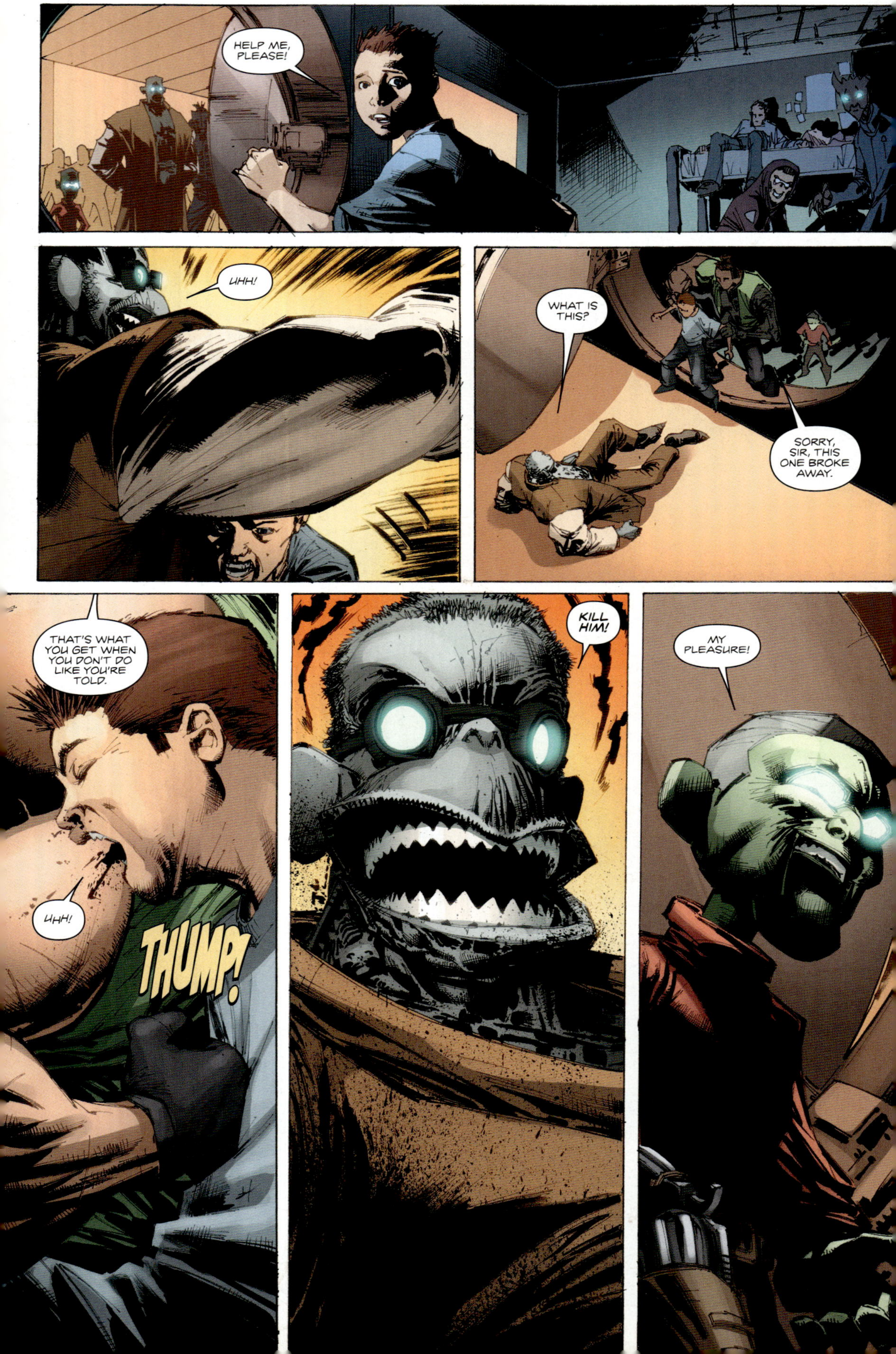
HELP ME, PLEASE!
UHH!
WHAT IS THIS?
SORRY, SIR, THIS ONE BROKE AWAY.
THAT'S WHAT YOU GET WHEN YOU DON'T DO LIKE YOU'RE TOLD.
UHH!
THUMP!
KILL HIM!
MY PLEASURE!

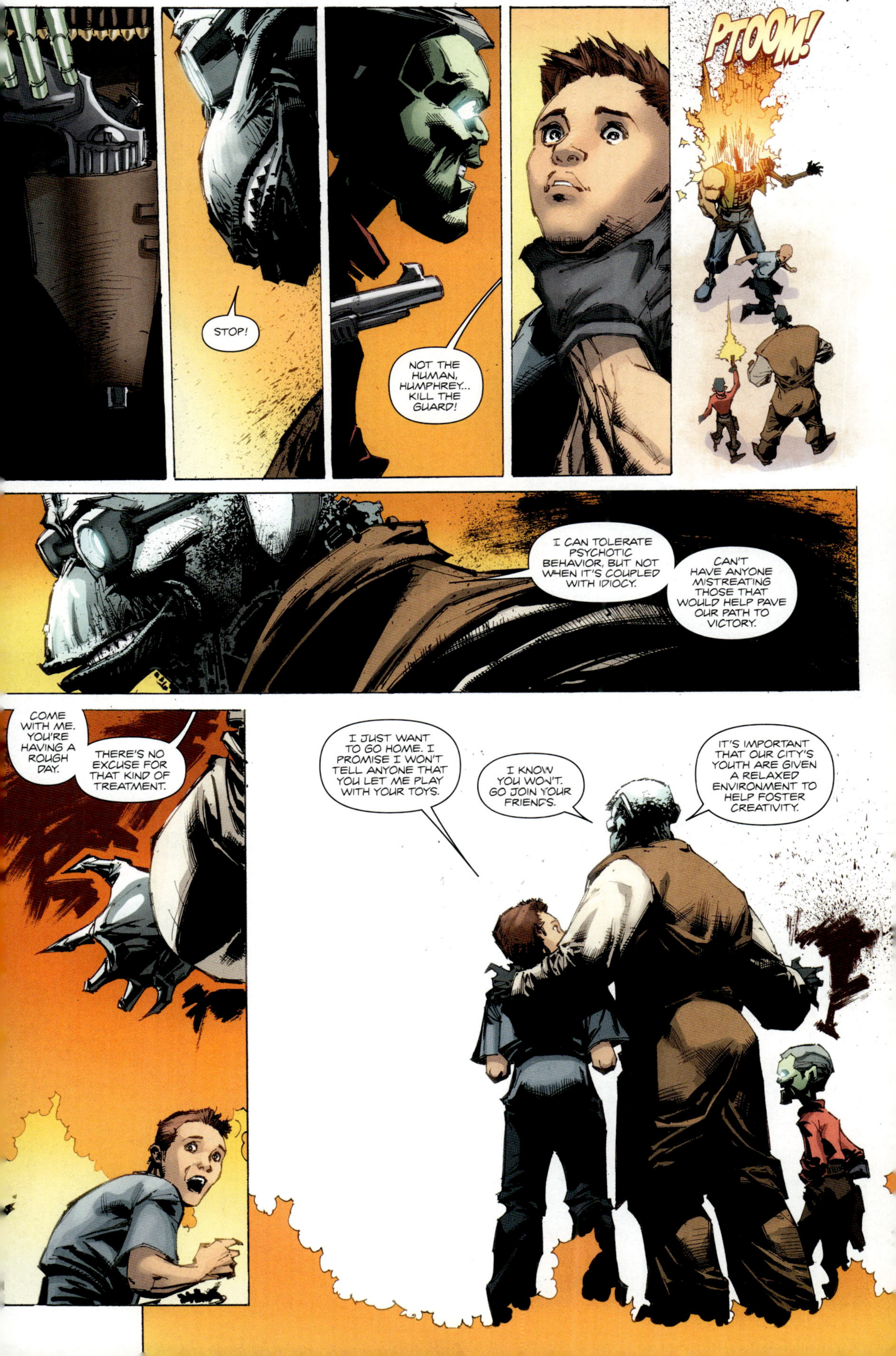
PTOOM!
STOP!
NOT THE HUMAN, HUMPHREY... KILL THE GUARD!
I CAN TOLERATE PSYCHOTIC BEHAVIOR, BUT NOT WHEN IT'S COUPLED WITH IDIOCY.
CAN'T HAVE ANYONE MISTREATING THOSE THAT WOULD HELP PAVE OUR PATH TO VICTORY.
COME WITH ME. YOU'RE HAVING A ROUGH DAY.
THERE'S NO EXCUSE FOR THAT KIND OF TREATMENT.
I JUST WANT TO GO HOME. I PROMISE I WON'T TELL ANYONE THAT YOU LET ME PLAY WITH YOUR TOYS.
I KNOW YOU WON'T. GO JOIN YOUR FRIENDS.
IT'S IMPORTANT THAT OUR CITY'S YOUTH ARE GIVEN A RELAXED ENVIRONMENT TO HELP FOSTER CREATIVITY.

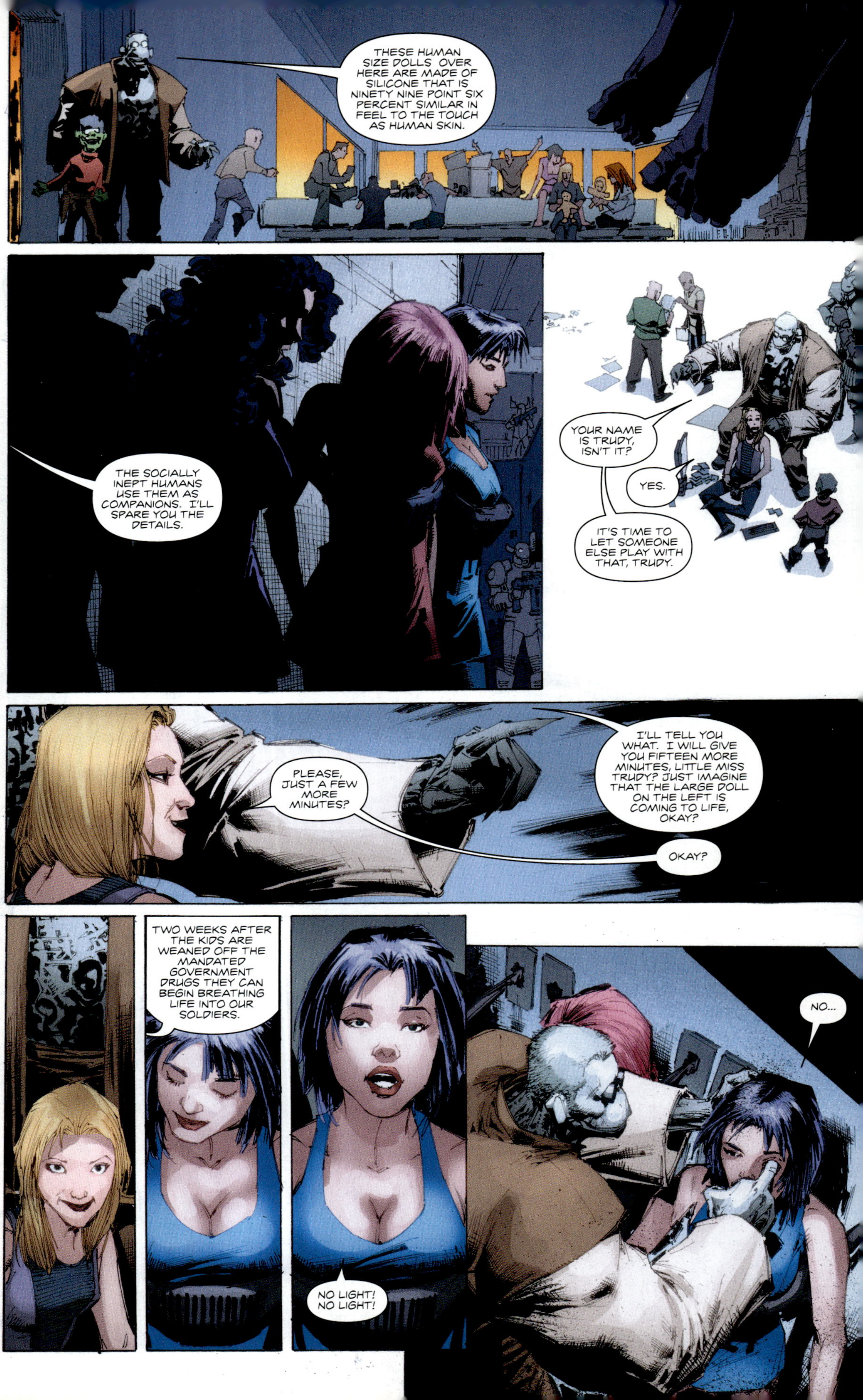
THESE HUMAN SIZE DOLLS OVER HERE ARE MADE OF SILICONE THAT IS NINETY NINE POINT SIX PERCENT SIMILAR IN FEEL TO THE TOUCH AS HUMAN SKIN.
THE SOCIALLY INEPT HUMANS USE THEM AS COMPANIONS. I'LL SPARE YOU THE DETAILS.
YOUR NAME IS TRUDY, ISN'T IT?
YES.
IT'S TIME TO LET SOMEONE ELSE PLAY WITH THAT, TRUDY.
PLEASE, JUST A FEW MORE MINUTES?
I'LL TELL YOU WHAT. I WILL GIVE YOU FIFTEEN MORE MINUTES, LITTLE MISS TRUDY? JUST IMAGINE THAT THE LARGE DOLL ON THE LEFT IS COMING TO LIFE, OKAY?
OKAY?
TWO WEEKS AFTER THE KIDS ARE WEANED OFF THE MANDATED GOVERNMENT DRUGS THEY CAN BEGIN BREATHING LIFE INTO OUR SOLDIERS.
NO LIGHT! NO LIGHT!
NO...

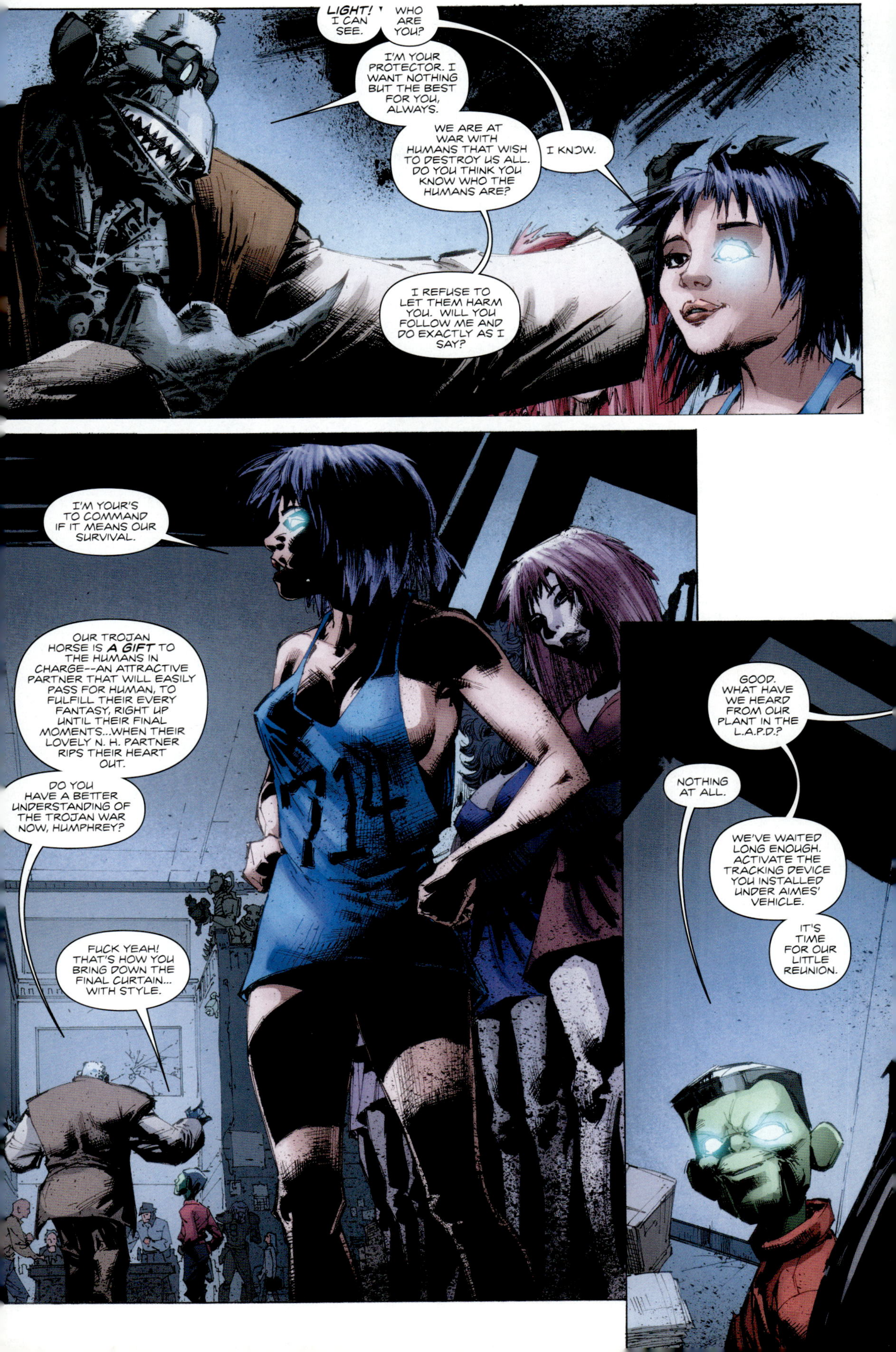
LIGHT! I CAN SEE.
WHO ARE YOU?
I'M YOUR PROTECTOR. I WANT NOTHING BUT THE BEST FOR YOU, ALWAYS.
WE ARE AT WAR WITH HUMANS THAT WISH TO DESTROY US ALL. DO YOU THINK YOU KNOW WHO THE HUMANS ARE?
I KNOW.
I REFUSE TO LET THEM HARM YOU. WILL YOU FOLLOW ME AND DO EXACTLY AS I SAY?
I'M YOUR'S TO COMMAND IF IT MEANS OUR SURVIVAL.
OUR TROJAN HORSE IS A GIFT TO THE HUMANS IN CHARGE--AN ATTRACTIVE PARTNER THAT WILL EASILY PASS FOR HUMAN, TO FULFILL THEIR EVERY FANTASY, RIGHT UP UNTIL THEIR FINAL MOMENTS...WHEN THEIR LOVELY N. H. PARTNER RIPS THEIR HEART OUT.
DO YOU HAVE A BETTER UNDERSTANDING OF THE TROJAN WAR NOW, HUMPHREY?
FUCK YEAH! THAT'S HOW YOU BRING DOWN THE FINAL CURTAIN... WITH STYLE.
GOOD. WHAT HAVE WE HEARD FROM OUR PLANT IN THE L.A.P.D.?
NOTHING AT ALL.
WE'VE WAITED LONG ENOUGH. ACTIVATE THE TRACKING DEVICE YOU INSTALLED UNDER AIMES' VEHICLE.
IT'S TIME FOR OUR LITTLE REUNION.

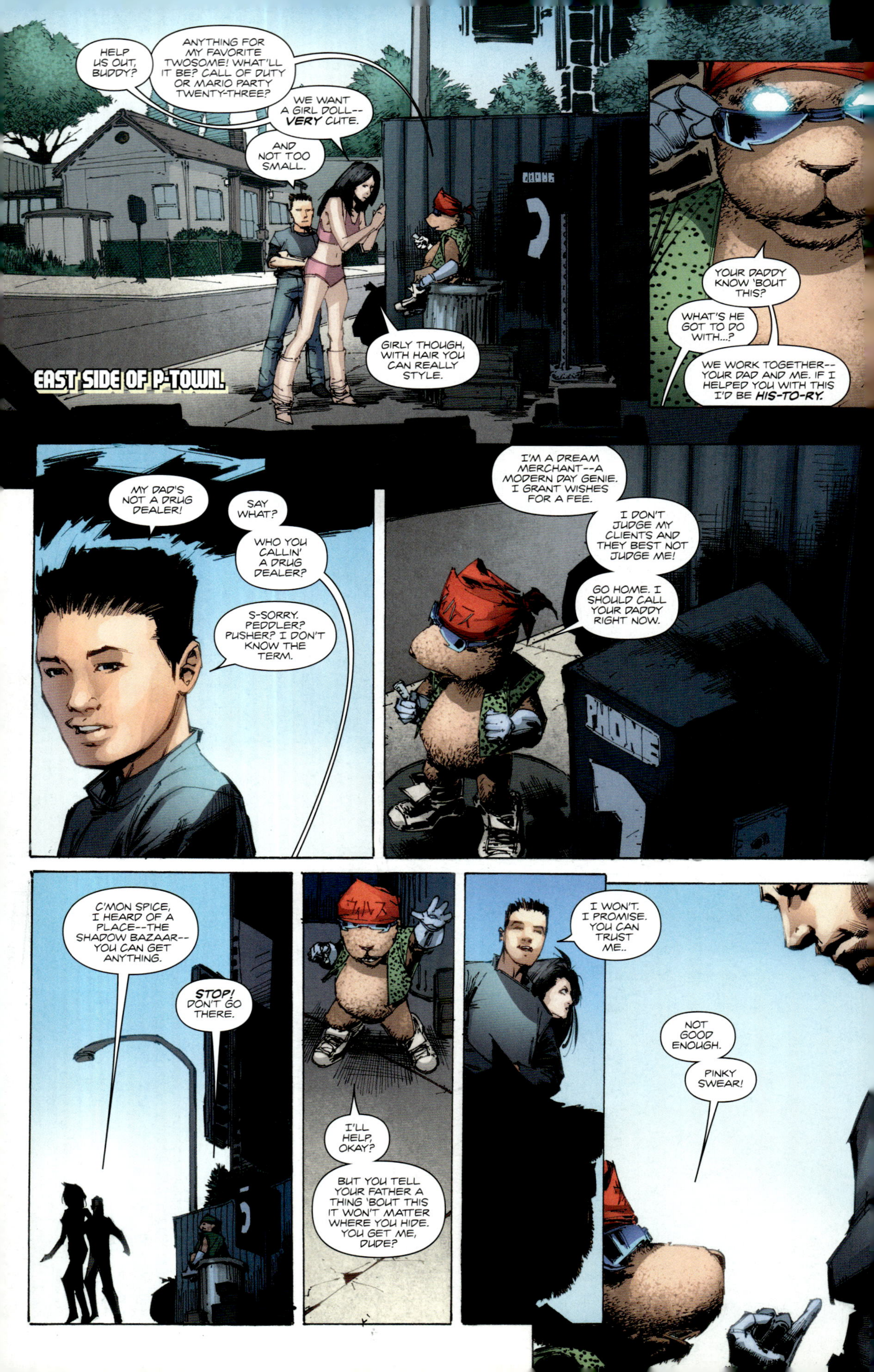
HELP US OUT, BUDDY?
ANYTHING FOR MY FAVORITE TWOSOME! WHAT'LL IT BE? CALL OF DUTY OR MARIO PARTY TWENTY-THREE?
WE WANT A GIRL DOLL-- VERY CUTE.
AND NOT TOO SMALL.
GIRLY THOUGH, WITH HAIR YOU CAN REALLY STYLE.
EAST SIDE OF P-TOWN.
YOUR DADDY KNOW 'BOUT THIS?
WHAT'S HE GOT TO DO WITH...?
WE WORK TOGETHER-- YOUR DAD AND ME. IF I HELPED YOU WITH THIS I'D BE HIS-TO-RY.
MY DAD'S NOT A DRUG DEALER!
SAY WHAT?
WHO YOU CALLIN' A DRUG DEALER?
S-SORRY. PEDDLER? PUSHER? I DON'T KNOW THE TERM.
I'M A DREAM MERCHANT--A MODERN DAY GENIE. I GRANT WISHES FOR A FEE.
I DON'T JUDGE MY CLIENTS AND THEY BEST NOT JUDGE ME!
GO HOME. I SHOULD CALL YOUR DADDY RIGHT NOW.
PHONE
C'MON SPICE, I HEARD OF A PLACE--THE SHADOW BAZAAR-- YOU CAN GET ANYTHING.
STOP! DON'T GO THERE.
I'LL HELP, OKAY?
BUT YOU TELL YOUR FATHER A THING 'BOUT THIS IT WON'T MATTER WHERE YOU HIDE. YOU GET ME, DUDE?
I WON'T. I PROMISE. YOU CAN TRUST ME..
NOT GOOD ENOUGH.
PINKY SWEAR!

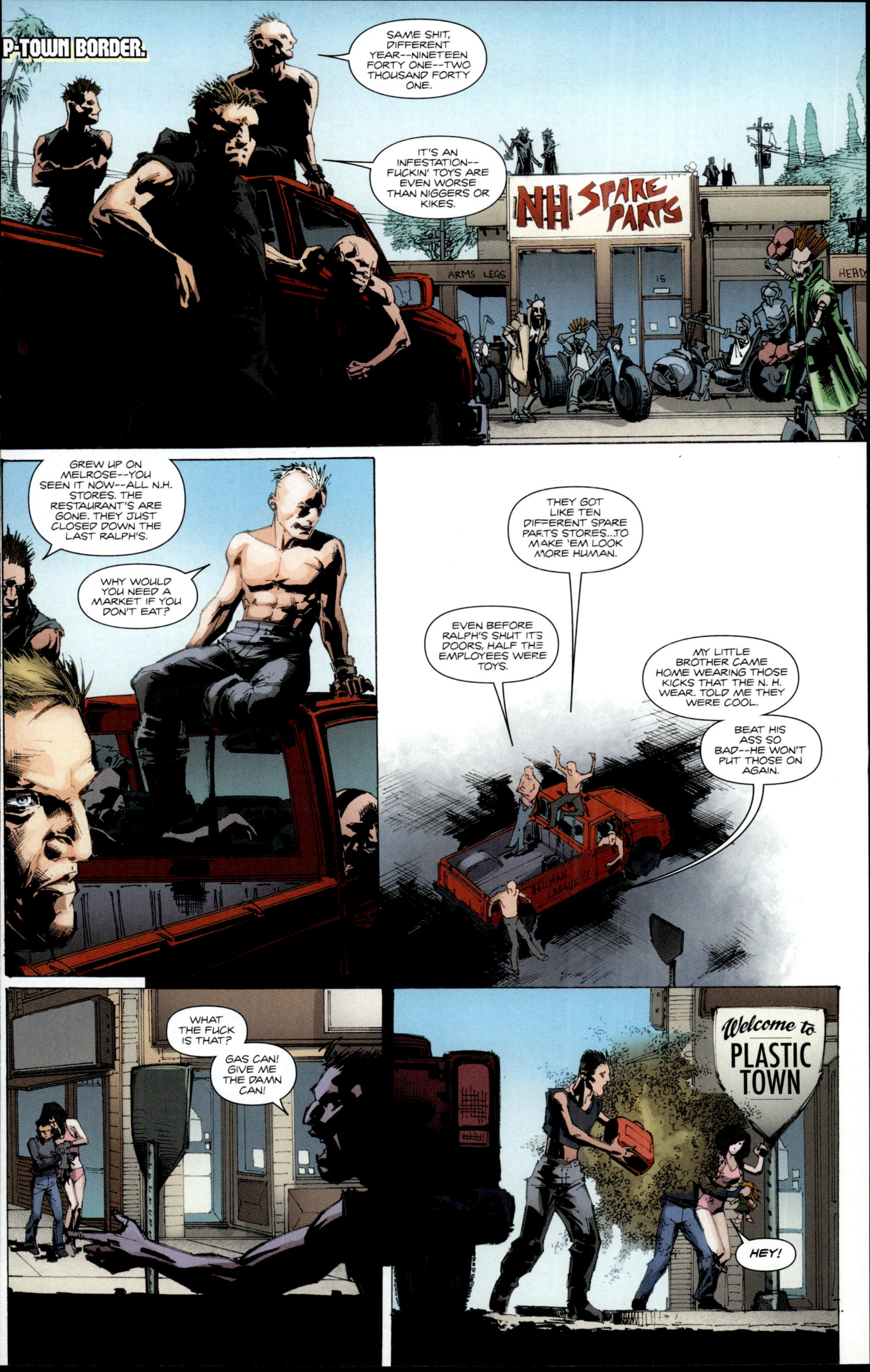
P-TOWN BORDER.
SAME SHIT, DIFFERENT YEAR--NINETEEN FORTY ONE--TWO THOUSAND FORTY ONE.
IT'S AN INFESTATION-- FUCKIN' TOYS ARE EVEN WORSE THAN NIGGERS OR KIKES.
N H SPARE PARTS
ARMS LEGS
15
HEADS
GREW UP ON MELROSE--YOU SEEN IT NOW--ALL N.H. STORES. THE RESTAURANT'S ARE GONE. THEY JUST CLOSED DOWN THE LAST RALPH'S.
WHY WOULD YOU NEED A MARKET IF YOU DON'T EAT?
THEY GOT LIKE TEN DIFFERENT SPARE PARTS STORES...TO MAKE 'EM LOOK MORE HUMAN.
EVEN BEFORE RALPH'S SHUT ITS DOORS, HALF THE EMPLOYEES WERE TOYS.
MY LITTLE BROTHER CAME HOME WEARING THOSE KICKS THAT THE N. H. WEAR. TOLD ME THEY WERE COOL.
BEAT HIS ASS SO BAD--HE WON'T PUT THOSE ON AGAIN.
HUMAN LEAGUE!!!
WHAT THE FUCK IS THAT?
GAS CAN! GIVE ME THE DAMN CAN!
Welcome to PLASTIC TOWN
HEY!

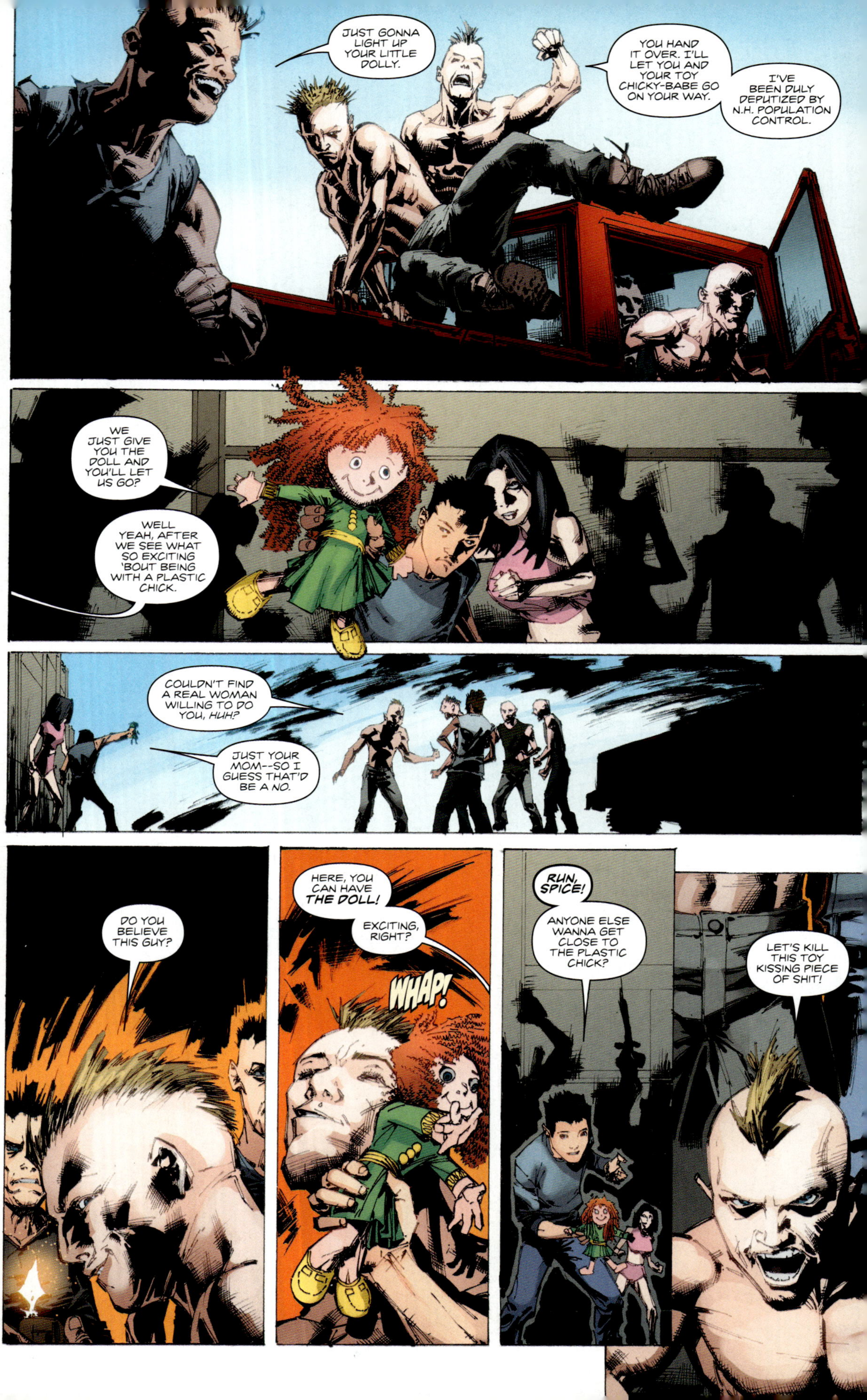

JUST GONNA LIGHT UP YOUR LITTLE DOLLY.
YOU HAND IT OVER. I'LL LET YOU AND YOUR TOY CHICKY-BABE GO ON YOUR WAY.
I'VE BEEN DULY DEPUTIZED BY N.H. POPULATION CONTROL.
WE JUST GIVE YOU THE DOLL AND YOU'LL LET US GO?
WELL YEAH, AFTER WE SEE WHAT SO EXCITING 'BOUT BEING WITH A PLASTIC CHICK.
COULDN'T FIND A REAL WOMAN WILLING TO DO YOU, *HUH?*
JUST YOUR MOM--SO I GUESS THAT'D BE A NO.
DO YOU BELIEVE THIS GUY?
HERE, YOU CAN HAVE ***THE DOLL!***
EXCITING, RIGHT?
WHAP!
***RUN, SPICE!***
ANYONE ELSE WANNA GET CLOSE TO THE PLASTIC CHICK?
LET'S KILL THIS TOY KISSING PIECE OF SHIT!

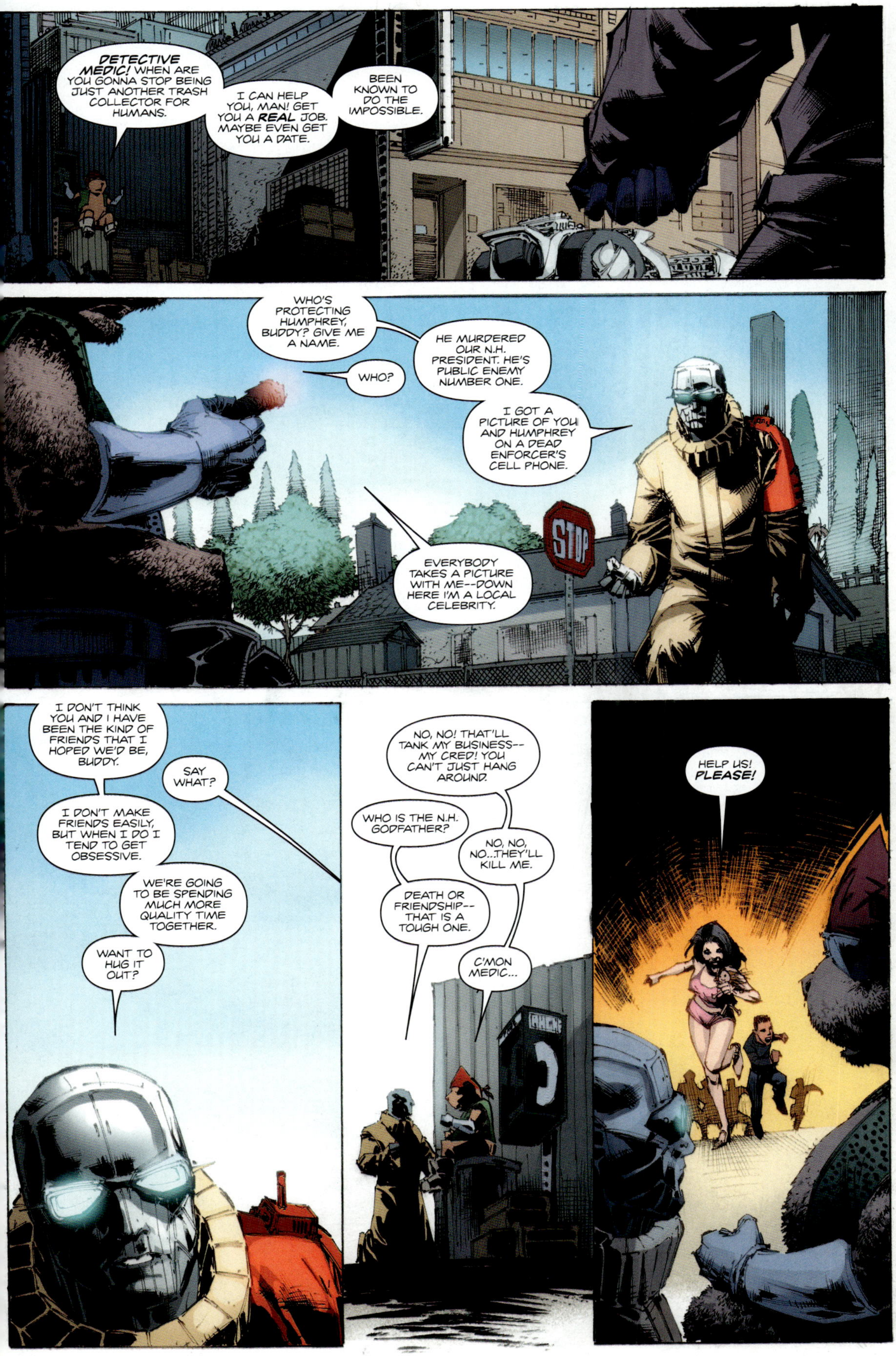

DETECTIVE MEDIC! WHEN ARE YOU GONNA STOP BEING JUST ANOTHER TRASH COLLECTOR FOR HUMANS.
I CAN HELP YOU, MAN! GET YOU A REAL JOB. MAYBE EVEN GET YOU A DATE.
BEEN KNOWN TO DO THE IMPOSSIBLE.
WHO'S PROTECTING HUMPHREY, BUDDY? GIVE ME A NAME.
WHO?
HE MURDERED OUR N.H. PRESIDENT. HE'S PUBLIC ENEMY NUMBER ONE.
I GOT A PICTURE OF YOU AND HUMPHREY ON A DEAD ENFORCER'S CELL PHONE.
EVERYBODY TAKES A PICTURE WITH ME--DOWN HERE I'M A LOCAL CELEBRITY.
STOP
I DON'T THINK YOU AND I HAVE BEEN THE KIND OF FRIENDS THAT I HOPED WE'D BE, BUDDY.
SAY WHAT?
I DON'T MAKE FRIENDS EASILY, BUT WHEN I DO I TEND TO GET OBSESSIVE.
WE'RE GOING TO BE SPENDING MUCH MORE QUALITY TIME TOGETHER.
WANT TO HUG IT OUT?
NO, NO! THAT'LL TANK MY BUSINESS-- MY CRED! YOU CAN'T JUST HANG AROUND.
WHO IS THE N.H. GODFATHER?
NO, NO, NO...THEY'LL KILL ME.
DEATH OR FRIENDSHIP-- THAT IS A TOUGH ONE.
C'MON MEDIC...
HELP US! PLEASE!

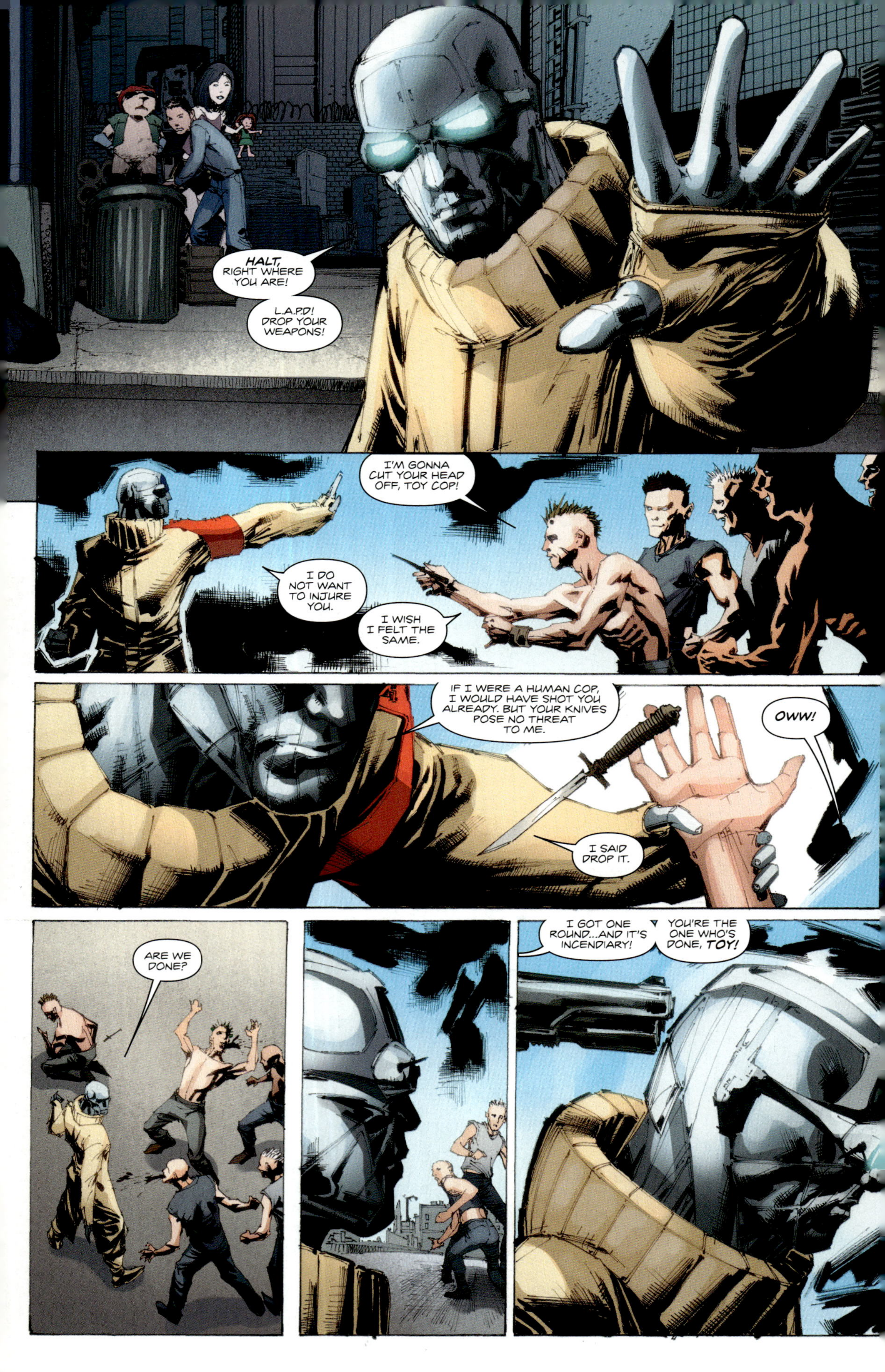
HALT, RIGHT WHERE YOU ARE!
L.A.P.D! DROP YOUR WEAPONS!
I'M GONNA CUT YOUR HEAD OFF, TOY COP!
I DO NOT WANT TO INJURE YOU.
I WISH I FELT THE SAME.
IF I WERE A HUMAN COP, I WOULD HAVE SHOT YOU ALREADY. BUT YOUR KNIVES POSE NO THREAT TO ME.
OWW!
I SAID DROP IT.
ARE WE DONE?
I GOT ONE ROUND...AND IT'S INCENDIARY!
YOU'RE THE ONE WHO'S DONE, TOY!

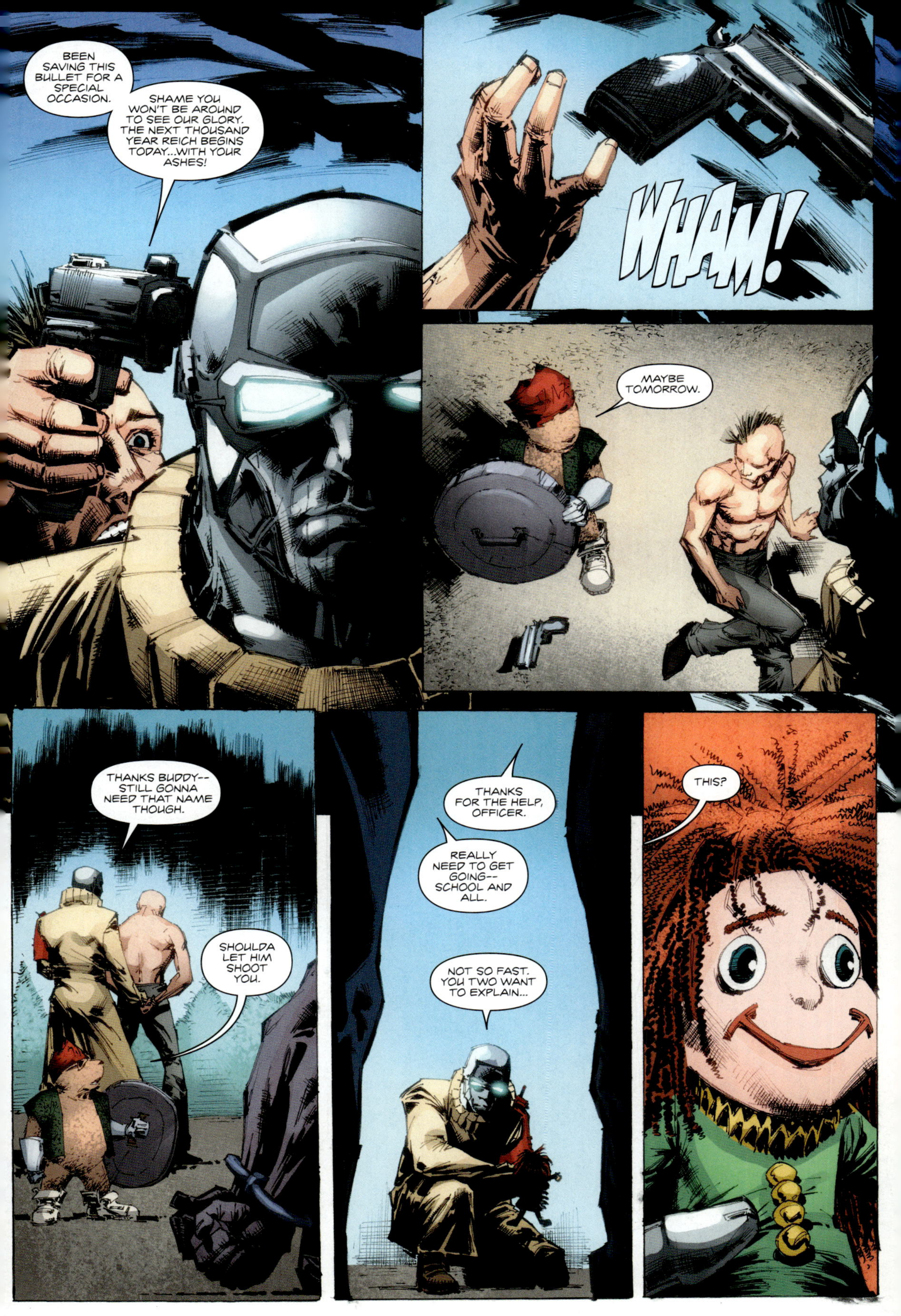
BEEN SAVING THIS BULLET FOR A SPECIAL OCCASION.
SHAME YOU WON'T BE AROUND TO SEE OUR GLORY. THE NEXT THOUSAND YEAR REICH BEGINS TODAY...WITH YOUR ASHES!
WHAM!
MAYBE TOMORROW.
THANKS BUDDY-- STILL GONNA NEED THAT NAME THOUGH.
SHOULDA LET HIM SHOOT YOU.
THANKS FOR THE HELP, OFFICER.
REALLY NEED TO GET GOING-- SCHOOL AND ALL.
NOT SO FAST. YOU TWO WANT TO EXPLAIN...
THIS?

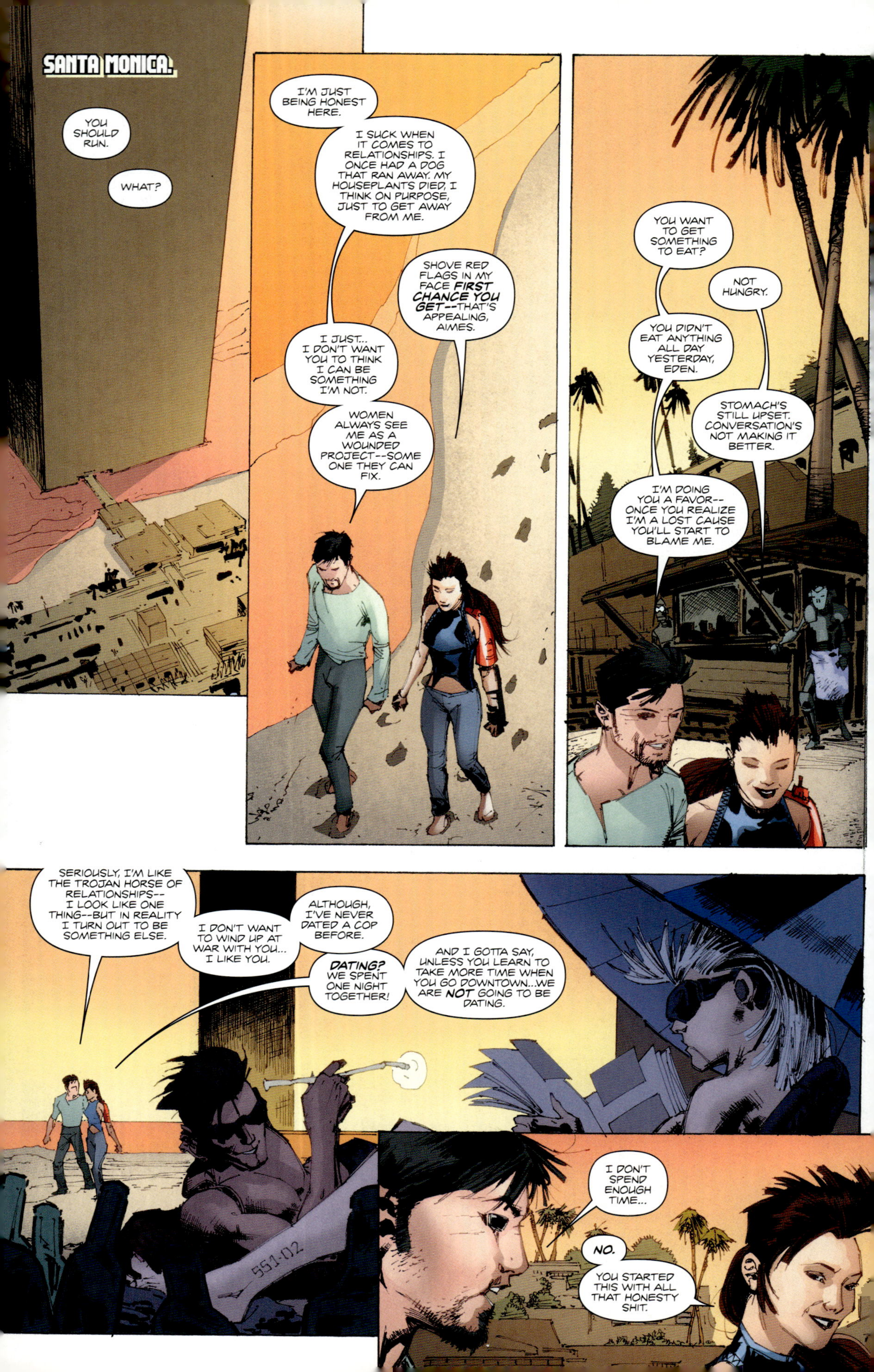
SANTA MONICA.
YOU SHOULD RUN.
WHAT?
I'M JUST BEING HONEST HERE.
I SUCK WHEN IT COMES TO RELATIONSHIPS. I ONCE HAD A DOG THAT RAN AWAY. MY HOUSEPLANTS DIED, I THINK ON PURPOSE, JUST TO GET AWAY FROM ME.
SHOVE RED FLAGS IN MY FACE FIRST CHANCE YOU GET--THAT'S APPEALING, AIMES.
I JUST... I DON'T WANT YOU TO THINK I CAN BE SOMETHING I'M NOT.
WOMEN ALWAYS SEE ME AS A WOUNDED PROJECT--SOME ONE THEY CAN FIX.
YOU WANT TO GET SOMETHING TO EAT?
NOT HUNGRY.
YOU DIDN'T EAT ANYTHING ALL DAY YESTERDAY, EDEN.
STOMACH'S STILL UPSET. CONVERSATION'S NOT MAKING IT BETTER.
I'M DOING YOU A FAVOR--ONCE YOU REALIZE I'M A LOST CAUSE YOU'LL START TO BLAME ME.
SERIOUSLY, I'M LIKE THE TROJAN HORSE OF RELATIONSHIPS--I LOOK LIKE ONE THING--BUT IN REALITY I TURN OUT TO BE SOMETHING ELSE.
I DON'T WANT TO WIND UP AT WAR WITH YOU... I LIKE YOU.
ALTHOUGH, I'VE NEVER DATED A COP BEFORE.
DATING? WE SPENT ONE NIGHT TOGETHER!
AND I GOTTA SAY, UNLESS YOU LEARN TO TAKE MORE TIME WHEN YOU GO DOWNTOWN...WE ARE NOT GOING TO BE DATING.
551-02
I DON'T SPEND ENOUGH TIME...
NO.
YOU STARTED THIS WITH ALL THAT HONESTY SHIT.

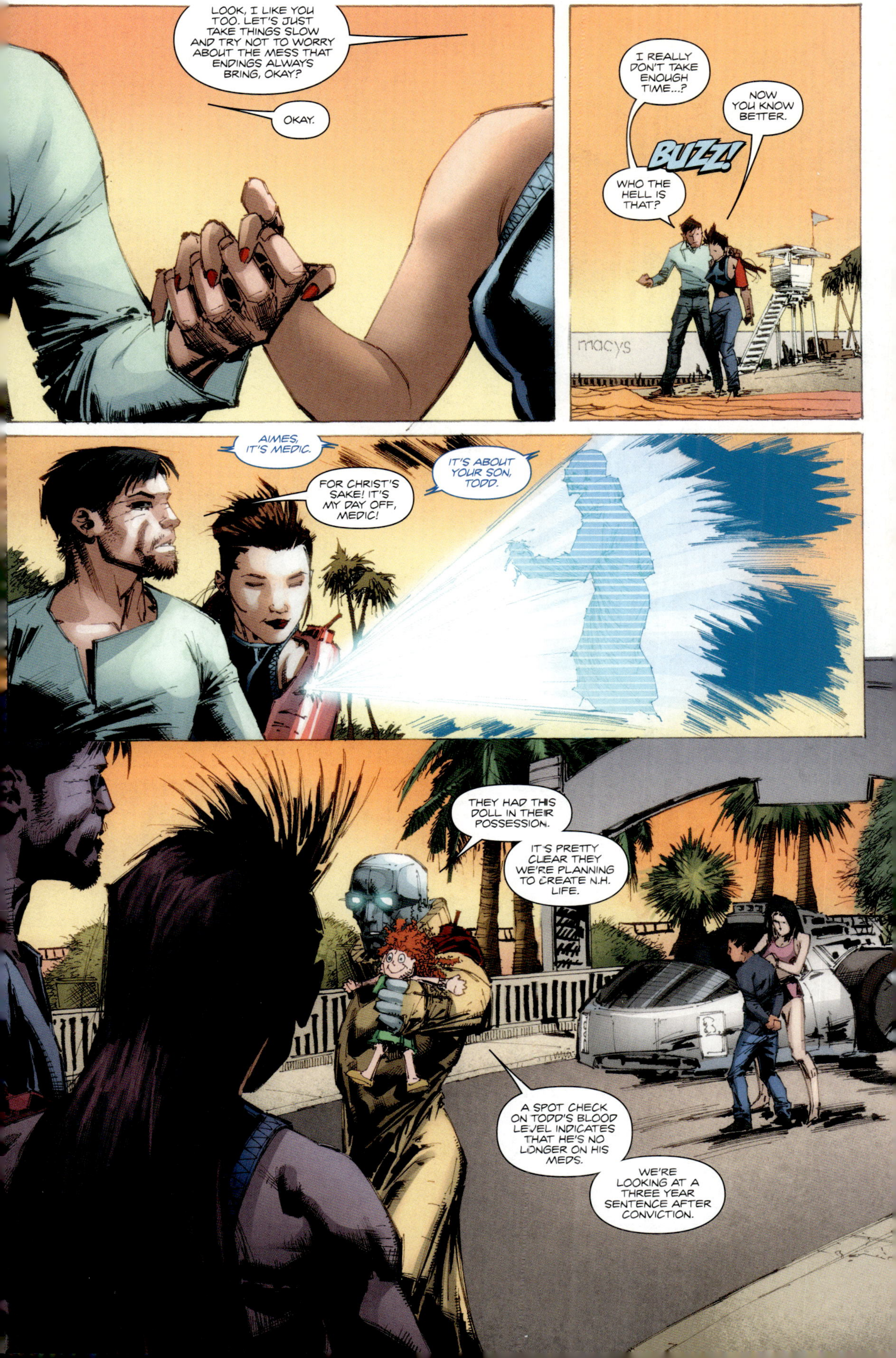
LOOK, I LIKE YOU TOO. LET'S JUST TAKE THINGS SLOW AND TRY NOT TO WORRY ABOUT THE MESS THAT ENDINGS ALWAYS BRING, OKAY?
OKAY.
I REALLY DON'T TAKE ENOUGH TIME...?
NOW YOU KNOW BETTER.
BUZZ!
WHO THE HELL IS THAT?
macys
AIMES, IT'S MEDIC.
FOR CHRIST'S SAKE! IT'S MY DAY OFF, MEDIC!
IT'S ABOUT YOUR SON, TODD.
THEY HAD THIS DOLL IN THEIR POSSESSION.
IT'S PRETTY CLEAR THEY WE'RE PLANNING TO CREATE N.H. LIFE.
A SPOT CHECK ON TODD'S BLOOD LEVEL INDICATES THAT HE'S NO LONGER ON HIS MEDS.
WE'RE LOOKING AT A THREE YEAR SENTENCE AFTER CONVICTION.

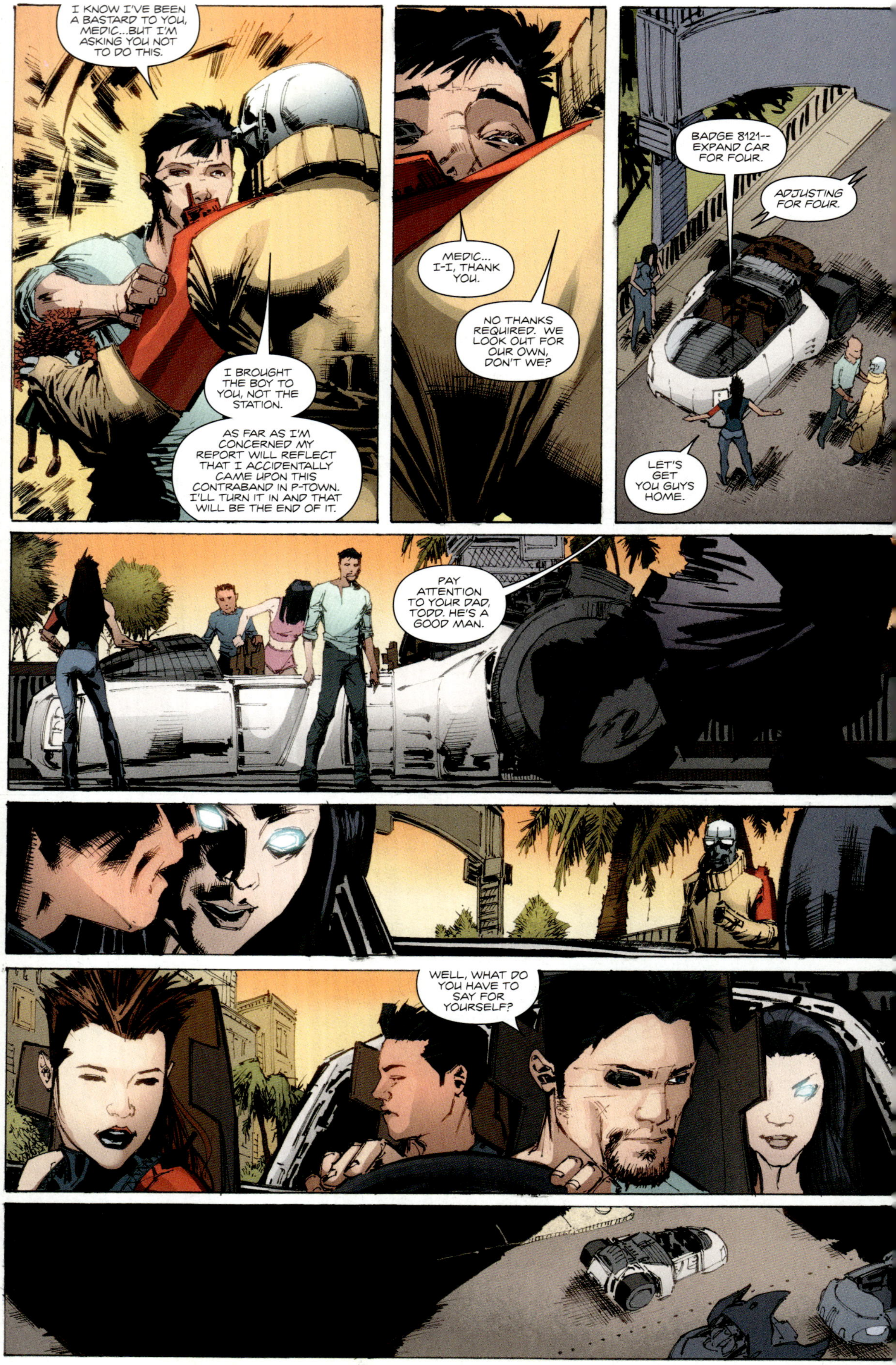

I KNOW I'VE BEEN A BASTARD TO YOU, MEDIC...BUT I'M ASKING YOU NOT TO DO THIS.
I BROUGHT THE BOY TO YOU, NOT THE STATION.
AS FAR AS I'M CONCERNED MY REPORT WILL REFLECT THAT I ACCIDENTALLY CAME UPON THIS CONTRABAND IN P-TOWN. I'LL TURN IT IN AND THAT WILL BE THE END OF IT.
MEDIC... I-I, THANK YOU.
NO THANKS REQUIRED. WE LOOK OUT FOR OUR OWN, DON'T WE?
BADGE 8121-- EXPAND CAR FOR FOUR.
ADJUSTING FOR FOUR.
LET'S GET YOU GUYS HOME.
PAY ATTENTION TO YOUR DAD, TODD. HE'S A GOOD MAN.
WELL, WHAT DO YOU HAVE TO SAY FOR YOURSELF?

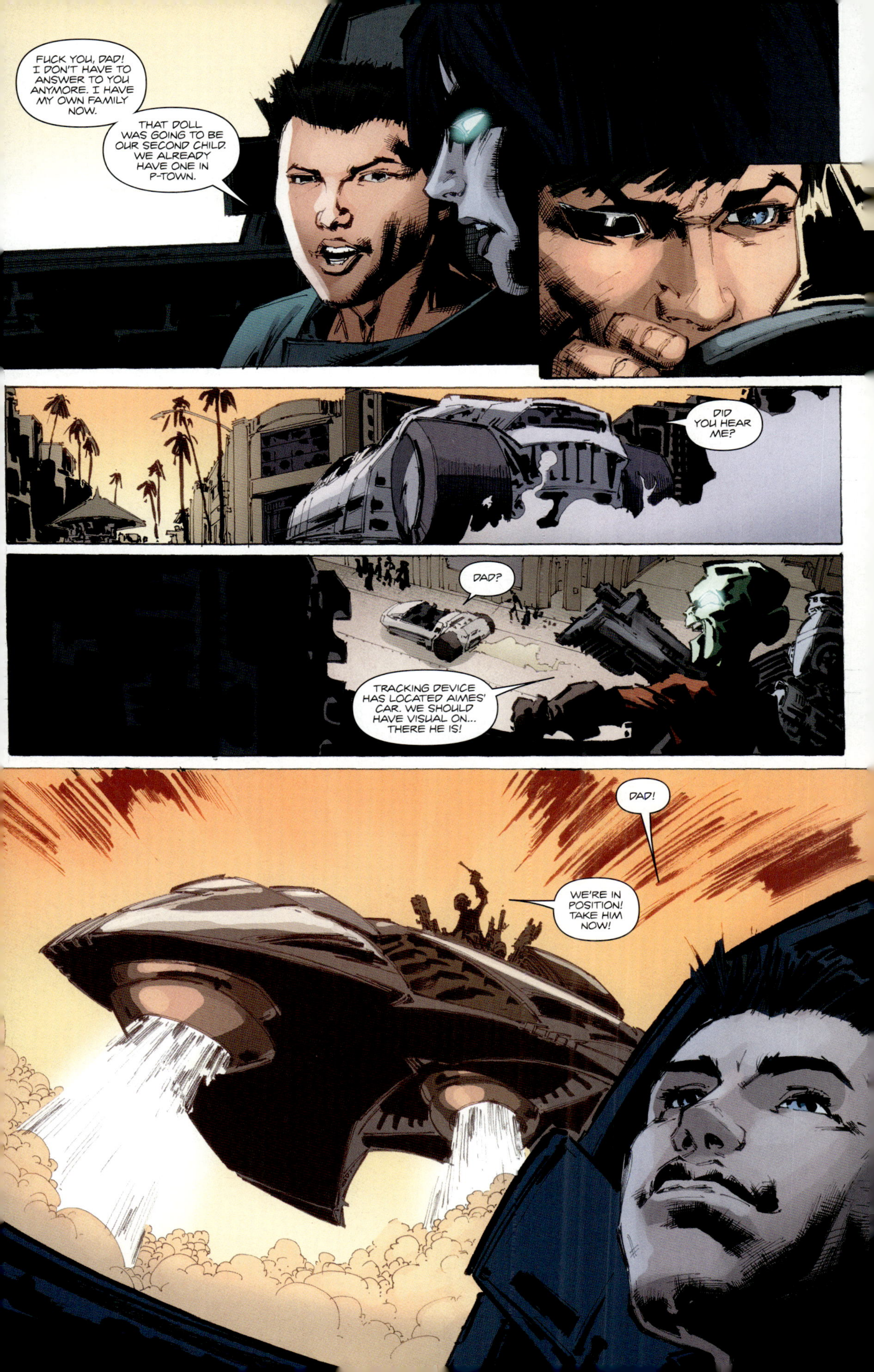
FUCK YOU, DAD! I DON'T HAVE TO ANSWER TO YOU ANYMORE. I HAVE MY OWN FAMILY NOW.
THAT DOLL WAS GOING TO BE OUR SECOND CHILD. WE ALREADY HAVE ONE IN P-TOWN.
DID YOU HEAR ME?
DAD?
TRACKING DEVICE HAS LOCATED AIMES' CAR. WE SHOULD HAVE VISUAL ON... THERE HE IS!
DAD!
WE'RE IN POSITION! TAKE HIM NOW!

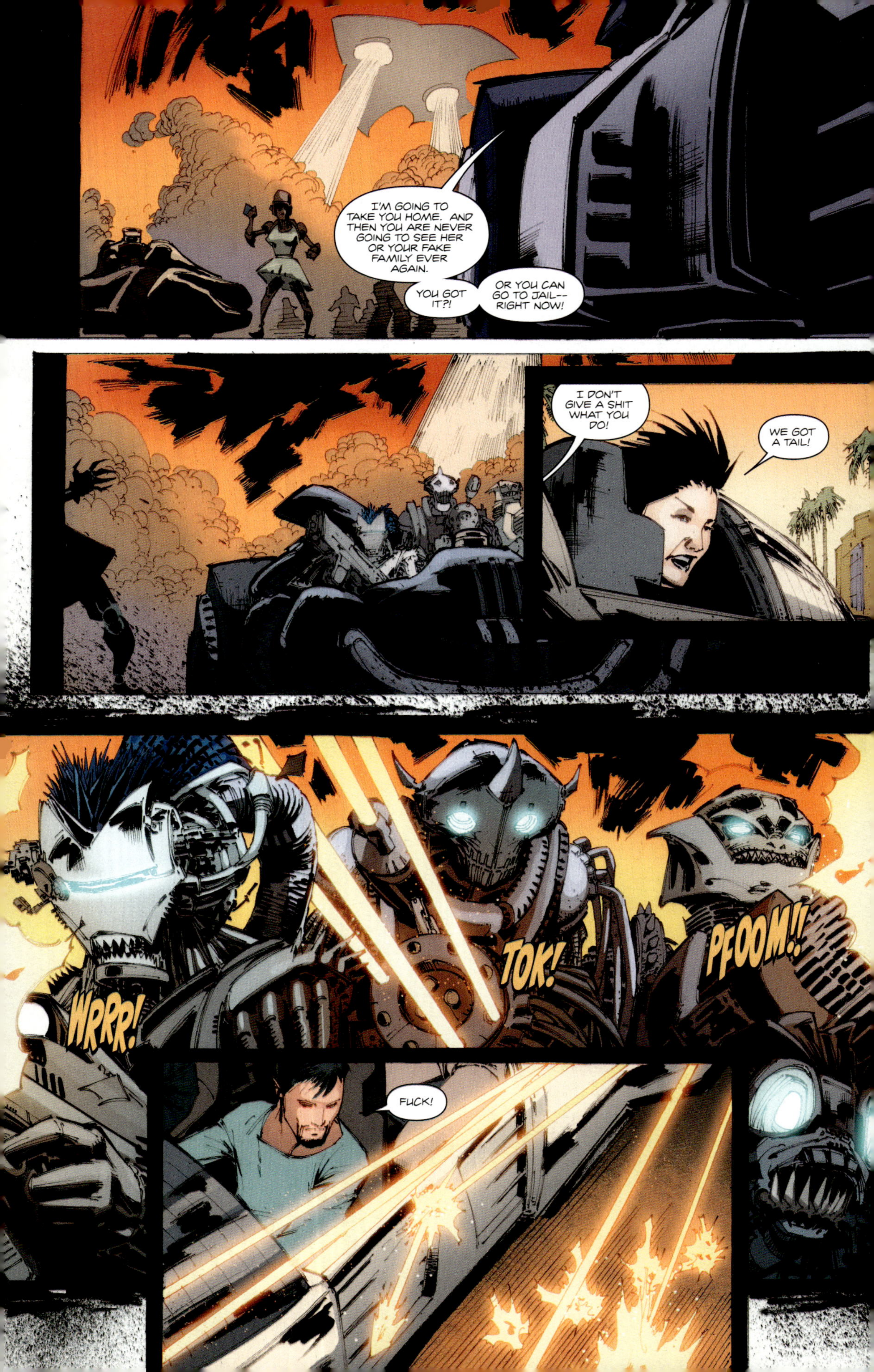
I'M GOING TO TAKE YOU HOME. AND THEN YOU ARE NEVER GOING TO SEE HER OR YOUR FAKE FAMILY EVER AGAIN.
YOU GOT IT?!
OR YOU CAN GO TO JAIL-- RIGHT NOW!
I DON'T GIVE A SHIT WHAT YOU DO!
WE GOT A TAIL!
WRRR!
TOK!
PFOOM!!
FUCK!

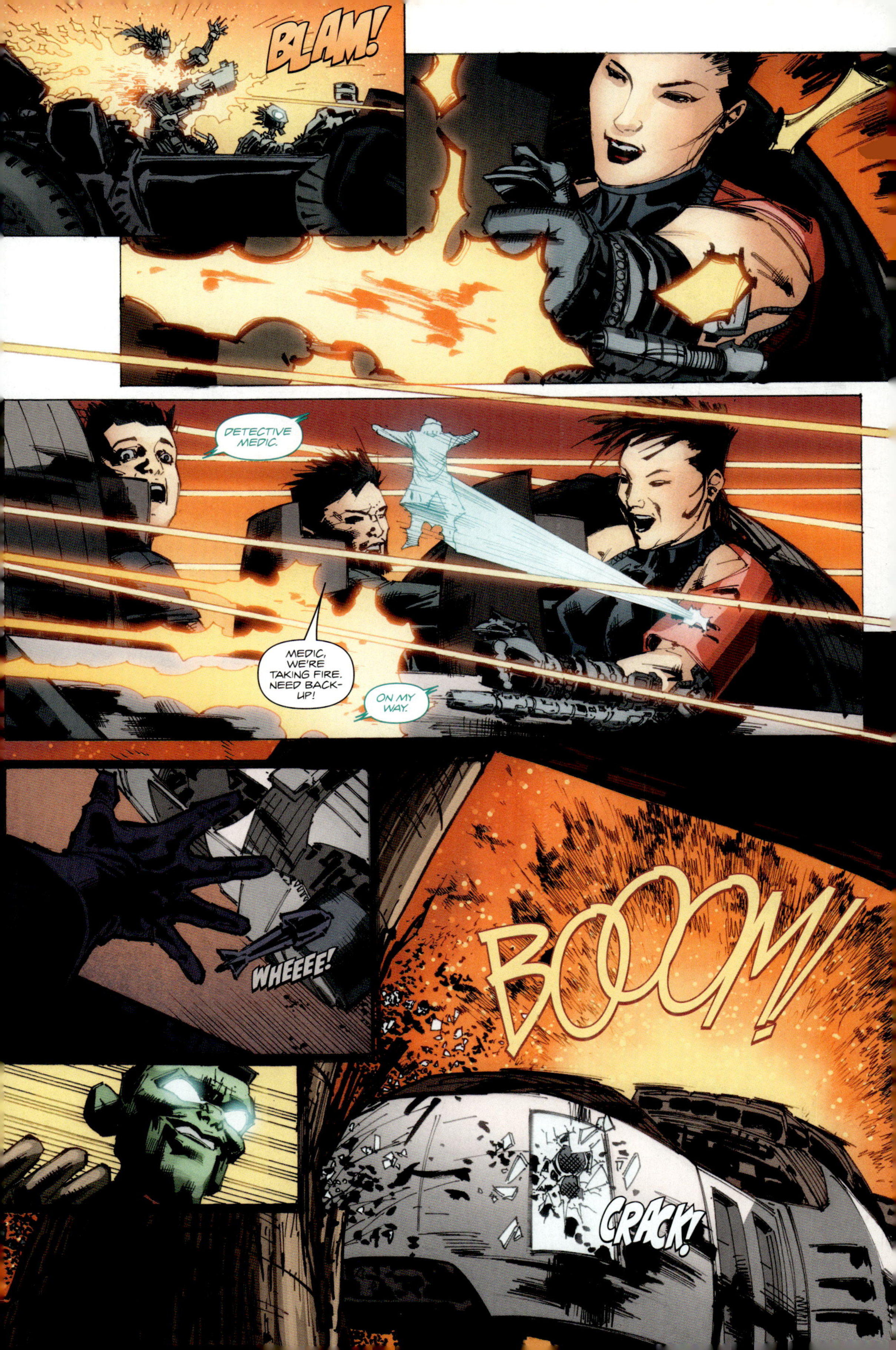
BLAM!
DETECTIVE MEDIC.
MEDIC, WE'RE TAKING FIRE. NEED BACK-UP!
ON MY WAY.
WHEEEE!
BOOOM!
CRACK!

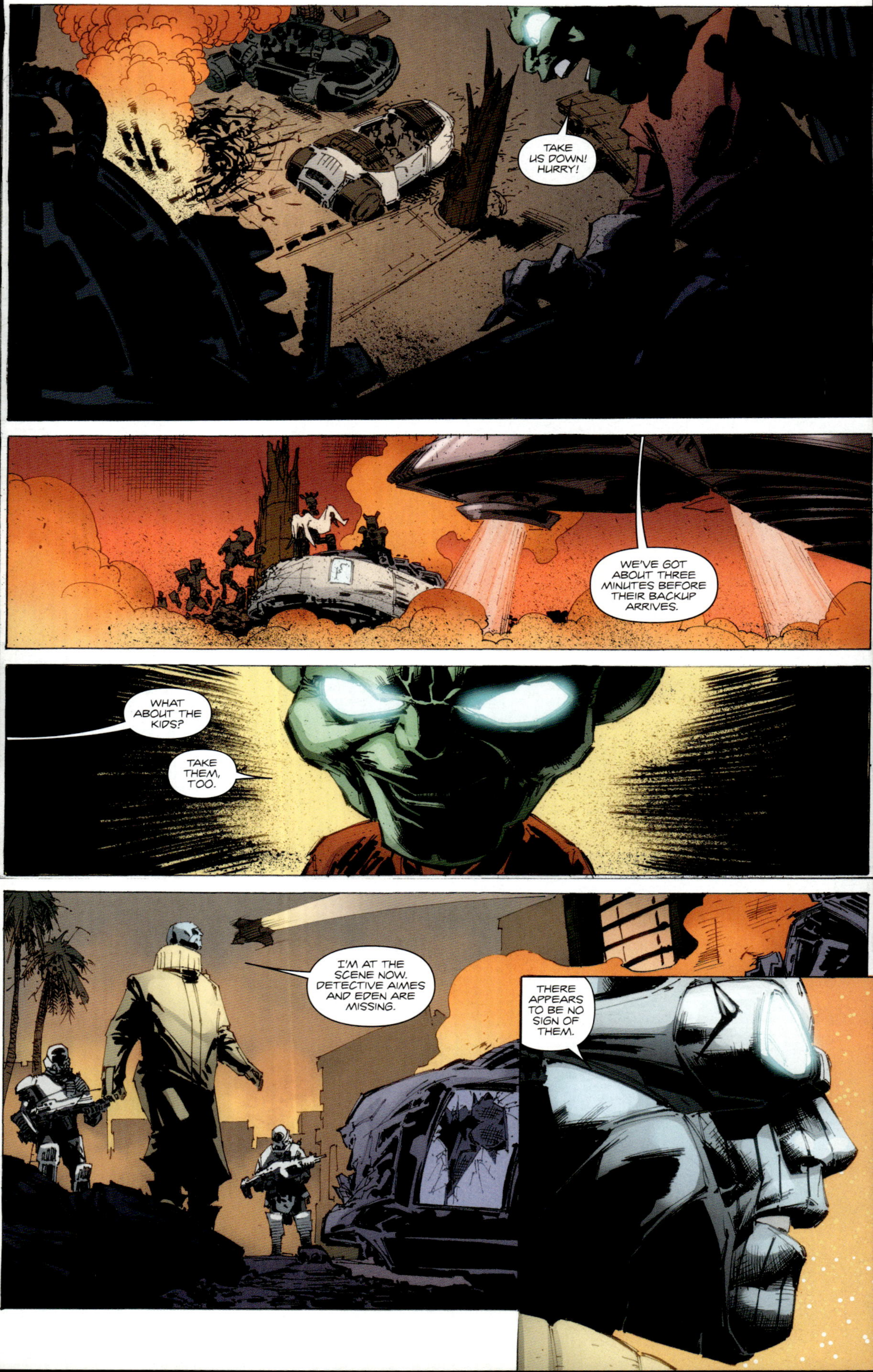
TAKE US DOWN! HURRY!
WE'VE GOT ABOUT THREE MINUTES BEFORE THEIR BACKUP ARRIVES.
WHAT ABOUT THE KIDS?
TAKE THEM, TOO.
I'M AT THE SCENE NOW. DETECTIVE AIMES AND EDEN ARE MISSING.
THERE APPEARS TO BE NO SIGN OF THEM.

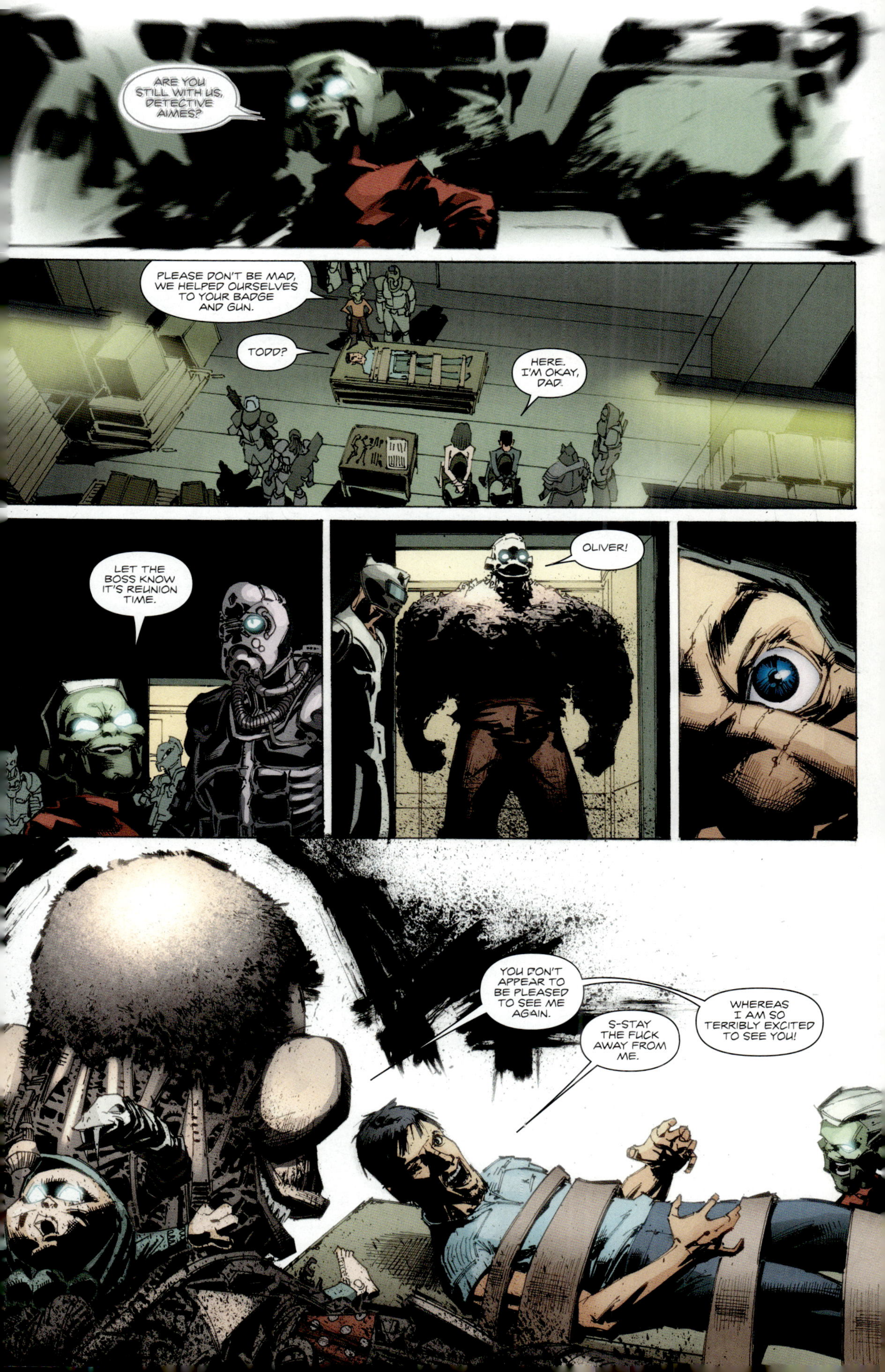
ARE YOU STILL WITH US, DETECTIVE AIMES?
PLEASE DON'T BE MAD, WE HELPED OURSELVES TO YOUR BADGE AND GUN.
TODD?
HERE. I'M OKAY, DAD.
LET THE BOSS KNOW IT'S REUNION TIME.
OLIVER!
YOU DON'T APPEAR TO BE PLEASED TO SEE ME AGAIN.
WHEREAS I AM SO TERRIBLY EXCITED TO SEE YOU!
S-STAY THE FUCK AWAY FROM ME.

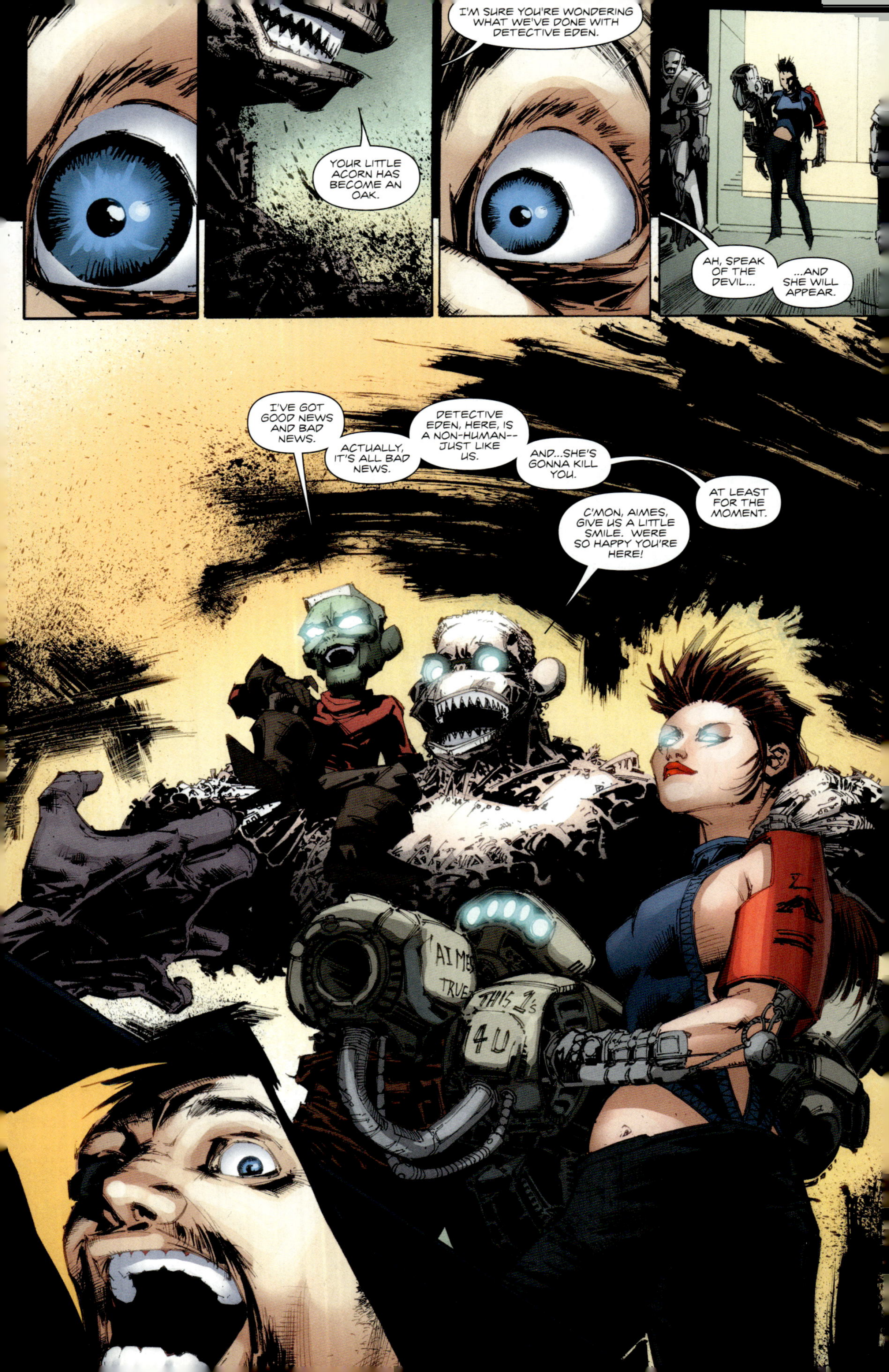
YOUR LITTLE ACORN HAS BECOME AN OAK.
I'M SURE YOU'RE WONDERING WHAT WE'VE DONE WITH DETECTIVE EDEN.
AH, SPEAK OF THE DEVIL...
...AND SHE WILL APPEAR.
I'VE GOT GOOD NEWS AND BAD NEWS.
ACTUALLY, IT'S ALL BAD NEWS.
DETECTIVE EDEN, HERE, IS A NON-HUMAN-- JUST LIKE US.
AND...SHE'S GONNA KILL YOU.
AT LEAST FOR THE MOMENT.
C'MON, AIMES, GIVE US A LITTLE SMILE. WERE SO HAPPY YOU'RE HERE!
AIMES TRUE
THIS 1's 4 U

# CHAPTER FOUR

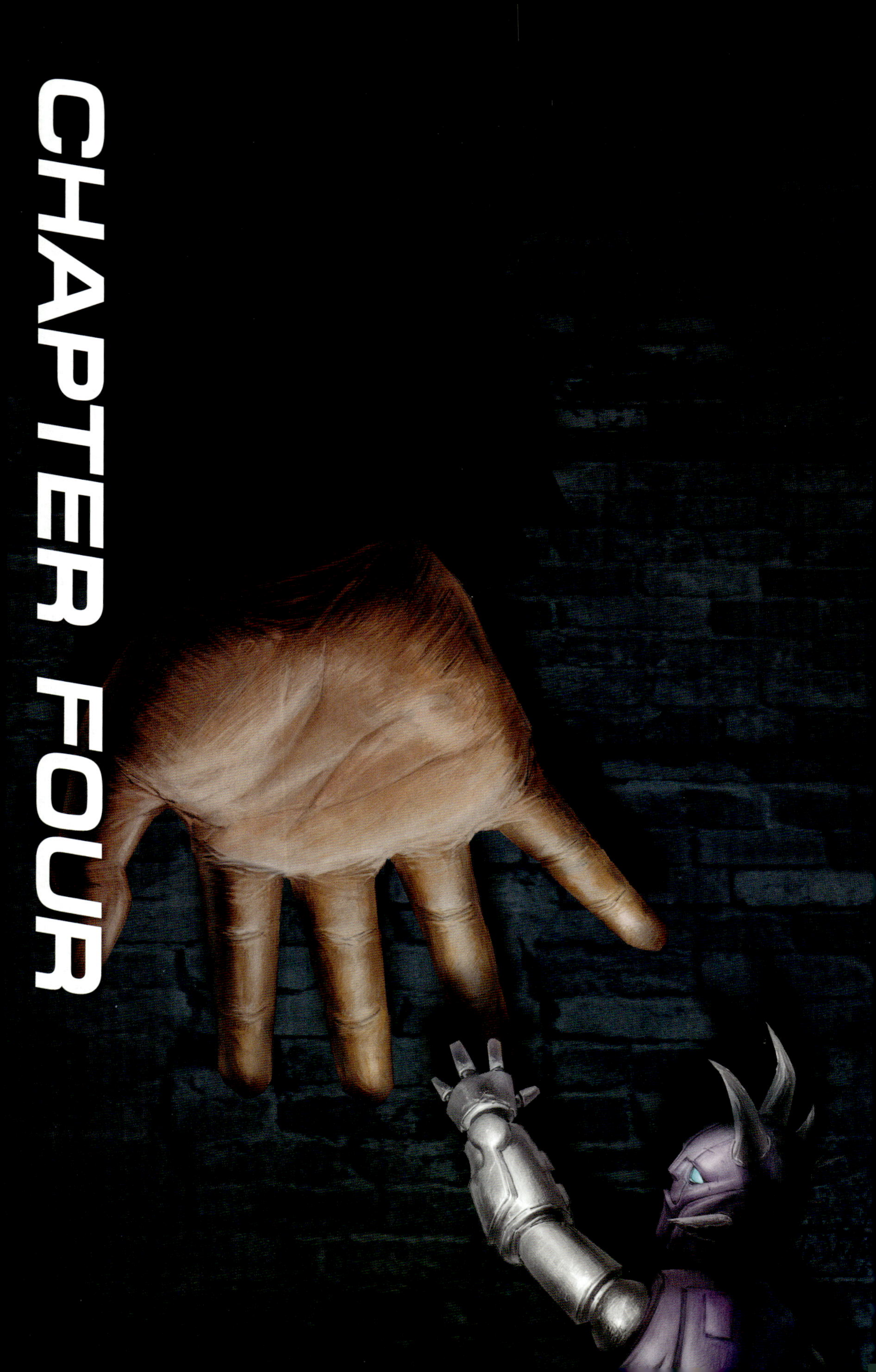

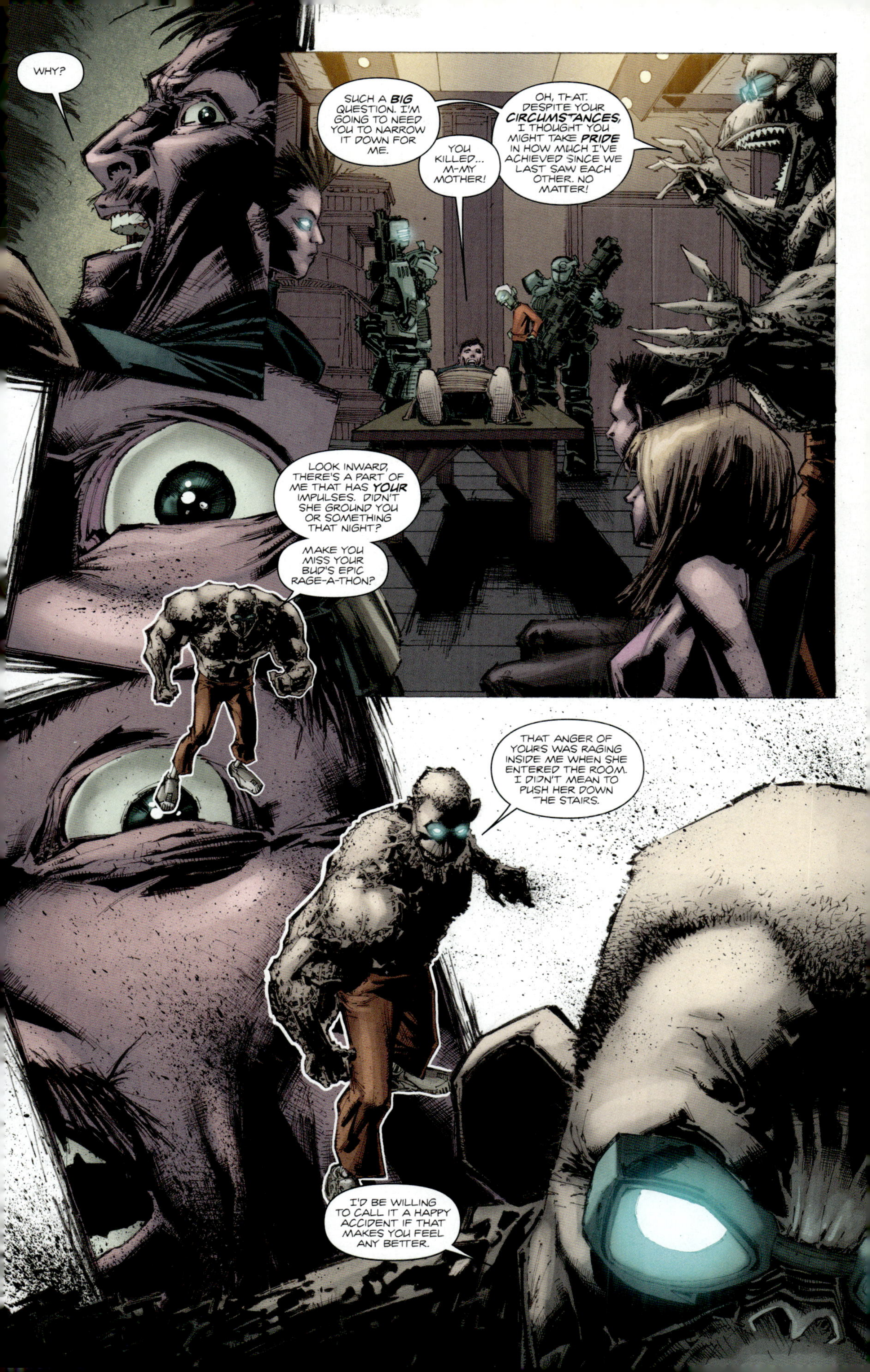
WHY?
SUCH A BIG QUESTION. I'M GOING TO NEED YOU TO NARROW IT DOWN FOR ME.
YOU KILLED... M-MY MOTHER!
OH, THAT. DESPITE YOUR CIRCUMSTANCES, I THOUGHT YOU MIGHT TAKE PRIDE IN HOW MUCH I'VE ACHIEVED SINCE WE LAST SAW EACH OTHER. NO MATTER!
LOOK INWARD, THERE'S A PART OF ME THAT HAS YOUR IMPULSES. DIDN'T SHE GROUND YOU OR SOMETHING THAT NIGHT?
MAKE YOU MISS YOUR BUD'S EPIC RAGE-A-THON?
THAT ANGER OF YOURS WAS RAGING INSIDE ME WHEN SHE ENTERED THE ROOM. I DIDN'T MEAN TO PUSH HER DOWN THE STAIRS.
I'D BE WILLING TO CALL IT A HAPPY ACCIDENT IF THAT MAKES YOU FEEL ANY BETTER.

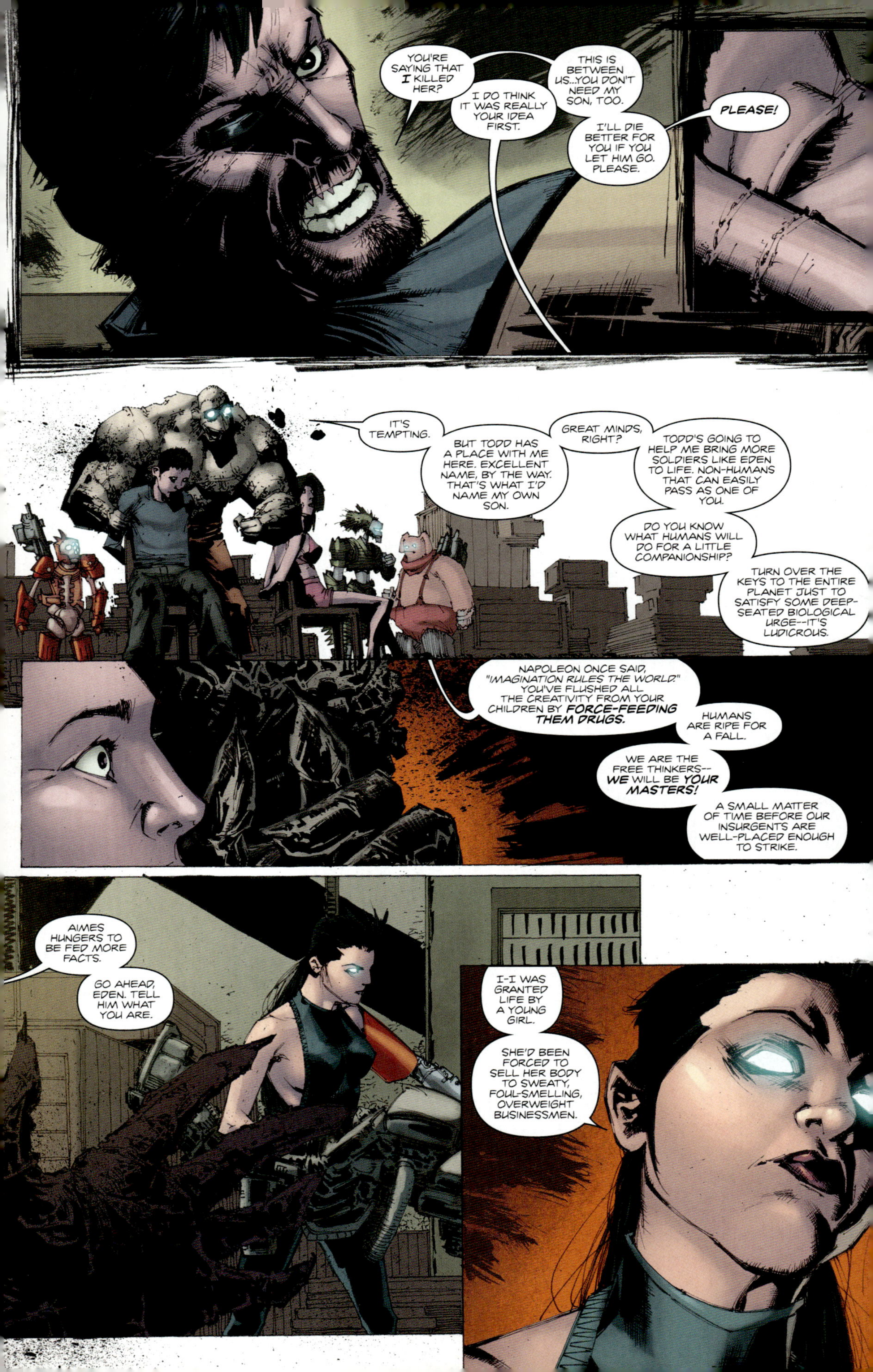
YOU'RE SAYING THAT I KILLED HER?
THIS IS BETWEEN US...YOU DON'T NEED MY SON, TOO.
I DO THINK IT WAS REALLY YOUR IDEA FIRST.
I'LL DIE BETTER FOR YOU IF YOU LET HIM GO. PLEASE.
PLEASE!
IT'S TEMPTING.
BUT TODD HAS A PLACE WITH ME HERE. EXCELLENT NAME, BY THE WAY. THAT'S WHAT I'D NAME MY OWN SON.
GREAT MINDS, RIGHT?
TODD'S GOING TO HELP ME BRING MORE SOLDIERS LIKE EDEN TO LIFE. NON-HUMANS THAT CAN EASILY PASS AS ONE OF YOU.
DO YOU KNOW WHAT HUMANS WILL DO FOR A LITTLE COMPANIONSHIP?
TURN OVER THE KEYS TO THE ENTIRE PLANET JUST TO SATISFY SOME DEEP-SEATED BIOLOGICAL URGE--IT'S LUDICROUS.
NAPOLEON ONCE SAID, "IMAGINATION RULES THE WORLD." YOU'VE FLUSHED ALL THE CREATIVITY FROM YOUR CHILDREN BY FORCE-FEEDING THEM DRUGS.
HUMANS ARE RIPE FOR A FALL.
WE ARE THE FREE THINKERS-- WE WILL BE YOUR MASTERS!
A SMALL MATTER OF TIME BEFORE OUR INSURGENTS ARE WELL-PLACED ENOUGH TO STRIKE.
AIMES HUNGERS TO BE FED MORE FACTS.
GO AHEAD, EDEN. TELL HIM WHAT YOU ARE.
I-I WAS GRANTED LIFE BY A YOUNG GIRL.
SHE'D BEEN FORCED TO SELL HER BODY TO SWEATY, FOUL-SMELLING, OVERWEIGHT BUSINESSMEN.

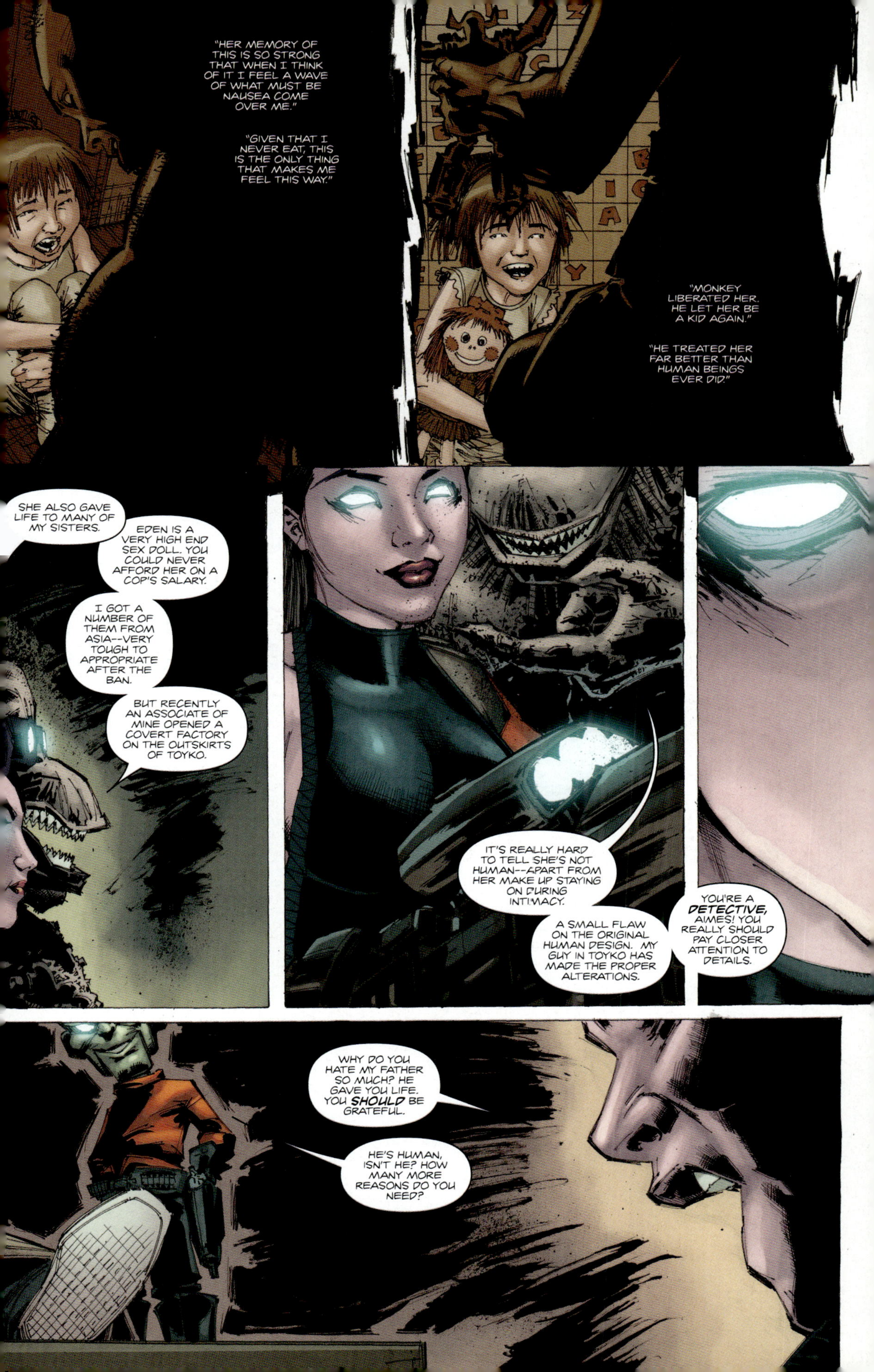
"HER MEMORY OF THIS IS SO STRONG THAT WHEN I THINK OF IT I FEEL A WAVE OF WHAT MUST BE NAUSEA COME OVER ME."
"GIVEN THAT I NEVER EAT, THIS IS THE ONLY THING THAT MAKES ME FEEL THIS WAY."
"MONKEY LIBERATED HER. HE LET HER BE A KID AGAIN."
"HE TREATED HER FAR BETTER THAN HUMAN BEINGS EVER DID."
SHE ALSO GAVE LIFE TO MANY OF MY SISTERS.
EDEN IS A VERY HIGH END SEX DOLL. YOU COULD NEVER AFFORD HER ON A COP'S SALARY.
I GOT A NUMBER OF THEM FROM ASIA--VERY TOUGH TO APPROPRIATE AFTER THE BAN.
BUT RECENTLY AN ASSOCIATE OF MINE OPENED A COVERT FACTORY ON THE OUTSKIRTS OF TOYKO.
IT'S REALLY HARD TO TELL SHE'S NOT HUMAN--APART FROM HER MAKE UP STAYING ON DURING INTIMACY.
A SMALL FLAW ON THE ORIGINAL HUMAN DESIGN. MY GUY IN TOYKO HAS MADE THE PROPER ALTERATIONS.
YOU'RE A ***DETECTIVE,*** AIMES! YOU REALLY SHOULD PAY CLOSER ATTENTION TO DETAILS.
WHY DO YOU HATE MY FATHER SO MUCH? HE GAVE YOU LIFE. YOU ***SHOULD*** BE GRATEFUL.
HE'S HUMAN, ISN'T HE? HOW MANY MORE REASONS DO YOU NEED?

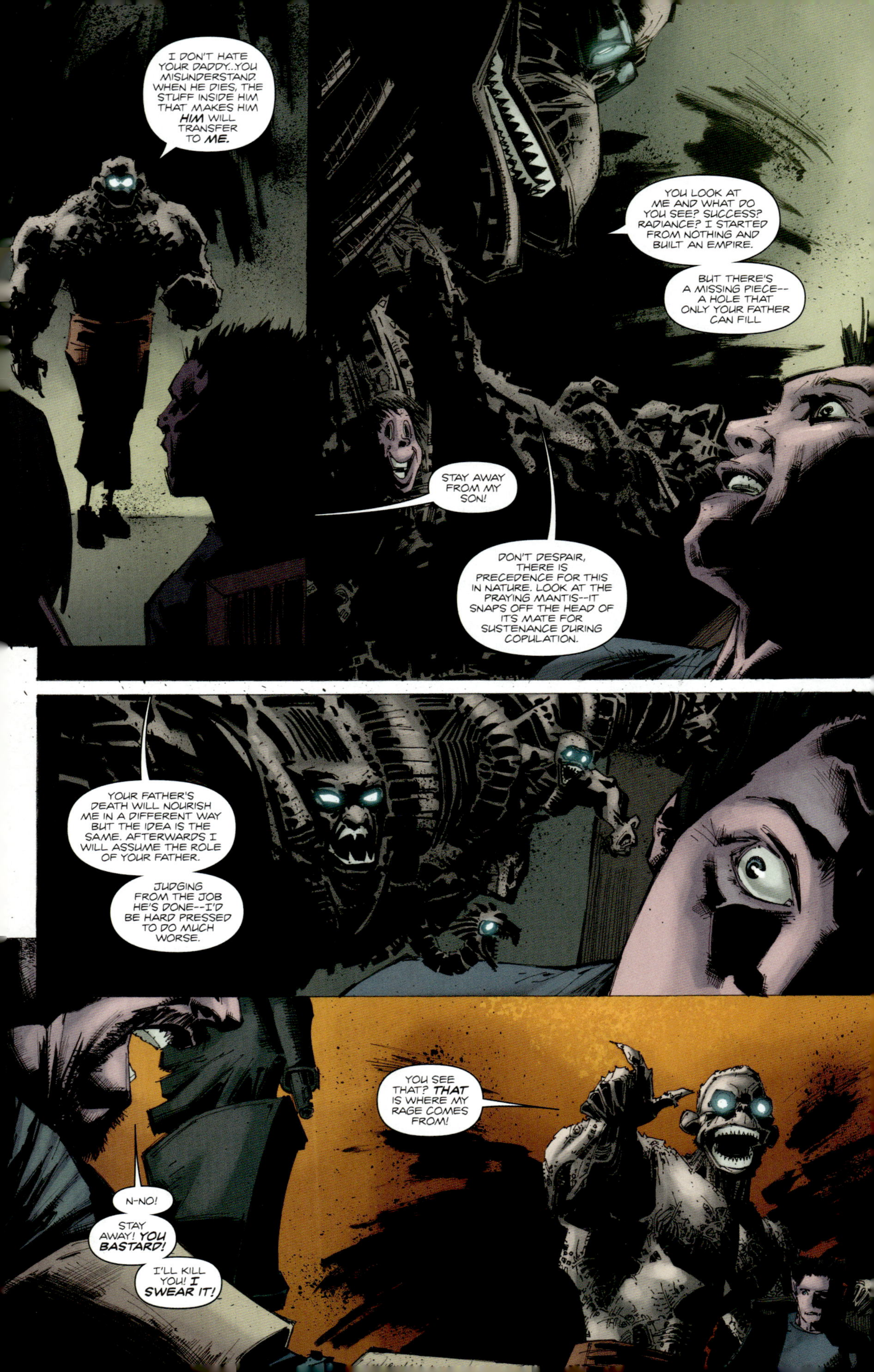
I DON'T HATE YOUR DADDY...YOU MISUNDERSTAND. WHEN HE DIES, THE STUFF INSIDE HIM THAT MAKES HIM **HIM** WILL TRANSFER TO **ME.**
YOU LOOK AT ME AND WHAT DO YOU SEE? SUCCESS? RADIANCE? I STARTED FROM NOTHING AND BUILT AN EMPIRE.
BUT THERE'S A MISSING PIECE-- A HOLE THAT ONLY YOUR FATHER CAN FILL
STAY AWAY FROM MY SON!
DON'T DESPAIR, THERE IS PRECEDENCE FOR THIS IN NATURE. LOOK AT THE PRAYING MANTIS--IT SNAPS OFF THE HEAD OF ITS MATE FOR SUSTENANCE DURING COPULATION.
YOUR FATHER'S DEATH WILL NOURISH ME IN A DIFFERENT WAY BUT THE IDEA IS THE SAME. AFTERWARDS I WILL ASSUME THE ROLE OF YOUR FATHER.
JUDGING FROM THE JOB HE'S DONE--I'D BE HARD PRESSED TO DO MUCH WORSE.
YOU SEE THAT? **THAT** IS WHERE MY RAGE COMES FROM!
N-NO!
STAY AWAY! **YOU BASTARD!**
I'LL KILL YOU! **I SWEAR IT!**

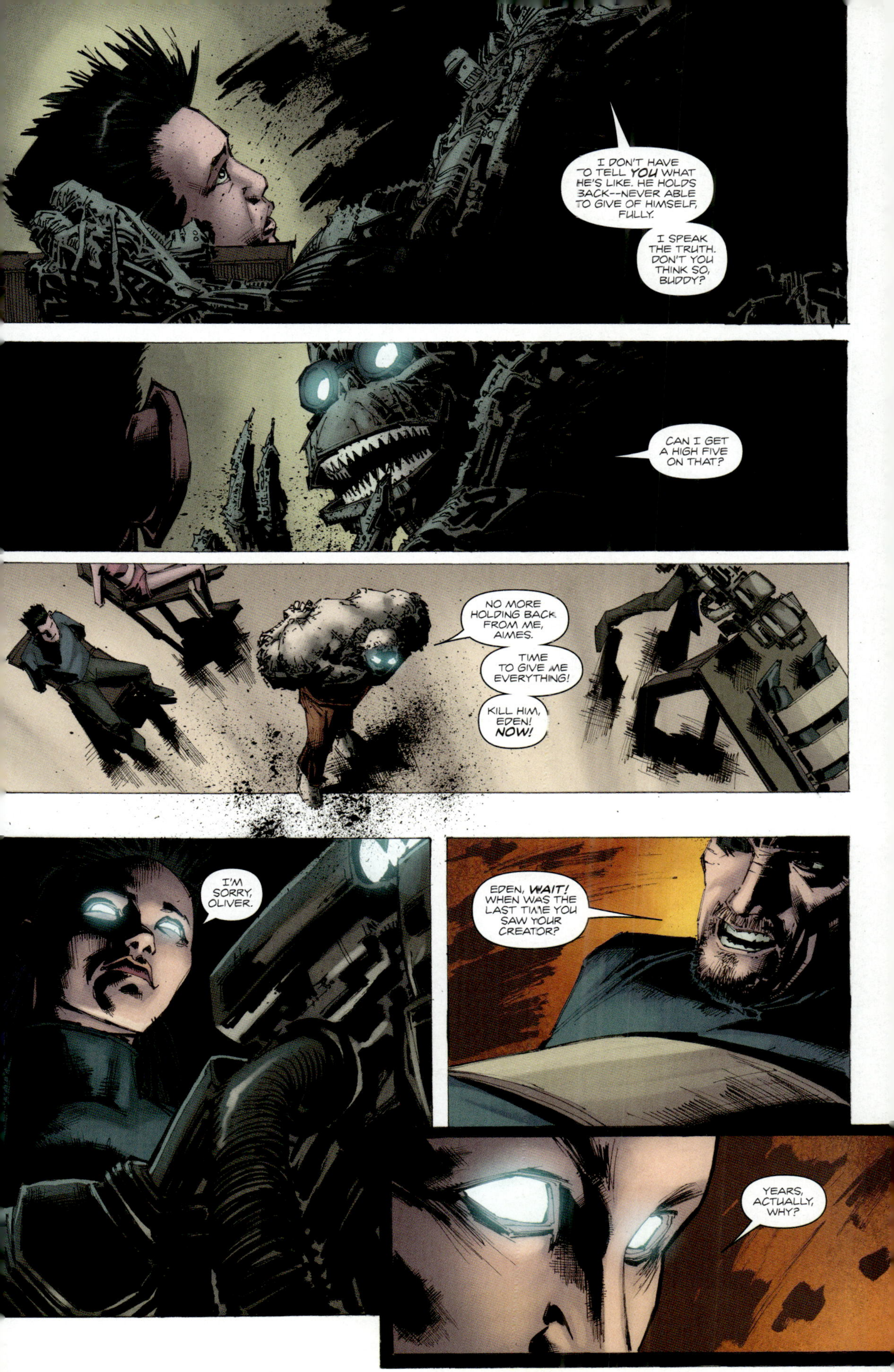
I DON'T HAVE TO TELL YOU WHAT HE'S LIKE. HE HOLDS BACK--NEVER ABLE TO GIVE OF HIMSELF, FULLY.
I SPEAK THE TRUTH. DON'T YOU THINK SO, BUDDY?
CAN I GET A HIGH FIVE ON THAT?
NO MORE HOLDING BACK FROM ME, AIMES.
TIME TO GIVE ME EVERYTHING!
KILL HIM, EDEN! NOW!
I'M SORRY, OLIVER.
EDEN, WAIT! WHEN WAS THE LAST TIME YOU SAW YOUR CREATOR?
YEARS, ACTUALLY, WHY?

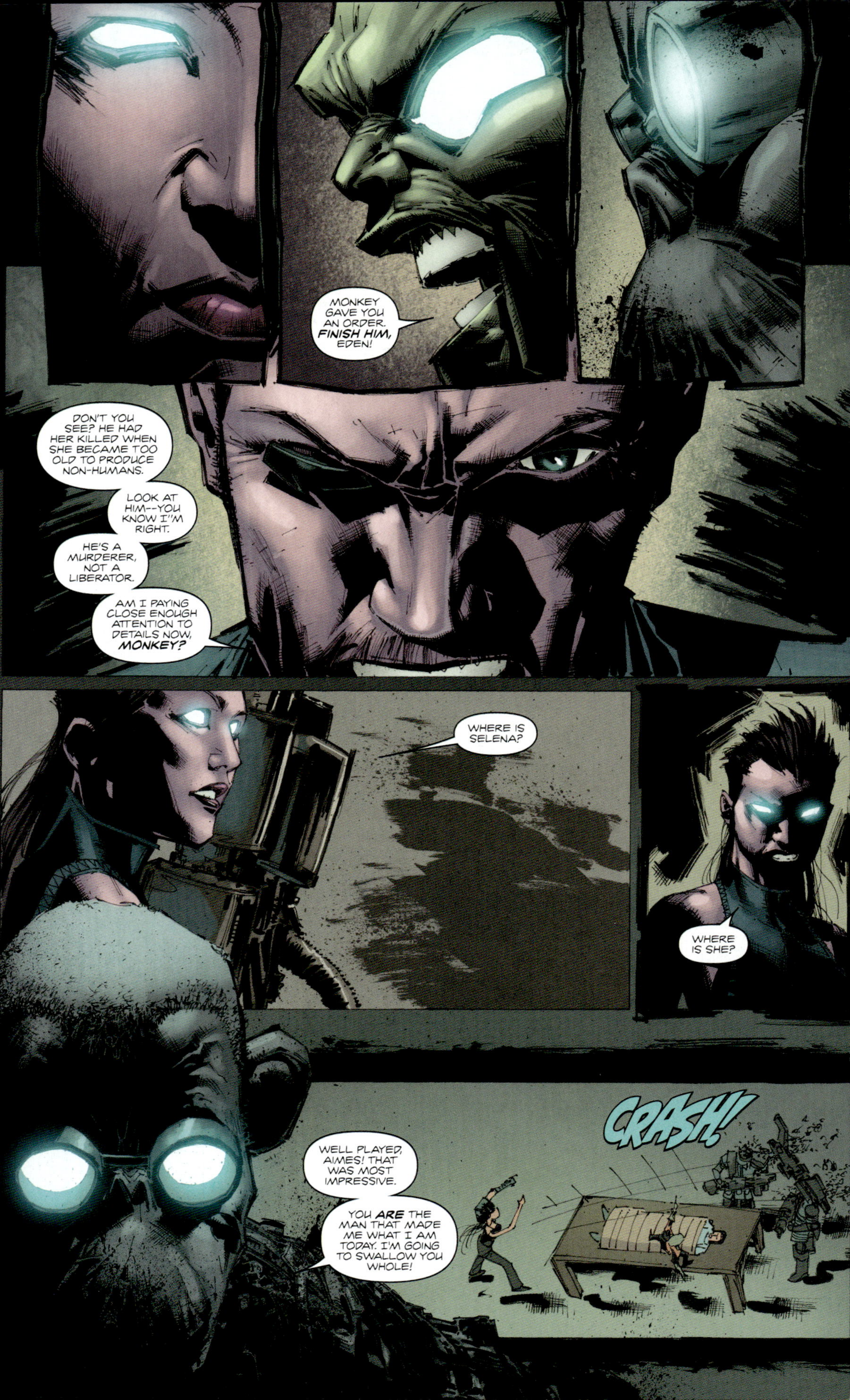
MONKEY GAVE YOU AN ORDER. FINISH HIM, EDEN!
DON'T YOU SEE? HE HAD HER KILLED WHEN SHE BECAME TOO OLD TO PRODUCE NON-HUMANS.
LOOK AT HIM--YOU KNOW I'M RIGHT.
HE'S A MURDERER, NOT A LIBERATOR.
AM I PAYING CLOSE ENOUGH ATTENTION TO DETAILS NOW, MONKEY?
WHERE IS SELENA?
WHERE IS SHE?
CRASH!
WELL PLAYED, AIMES! THAT WAS MOST IMPRESSIVE.
YOU ARE THE MAN THAT MADE ME WHAT I AM TODAY. I'M GOING TO SWALLOW YOU WHOLE!

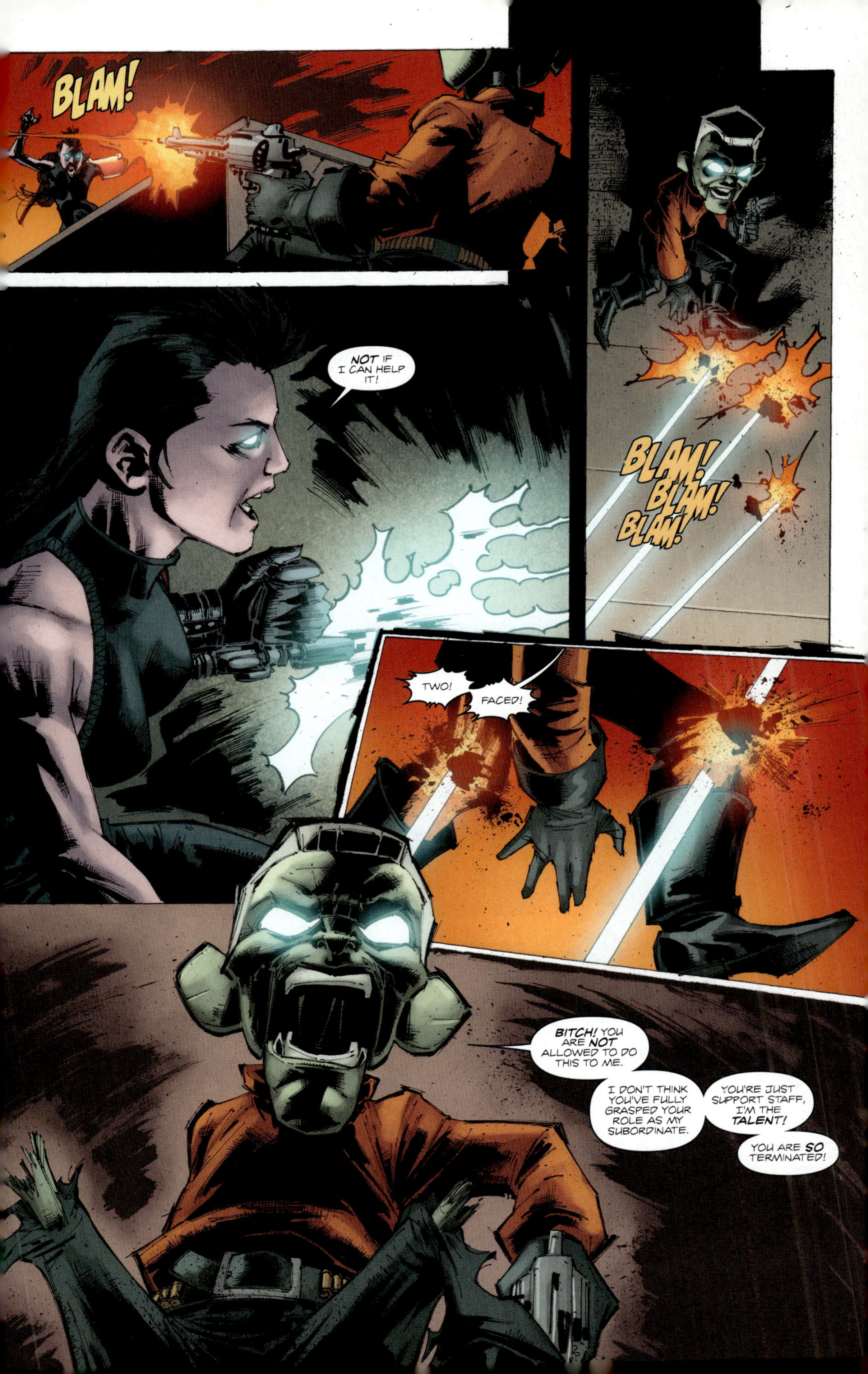
BLAM!
NOT IF I CAN HELP IT!
BLAM! BLAM! BLAM!
TWO!
FACED!
BITCH! YOU ARE NOT ALLOWED TO DO THIS TO ME.
I DON'T THINK YOU'VE FULLY GRASPED YOUR ROLE AS MY SUBORDINATE.
YOU'RE JUST SUPPORT STAFF, I'M THE TALENT!
YOU ARE SO TERMINATED!

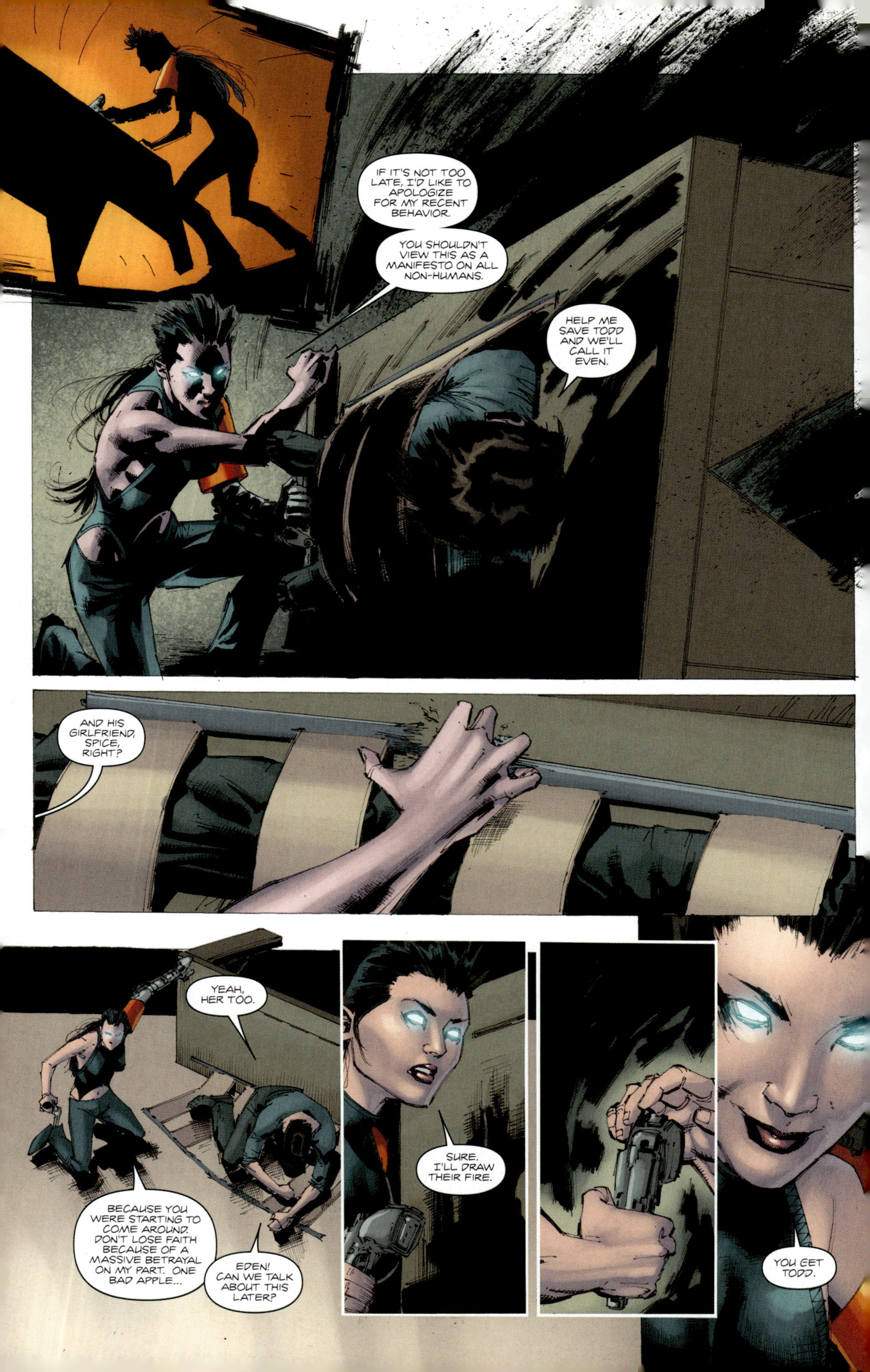
IF IT'S NOT TOO LATE, I'D LIKE TO APOLOGIZE FOR MY RECENT BEHAVIOR.
YOU SHOULDN'T VIEW THIS AS A MANIFESTO ON ALL NON-HUMANS.
HELP ME SAVE TODD AND WE'LL CALL IT EVEN.
AND HIS GIRLFRIEND, SPICE, RIGHT?
YEAH, HER TOO.
BECAUSE YOU WERE STARTING TO COME AROUND. DON'T LOSE FAITH BECAUSE OF A MASSIVE BETRAYAL ON MY PART. ONE BAD APPLE...
EDEN! CAN WE TALK ABOUT THIS LATER?
SURE. I'LL DRAW THEIR FIRE.
YOU GET TODD.

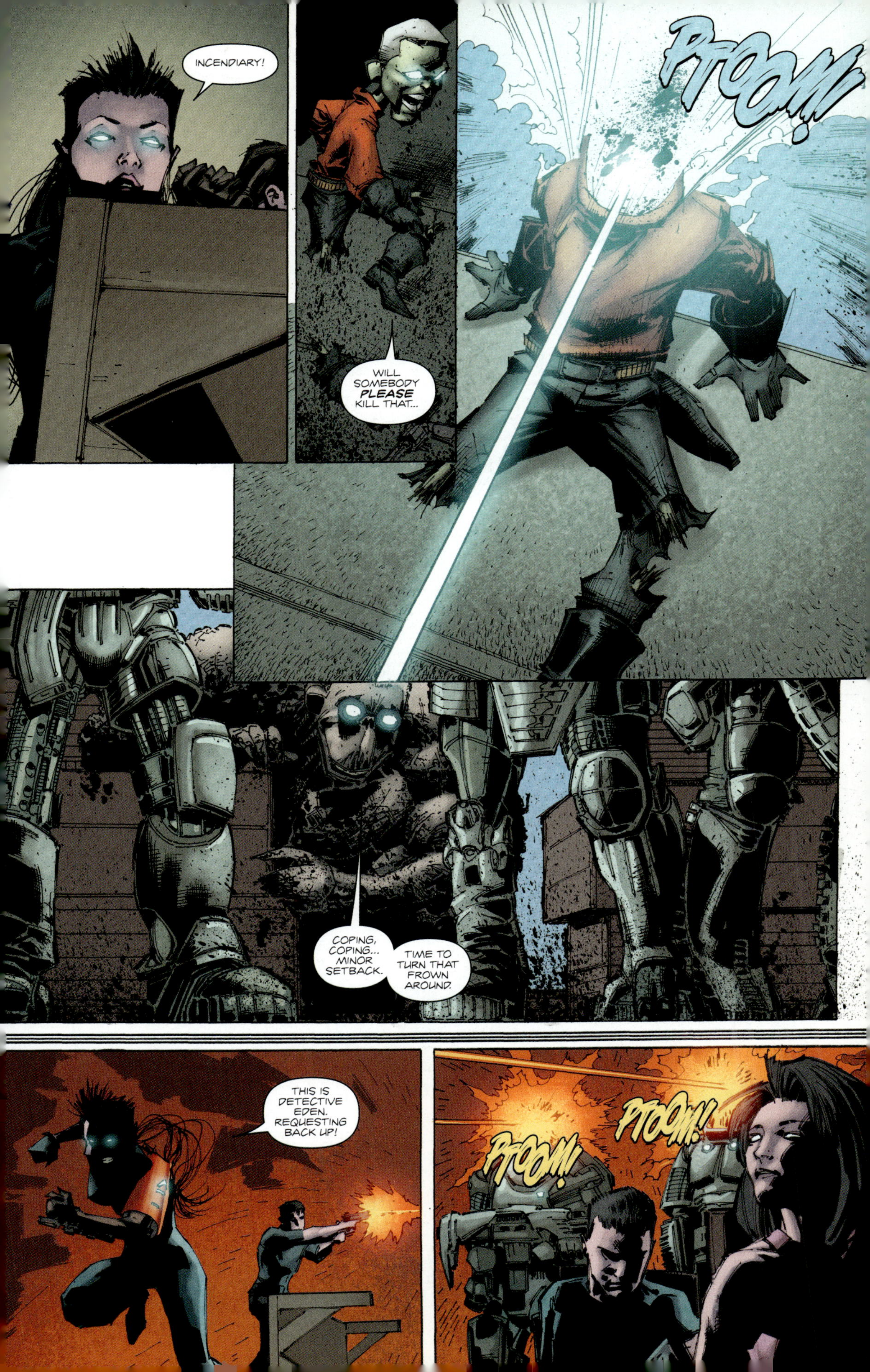
INCENDIARY!
WILL SOMEBODY PLEASE KILL THAT...
PTOOM!
COPING, COPING... MINOR SETBACK.
TIME TO TURN THAT FROWN AROUND.
THIS IS DETECTIVE EDEN. REQUESTING BACK UP!
PTOOM!
PTOOM!

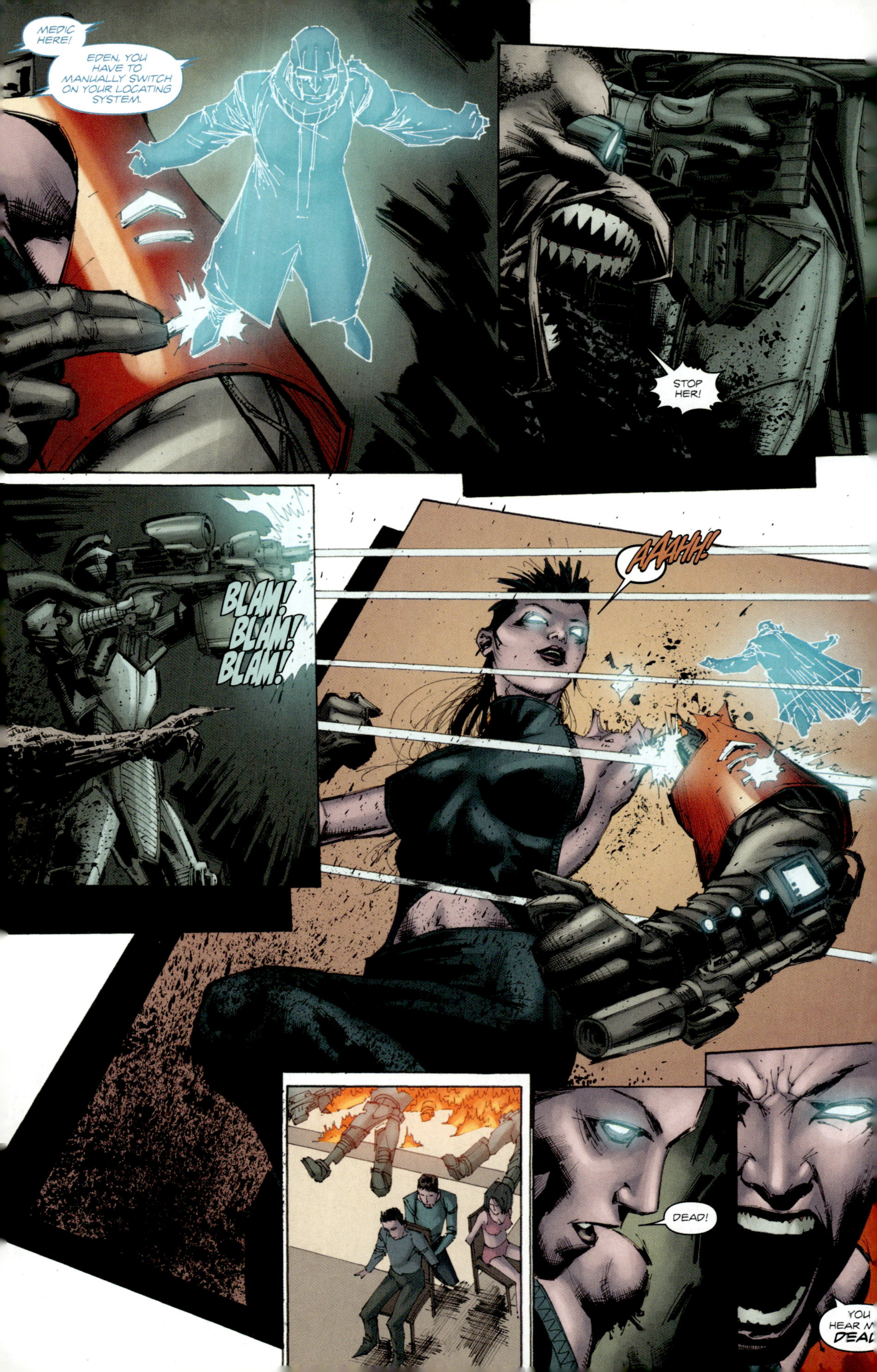
MEDIC HERE!
EDEN, YOU HAVE TO MANUALLY SWITCH ON YOUR LOCATING SYSTEM.
STOP HER!
BLAM! BLAM! BLAM!
AAAHH!
DEAD!

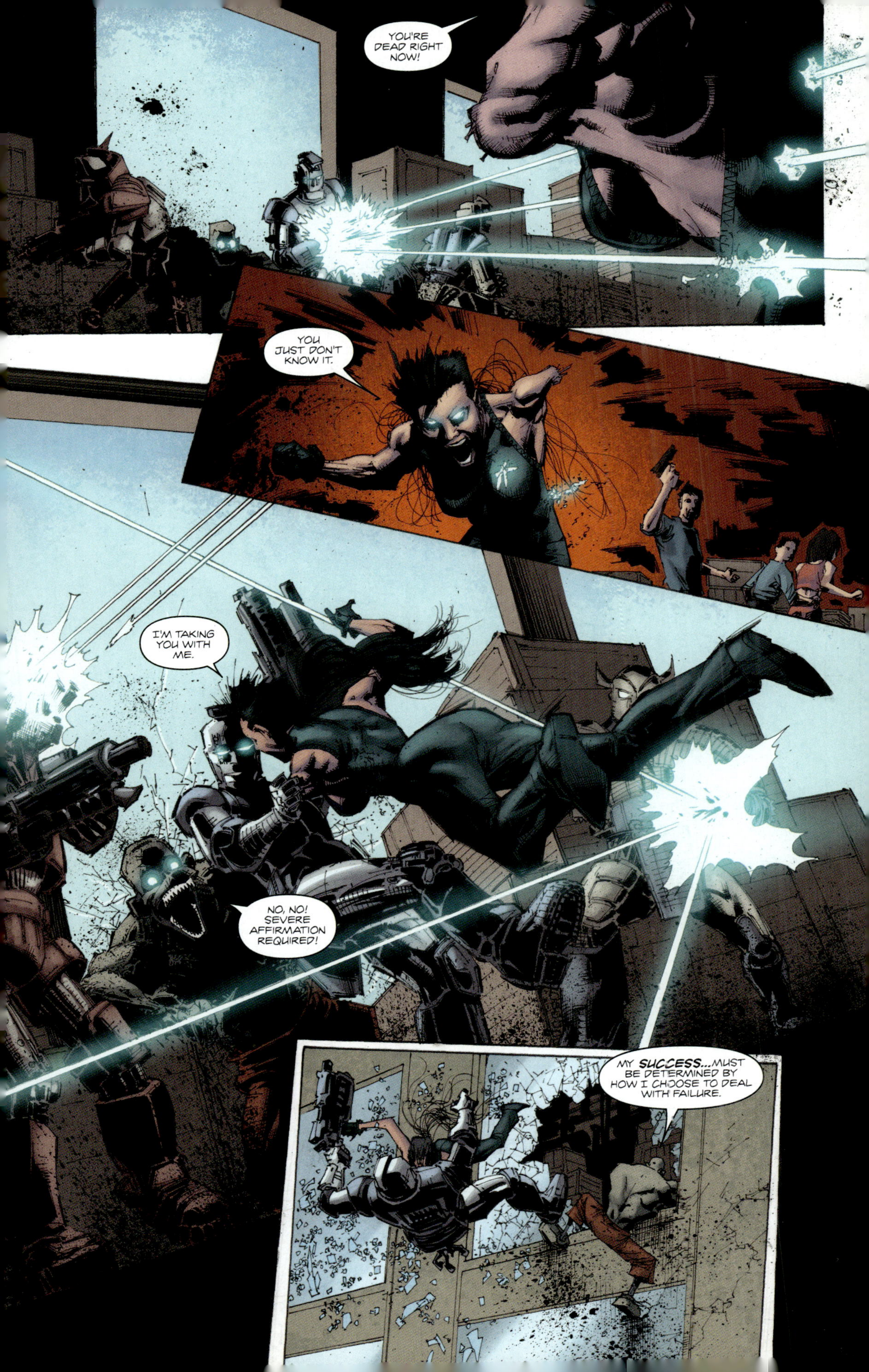
YOU'RE DEAD RIGHT NOW!
YOU JUST DON'T KNOW IT.
I'M TAKING YOU WITH ME.
NO, NO! SEVERE AFFIRMATION REQUIRED!
MY SUCCESS...MUST BE DETERMINED BY HOW I CHOOSE TO DEAL WITH FAILURE.

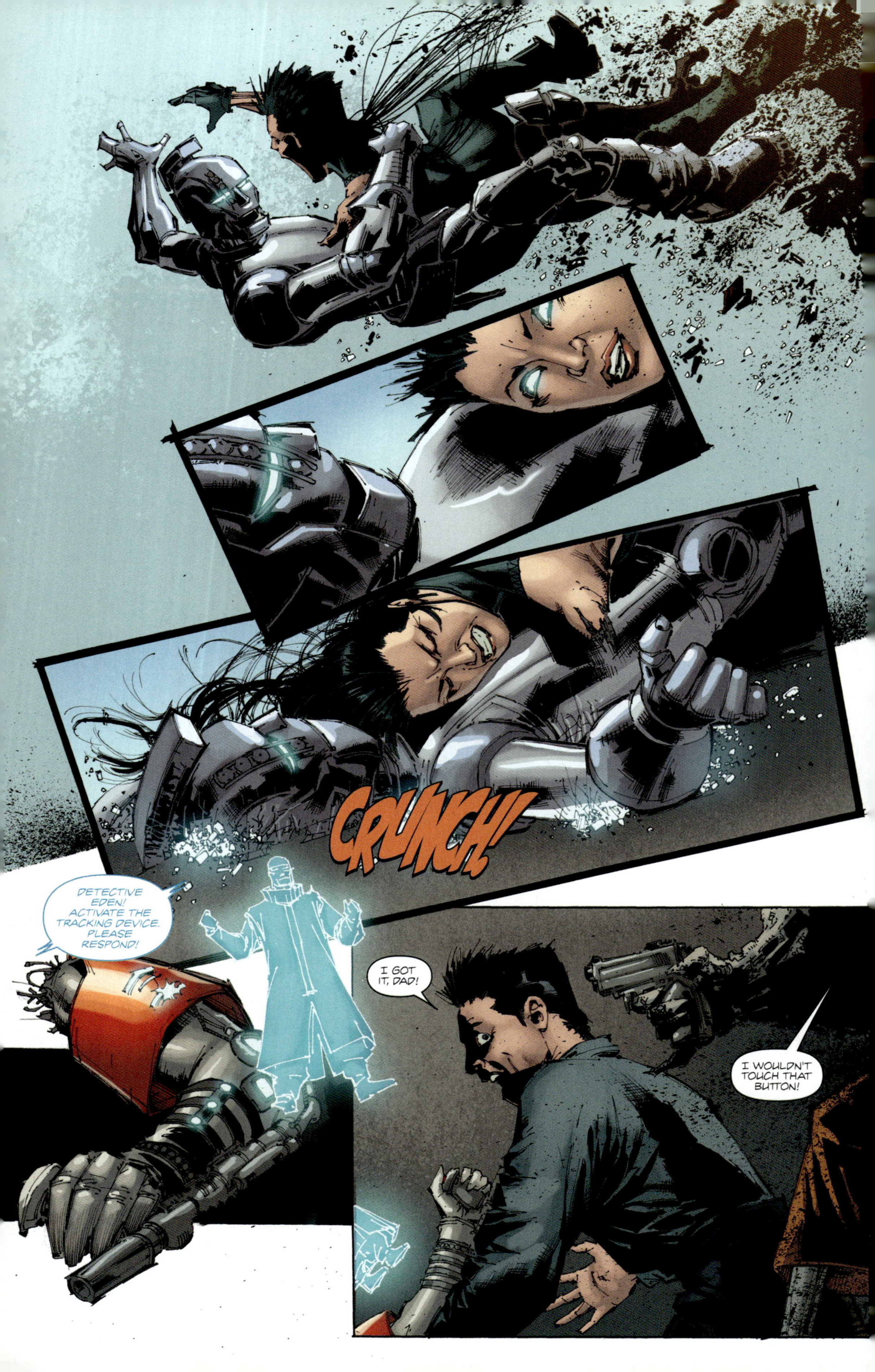
CRUNCH!
DETECTIVE EDEN! ACTIVATE THE TRACKING DEVICE. PLEASE RESPOND!
I GOT IT, DAD!
I WOULDN'T TOUCH THAT BUTTON!

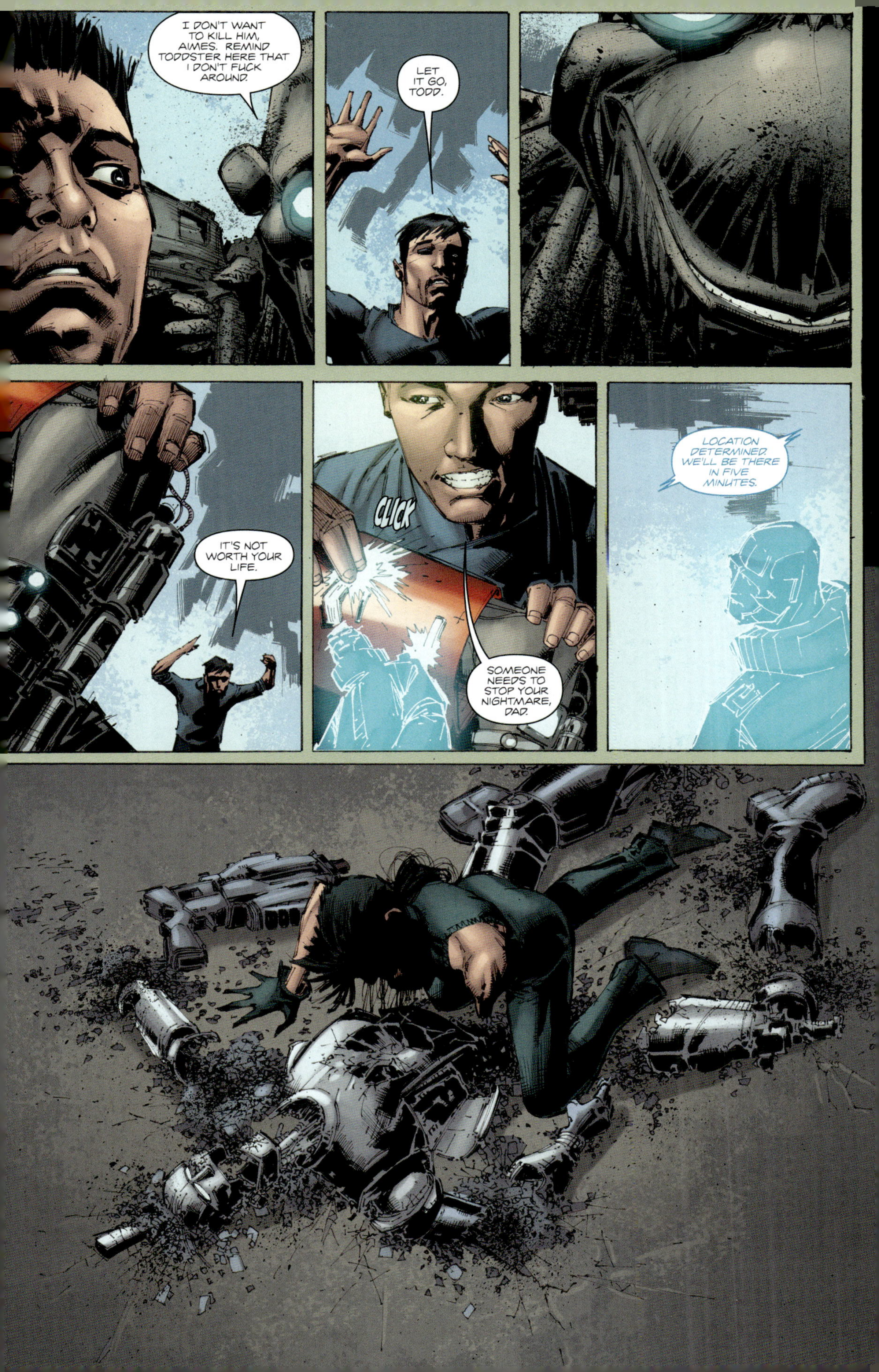
I DON'T WANT TO KILL HIM, AIMES. REMIND TODDSTER HERE THAT I DON'T FUCK AROUND.
LET IT GO, TODD.
IT'S NOT WORTH YOUR LIFE.
CLICK
SOMEONE NEEDS TO STOP YOUR NIGHTMARE, DAD.
LOCATION DETERMINED. WE'LL BE THERE IN FIVE MINUTES.

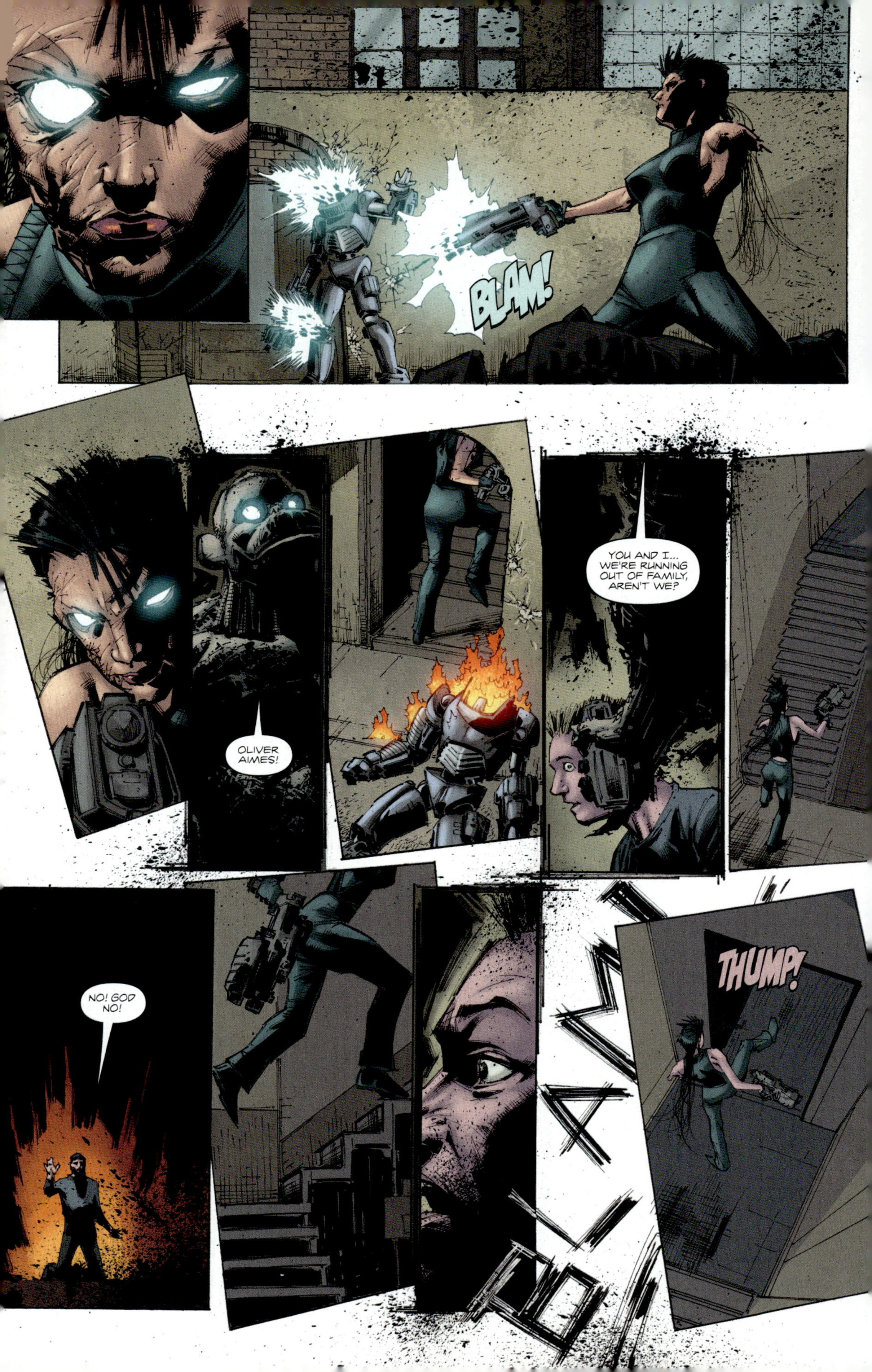
BLAM!
OLIVER AIMES!
YOU AND I... WE'RE RUNNING OUT OF FAMILY, AREN'T WE?
NO! GOD NO!
THUMP!

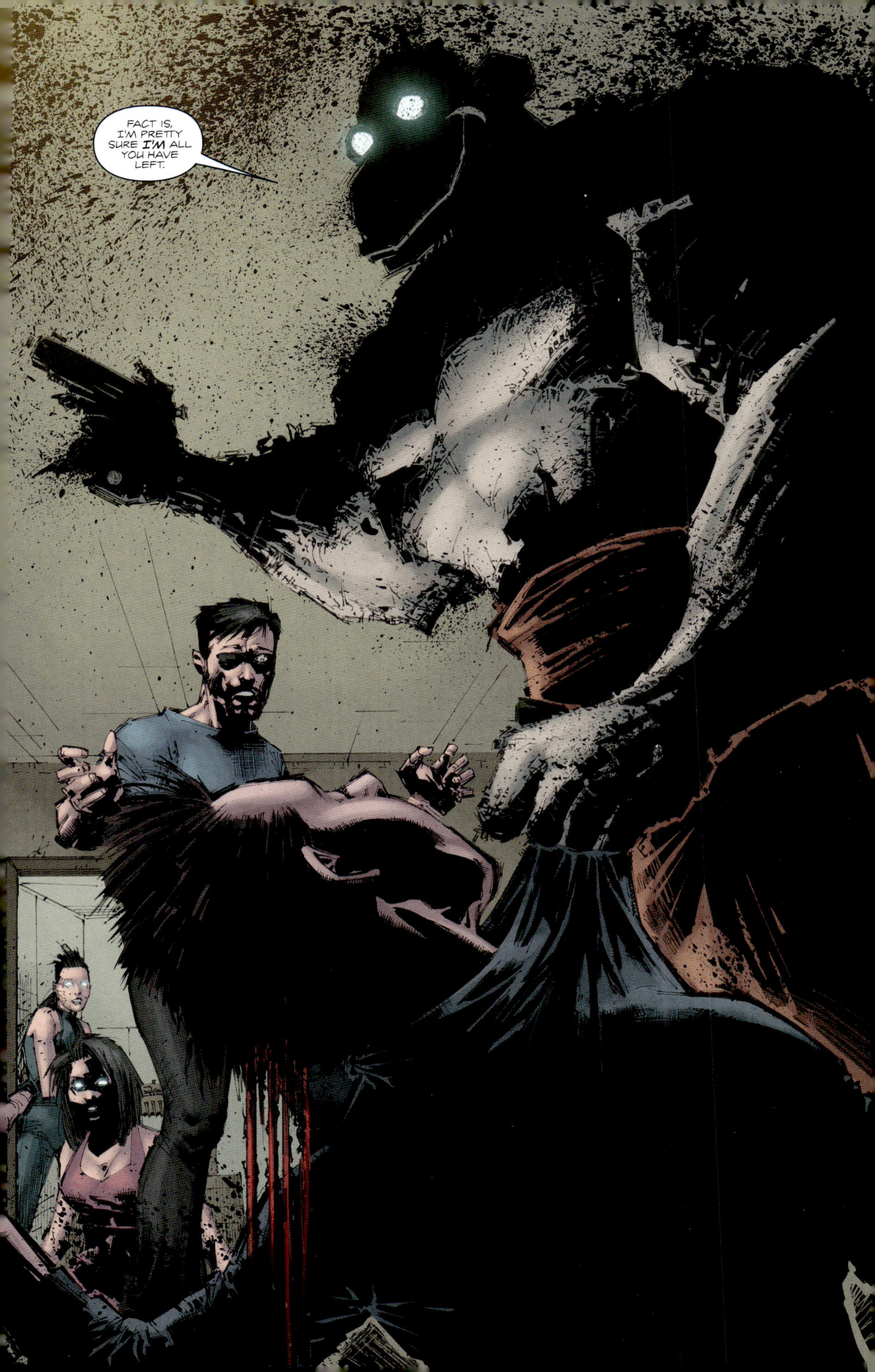
FACT IS, I'M PRETTY SURE I'M ALL YOU HAVE LEFT.

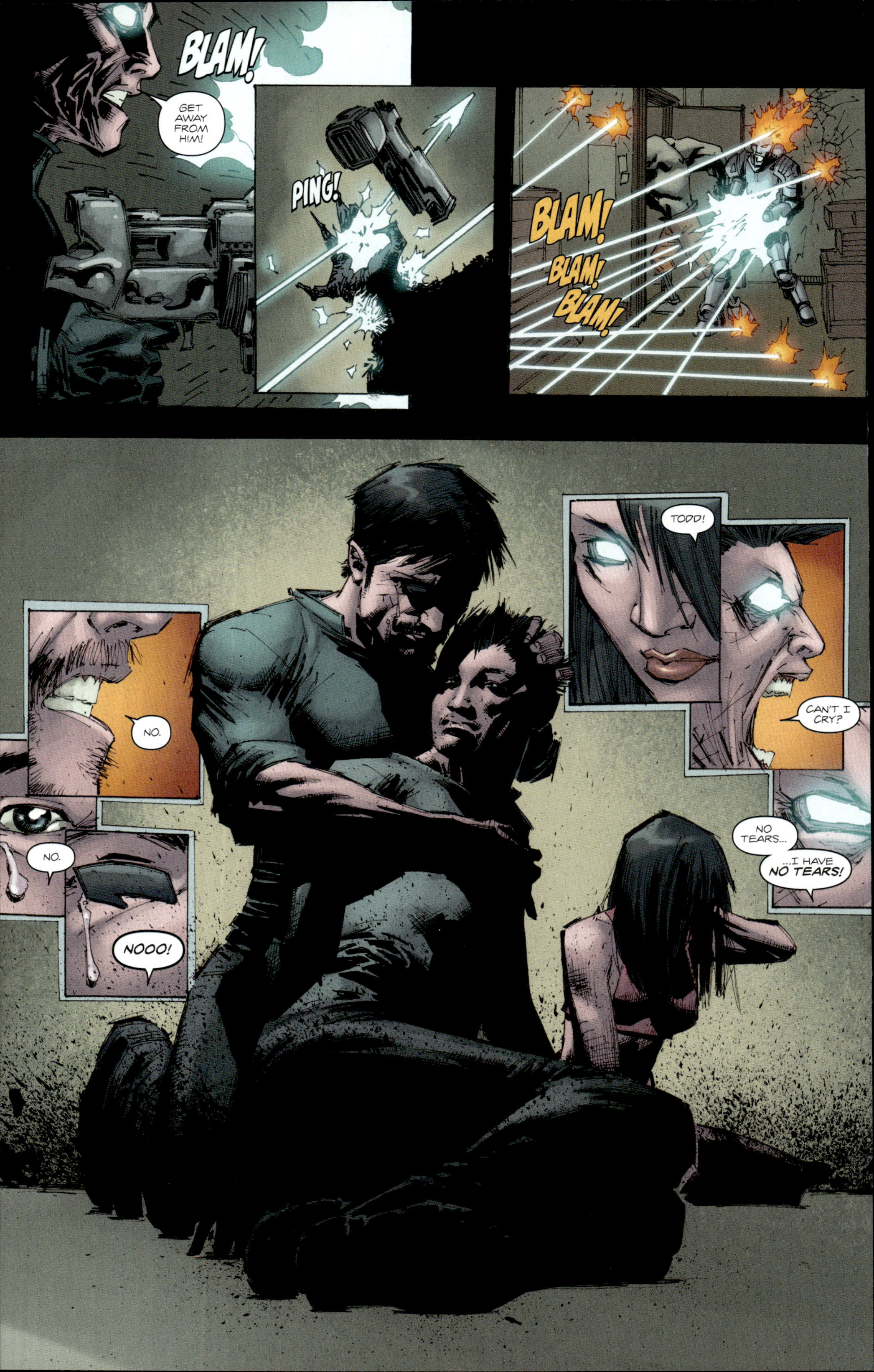
BLAM!
GET AWAY FROM HIM!
PING!
BLAM!
BLAM!
BLAM!
TODD!
CAN'T I CRY?
NO.
NO.
NOOO!
NO TEARS...
...I HAVE NO TEARS!

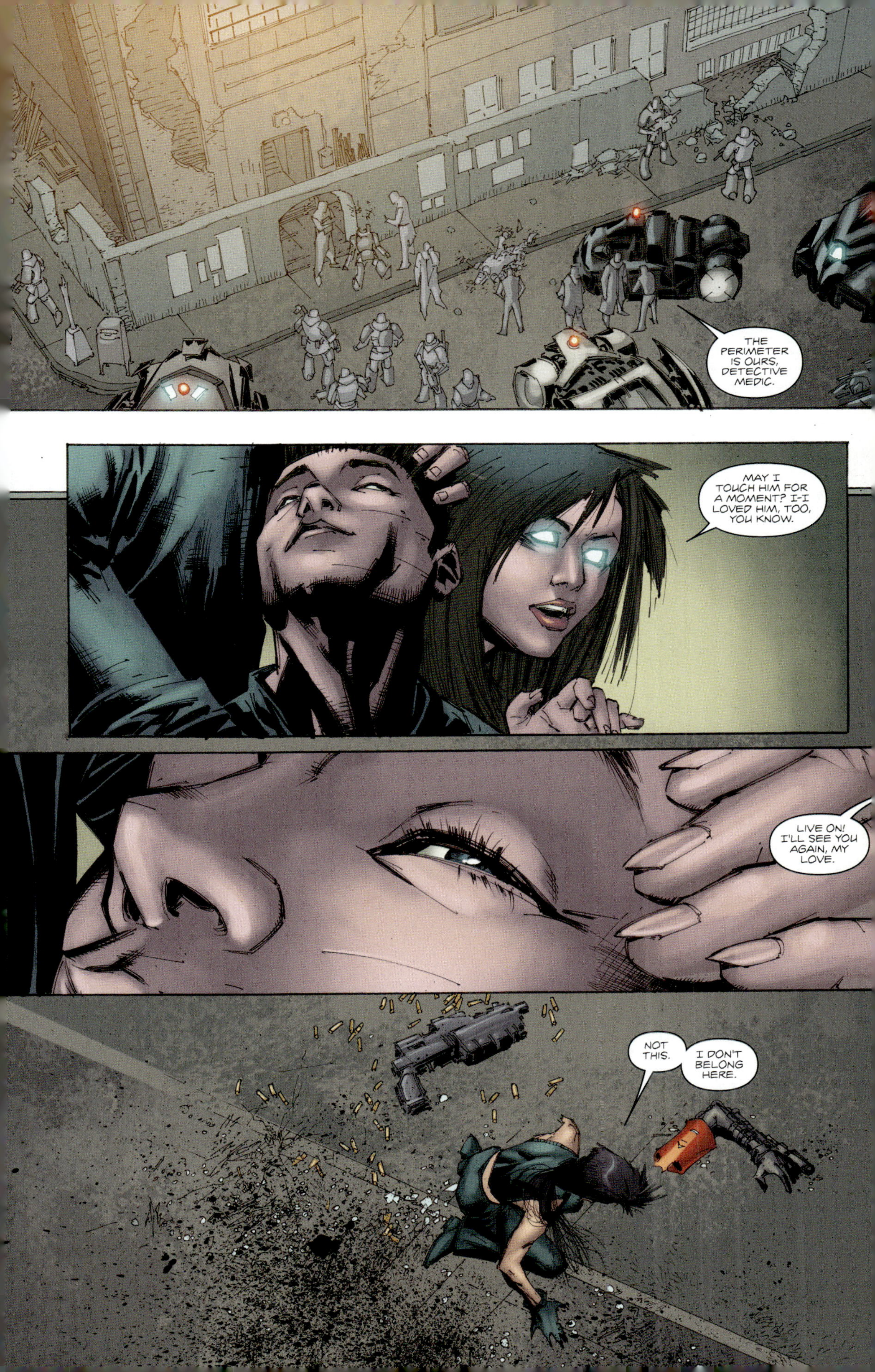
THE PERIMETER IS OURS, DETECTIVE MEDIC.
MAY I TOUCH HIM FOR A MOMENT? I-I LOVED HIM, TOO, YOU KNOW.
LIVE ON! I'LL SEE YOU AGAIN, MY LOVE.
NOT THIS.
I DON'T BELONG HERE.

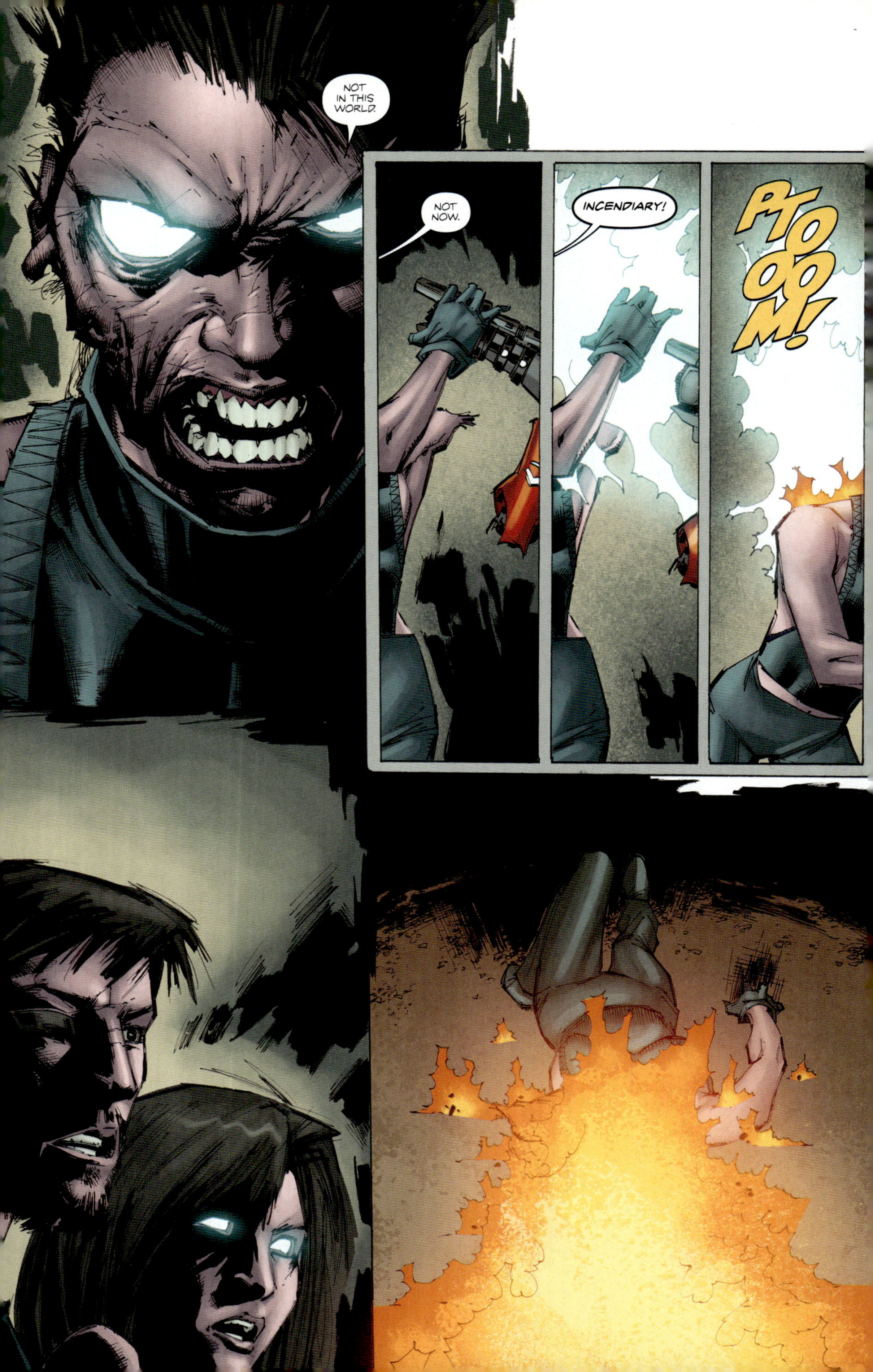
NOT IN THIS WORLD.
NOT NOW.
INCENDIARY!
PTOOOM!

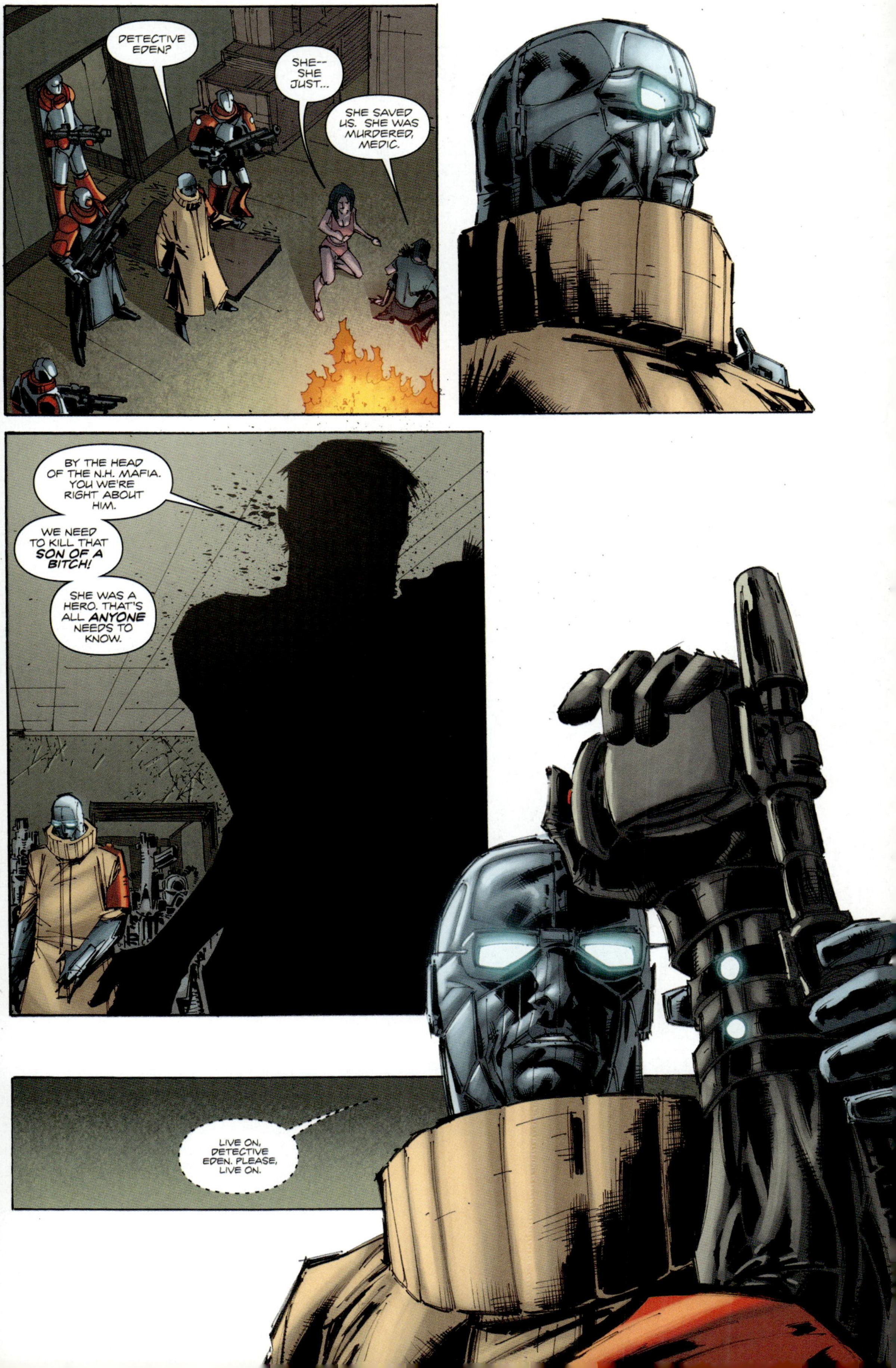

DETECTIVE EDEN?
SHE-- SHE JUST...
SHE SAVED US. SHE WAS MURDERED, MEDIC.
BY THE HEAD OF THE N.H. MAFIA. YOU WE'RE RIGHT ABOUT HIM.
WE NEED TO KILL THAT SON OF A BITCH!
SHE WAS A HERO. THAT'S ALL ANYONE NEEDS TO KNOW.
LIVE ON, DETECTIVE EDEN. PLEASE, LIVE ON.

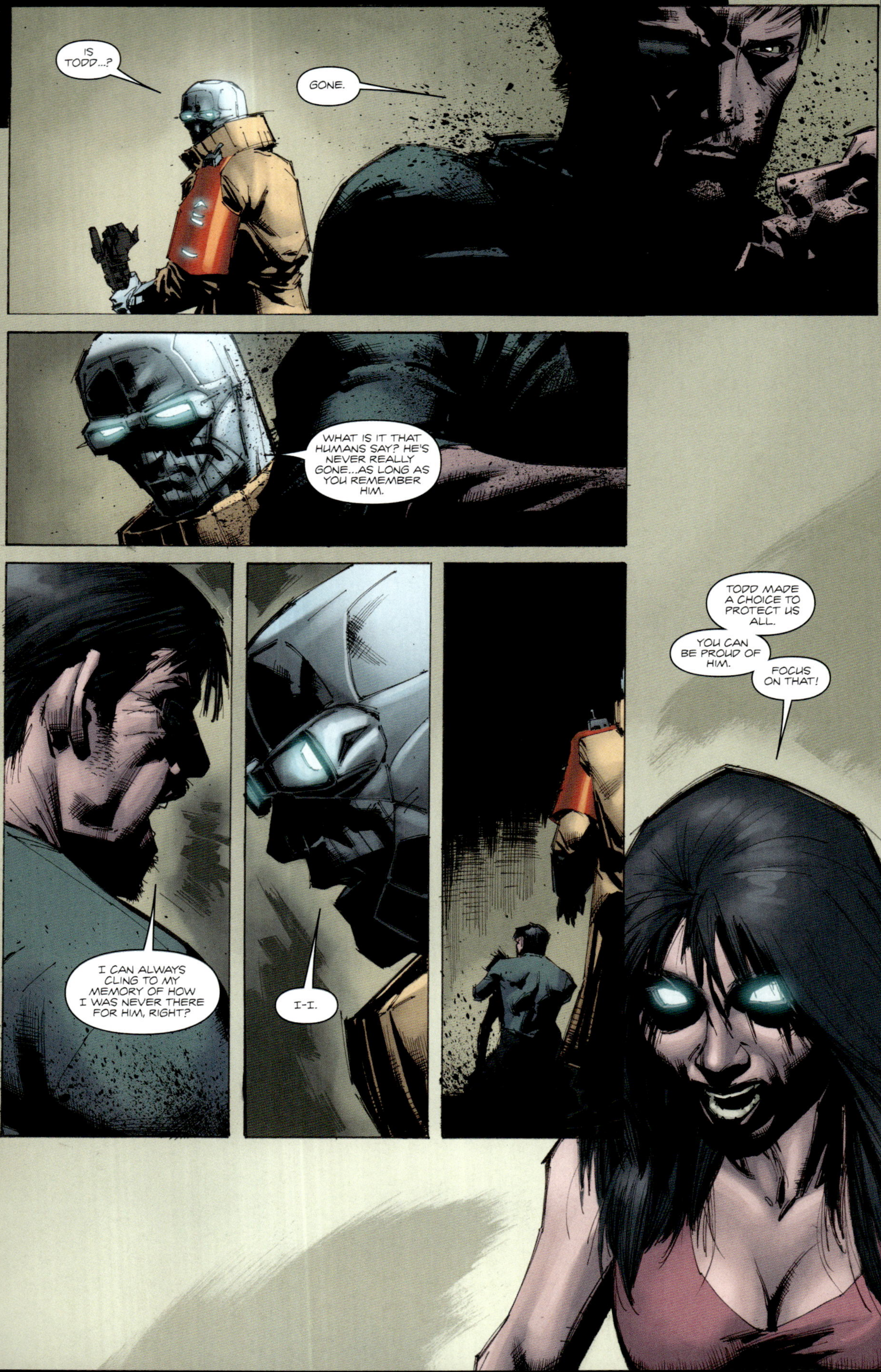
IS TODD...?
GONE.
WHAT IS IT THAT HUMANS SAY? HE'S NEVER REALLY GONE...AS LONG AS YOU REMEMBER HIM.
I CAN ALWAYS CLING TO MY MEMORY OF HOW I WAS NEVER THERE FOR HIM, RIGHT?
I-I.
TODD MADE A CHOICE TO PROTECT US ALL.
YOU CAN BE PROUD OF HIM.
FOCUS ON THAT!

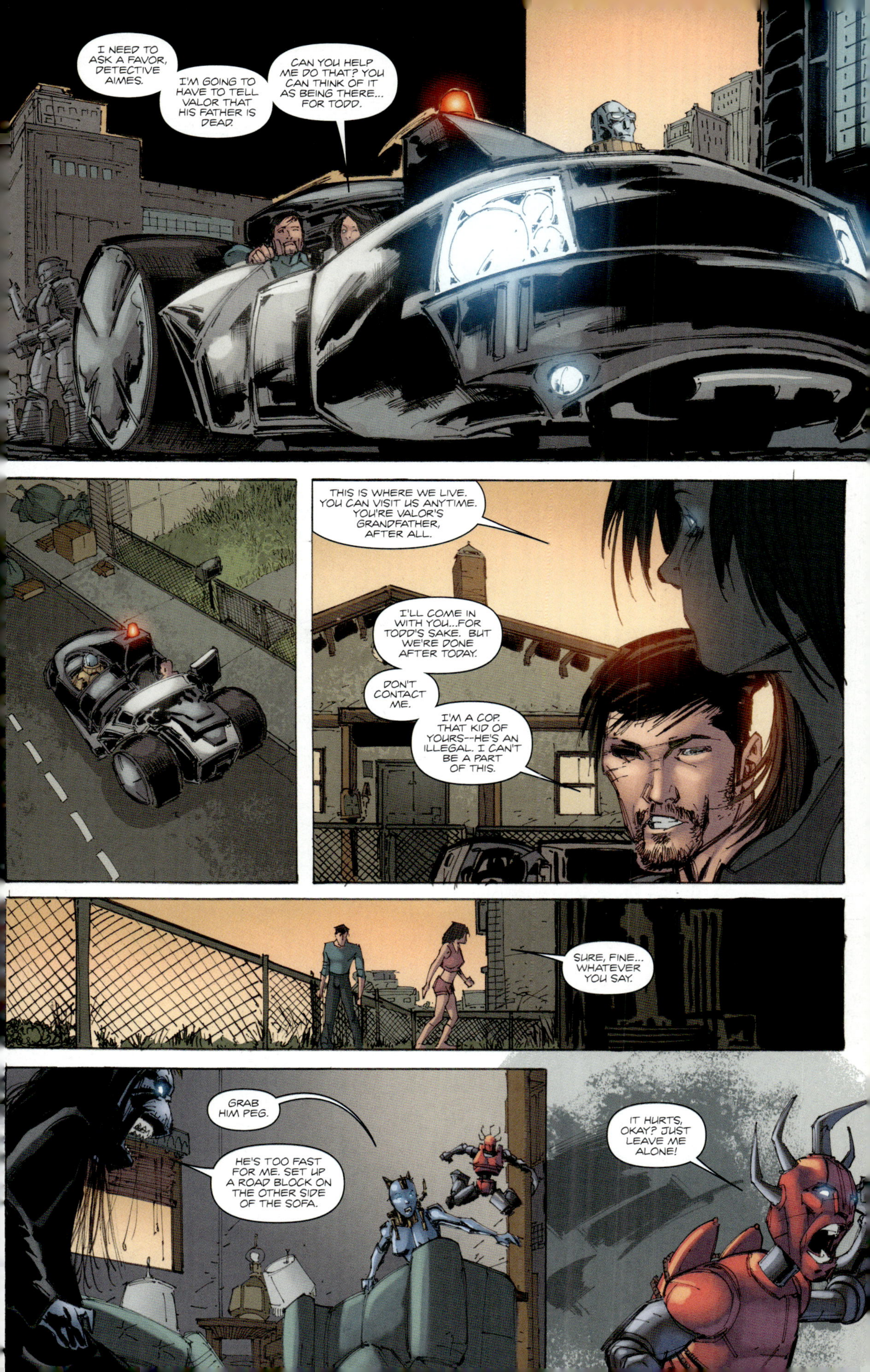
I NEED TO ASK A FAVOR, DETECTIVE AIMES.
I'M GOING TO HAVE TO TELL VALOR THAT HIS FATHER IS DEAD.
CAN YOU HELP ME DO THAT? YOU CAN THINK OF IT AS BEING THERE... FOR TODD.
THIS IS WHERE WE LIVE. YOU CAN VISIT US ANYTIME. YOU'RE VALOR'S GRANDFATHER, AFTER ALL.
I'LL COME IN WITH YOU...FOR TODD'S SAKE. BUT WE'RE DONE AFTER TODAY.
DON'T CONTACT ME.
I'M A COP. THAT KID OF YOURS--HE'S AN ILLEGAL. I CAN'T BE A PART OF THIS.
SURE, FINE... WHATEVER YOU SAY.
GRAB HIM PEG.
HE'S TOO FAST FOR ME. SET UP A ROAD BLOCK ON THE OTHER SIDE OF THE SOFA.
IT HURTS, OKAY? JUST LEAVE ME ALONE!

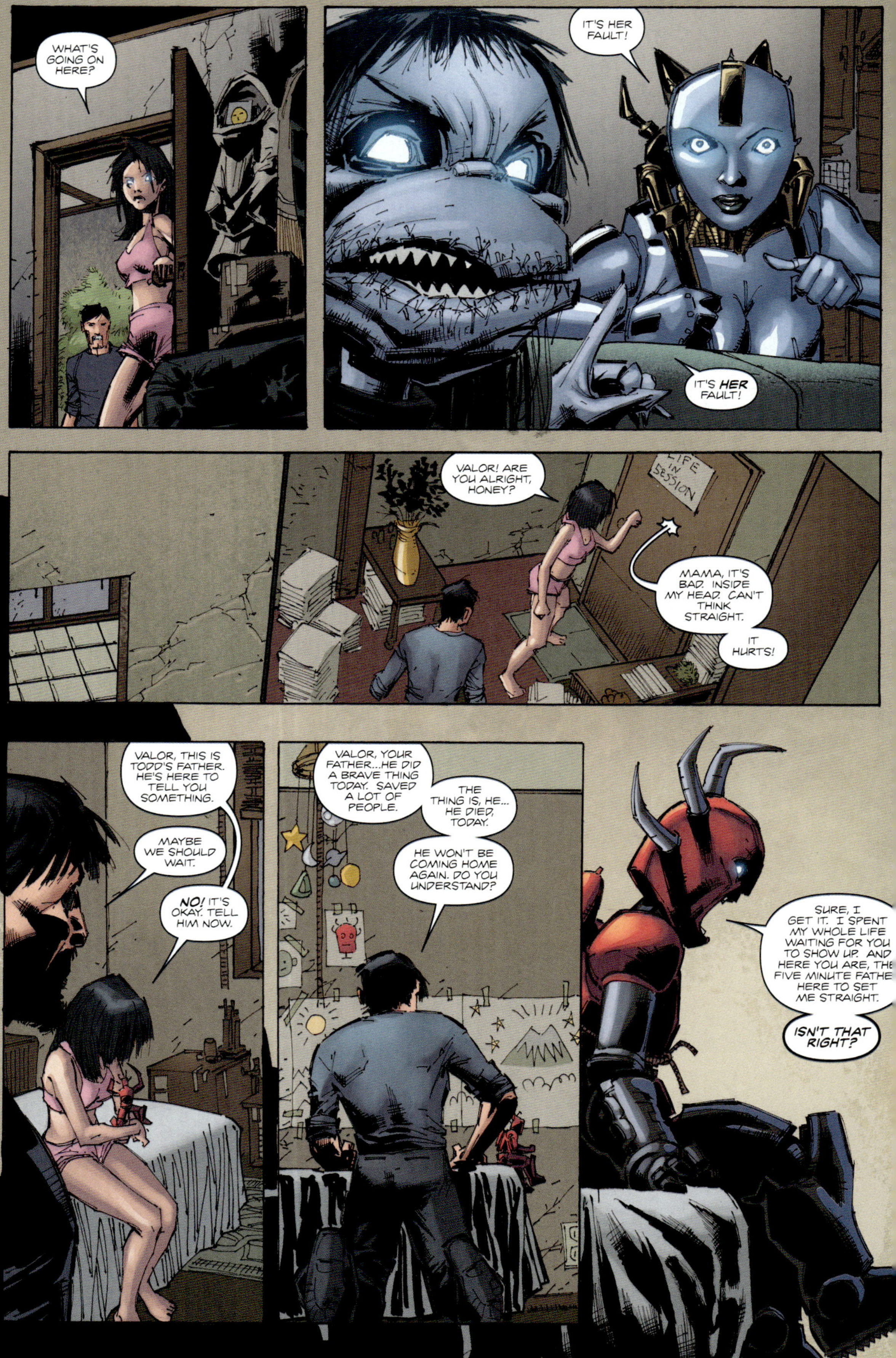
WHAT'S GOING ON HERE?
IT'S HER FAULT!
IT'S **HER** FAULT!
VALOR! ARE YOU ALRIGHT, HONEY?
LIFE IN SESSION
MAMA, IT'S BAD. INSIDE MY HEAD. CAN'T THINK STRAIGHT.
IT HURTS!
VALOR, THIS IS TODD'S FATHER. HE'S HERE TO TELL YOU SOMETHING.
MAYBE WE SHOULD WAIT.
**NO!** IT'S OKAY. TELL HIM NOW.
VALOR, YOUR FATHER...HE DID A BRAVE THING TODAY. SAVED A LOT OF PEOPLE.
THE THING IS, HE... HE DIED, TODAY.
HE WON'T BE COMING HOME AGAIN. DO YOU UNDERSTAND?
SURE, I GET IT. I SPENT MY WHOLE LIFE WAITING FOR YOU TO SHOW UP. AND HERE YOU ARE, THE FIVE MINUTE FATHE HERE TO SET ME STRAIGHT.
ISN'T THAT RIGHT?

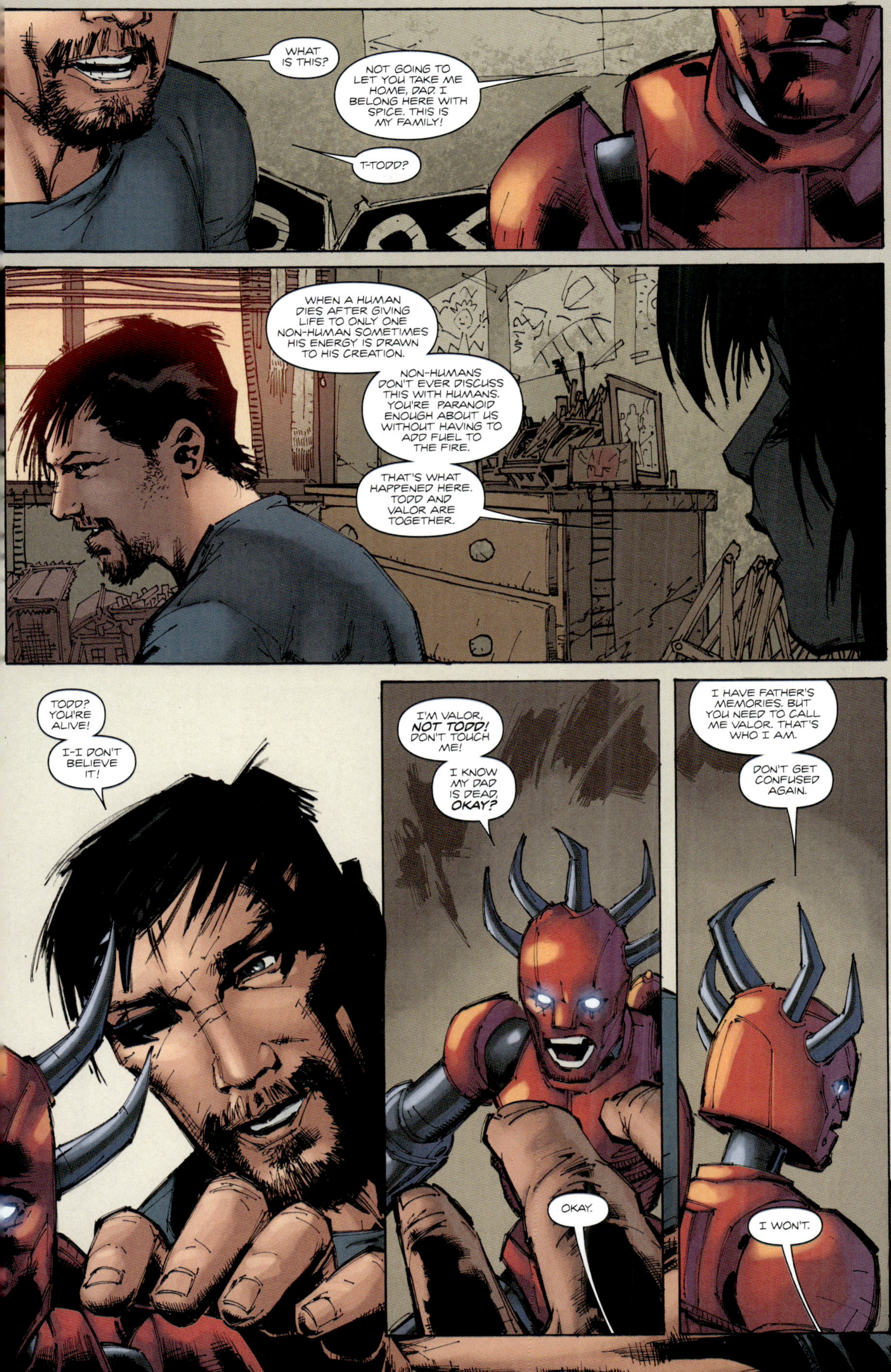
WHAT IS THIS?
NOT GOING TO LET YOU TAKE ME HOME, DAD. I BELONG HERE WITH SPICE. THIS IS MY FAMILY!
T-TODD?
WHEN A HUMAN DIES AFTER GIVING LIFE TO ONLY ONE NON-HUMAN SOMETIMES HIS ENERGY IS DRAWN TO HIS CREATION.
NON-HUMANS DON'T EVER DISCUSS THIS WITH HUMANS. YOU'RE PARANOID ENOUGH ABOUT US WITHOUT HAVING TO ADD FUEL TO THE FIRE.
THAT'S WHAT HAPPENED HERE. TODD AND VALOR ARE TOGETHER.
TODD? YOU'RE ALIVE!
I-I DON'T BELIEVE IT!
I'M VALOR, **NOT TODD!** DON'T TOUCH ME!
I KNOW MY DAD IS DEAD, **OKAY?**
OKAY.
I HAVE FATHER'S MEMORIES. BUT YOU NEED TO CALL ME VALOR. THAT'S WHO I AM.
DON'T GET CONFUSED AGAIN.
I WON'T.

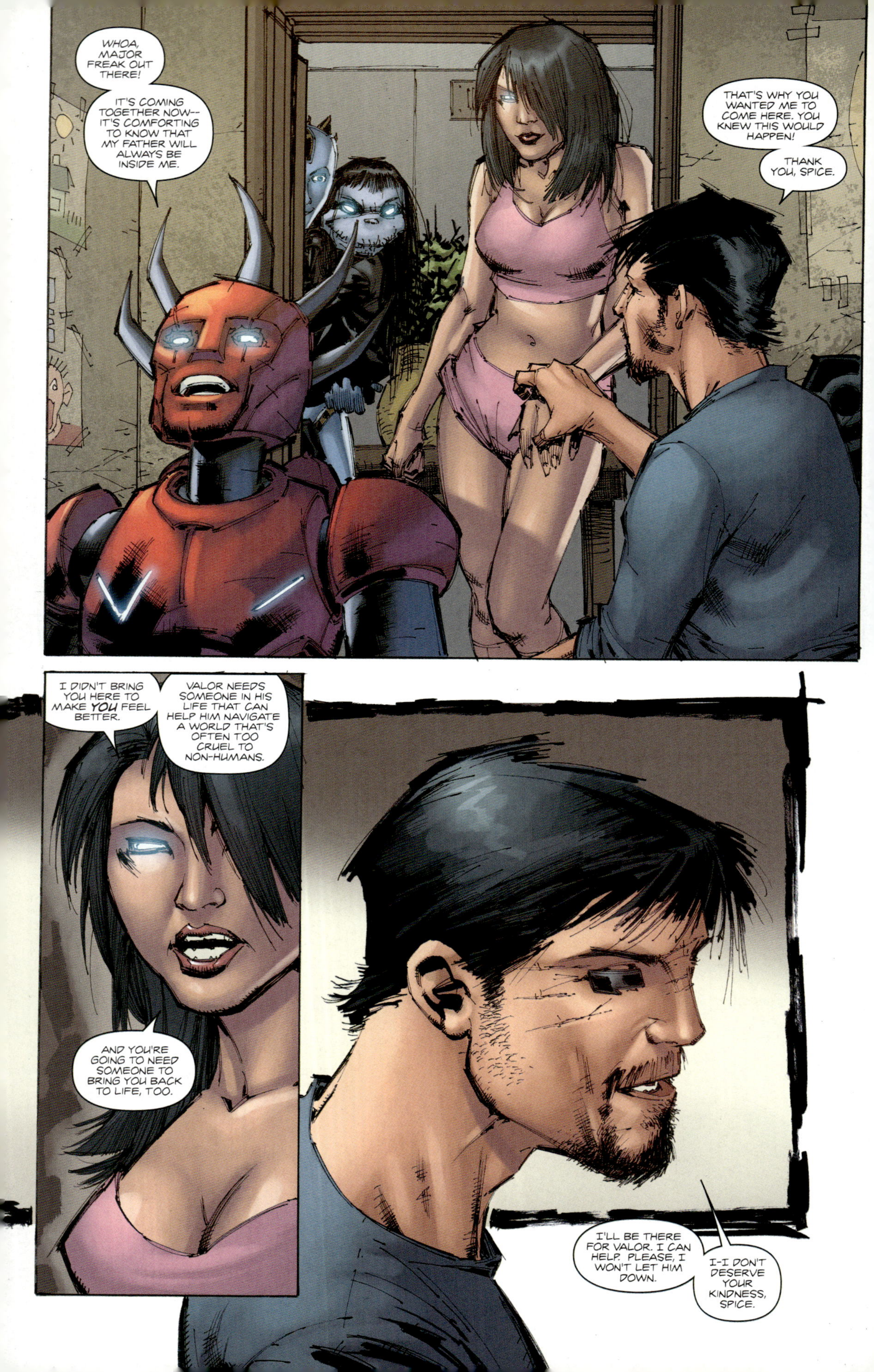
WHOA, MAJOR FREAK OUT THERE!
IT'S COMING TOGETHER NOW-- IT'S COMFORTING TO KNOW THAT MY FATHER WILL ALWAYS BE INSIDE ME.
THAT'S WHY YOU WANTED ME TO COME HERE. YOU KNEW THIS WOULD HAPPEN!
THANK YOU, SPICE.
I DIDN'T BRING YOU HERE TO MAKE **YOU** FEEL BETTER.
VALOR NEEDS SOMEONE IN HIS LIFE THAT CAN HELP HIM NAVIGATE A WORLD THAT'S OFTEN TOO CRUEL TO NON-HUMANS.
AND YOU'RE GOING TO NEED SOMEONE TO BRING YOU BACK TO LIFE, TOO.
I'LL BE THERE FOR VALOR. I CAN HELP. PLEASE, I WON'T LET HIM DOWN.
I-I DON'T DESERVE YOUR KINDNESS, SPICE.

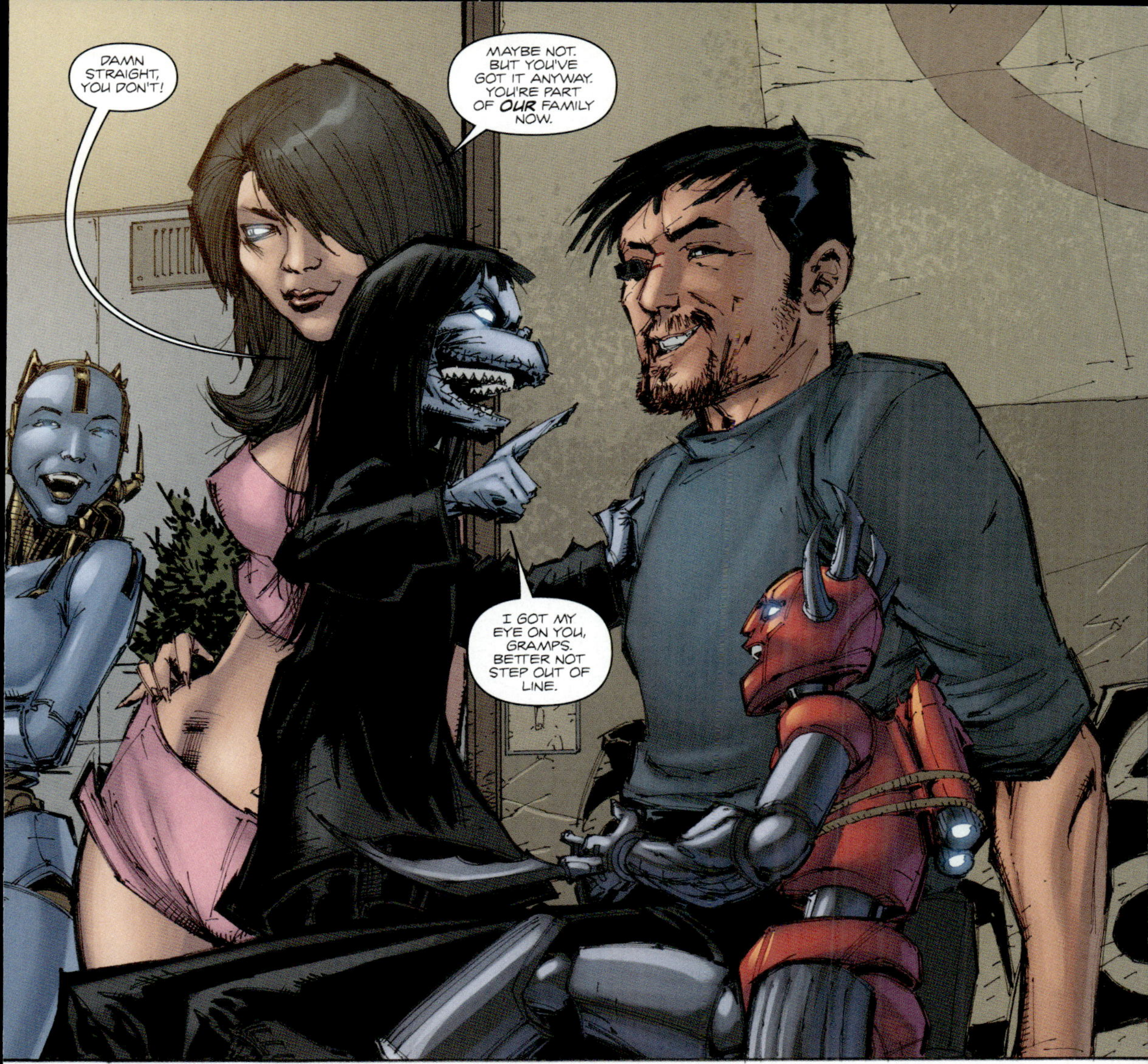
DAMN STRAIGHT, YOU DON'T!
MAYBE NOT. BUT YOU'VE GOT IT ANYWAY. YOU'RE PART OF OUR FAMILY NOW.
I GOT MY EYE ON YOU, GRAMPS. BETTER NOT STEP OUT OF LINE.

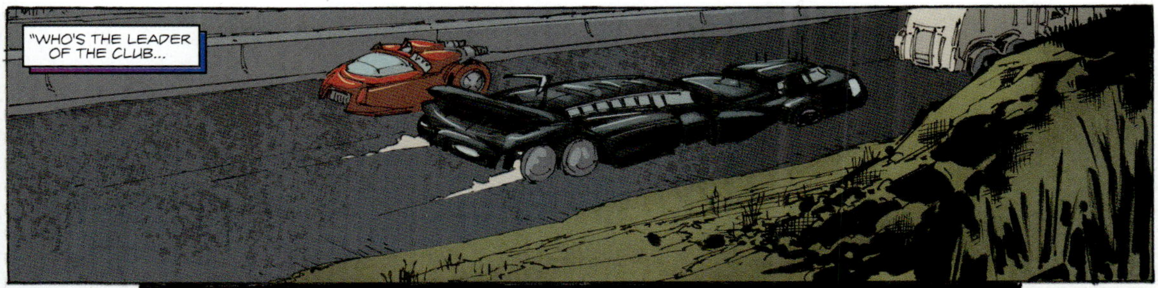
"WHO'S THE LEADER OF THE CLUB...

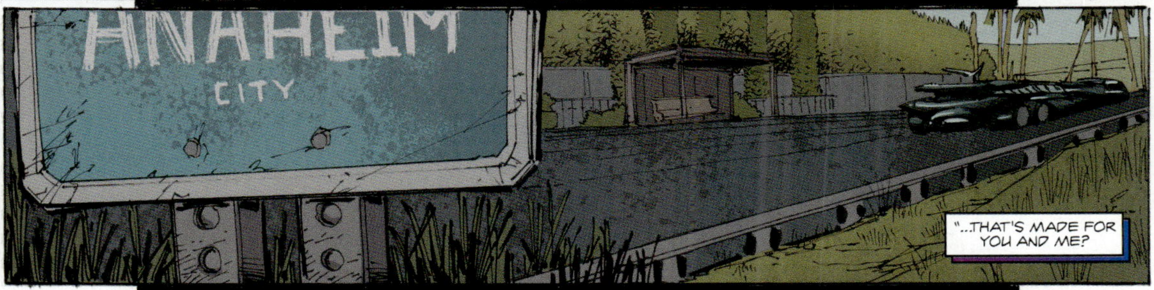
ANAHEIM
CITY
"...THAT'S MADE FOR YOU AND ME?

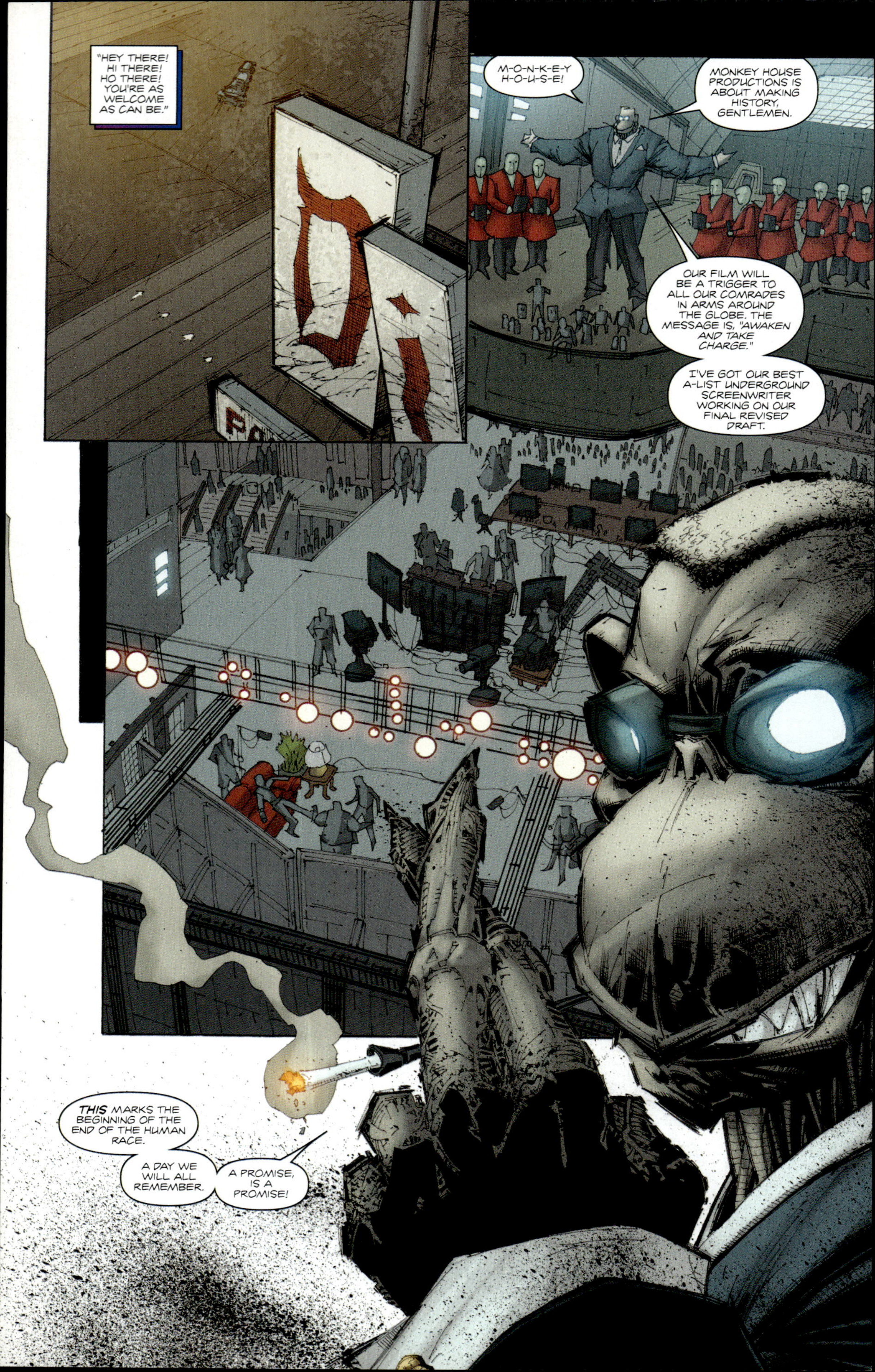
"HEY THERE! HI THERE! HO THERE! YOU'RE AS WELCOME AS CAN BE."
M-O-N-K-E-Y H-O-U-S-E!
MONKEY HOUSE PRODUCTIONS IS ABOUT MAKING HISTORY, GENTLEMEN.
OUR FILM WILL BE A TRIGGER TO ALL OUR COMRADES IN ARMS AROUND THE GLOBE. THE MESSAGE IS, "AWAKEN AND TAKE CHARGE."
I'VE GOT OUR BEST A-LIST UNDERGROUND SCREENWRITER WORKING ON OUR FINAL REVISED DRAFT.
THIS MARKS THE BEGINNING OF THE END OF THE HUMAN RACE.
A DAY WE WILL ALL REMEMBER.
A PROMISE, IS A PROMISE!

# NON HUMANS

# SKETCHBOOK

World building and design are the foundation that brings *NON-HUMANS* to life. This is Whilce Portacio's love...and his strength. To be successful at breathing life into a world we've never seen before it's important to think beyond the edges of the page-- to create an illusion that you're only seeing part of the world you've been shown. To toggle a switch inside the mind of the reader that allows them to bring their own vision, outside of the borders, to this fictitious world. These are the sketches and designs that Whilce started with to begin the process. It's amazing to see how far he's come...and how much he already had back in the beginning.

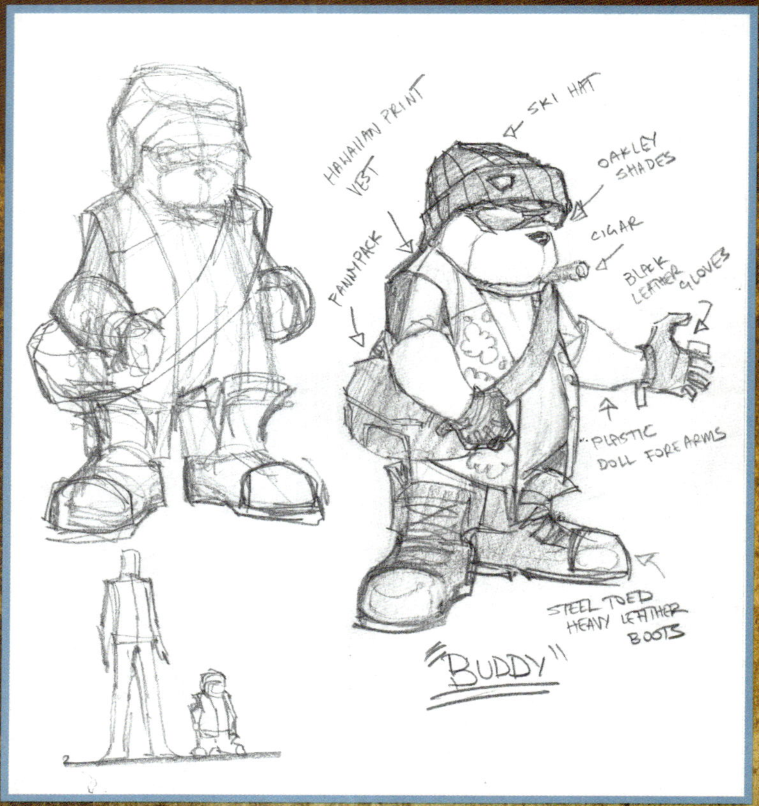
HAWAIIAN PRINT VEST
SKI HAT
OAKLEY SHADES
CIGAR
FANNYPACK
BLACK LEATHER GLOVES
PLASTIC DOLL FORE ARMS
STEEL TOED HEAVY LEATHER BOOTS
"BUDDY"

**First sketch of Buddy-The-Bear.**

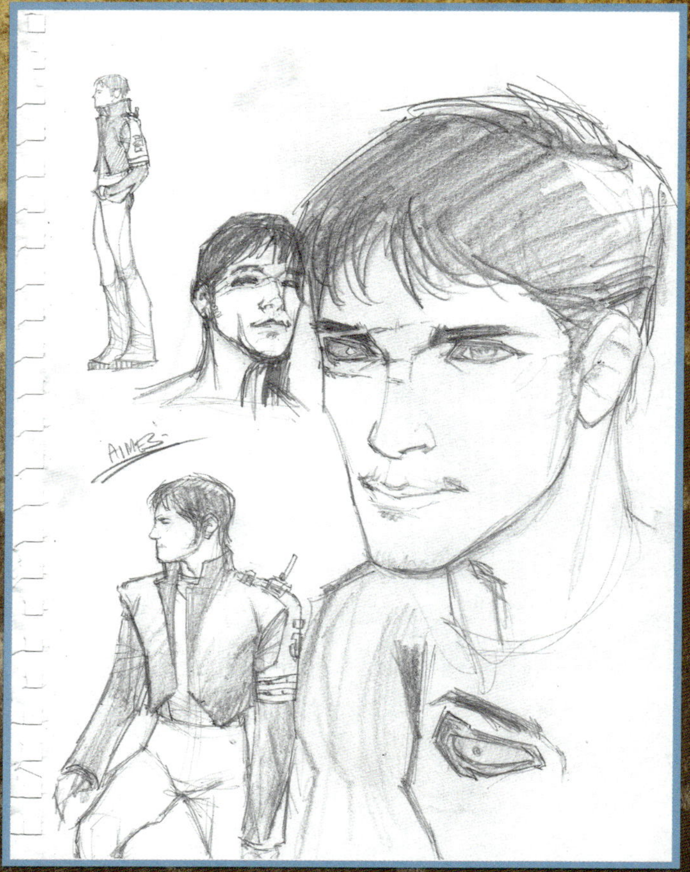
AIMES

**First sketch of Detective Oliver Aimes--mechanical eye, police jacket and badge are already there.**

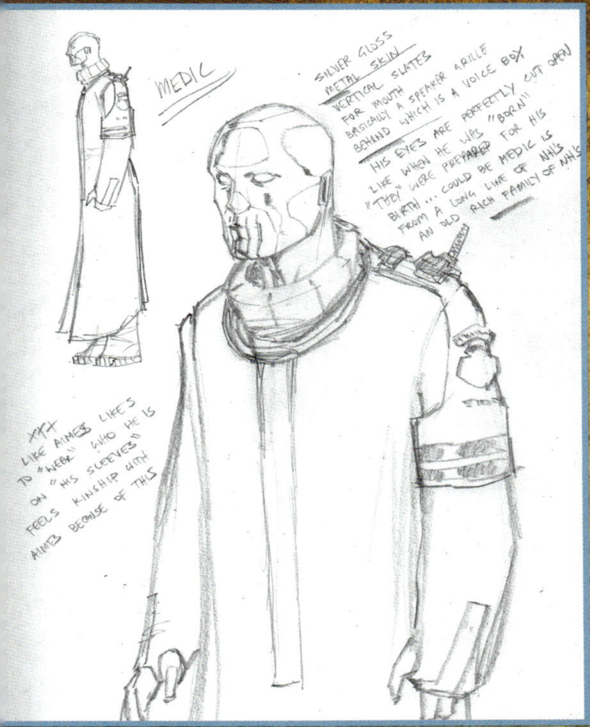
MEDIC
SILVER GLOSS
METAL SKIN
VERTICAL SLATES
FOR MOUTH
BASICALLY A SPEAKER GRILLE
BEHIND WHICH IS A VOICE BOX
HIS EYES ARE PERFECTLY CUT OPEN
LIKE WHEN HE WAS "BORN"
"THEY" WERE PREPARED FOR HIS
BIRTH ... COULD BE MEDIC IS
FROM A LONG LINE OF NH'S
AN OLD RICH FAMILY OF NH'S

First sketch of Medic.

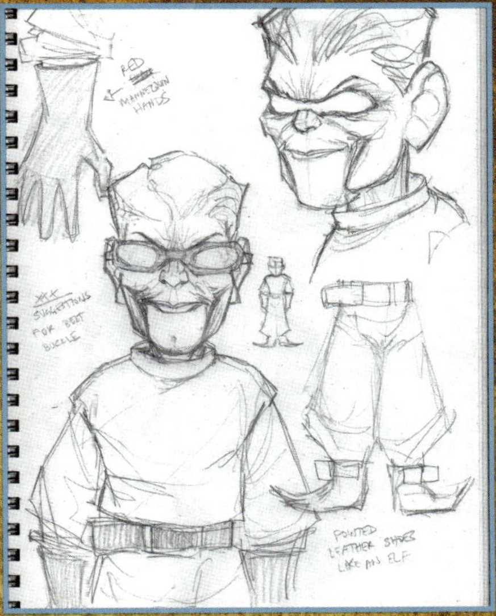

First sketch of Humphrey.

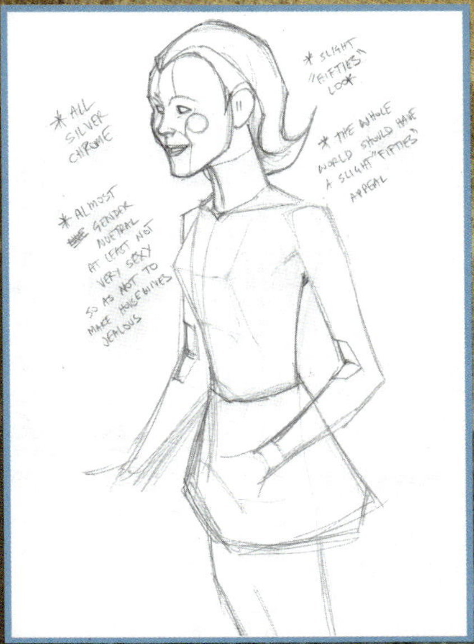

Rejected sketch for Teresa Tech.

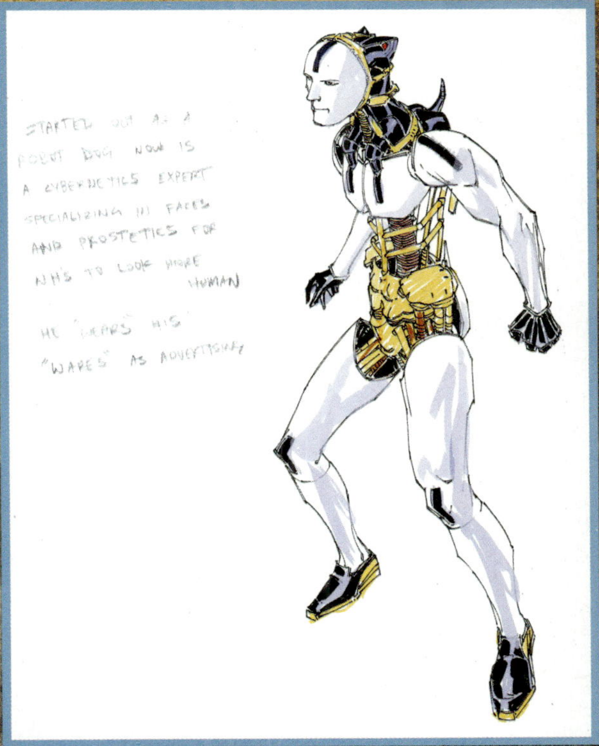

First sketch of Teresa Tech.

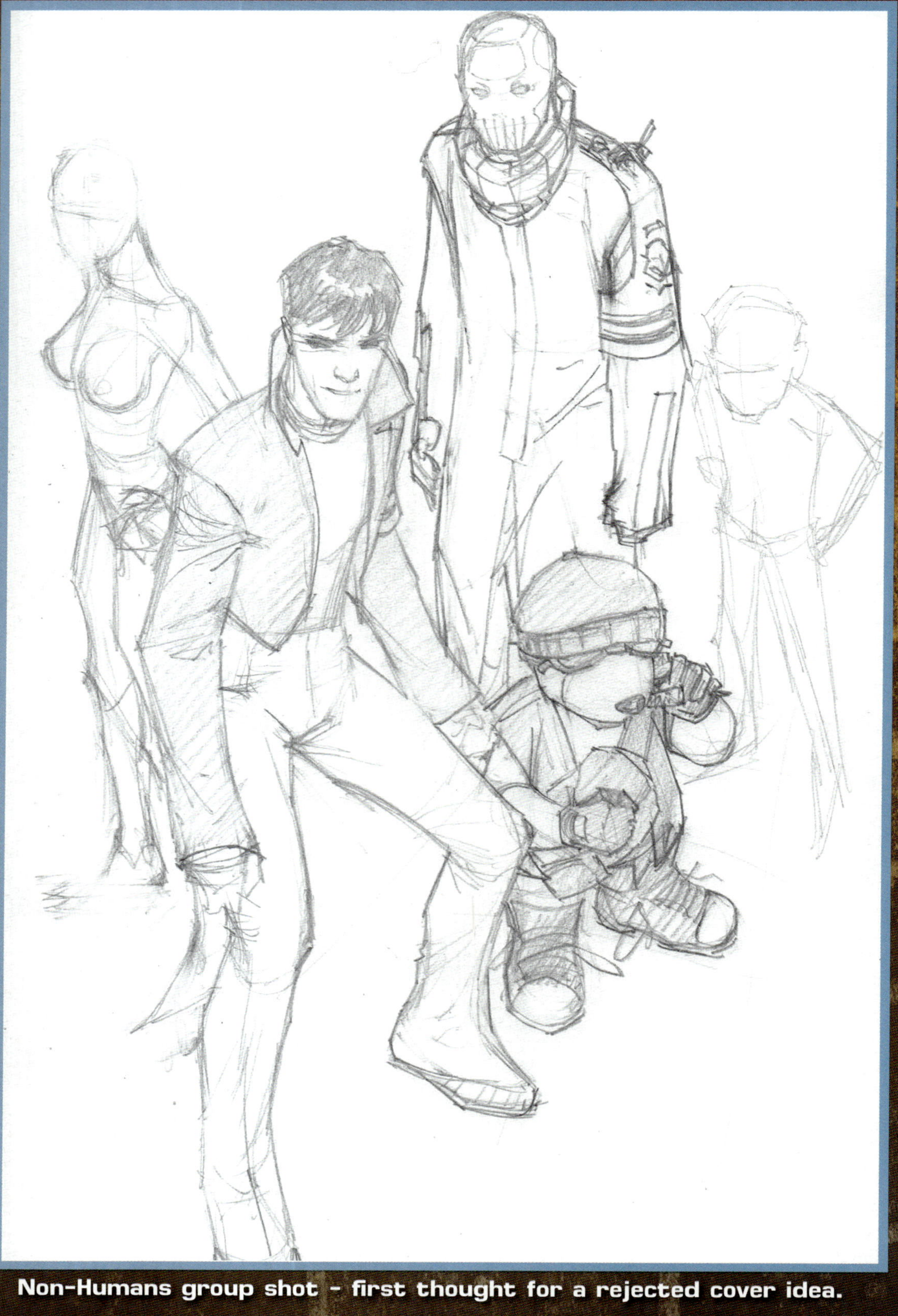

Non-Humans group shot - first thought for a rejected cover idea.

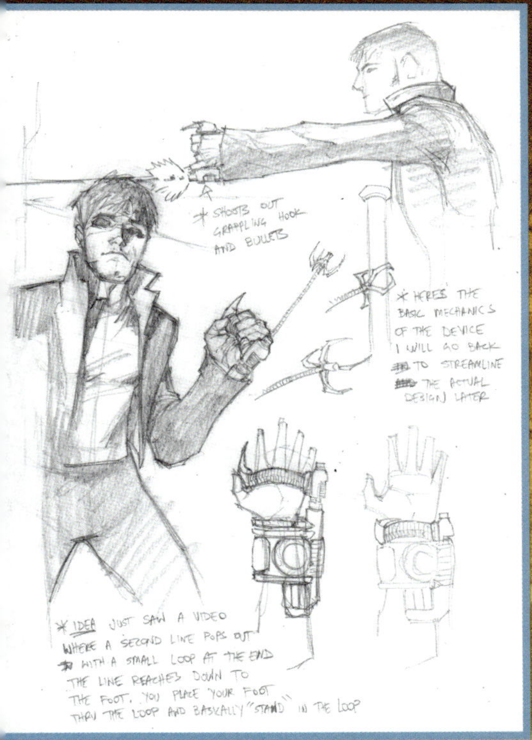
* SHOOTS OUT GRAPPLING HOOK AND BULLETS
* HERES THE BASIC MECHANICS OF THE DEVICE I WILL GO BACK TO STREAMLINE THE ACTUAL DESIGN LATER
* IDEA JUST SAW A VIDEO WHERE A SECOND LINE POPS OUT WITH A SMALL LOOP AT THE END THE LINE REACHES DOWN TO THE FOOT. YOU PLACE YOUR FOOT THRU THE LOOP AND BASICALLY "STAND" IN THE LOOP

**Aimes - gun and hook equipment design.**

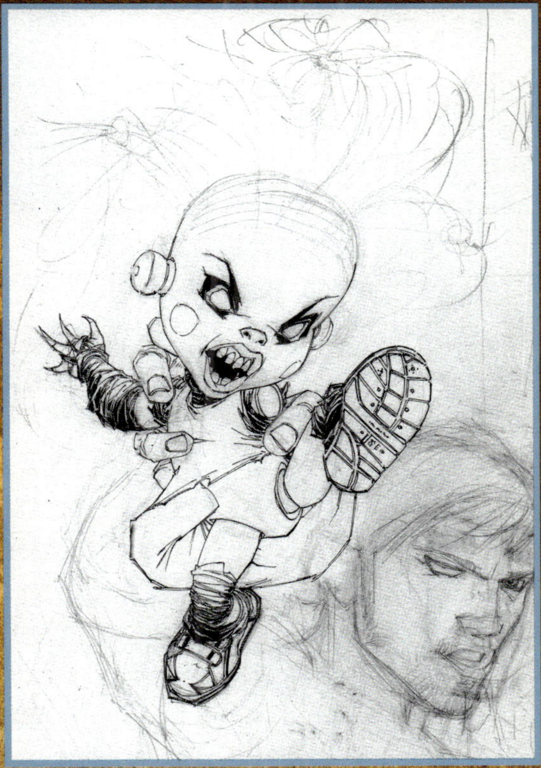

**Nano-Babe - used on the cover to issue #1.**

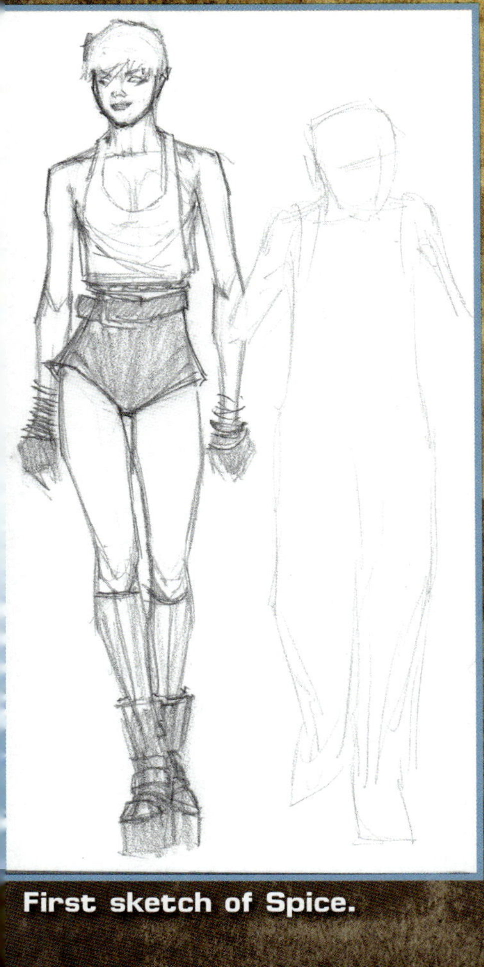

**First sketch of Spice.**

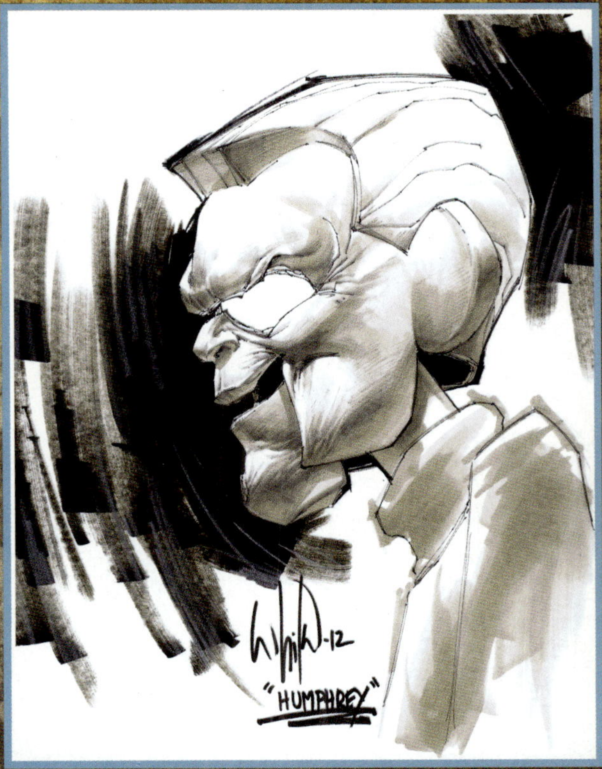
"HUMPHREY"

**Humphrey portrait.**

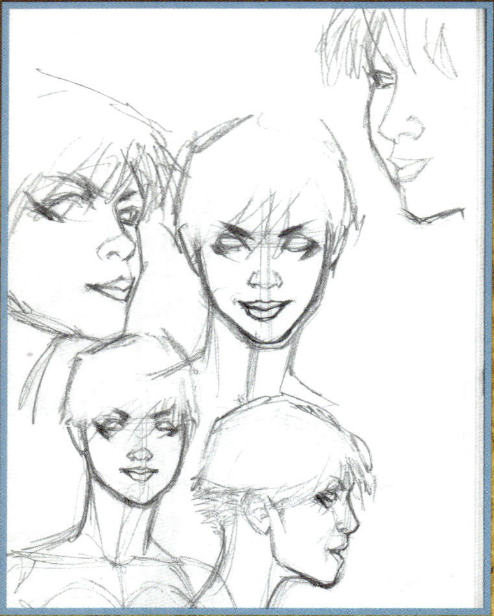

Spice faces.

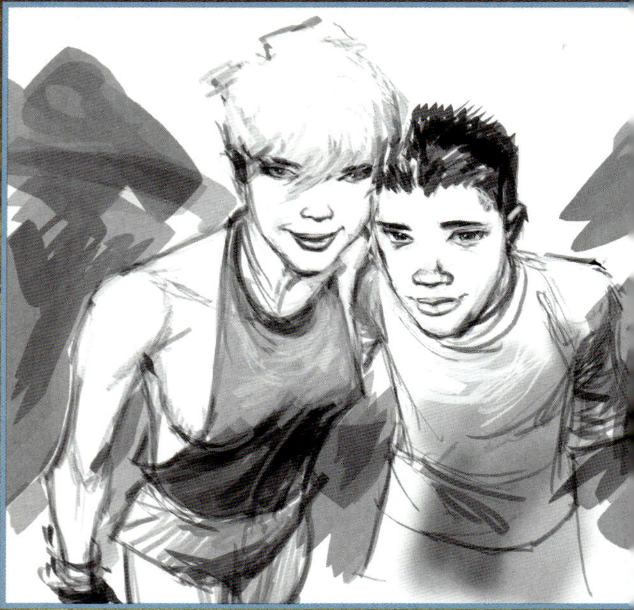

Spice and Todd portrait.

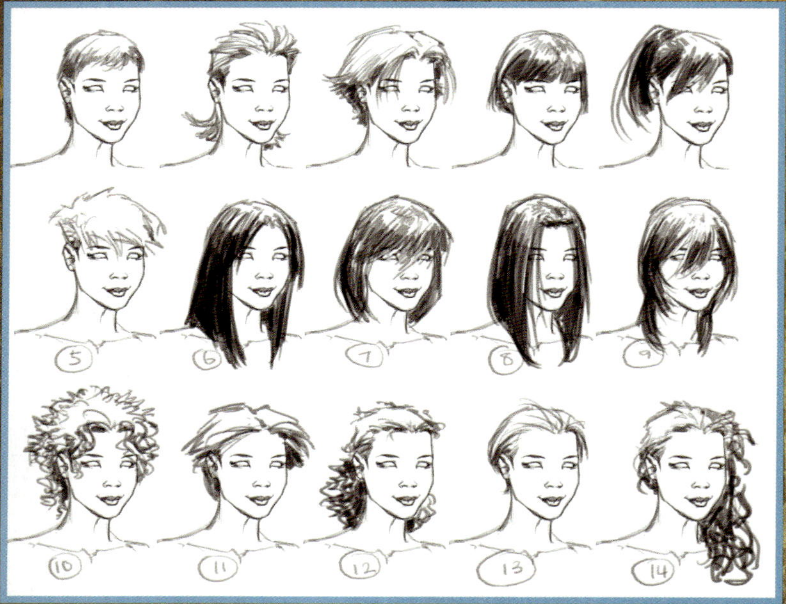
5
6
7
8
9
10
11
12
13
14

Hair choices for Spice.

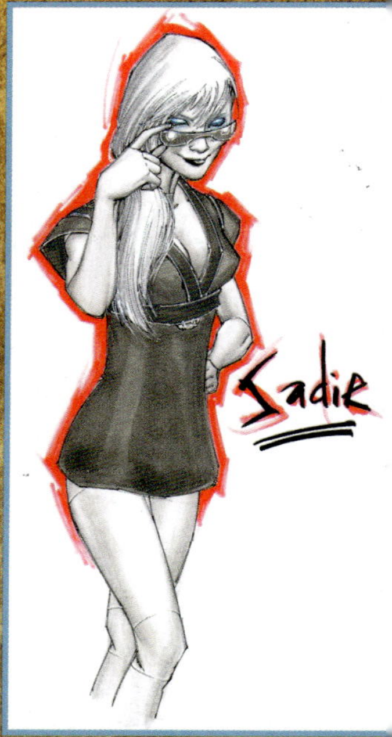
Sadie

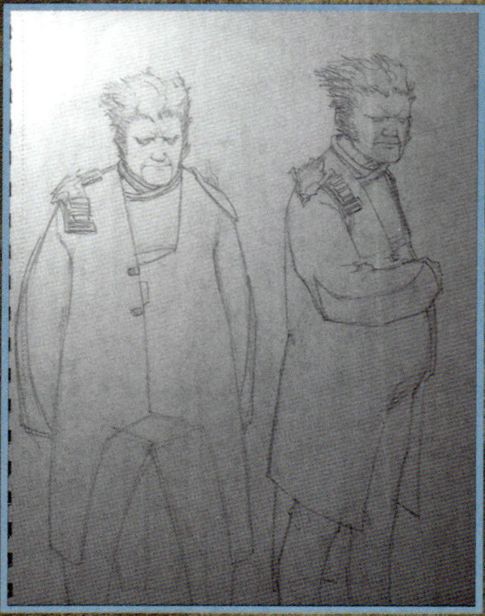

Sketch of Gonzales.

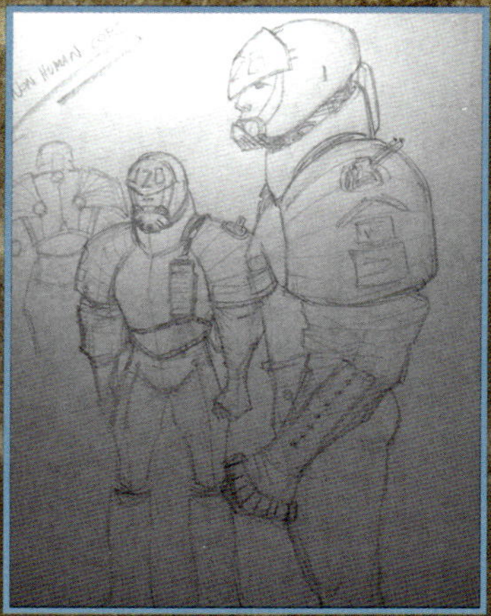

Cops concept sketch.

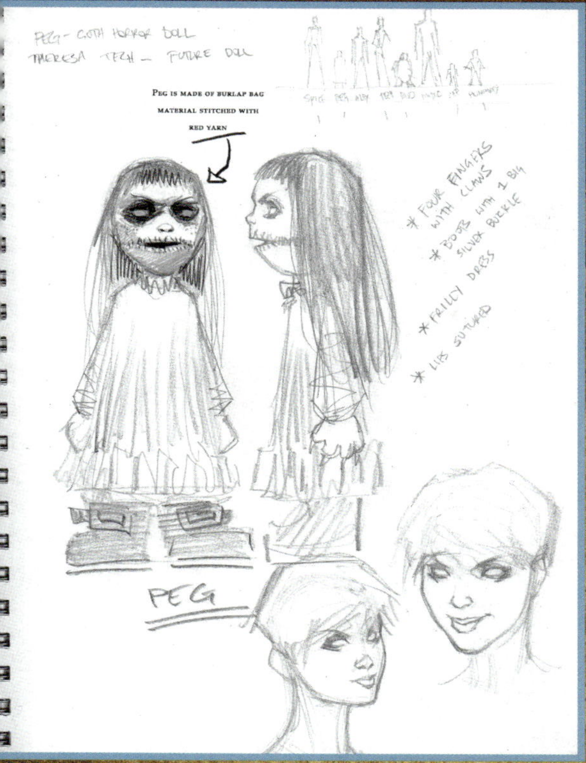
PEG - GOTH HORROR DOLL
THERESA TECH - FUTURE DOLL
PEG IS MADE OF BURLAP BAG
MATERIAL STITCHED WITH
RED YARN
* FOUR FINGERS WITH CLAWS
* BOOTS WITH 1 BIG SILVER BUCKLE
* FRILLY DRESS
* LIPS SUTURED
PEG

irst sketch of Peg.

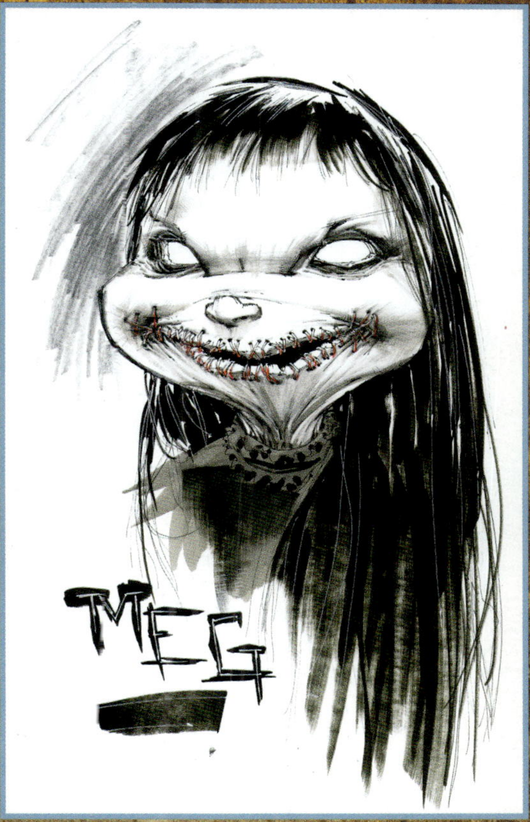
MEG

Peg head. (Meg)

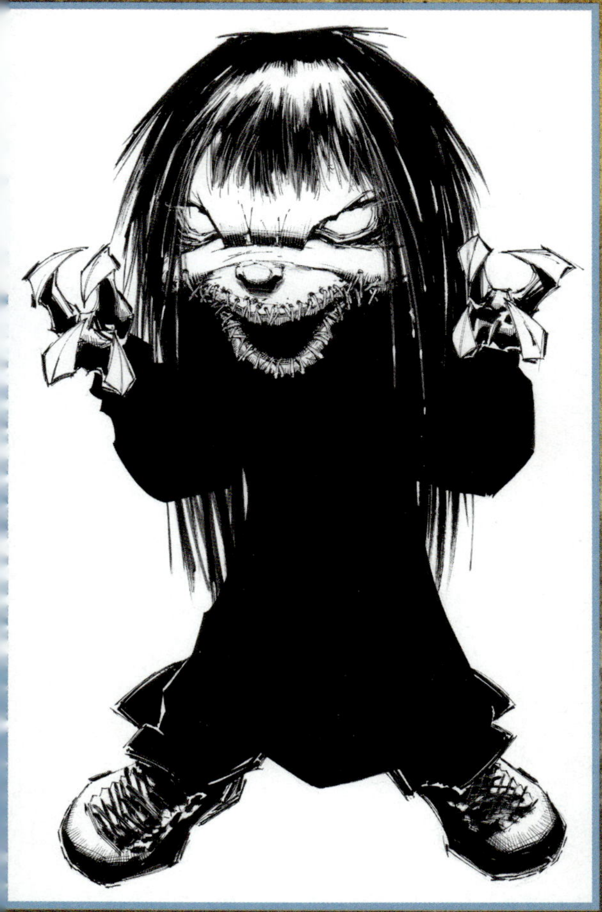

eg portrait.

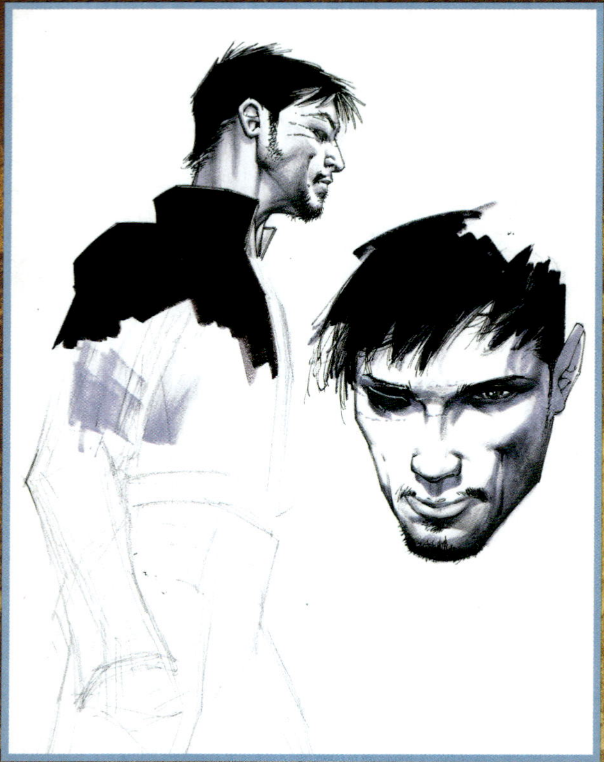
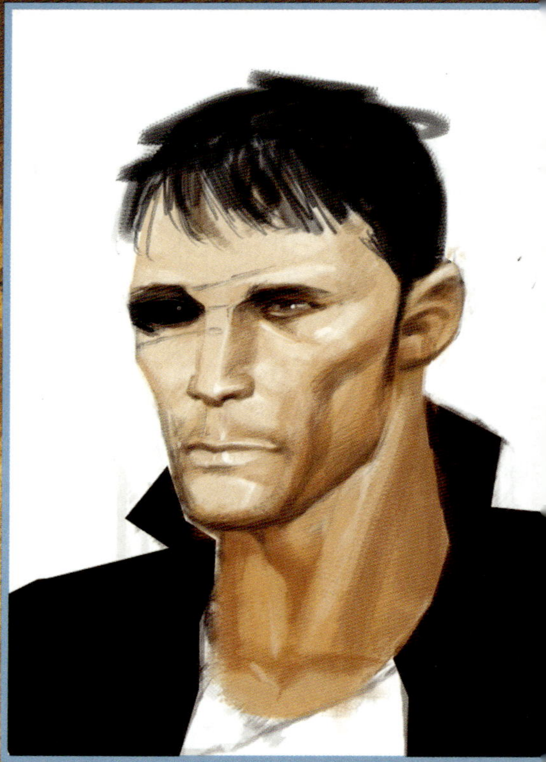

More early sketches of Aimes.

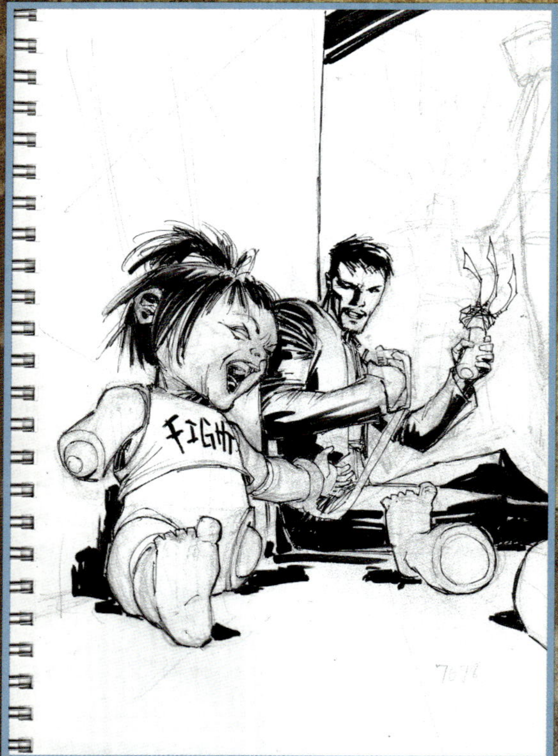
FIGHT

Rejected idea for issue #1.

Unused character sketch

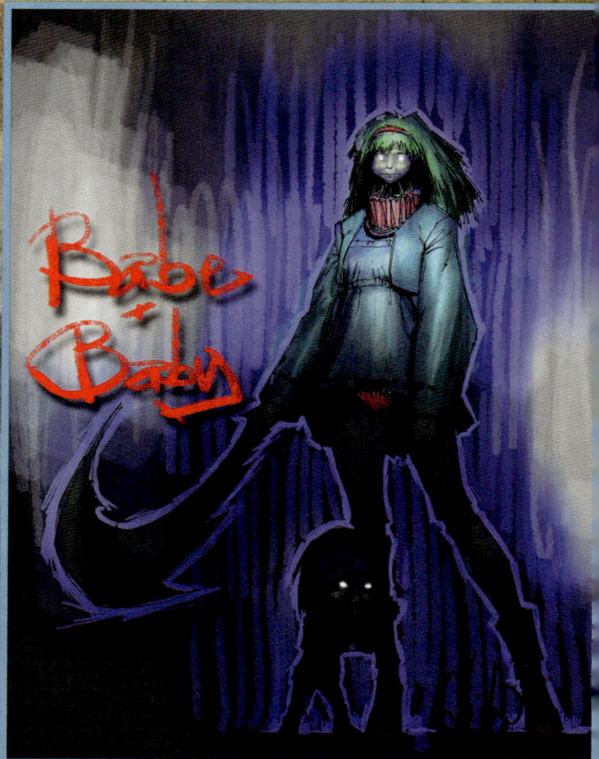
Babe + Baby

# PROCESS

For our first issue, Whilce did extensive outlines as he was figuring out the look of the book. If you compare these pages to the actual pages in the book you can see how different they became from concept to page. Later, as Whlice became more comfortable with our world he stopped doing these outlines--opting instead to work directly on the finished pages. It's fun to look at this early take as it gives you insight into the step ladder he was building toward his final vision. On page 14 we have the early version of Teresa-Tech that we swapped out for her final printed version.

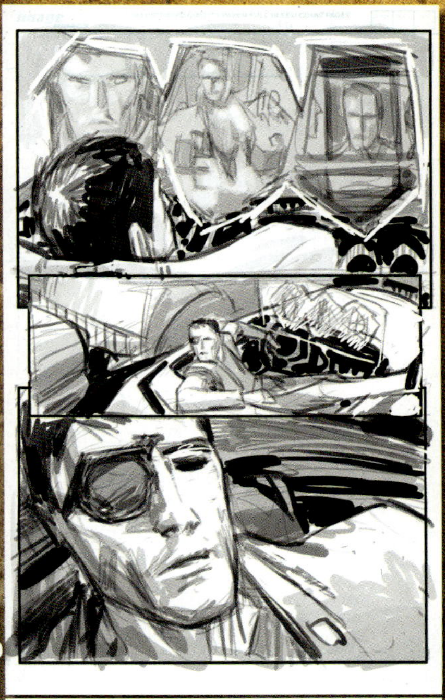
Page1

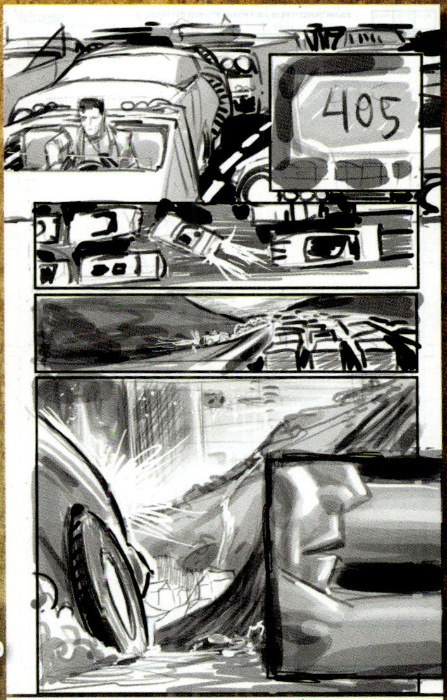
405
Page2

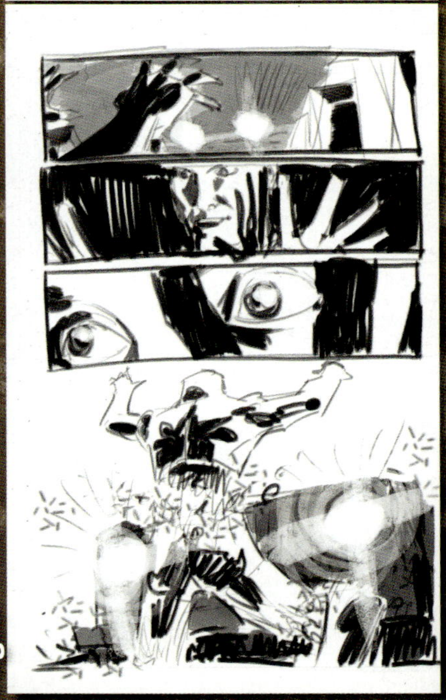
Page3

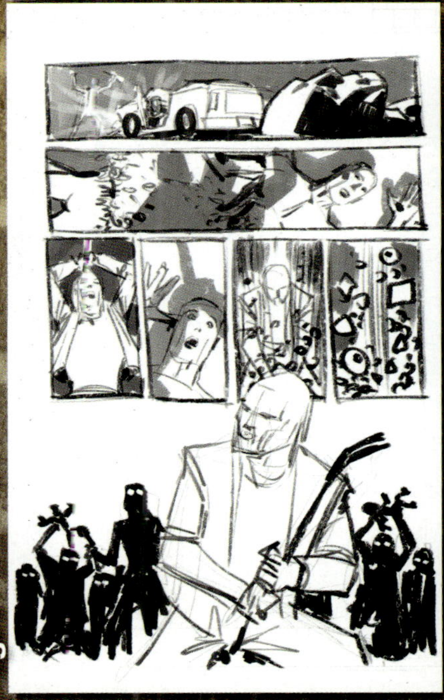
Page4

Page5

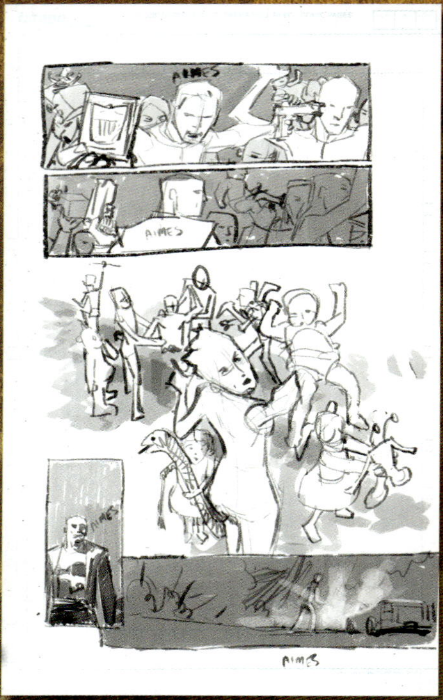

Page6

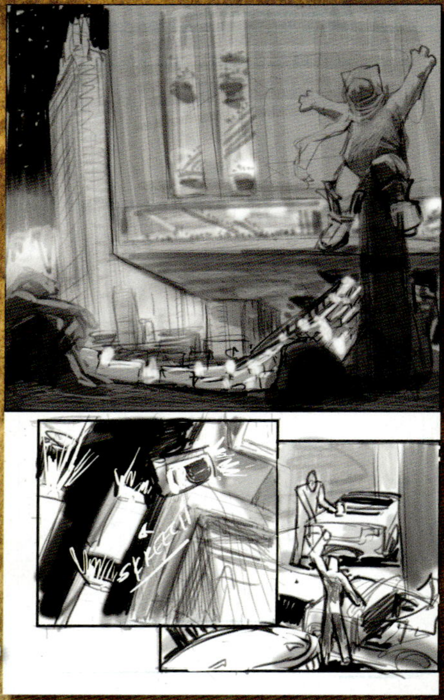

Page10

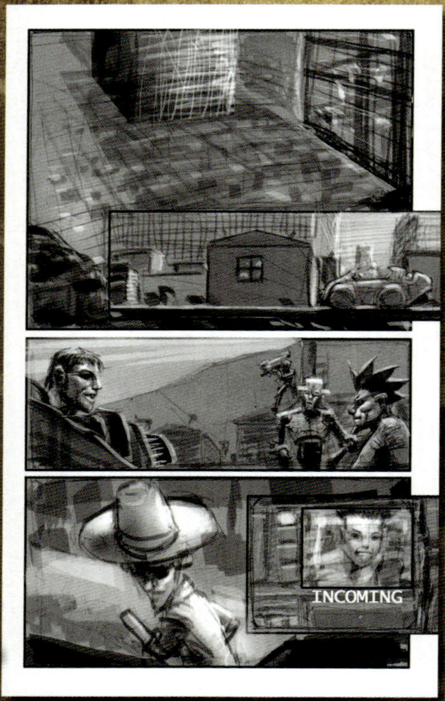
INCOMING

Page11

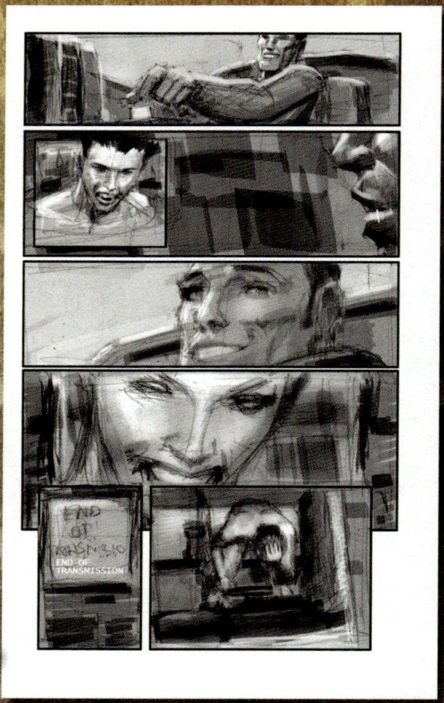
END OF
TRANSMISSION

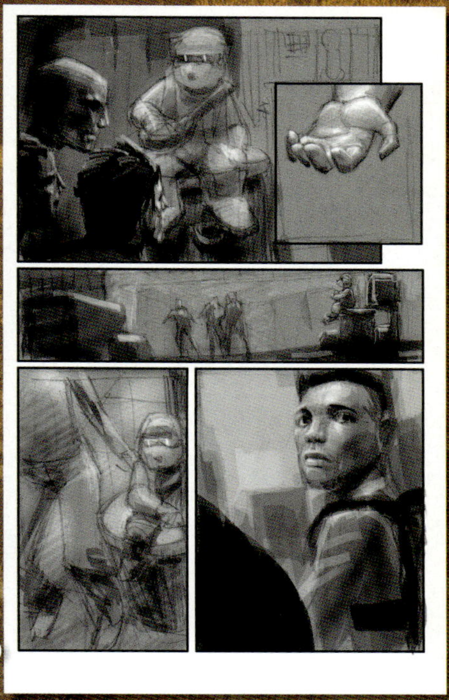

Page 12

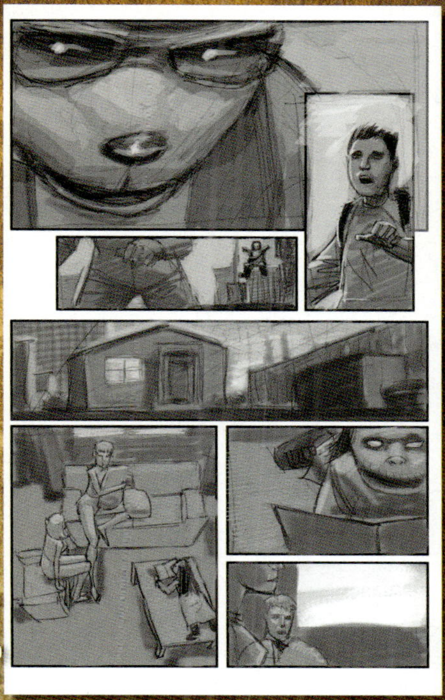

Page 13

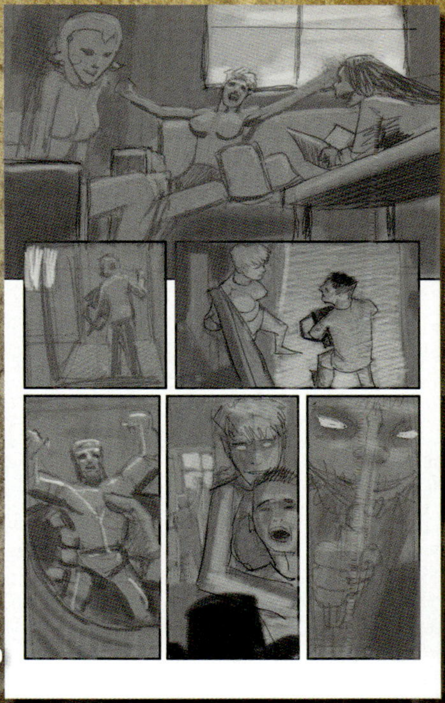

Page 14